THE
ASSASSIN

THE
ASSASSIN

ANDREW BRITTON

KENSINGTON BOOKS
http://www.kensingtonbooks.com

KENSINGTON BOOKS are published by

Kensington Publishing Corp.
850 Third Avenue
New York, NY 10022

All Kensington titles, imprints and distributed lines are available at special quantity discounts for bulk purchases for sales promotion, premiums, fund-raising, educational or institutional use.

Special book excerpts or customized printings can also be created to fit specific needs. For details, write or phone the office of the Kensington Special Sales Manager: Kensington Publishing Corp., 850 Third Avenue, New York, NY 10022. Attn. Special Sales Department. Phone: 1-800-221-2647.

Kensington and the K logo Reg. U.S. Pat. & TM Off.

Library of Congress Control Number: 2006938489
ISBN-13: 978-0-7582-1334-1
ISBN-10: 0-7582-1334-4

First Printing: March 2007
10   9   8   7   6   5   4   3   2   1

Printed in the United States of America

For my sister, Roxanne,
and my cousins in Camlough, Yasmin Gene and
Leah Madeline Britton

ACKNOWLEDGMENTS

To Kristine Murphy at Wood TV in Grand Rapids, Michigan, for answering all my questions about live reporting (with a detailed written report, no less). To Pete Pagano and everybody at Tir Na Nog Irish Pub in Raleigh, NC, for putting together a great publicity party in March 2006. To the Raleigh-based Irish community at large, for throwing their support behind my work. To D.G. Martin at UNC-TV's *Bookwatch*, for including me on his excellent show. To Paddy Gibney, an outstanding musician and a great guy in general, for putting me in touch with all the right people. Be sure to check out his website (www.paddygibneymusic.com).

Special thanks go to Officer Jack Libby of the Raleigh Police Department, for taking time out of his busy schedule to show me the ins and outs of police work. To Brad Thor and Stephen Frey, two extremely talented authors who took time from their own writing to read *The American* and offer some praise; I'm indebted to both of them. To Carol Fitzgerald and her extraordinary team at www.bookreporter.com, for setting up an outstanding website and supporting my work in general.

As always, thanks to the talented team at Kensington: Steven Zacharius, Laurie Parkin, Joan Schulhafer, Maureen Cuddy, Robin E. Cook, and Meryl Earl in particular, for the amazing work she's done with foreign rights to *The American*. Also, sincere thanks to my exceptionally patient, hard-working editor, Audrey LaFehr. It's a privilege to work with such a dedicated group of individuals.

And to my literary agent, Nancy Coffey, for her unwavering support and encouragement; I couldn't have done it without you.

PROLOGUE

BAGHDAD

Anita Zaid folded her arms as she glared across the cavernous lobby of the Babylon Hotel. Not for the first time, she found herself hoping that the target of her righteous anger would suddenly come down with some sort of exotic fever, something specific to overly glamorous, thunder-stealing network reporters. Better yet, maybe her menacing stare could somehow infect the woman with subconscious doubt, leading to an irrepressible stutter whenever she stepped in front of the cameras. Anita momentarily brightened with this notion but knew it was asking a lot; unfortunately, Penelope Marshall had a reputation for handling the crushing pressure of televised journalism with the skill of a seasoned pro, despite her relative youth.

It should have been perfect. Anita was fortunate enough to have the best source possible, a cousin assigned to the Ministry of Defense. The man's access was incredible and well worth a generous stipend, which her employer would have gladly paid. In this respect, however, she was lucky again. All her cousin's assistance cost her was the occasional visit to his modest home on the outskirts of Baghdad, where he was given to bad cooking and good-natured but endless complaints about the Americans, much to the dismay of his long-suffering wife. His latest tip had arrived just forty minutes earlier, and for once, Anita was in the perfect position to act on it, bored senseless and lounging over cold coffee in a Green Zone café with Tim Hoffman, her American cameraman. Twenty minutes and a couple of irritating stops at various checkpoints had seen her out of the zone and into the leafy streets of the Jadriya residential district, the unlikely site of the Babylon Hotel.

As she looked for a hole in the building crowd, Anita brushed her hair back from her face and sighed in mounting frustration. She had worked for London-based Independent Television for five years now and was beginning to wonder how much longer she could put up with the long hours and low pay. Her position as ITV's Middle East correspondent was a natural fit, as she'd been born and raised in Mosul before immigrating to England at the age of seventeen, where she'd earned a BA with honors in English at Cambridge. Intellectually speaking, she knew she was too young to be burned out—she had just turned thirty-six, after all—but at the same time, she couldn't help but feel that she might be missing out on better-paying, less-demanding opportunities. The desire to move on to something better had grown stronger in recent months, and days like today definitely didn't help.

The trouble had started soon after they'd arrived at the hotel. Spotting the bulky black cases in Hoffman's hands, the manager had stopped them as soon as they'd walked in, insisting that Zaid pay for "a room" if she intended to set up camp in his lobby. What the man really wanted was glaringly obvious and not at all surprising. Anita was very familiar with the way things had worked before the American invasion, when bribes had been the rule rather than the exception. In the months leading up to the war, Saddam's Information Ministry had strictly controlled the movements and access of every Western journalist, and she had quickly learned to adapt, though not before enduring several heated arguments with the tightfisted accountants at ITV.

Unfortunately, the Babylon's manager had demanded immediate payment in cash, which Anita didn't have on hand, and the delay had given somebody time to send word up to Marshall's room. Penny Marshall was CNN's latest and brightest star, a twenty-something blonde from New Zealand. After hearing the news, the young woman had somehow managed to hustle downstairs in the space of three minutes, looking like she'd just stepped out of make-up. As it turned out, her presence at the hotel was pure coincidence. Her cameramen—she had two of them, Anita noticed, with a twinge of jealousy—had followed her down a few minutes later, shabbily dressed men with identical beer bellies. On arrival, they'd staked their claim in loud and spectacular fashion, which was exactly what Anita had hoped to avoid. The presence of both camera crews had opened the floodgates, and now every journalist in the city seemed to be aware of the man's imminent arrival. Zaid had clearly suffered the most; what had started as a respectable shot was now obscured by a rectangular lens hood and the heavily teased hair of the regional correspondent for CBS News.

"Anita, we've got to find something better," Hoffman finally said, poking his bearded face out from behind his camera. "From this position, I'll have him on-screen for less than five seconds, and that's a best-case scenario. The interview's out, you know. He won't hear one word over this bloody lot."

She turned away, rolling her eyes in exasperation. Despite having been born and raised in New Hampshire, Hoffman had been adopting British speech patterns for as long as she'd known him. At first, she had shrugged it off, thinking it was a joke, but then, less than two weeks into their partnership, she'd been disheartened to learn just how seriously he took his British "heritage." Anita had coached him against the annoying habit on several occasions, but this time she let it slide and began weighing her options, trying to visualize the shot from various locations. The second-floor balcony was no good; from where she was standing, she could see that the angle was all wrong, and besides, there seemed to be a number of security men blocking the stairs. At the same time, pulling back wouldn't help in the least; in fact, it would put her on the outskirts, where her separation from the crowd, ironically, would be too great. Viewers wanted a sense of excitement, a sense of being in the thick of things, but they also wanted exclusive material. A good compromise was nearly impossible to find, and Hoffman wasn't helping at all.

"You know, I'd be surprised if the man even shows up," he remarked in a languid drawl. "Once he finds out the press is here, he'll probably stay in the zone. Besides, if he *was* coming, he would have been here an hour ago."

"He'll come," Anita said, trying to push down her own rising doubts. Although the Sunni-dominated insurgency had been surprisingly quiet of late, the number of attacks had been increasing steadily since 2003, rising at a rate of approximately 14 percent per year. In accordance with the growing threat, Baghdad's major hotels—especially those that catered primarily to Westerners—had substantially enhanced their collective security measures, but the danger was still very real. "This place is like a fortress, Tim. Didn't you see the gates outside? Besides, the man has bodyguards, police escorts . . . He'll come. You'll see."

As Zaid maneuvered for position in the lobby, radio calls were steadily streaming out to the static posts that had already been set up on both ends of Abu Nuwas Street, 300 yards in either direction. Inside the building, the reporters had been watched from the start by a rotating group of plainclothes officers with the Iraqi Police Service. The men who comprised the advance team had been carefully selected for their religious and political affiliations; all were Shiite Muslims, and most belonged to the Dawa Party, not unlike the man they were assigned to protect. From their position on the second floor, the security officers were able to maintain a constant watch on the crowd below. As they scanned for suspicious activity, the frequent reports they muttered into their radios were routed straight through to the lead vehicle of the approaching convoy.

Five minutes after the advance team vetted the group of reporters, a black Ford Explorer squealed to a halt in front of the building. The doors swung open, revealing four additional security officers. Each man carried an M4A1 assault rifle and an M9 Beretta pistol, weapons supplied by the U.S. Department of Defense. They climbed out of the vehicle and scattered, two moving across the road as the other two formed an identical pattern in front of the Babylon Hotel. The goal was to set up a hasty perimeter for the car that would follow, a close-quarter protection technique perfected by the State Department's Diplomatic Security Service many years earlier. Having learned the maneuver from their American training officers, the guards put it to use with rapid precision, calling in on a dedicated radio link once the area was secure. A white Mercedes sedan appeared a moment later, hunkering low on its wheels, gliding to a gentle halt beside the curb. A security officer reached for the door handle; the man stepped into the street, carefully avoiding a minefield of muddy puddles. The officers converged, and the man was swept from view.

Inside the building, Anita Zaid was navigating the outskirts of the crowd when the reporters pressed forward without warning, their voices erupting in a torrent of unintelligible questions.

"Oh, shit," Hoffman said. "Come on, we've got to—"

"No! We do it right here." Anita swore under her breath, furious at being caught out of position, but determined to make the best of it. She turned her back to the crowd and fixed her hair, checked her mic, and smoothed her shirt in one fast motion. "Give me the count, Tim. Let's go. We'll make it work."

As Hoffman settled the camera onto his shoulder, Anita felt herself slipping into the mode she knew so well: restrained enthusiasm, shoulders back, chin up . . . She was completely calm, a poised professional. This was the best part of her job, and as she looked into the lens and silently composed her introduction, she was reminded of why she loved her work so much.

"Okay, you're on in five, four—"

Hoffman's voice was suddenly drowned out by a thunderous boom overhead. Confined by the building's walls, the sound was strangely muffled, and Anita didn't immediately recognize it for what it was. Apparently, neither did anyone else; they were all looking up in confusion, except for the visitor's bodyguards, who were already dragging their charge back to the doors. The noise was almost like thunder, but sharper, not as prolonged. . . .

And then came the second explosion.

Turning to the right, she saw it unfold with terrible clarity. A massive fireball emerged from the eastern stairwell, engulfing Penny Marshall, her crew, and a dozen bystanders in a blossoming cloud of orange fire. Anita had no time to react as something hard and hot heaved her into the air, twisting her limbs in directions they were simply not designed for.

When she finally hit the ground, she did so awkwardly, something sharp lancing up her right arm. She blacked out for a split second, and when she came back, the pain was the first thing she noticed, but it was more than pain; it was pure agony.

She hurt all over, but her injuries, as bad as they were, were eclipsed by the surrounding images. She couldn't hear for some reason, and the silent scenes played out in a nightmarish collage: bloodied arms and splayed fingers tearing the air, mouths stretching open in silent screams, the dancing, blazing figures of those who'd been closest to the opposite stairwell.

It was just too much. Too much, too fast. Anita tried to let out her own scream of horror and pain, but it lodged in her throat. She squeezed her eyes shut in an attempt to block out what she was seeing, but it was too late; the images were already seared into her mind. If that wasn't enough, an elusive piece of information was pressing against her subconscious, trying to inform her of a more serious problem.

And then she realized she didn't hurt anymore.

The knowledge swept over her in a terrible wave. No pain meant no chance . . . She didn't know where that thought had come from, but it played over and over in her mind like a terrible mantra, and she knew it was right. *No pain, no chance. No pain, no chance. No pain . . .*

She desperately wanted to feel something, *anything*, but her surroundings were already slipping away. As the darkness moved in, she wasn't sure if the debris falling around her was real or part of a panic-induced hallucination. Pieces of plaster and marble were dropping down from the ceiling, smaller chunks at first, and then giant slabs of heavy material, crashing down to the blood-streaked floor.

Only a few seconds had passed, but no one was dancing anymore; the bodies lay still, black figures wreathed in orange flames. Anita tried to move her arms, her eyes fixed on the shattered main entrance and the open air beyond, but nothing was working.

And then she felt a sharp, sudden pressure at the back of her neck, and the darkness closed in once and for all.

CHAPTER 1

WASHINGTON, D.C.

Dusk was settling over the city skyline, layers of gray falling through rain-laden clouds as a black Lincoln Town Car sped south along the river on the George Washington Parkway. From the front passenger seat, Jonathan Harper gazed out across the Potomac as riverside lamps pushed weak yellow light over the black water. Although his eyes never strayed from the passing scenery, his mind was in another place altogether, fixed on the news that had come into his office less than four hours earlier. As a result, he wasn't really paying attention to the radio, which was tuned to a local news station and playing softly in the background. When the commentary began to align with his own ruminations, though, he leaned forward and turned up the volume.

"In Baghdad today, U.S. and Iraqi forces were put on high alert. Additional checkpoints were set up throughout the city, and the State Department updated the travel warnings already in place. This, following the attempted assassination of Nuri al-Maliki in the Iraqi capital. At approximately 12:14 AM Baghdad time, a pair of massive bombs tore apart the second and third floors of the Babylon Hotel, located just south of the International Zone. According to embassy officials, the prime minister survived the near-simultaneous blasts, although his condition is believed to be critical. Preliminary reports indicate that as many as twenty-five American civilians, mostly reporters embedded with the U.S. forces, are still unaccounted for and believed dead in the aftermath of the attack.

"In a press briefing held earlier today at the White House, President David Brenneman condemned the bombing and offered condolences to the families of those who were killed. In a surprising sidebar, he also reaffirmed his commitment to the goal of force reductions in the region. These reductions are an integral part of the president's reelection platform, as they provide for the scaled withdrawal of U.S. forces over the course of five years. The president's plan, which also calls for the return of four of eighteen provinces to Iraqi control by next April, has been ridiculed by the Democratic leadership as too conservative in scope. Even so, with this most recent incident, many are wondering if the president will be forced to rescind his promise to the families of America's servicemen and women, a move which would almost certainly cost him the election in November.

"Moving on to other news, demonstrations in Beirut were brought to a halt yesterday when—"

Harper switched off the radio. The report hadn't told him anything new, which wasn't surprising. He already knew far more about the current situation than the Washington press corps ever would, despite their collective fact-gathering abilities.

As both the deputy director of operations (DDO) and director of the newly formed National Clandestine Service, Jonathan Harper shared the number three spot in the Central Intelligence Agency with his counterpart in the Intelligence Directorate. Despite his seniority, only a handful of people on the Hill could have picked him out of a crowd. The reason for this was simple: the name of the presiding DDO was almost never released to the public, the sole exception being Jim Pavitt's appearance before the 9/11 Commission in 2004. Even Harper's appearance seemed to lend itself to anonymity. His wife often joked that the conservative Brooks Brothers suits he favored were hardly worth the cost, as they made him all but invisible in a well-dressed city such as Washington, D.C.

It was, of course, an image he had long cultivated, and for good reason; his ability to blend into the background had saved his life on more than one occasion in his early years with the Agency. He'd spent much of the eighties running agents in the former Soviet Union, as well as sneaking high-value defectors out of the country through the western wastelands of Belarus and Bulgaria. Recently, his roles had been better suited to his age and station, which made them more ambiguous and much less interesting. Among other things, he had been assigned to the National Reconnaissance Office and a number of foreign embassies before assuming his current position four years earlier.

Harper's gaze drifted back to the window as his driver turned left on 17th Street. He wasn't looking forward to the upcoming meeting, as he knew it probably wouldn't go well for him. As it stood, the Agency's presence in Iraq was extremely limited, despite popular belief to the contrary. He had made a case for additional funding and personnel earlier in the year, only to see his proposal shot down by the newly installed deputy executive director. This fact, he was sure, had not been revealed to the president. Harper's immediate supervisor was a skilled politician in her own right and more than capable of presenting the facts in accordance with her own ambitions. As a result, Harper was sure that she had managed to relieve herself of most of the blame for this latest intelligence failure.

Worst of all was the timing. With the presidential election looming on the horizon, Brenneman was facing public unrest over the ongoing war, sagging approval ratings, and a popular adversary in California Governor Richard Fiske. Iraq, of course, was the key issue; the governor's proposal called for a rapid withdrawal of U.S. forces on the order of 72,000 soldiers over the course of eighteen months, with scaled reductions to follow. Privately, Harper believed it to be an empty promise, but the American public had seized the opportunity to rid itself of a war for which the costs were rapidly becoming untenable. Brenneman's proposal was far less ambitious by comparison, calling for the gradual replacement of U.S. forces by combat-ready units of the Iraqi Army. Since the latest statistics suggested that less than 20,000 Iraqi troops currently met the requirements, the president's plan had taken fire from politicians on both sides of the partisan divide, as well as from the public at large.

Harper's vehicle approached the southwest gate of the White House, braking to a gentle halt next to the guardhouse. A pair of officers from the Uniformed Division of the Secret Service emerged immediately and proceeded with the security check. The gates swung open a moment later, and the Town Car rolled up West Executive Avenue to the first-floor entrance of the West Wing.

Harper climbed out of the vehicle and immediately caught sight of his escort. Darrell Reed was a senior advisor to the president and the deputy chief of staff. He was a lean black man with an easy smile and a genteel manner, but Harper knew that Reed's affable nature did not extend to the cutthroat world of D.C. politics. The deputy chief could be as ruthless as the next man in the exercise of his considerable power, as he had demonstrated on countless occasions.

Reed smiled as he approached and offered his hand. "John, how are you?"

"Well, I think that remains to be seen. Ask me again when this meeting is over."

The deputy chief shook his head, the small grin fading. "The president is not a happy man, I can tell you that much. Ford's already here, and they've had some words."

Harper grimaced. "She's supposed to be in Israel with the director."

"She was on her way back to take care of some routine business," Reed replied. "The president called her in this morning." He cleared his throat. "It's the timing, John, and the civilian casualties. He wants some answers."

"So do I, but it's going to take some time."

"Unfortunately, that's the one thing we don't really have."

Harper nodded glumly; he knew what Reed was referring to. In the press briefing earlier that day, the president had assured the American public that the murder of U.S. civilians in Iraq would not go unpunished. With the election less than two months away, those words would not be soon forgotten.

"We haven't even seen a claim of responsibility yet. I just hope he can follow through on the promise."

"Well, that's where you come in. He's expecting you."

Harper shrugged. "Lead the way."

CHAPTER 2

WASHINGTON, D.C.

Once inside, they passed through another security check and began the 70-foot walk to the Oval Office. As always, Harper couldn't help but think about how easy it was to get into this building. It was all an illusion, of course; despite the apparent lack of security, he was well aware that the Secret Service had eyes, electronic or otherwise, on virtually every part of the West Wing, including the adjacent hallways that led to the president's corner office. When they stepped into the room, the deputy chief of staff gestured to one of the couches scattered over the presidential rug and said, "Take a seat, John. I'll go and see what's holding him up."

"Thanks, Darrell."

Reed walked out, giving the DDO the opportunity to briefly examine his surroundings. It wasn't often that he found himself alone in the president's office, and the small space contained enough of his country's past to keep Jonathan Harper, a self-proclaimed history buff, absorbed for hours. His eyes drifted over numerous oil paintings, most of which had nautical themes, before coming to rest on the towering colonnade windows. Soft light from the bulbs in the Rose Garden spilled through the panes, working with the dim interior lamps to illuminate the polished surface of the president's desk.

Harper knew that the beautifully detailed piece had been crafted from the hull of the HMS *Resolute*, a British vessel abandoned in the Arctic Circle in 1854. In 1855, the ship was discovered by an American whaler as it was drifting over 1,200 miles from its original position, having dislodged itself from the ice in which it was mired. Over the course of the following year, the vessel was restored by the American government and returned to England as a gesture of goodwill. When the *Resolute* was retired in 1879, Queen Victoria commissioned a desk made from the timbers, which she then presented to Rutherford B. Hayes. Almost every president since had used the desk during the course of his administration.

He was about to stand to get a closer look when the door leading to the Cabinet Room was pulled open. Harper rose as President David Brenneman walked in, followed soon thereafter by Rachel Ford. The deputy director of Central Intelligence, or deputy DCI, was a pale, trim woman in her early forties. As usual, her shoulder-length hair was slightly askew, tendrils of dark red framing her attractive, albeit sharp-featured, face.

Brenneman approached and offered his hand. "Good to see you, John. How's Julie?"

Harper nearly smiled at the mention of his wife, but stopped himself when he saw the president's grave expression. "She's doing well, sir, thanks."

"Glad to hear it." Brenneman forced a tight smile of his own and gestured to the couch. "Please, take a seat, both of you. Make yourselves comfortable."

The president walked behind his desk, shrugging off his suit jacket as the two CIA officials picked out chairs. A navy steward moved into the room and deposited a tray bearing a small carafe, cups, and creamer. The man withdrew as Brenneman joined them in the meeting area, smoothing a blue silk tie against his crisp white shirt.

"So," he said, fixing them both with a serious look. "I have quite a few questions for both of you, but first, let's make sure we're on the same page. My advisors seem to agree that this was a deliberate assassination attempt, as opposed to a random attack on a target of opportunity. I know how it's being carried in the press, but I'd like to hear your opinions."

"I don't think there's any question." Ford crossed her legs and focused her gaze on the president. "Of course, I'd like to know what he was doing outside the zone in the first place. Setting that aside, though, it's just too much of a coincidence. A 'target of opportunity' would warrant nothing more than a suicide bomber on foot or an RPG. We certainly wouldn't be seeing anything like the devastation that actually transpired." She didn't need to expand on this; they had all seen the video footage aired by CNN.

"I agree," Harper said. "And there's something else: the Babylon has gates that are manned by the Iraqi Police Service. It would have been almost impossible to get something past them without a great deal of planning."

"Or their help," Brenneman muttered.

"That, too," Harper conceded. "We'll be looking into that, sir, but it might be difficult, since they'll be the ones tasked with the investigation."

"That's true." Ford fired her subordinate a disapproving glance. "We *do* need to be careful about whom we trust in the IPS, but I wouldn't recommend trying to cut them out of the loop. That will set a negative tone at a very sensitive time, especially if al-Maliki doesn't survive the assassination attempt."

And you're advising the president on things that don't concern you, Harper thought. Ford was an outside appointee; most of her career had been spent serving the constituents of Michigan's 3rd Congressional District. After four terms in the House, she had turned her attention to Harvard's Kennedy School of Government, where she'd served as dean prior to accepting the president's nomination earlier in the year. In Harper's opinion, she still had a lot to learn about her new position, particularly the limits of her questionable expertise.

It looked like Brenneman caught it, too. He glanced sideways at his deputy DCI, the message clear in his stern expression, but she missed it entirely as a noise intruded. Ford snatched her cell phone off the table and flipped it open impatiently. "What is it?" She listened intently, then turned to the president. "Sir, this is urgent. May I . . . ?"

He nodded abruptly. Ford jumped to her feet and walked into the adjacent Cabinet Room, closing the door behind her somewhat harder than necessary. Brenneman shot his subordinate a bemused glance. Harper worked to keep his face impassive, but suspected the president knew exactly what he was thinking.

His suspicions were confirmed an instant later. "Something on your mind, John?"

Harper shook his head in the negative. Leaning forward to pour himself some coffee, he idly wondered why he harbored such an intense, transparent dislike for Rachel Ford. It wasn't that he found her lacking in intellect; her education, beginning with Sarah Lawrence and culminating in a JD from Harvard Law, could hardly be found wanting. The fact that she was technically his superior didn't bother him, either; Jonathan held no reservations when it came to working for a woman. After all, he had done so often enough in the past, and it had never been a problem before. In short, he didn't know how the animosity, which was decidedly mutual, had come about.

The president was leafing through a briefing folder. "Seventeen American casualties? Is that right?"

The DDO cleared his throat and said, "Actually, sir, that report is several hours old. The latest numbers in from the embassy confirm nineteen dead. Five more are critically injured."

Brenneman's dark brown eyes grew darker still, but he didn't respond. Instead, he tossed the folder onto the table and appraised his visitor for a long moment. Finally, he said, "She brought up a good point, you know."

Harper was momentarily caught off-guard. "Al-Maliki," Brenneman reminded him. "What *was* he doing outside the zone?"

The other man considered his response for a moment, wondering if the president's main concern lay with the American loss of life or the attempted assassination of the Iraqi prime minister. "Sir, when was the last time you were in Baghdad?"

"Six months ago, I think. I went to address the troops and to take a look at the new embassy."

"What were the roads like?"

"God awful, and that's probably generous on my part. Of course, it's a straight shot from the airport to the zone, so at least the travel time wasn't too bad."

"A straight shot for *you*, sir. Moving around Baghdad is different for everyone else, even senior Iraqi officials."

A slight frown appeared on the president's face. "How so?"

"Well, first they have to fill out a form that states where they're going and why. Then they have to request vehicles and bodyguards. All of this has to be done the day before a scheduled movement. It's very inconvenient, especially when, even after all of that, you still get stopped at three different checkpoints on your way in and out. Most of the top guys look for ways to avoid it."

"Like avoiding the zone entirely."

"Exactly. Only problem is, once you're outside, you're fair game."

Brenneman nodded slowly, a little piqued at Harper's description. Iraq had topped his foreign policy agenda for the past four years; he didn't care to hear the place described as a war zone, though, in fact, it could hardly be described as anything else. "Okay, next question. How did they know he would be there?"

"It's all speculation at this point. I'm guessing we'll have to wait until they come up with a list of casualties. Then we'll focus on who's missing, such as bodyguards and hotel employees. We'll also take a look at building security . . . Like I said, sir, the gates were manned by the IPS. That might be a good place to start."

Brenneman sighed heavily and ran a hand through his silver brown hair. "It doesn't sound like we have much to work with."

"I know," Harper agreed. "But we're just getting started, sir."

"Fair enough. What kind of fallout can we expect from this?"

The DDO mulled over the question for a moment. "It's been unusually quiet over the past several months, but this could definitely serve as a catalyst. We'll probably see increased insurgent activity in the major cities, particularly Baghdad and Fallujah. Of course, some of that depends on what happens with the prime minister."

Brenneman got to his feet and moved to the windows, looking over the South Lawn for a long moment. "This couldn't come at a worse time," he finally murmured. "Even if he makes it through. It's hard to justify troop withdrawals when we can't guarantee the safety of the senior leadership."

He suddenly seemed to come back to reality. "What kind of assets do you have over there?"

Harper ran through the list in his head. "Exley, sir. He's one of our guys in the embassy, used to be army intelligence. He's connected in all the right places. Keith Moore is chief of station. Jenna Thompson's the head tech officer—"

"What about Kealey?"

The question seemed to hang in the air for a long time. "He's in the area. A little farther to the west," Harper replied cautiously. "But I don't know if he's . . ."

"Available?" The president turned from the window to stare at his subordinate. "Is that what you were going to say?"

Harper frowned but didn't respond.

"Is he up to speed in the Middle East?"

"As much as anyone."

"You may not be aware of this, John, but I took an interest after what happened last year. I know he asked to come back in an official capacity. I also know that his request was initially rejected by Director Andrews, and that you intervened and signed the waiver when he wouldn't talk to the in-house counselors."

The president paused and shot the DDO a curious glance. "Why did you do that, by the way? I never had the chance to ask you."

Harper was uncomfortable with the question, and it showed. "Kealey's a good man, sir. He's been through a lot, but he's not the type to respond to any kind of counseling. It wouldn't have helped. As for bringing him back inside . . . Well, let's just say I couldn't turn him down. Not after what happened."

Brenneman considered this for a long moment, finally turning back to his guest. "John, I need to know if this goes any deeper. The press will be all over me if I don't stick to the timetable, but I can't start pulling soldiers out with the knowledge that I'll have to send them back in six months. More to the point, someone has to be held accountable for this. I need someone who can move fast and get results. If Ryan's already over there, so much the better."

Harper shook his head. "I'm sorry, sir, but I don't think he's the right man for this."

The president did not respond. Instead, he assumed a neutral expression and motioned for Harper to continue.

"For most things, I'd put him out there in a heartbeat. But not in this case. There's too much riding on it, and lately, he's been . . . taking chances."

Brenneman furrowed his brow. "I know he got hurt. Is that the problem? Because if that's an issue . . ."

"Physically, there's nothing wrong with him. That's not what concerns me."

Another aching silence. "Look, John, I appreciate your honesty. At the same time, you brought him back to the Agency for a reason. Unless you can point to something specific, we need him on this. *I* need him on this."

Reluctantly, Harper nodded. Brenneman glanced at his watch and stood, ending the conversation. As the other man got to his feet and started toward the door, the president's voice brought him to a halt.

"This will not pass, John. Find your man, and bring him up to speed. I want to know who was responsible, and soon."

CHAPTER 3

FALLUJAH

A dirty gray dawn was just beginning to lift as a helicopter beat a steady path east from the Habbaniyah air base, a small facility located 80 kilometers west of Baghdad. The Soviet-designed aircraft, now passing over the Euphrates River valley, had been used by both Taliban and Northern Alliance forces during the U.S. invasion of Afghanistan. Since the enemy on the ground had been reluctant to open fire for fear of engaging their own commanders, the Mi-17 had been adopted by the CIA as a preferred means of travel in the region. Its popularity had begun to fade in recent months, as its role in the American fleet was becoming a well-known fact in all the wrong circles, but it still offered better protection than some of the Agency's more conspicuous aircraft.

From his seat just aft of the cockpit, Mark Walland peered through a grimy window on the starboard side as the outskirts of Fallujah appeared through scattered clouds, revealing broken walls of pale stone and low-slung cinder block homes. Although the view was far from scenic, Walland knew that things would look much worse on the ground. He wasn't looking forward to going down there, but it seemed as if he had been doing just that—heading into harm's way—for the better part of his short career.

Like the men in the cockpit, Walland was attached to the Special Activities Division, the Agency's elite paramilitary force. He was short but well built, with dark, restless eyes set deep in a sunburnt face.

His light brown hair was trimmed close, which put it at odds with the thick beard he had grown over the past few months. Walland had joined the CIA following his departure from the army three years earlier, at the surprisingly young age of twenty-seven. He'd seen plenty of action as a captain in the 82nd Airborne Division, particularly in the mountains of Afghanistan. Still, the former Ranger knew that his experience was nothing compared to that of the individual who was seated directly across from him, on the other side of the wide, empty aisle.

Walland had been working on and off with Ryan Kealey for the past six months, yet the man remained a mystery. He'd heard a few things, of course, brief snatches of conversation caught during his time at the forward operating bases to the east. Mostly, they were rumors with respect to Kealey's military record: his time with the 3rd Special Forces Group, his role in the death of a senior Islamic militant in Syria, the two lost years during which his name had been placed on the Security Roster, the army's list of covert operators. Walland knew something of his recent work as well; Kealey's role in the prevention of a major terrorist attack the previous year was too big to have been covered up entirely, despite the best efforts of the operations directorate. For the most part, however, the man—and his past—remained a closed book.

The young operative broke from his thoughts as the airframe shuddered, the engines flaring as the pilot applied the aft cyclic. The helicopter dropped through the clouds with startling speed, the wheels bouncing once, then settling into the dirt a moment later. Walland stripped off his in-flight headset and saw Kealey do the same. The side door was pulled open after a few seconds, and they jumped down from the elevated fuselage, shielding their eyes from the rotor wash as they hurried toward the waiting vehicles.

The dust began to clear as they approached, revealing half a dozen soldiers in civilian clothes and three battered Toyota pickups. The soldiers were spread out in a loose perimeter around the vehicles, which were parked next to the train station, a low-slung building marked by bullet holes and large areas of blackened cement. Located just north of the city, the station had been carefully selected for its value as a defensive position and its proximity to the meeting point. Kealey adjusted his load as he waited for Walland to catch up, slinging his AK-74M over his shoulder so that the black plastic grip of the rifle dangled a mere few inches from his right hand. When Walland appeared at his side, they walked over to the lead Tacoma. A lanky, dark-haired individual was leaning against the passenger-side fender. He straightened as they approached.

"Good to see you, Ryan," he said. "It's been a long time."

Kealey took the proffered hand. "You're right about that, Paul. It's good to see you, too." He gestured to Walland and made the introductions. The two men shook hands in turn.

Paul Owen was an army officer based out of Camp Fallujah, the marine base located fifteen miles east of the city. As a lieutenant colonel in the 1st SFOD-D, he'd been one of Kealey's commanding officers during the younger man's time at Fort Bragg. Due to the peculiar relationship between the CIA and the Special Forces community, the thirty-three-year-old Kealey now more or less shared command with the man who had once been his superior officer. On the ride east from Habbaniyah, Kealey had wondered, with some trepidation, about how this turn of events might play out, but his fears were soon abated. With the introductions out of the way, Owen turned back to him and said, "So, how exactly do you want to handle this?"

"What have you been told?"

"The bare minimum. We have a location and a guarantee of safe passage on your end. At least, that's what you said when you called to set this up."

"And that still holds." He caught the Delta officer's skeptical expression. "Look, Paul, we've dealt with this guy before. It's in his best interest to get us in and out of there without an incident. He definitely has the influence; he could probably lock down the entire district if he wanted to."

Owen nodded in reluctant agreement. "Fair enough. I've heard the same thing. How long will it take?"

"About ten minutes." Kealey slapped the hand guard of his weapon. "I'll be leaving this with you. They'll disarm me when I go in, anyway."

"Okay. You said you had some imagery for me."

Kealey was carrying a black Jansport backpack in addition to his rifle. Shrugging the pack off his shoulders, he unzipped the front compartment and extracted a thin manila folder. The folder was placed on the warm hood of the first Tacoma, and the contents withdrawn. Both Owen and Walland leaned in for a closer look.

"These shots were taken when we first set up shop in Fallujah," Kealey explained. "Two years ago this guy was low priority, and nothing's really changed in that department. The DO was never able to justify satellite imagery, so all we have are digital shots from the air."

Selecting one of the closer shots, he pointed out a squat, dun-colored two-story structure. "This is it. I know it looks like every other house on the street, but they'll have armed guards posted outside and possibly in the buildings across the road." He fixed Owen with a serious look. "Tell your men to watch how they handle their weapons. These guys will be jumpy, and I don't want any accidents."

"I'll tell them, but I didn't bring rookies."

Kealey cast a glance around, reappraising the faces. His twelve years of experience told him that Owen had chosen well. They all had dark hair and complexions, and the weapons they carried, combined with their style of dress, would enable them to blend into the city landscape. "Are they yours?"

"Every one of them."

The younger man was satisfied. "You already have your route, right?"

"Yeah. It's pretty straightforward, but we set up the GPS just in case. It's easy to get turned around if the bullets start flying. I figure it's about three minutes in, once we cross the tracks. Then ten minutes for you to take care of business, and another few minutes out."

The Delta officer straightened and seemed to hesitate. "This is a bad place to waste time, Ryan. I want to limit the risk to my men."

"I know," Kealey replied. "I'll make it quick."

Another hesitation, as though Owen could see through the younger man's façade. "This is just a drop, right? I mean, we're not equipped for—"

"It's just like I told you," Kealey said. "A simple drop."

It was something new for him. He had made a decision back at the air base, a decision that, at the very least, would likely cost him what was left of his career. With the helicopter blades already turning, he had tracked down the necessary materials . . . He had lied to Owen, lied to all of them. A year earlier he would not have considered it. He waited for a tinge of guilt, but it didn't come.

He realized that Owen was staring at him. To break the awkward silence, he said, "Are the patrols still going out?"

"No. I personally spoke to the brigade staff for the 1st MEB. We're gonna be all alone out there."

"Good." Kealey closed the folder and handed it over. "Show this to your guys. Maybe they'll have some suggestions. Let me know when you're ready to move."

Owen took the folder and walked off. Kealey picked up his pack and started walking back to the last vehicle.

"Where are you going?" Walland called out.

"I saw a cooler back there. I'm going to grab some water. Just sit tight."

The small convoy rolled out a few minutes later. Kealey rode in the first vehicle with Owen, who was behind the wheel. They pulled away from the train yard, wheels bouncing over the twisted remains of the rails as they crossed the 300 yards of open ground leading into the densely packed warren of the Jolan district.

The state of the city grew steadily worse as they headed south through the narrow streets. The rubble-strewn roads were bordered on both sides by shattered buildings and scorched cement. Although most of the damage could be attributed to the fighting, Kealey doubted that Fallujah would have been much to look at before the American invasion. The mosques in the city center were hardly visible from his location, the skyline obscured by thousands of drooping power lines. The buildings all looked alike; the only color to be seen was the occasional green of the date palm and olive trees that had survived the bombing runs.

Kealey was lost in thought as he watched the passing structures for movement. It had been four days since the failed assassination attempt on Nuri al-Maliki, four days since Harper's call. Since then, he had talked to two other men, both of whom were prominent figures on the American payroll, but neither of whom could be trusted. Sitting across from him, they had plied him with strong tea and offered their justification for the monetary assistance of the Central Intelligence Agency. When pressed for specifics, they were quick to provide what appeared to be hard numbers, but it was all meaningless. The Agency's lack of assets and infrastructure in the region was not a well-guarded secret. Stories were rarely checked out with due diligence, and it was not expensive for these men to push the lies down the line. Eventually, it always seemed to come down to a staff officer in the Iraqi National Guard who would swear that, yes, those funds *had* been made available to the target organization. They had turned over their weapons, they were now beholden to the United States . . . Kealey could not accept these words at face value, because nothing ever seemed to change.

For this reason, he had decided to take a chance in the upcoming meeting. He had proof of financial irregularities in this case, but that wouldn't justify his actions if it all went wrong. What he was about to do was completely off the reservation, and if it yielded anything less than a flood of information, Harper would almost certainly run him out of the Agency. In all honesty, though, Kealey didn't care too much if that happened. He was tired of the work, tired of the Agency— tired of everything.

They turned off the main road, bringing them into an area that had obviously seen some of the worst fighting. A small boy watched the passing vehicles for a few seconds, then ducked out of view behind a low cement wall marked with Arabic graffiti. Kealey had just enough time to read the message: THE AMERICANS ARE MURDERERS OF WOMEN AND CHILDREN. SADDAM IS STILL THE LEADER. Up ahead, he could see a pair of fighters standing outside one of the few structures that was still intact. Apart from the two men, the street was empty. "Stop here for a second."

The Tacoma slowed to a halt as he used a handheld radio to call back to the following vehicles. The other man was studying the scene through the windshield. "What do you think?"

"I don't like it," Kealey replied. "But then again, there isn't much I *do* like about this place." He thought about it for a few seconds. "I'll have Walland turn around and stay back with the third vehicle. That should give him clear shots from the back of his truck, if it comes to that. I want coverage on these guys up here, but like I said, they'll probably have people in the surrounding buildings."

He turned to face Owen. "Once I'm inside, give it a few minutes; then do the same. Turn your vehicle around. If something happens, they'll expect us to go straight for Highway 10. This way, we catch them off-guard."

The other man nodded; Highway 10 ran through the heart of the city, east to west, and was the quickest route back to the marine base east of the city. "When you start moving," Kealey continued, "watch those guards to see what they do. If you see something you don't like, hit your SQUELCH button twice, okay? They'll let me keep the radio."

Another nod. Kealey made the necessary call to the following vehicles, and then they rolled forward, braking to a halt once more next to the guards. He handed over his rifle, stock first.

The Delta colonel took it reluctantly. "You know, if something goes wrong, we won't be able to help you in there."

"I know," Kealey replied. "Don't worry about me. Just watch these guys." He slung the pack over his shoulder and climbed out of the vehicle.

As he approached the door, one of the fighters gestured for him to raise his hands. He complied, and the man performed a quick search, briefly examining the PRC-148 handheld radio hanging from Kealey's right hip. When he was satisfied, the guard made a move for the backpack, but it was pulled out of reach.

"This is for Kassem." Kealey spoke softly in Arabic, but his tone left no room for argument. "Go and ask him if you must, but no one else touches it. He will tell you the same."

The fighter, his face partially concealed by a wound kaffiyeh, measured him up with calm brown eyes. Kealey simply returned the stare, his face devoid of expression. Finally, the man stepped back, and Kealey passed through into the darkened hallway.

CHAPTER 4

LONDON

A light rain was falling steadily as a young woman hurried along New Bond Street, pulling the lapels of her coat together in a vain attempt to save her blouse from further damage. She was already soaked to the skin, despite having left the small café on Oxford Street just five minutes earlier. She had eaten her lunch alone, as usual, and the clouds had waited for her to step onto the sidewalk before opening up. Looking up at the swirling sky, Naomi Kharmai wondered if the weather had joined the rest of the world in working against her. As her green eyes flickered over the surrounding sea of umbrellas, she couldn't help but feel a little naïve, like a tourist in her own city. She briefly considered hailing a cab, but then decided she was already too wet for it to make a difference.

Kharmai had recently celebrated her thirty-first birthday, but her small, slender build belied her years. Her caramel-colored skin betrayed her Indian heritage, as did her jet-black hair, but she had never set foot on the Asian continent. She was British by birth, but she was also a naturalized American citizen. This last qualification was something of a necessity, as her office was located in the U.S. Embassy in Grosvenor Square, where she was officially listed as a senior analyst with the Office of Defense Cooperation. This description was not, however, entirely accurate. Naomi *was* an analyst, but not for the ODC. In reality, she was employed by the Central Intelligence Agency.

The recruiters had come looking for her nearly five years earlier. She'd been working at Bell Labs at the time, in the Computer Science and Software center in Murray Hill. Kharmai had truly despised the job, an entry-level position with little hope of advancement. She had graduated third in her class at Stanford, but that could only take her so far in a company that was home to some of the most brilliant minds in the field of computer engineering. Feeling more than a little neglected, she'd jumped at the chance to work in the CIA's Directorate of Science and Technology, where she was given access to some of the latest innovations and, more importantly, the opportunity to actually use the technology in a meaningful way. But Naomi's talents were not limited to the science of cryptography. It wasn't long before her language skills earned her a place in the CTC, the Agency's Counterterrorism Center. It was there that Jonathan Harper, in desperate need of an Arabic language specialist for an upcoming operation, had found her the previous year.

The rain started coming harder. She tucked her head down a little and increased her pace as she crossed the square for the shelter of the embassy. Climbing the short flight of marble stairs, she pulled open the door to the service entrance, then dug her ID out of her purse for the benefit of the armed marine at the security checkpoint.

He gave her a smile, which she tried to return as they went through the ritual. After being passed through, she made her way directly to the elevator. Soon she was in her office on the third floor. The term "office" was perhaps overly generous, as it was nothing more than a small, windowless cubbyhole. Secretly, Naomi suspected the room had been hijacked from some unfortunate janitor to make room for her. She sometimes caught herself sneaking little glances at the custodians she passed in the halls, searching for the smallest hint of forthcoming retribution.

She turned on her computer, then shrugged off her coat and draped it over the radiator. She was doing her best to wring the water out of her hair when someone tapped on the door. "Yeah?"

One of her fellow analysts poked her head in. "Hey, Naomi." A little grin appeared on her face. "You forgot your umbrella again, didn't you?"

Kharmai sighed in acknowledgment. "You'd think I would know better. I mean, I *did* live here until I was eighteen."

"Well, if you haven't learned by now, you never will. Anyway, the boss wants to talk to you."

"Okay. What's the agenda?"

"I'm not sure," the woman replied. "But you're the only one invited to the party. He wants you to bring these."

She took the proffered list and glanced at the numbered files. "Where is he?"

"Room C."

Naomi raised an eyebrow. Conference Rooms A through E were secure, with cipher locks on the doors and lead shielding in the walls. They were reserved for the most delicate embassy business, and since most of what was said in the building was not for public consumption, the rooms were usually occupied. Still, it wasn't often that she was summoned for a private discussion with the ranking CIA officer in the embassy. In fact, she couldn't think of a single precedent, which made her slightly uneasy.

She shrugged in resignation; she'd find out soon enough. "I'm on my way."

As usual, Naomi nearly missed Emmett Mills when she finally made it to the conference room, balancing a steaming cup of coffee and a stack of paperwork in her arms. At five feet three, Naomi was only a few inches shorter than the silver-haired chief of station, but she knew that the man's slight stature merely served to disguise a powerful intellect. By his midthirties, Mills had already earned four master's degrees from three different schools, as well as an honorary doctorate from the University of Pennsylvania.

Now fifty-four and approaching mandatory retirement, he was something of a legend at Langley. Naomi knew about most of the things he had pulled off during his illustrious career, but even if she'd been kept in the dark, she would have recognized the man's experience in his confident, finely drawn features. Mills was constantly wearing a slightly bemused smile, as though appraising the talent—or ineptitude—of the next generation. It always made her feel self-conscious, feelings that were not quite canceled out by the knowledge that he needed her. Mills had spent the majority of his career in the operations directorate; as a result, he relied heavily on Naomi when it came to technical matters. Since her posting to the embassy, she had been responsible for most of the electronic traffic between their department and the various British intelligence agencies.

"Glad you could finally make it, Kharmai." She started in on a feeble apology, but he held up a hand to stop her. "Do me a favor and kick on that doorstop. We've only got a few minutes before the defense attaché shows up to claim the room, so I'll make this brief. Did you find everything I asked for?"

She nodded as she took the seat across from him, nearly spilling her coffee in the process. Behind her, the door eased shut with a gentle click, locking automatically. She held up a folder. "This is a copy of our current watch list. All of these people have been linked in some way to one of the nine major terrorist groups in Iraq, and they're all based here in London. It's hard to keep track with our limited resources, but we do the best we can. Most of the ties are incidental: family relations, for example. Anything involving a financial transaction gets kicked over to Scotland Yard, MI5, and MI6. Unfortunately, they're a little less generous when it comes time to reciprocate, but that's understandable. This *is* their country, after all."

Mills nodded along, neatly concealing his vague amusement. He'd long ago noticed Kharmai's peculiar lapses when it came to her own national identity.

She set the file to one side, then selected another, much heavier folder. "This one came courtesy of the Ministry of Defense. It's a compilation of all the voiceprints they have on file at Whitehall, arranged in numerical order and based on cell phone intercepts here in the U.K. This is only a sample, of course. They've been fine-tuning the system, but they face the same problem we do in terms of geographical limitations. For us, the towers are based in Fort Meade, which confines the intercepts to the metro area. Here it's the M41 to the west and the A10 to the east." She was referring to the main roads that circled the city. "All in all, it's a seven-mile radius, or about twenty-five square miles, total, with the MoD as the epicenter."

"Okay. Do we have an idea of the daily take?"

"More than an idea, sir." Her smile was almost coy; she was on steady ground now, sure of herself and what she was saying. "Don't forget, I know a lot of people over there. Right now, they're picking off between two and three hundred transmissions a day."

He was surprised. "That many?"

Naomi shrugged. "Most of it's worthless. They've talked about pulling some of the keywords to narrow the scope. The NSA is playing around with the same idea, but the towers on the roof at Whitehall are much, much smaller, which limits both the range and the amount of traffic they can handle."

"Will they give us access to their database?"

"If we can come up with a good reason. We'll still need some search parameters, though. They have thousands of intercepts on file."

"What about going the other way? If you had a recording, for example, could you run it through the system to look for a match?"

"Of course. In fact, that's the easiest way, but it still takes some time."

"What kind of time are we talking about? Hours or days?"

She considered the question. "Again, you're better off if you have someplace to start, like age or gender. Ninety percent of the flagged intercepts are male voices, anyway, but everything helps. Maybe a couple of days, if you were starting with nothing." She tilted her head and frowned. "Sir, what's going on? If this is about the Iraqi prime minister, we can send it to the top of the list. If there's a match on file, you'll cut down on a lot of your wait time. I think I can guarantee cooperation on the British end. The default position in a situation like this is to share everything."

His smile was fading fast. "What makes you think that—"

"Sir, give me some credit. You ask me to bring you our watch list and this"—she held up the voiceprint folder—"which is worthless without the recordings, but you already knew that." She paused for a moment. "They found something in Baghdad, didn't they? A tape?"

He hesitated, then nodded reluctantly. "Yeah, it's a tape. But they didn't find it. *We* found it, here in London."

That surprised her; it was standard practice to work with MI5 on such occasions. The Agency rarely took things into its own hands on friendly soil. "And?"

Mills exhaled slowly and leaned back in his chair, debating his options. It was a tough call. If he brought her in all the way, he might end up losing her back to Langley. Naomi was a valuable part of his team, but if the recording gave them something to work with, she would probably use it to push her own self-interests.

He knew that she wasn't happy at the embassy. After what she'd managed to pull off the previous year, she would have expected a bump in the CTC, maybe to section chief. From what he had seen of her work, Emmett Mills was inclined to agree. He made his decision.

"Okay, Naomi, here's the deal. The final casualty list for the bombing at the Babylon Hotel was released two days ago. You know about al-Maliki?"

She nodded. The Iraqi prime minister had sustained serious injuries and was still listed in critical condition at an undisclosed location. The press had engaged in wild speculation, of course, one news agency going so far as to air an in-depth profile of al-Maliki's potential successors. The hysteria was beginning to die down, though, as it now appeared he was going to pull through.

Mills continued. "We had to wait for the list to see who was missing. The hotel manager was killed in the blast, along with most of the prime minister's security detail. He was careful in that respect; the bodyguards were screened beforehand, so the survivors were cleared in a hurry. The gate guards were cleared as well. They were rotated on a daily basis, but in that case, the interrogations did yield some useful information. In the first week of September, a crew was brought in to repair electrical problems on the second and third floors of the hotel. The work took ten days to complete. During that time, the assistant manager, Rashid Amin al-Umari, spoke to each of the shift leaders, asking them to pass the vehicles through without a security check."

"That's interesting." Naomi leaned forward in her seat. "That's *very* interesting. Let me guess. Rashid has dropped off the face of the earth."

Mills aimed a finger at her. "Exactly. We can't find him anywhere, but it's certainly not for lack of trying. The Iraqi Police Service raided his house in Baghdad yesterday, and"—he handed her a glossy 8 x 10—"this morning we sent a team into this residence in Knightsbridge."

Naomi accepted the photograph and studied it briefly. She was looking at a large home with carefully kept gardens and a beautiful stone façade. "How does a hotel manager afford a house like this?"

"Inheritance," Mills replied. "It belonged to his father, but al-Umari lived there until three months ago."

"*Belonged* to his father?"

"Karim al-Umari died during a U.S. airstrike over Baghdad in 2003. His wife—Rashid's mother—was also killed in the blast, as was his baby sister. Since the elder al-Umari had connections that went right to the top of the Baath regime, the bombing of his personal residence wasn't quite seen as . . . accidental. Rashid gave an interview to Al-Jazeera a few weeks after he buried his family, in which he made some fairly candid remarks about his feelings toward the United States."

Naomi took a few seconds to interpret that last remark; Mills was known to favor the British trait of understatement. "Well, that explains his motivation, I guess. But why that hotel in particular?"

"Because the prime minister frequently stayed there if he had an early appointment the next day. In this case, al-Maliki was scheduled to leave for Paris at seven a.m., so to avoid the traffic moving in and out of the Green Zone, he booked an entire floor at the Babylon for himself and his aides. The summit was scheduled a month or so in advance. Al-Maliki's plans to attend were public knowledge, so the bombers made a decision based on precedent, which obviously turned out to be right. They had plenty of time to set up an electrical malfunction, which al-Umari used to get them into the building."

"How did they plant the devices?"

"They built them into the walls on long-delay timers. Ingenious, really. The IRA tried something similar in '84. They failed as well, by the way, only their target was Margaret Thatcher and her entire cabinet."

"What about the tape? Where was it found?"

"In a wall safe in the house. He didn't do a good job of hiding it, to be honest. He might as well have left it on the kitchen table."

Naomi thought about that for a second. "He didn't feel the need to hide it, probably because it wasn't supposed to exist in the first place. Al-Umari recorded it himself, right? For insurance?"

"It looks that way."

"But you can't identify the other voice." The chief of station shook his head in the negative. "What about the gate guards? Maybe one of them—"

"Not yet. Remember, this is a new development, Naomi. They only found the tape this morning, but it's already in the works. The Iraqis will have a copy sometime tomorrow."

"And the men who planted the bomb?"

"They've disappeared as well. One point of interest: the team leader was a German by the name of Erich Kohl. That comes from the gate guards, by the way; they didn't do the security checks, but they did sign the workers in each morning. Kohl only showed up in the second week. Interestingly enough, the German government doesn't have a contractor by that name in the region, at least not in an official capacity."

Naomi nodded and reached for her coffee, which was already growing cold. "So, Kohl might be the mystery man on the tape?"

"I'd say there's a good chance. What I want you to do is bring it to our British friends and see if they can dig up a matching voiceprint on file. The conversation takes place in Arabic . . . Will that be a problem?"

She shook her head. "No, probably not. We can work around it."

"Good. There's a copy waiting for you in Operations." Mills leaned back in his chair and studied her plaintively. "If you need me to get involved, that's not a problem, but I'd prefer to handle it at our level. You can see the problem . . . We are *not* supposed to have this tape. I hope someone owes you a favor."

Naomi smiled as she gathered her things. "Actually, sir, I think I have just the man in mind."

CHAPTER 5

FALLUJAH

Mark Walland was on one knee in the dusty bed of the third Tacoma, which was turned around and facing north, back toward the train station. The other vehicles, parked about 30 meters away, had yet to pull the same maneuver. From his position, he could clearly see the two Iraqis standing guard, as well as the AK-47 rifles they held, which were vaguely pointed in the direction of the American visitors.

The scenario made him distinctly uneasy, even though he had performed similar tasks with Ryan Kealey on two other occasions in the past few days, and many times before that. The exchange of money for information and regional support was nothing new in the intelligence business, but Walland, despite his youth and limited experience, knew a few things about how effective the practice really was. A stack of American dollars could get you all kinds of promises, but it couldn't reveal a man's true nature, and the Arabs, at least the ones the Agency dealt with, were skilled dissemblers. Walland knew it was just a matter of time before one of their "clients" decided that the money just wasn't worth it.

He glanced at his watch, then lifted his left hand to adjust his ball cap. His right was wrapped around the grip of his M4 carbine. The weapon was specially modified, with a Rail Interface System that included a Visible Laser and a forward handgrip. Mounted to the upper receiver was an ACOG low-light, 4-power telescopic sight. Despite the rifle's proven worth in combat, it didn't offer Walland a great deal of comfort, as his intuition told him that the surrounding buildings were probably filled with armed insurgents. He was in a very dangerous place, and he knew it. Still, at least he had the advantage of a weapon at hand. Kealey's position was much more precarious. At the moment, Kealey had nothing but a backpack full of cash and the word of a Sunni warlord.

The dark hallways seemed far more extensive than he would have guessed from the front of the building. From the search at the entrance, Kealey had passed into the custody of two more fighters, each of whom wore kaffiyehs to shield their identities. He walked between the two men, their feet shuffling forward on cracked tile. The dim light prevented him from seeing who else might have been lurking in the shadows, but it did give him the opportunity to carefully withdraw an object from the main compartment of his pack, which he slid into the waistband of his utility pants. He then pulled his T-shirt over the slight bulge. His escorts didn't seem to notice the small movement.

A few more paces, and they stopped at a plain wooden door. One of the Iraqis ducked in first, then reemerged and gestured for Kealey to enter.

The room was spare and cramped, with a small window to the right. The hazy light that drifted through the dirty panes was enough to pull two men out of the shadows. The first was a guard armed with a battle-scarred AK-47. He stood in a corner, behind and to the left of his charge. The second man sat in the middle of the room, his thick arms resting on a bare metal table. When their eyes met, he smiled and gestured at the chair opposite his own. Kealey took the seat, dropping the backpack onto the floor next to him. As he did so, he heard another guard settle into position behind him. The door closed a moment later, and it was just the four of them.

The man smiled once more at Kealey, but it was a gesture devoid of warmth. "You've come a long way. Would you like something to drink? Something to eat, perhaps?"

He knew that to refuse would be seen as an insult, and he didn't want to set them on edge. At least not yet. "Just water."

The order was given to the guard behind Kealey. Hearing the door open and close once again, he took advantage of the brief distraction to study his host.

As far as the U.S. intelligence community was concerned, Arshad Abdul Kassem was a blank page. Even his age could not be verified, though Kealey's briefing officer in Baghdad had suggested that it probably fell somewhere between forty-five and fifty. This estimate was based on the fact that Kassem had served as a captain in the Republican Guard during the early years of the Iran-Iraq war, and then as a brigadier general in the months leading up to the second gulf war. When the Americans invaded in 2003, Kassem had made arrangements that resulted in the quiet surrender of his entire mechanized brigade outside Karbala. After several months in U.S. custody, Kassem was offered an even quieter deal by the CIA.

With the fall of the Baath regime in 2003, the former officer had narrowly avoided sharing the fate of his party leader. At least, that was the official line of the U.S. government. In truth, his name had never appeared on a watch list, for the Agency had a use for men like Arshad Kassem, high-profile figures in the former regime, with all the right connections. It made Kealey sick to deal with people like this, men who had, in all probability, committed unspeakable crimes under Saddam. Unfortunately, it was hard to find clean hands in high places, especially in this part of the world.

"So . . ." Kassem let the word trail off. He was rotating his hands on the surface of the table. The movement was strange; it made Kealey think of a sleight-of-hand artist on a city street. "I believe you have something for me."

"Yes." He didn't bother looking down at the pack. "But before we get to that, I need to ask you a few things."

Kassem grinned broadly, revealing stained, irregular teeth. He spread his arms wide. "Of course. A man must earn his wages. What do you want to know?"

Kealey looked him dead in the eye. It all came down to this, the defining moment. He could still turn back. He could find a way out to the vehicles, he could walk back in with what was expected . . . but it would be the same as before, and he'd be no further forward.

"I want you to tell me about the Babylon Hotel."

The Iraqi's face became suddenly cautious, the insolent grin sliding away. "I don't think I understand."

Kealey shook his head and leaned back in his seat, carefully appraising his host. "I think you do," he said, "but we'll come back to that. Let me ask it this way. Who, in your opinion, would benefit from al-Maliki's death?"

"That's a very long list, my friend."

"I'm aware of that. I was hoping you might be able to narrow it down for me."

Kassem didn't respond for a long time, but his curiosity finally won out. "And why would you think that?"

"Because there's a good chance the same people you used to work for are responsible," Kealey replied. Then he added, "And because we pay you to know."

The older man shook his head slowly. "I know a great many people. Some of them—most of them, even—are opposed to your presence here. That much is true, but I am not paid to spy on my own people. I have never agreed to such a thing, nor would I. Not for any amount of money."

"That's not good enough," Kealey said. Pushing it forward now, clipping his words, he added, "And if you can't come up with something better than that, we're going to have a problem."

Something flashed in the older man's eyes. "Young man, I've worked with your government for several years. What possible reason could I have to involve myself in such a thing?"

"That's what I'm here to find out," Kealey shot back. "We've been throwing cash at you since the fall of Baghdad, and in my opinion, we don't have a lot to show for it. So here's my next question, Arshad. Where does the money go?"

Kassem, caught off-guard, did not respond right away. This was his first time dealing with this man, this arrogant American. Did he not know where he was? Who he was talking to?

True, he did not resemble his predecessors. Most of the men sent to Kassem were throwbacks to the Cold War, former field men in their fifties and sixties. They were all the same: fattened on rich food, full of false smiles, soft in semiretirement and eager to please. This one was different.

The man who sat before him was young, lean, and exceptionally fit. His lank black hair was long and unkempt, drifting over his forehead in places, and the lower half of his tanned face was obscured by a matted beard. In many ways, he looked like one of the elite U.S. soldiers so prevalent in the city. At the same time, his clothes, a plain black T-shirt and threadbare utility pants, were decidedly civilian in style. Kassem took note of everything he saw, as was his habit, but it wasn't these things that bothered him.

It was the eyes. They were dark gray and completely empty. He had seen the same vacant look in men who had suffered a terrible loss, men who had surpassed the pain and found nothing to take its place. Kassem idly wondered what could have happened to this young American, but he was more concerned about what it might mean for him. He was beginning to think that his guest did not understand how the game was played.

"The money," he replied carefully, "goes to men who, without a way to feed their families, might take up arms. The money goes to trained fighters who, without hope, might offer your country more than petty resistance. It is what we agreed on."

"I understand the agreement. What I don't understand is how we're supposed to measure your progress. What guarantees can you offer us?"

"You have seen the proof," Kassem boasted. Despite his best efforts, he couldn't hold the arrogance down for long. "How many soldiers have you lost in the last month? Or the month before that?"

"That's a fair point," Kealey conceded. "I wonder what happened to those men. The ones who, according to you, have turned away from the insurgency. Maybe some of them have accepted the new government. Perhaps your peers to the east are as successful as you in their efforts to reform those who served under Saddam."

Kassem nodded solemnly. "Perhaps you are right. It takes time to—"

"On the other hand, maybe they didn't turn away at all."

The Iraqi furrowed his brow, clearly annoyed by the interruption. "What do you mean?"

Kealey leaned forward, stabbing his words across the table. "The timing seems very convenient, Arshad. You've been on the Agency payroll for nearly two years, but you didn't seem to care too much about fulfilling your end of the deal until the president decided to start pulling out troops. I can't help but wonder who else is dumping money into your bank account."

Kassem did not respond for a long moment. When he finally spoke, his words were slow and measured. "I can see that you are new to this line of work. You are very quick to make accusations."

Kealey shrugged. "Let me tell you that—"

"No, let me tell *you.*" Something had changed in the Iraqi's demeanor. "Have you ever been to Najaf?"

For Kealey, the lie came easily. "No."

"I know a man who lives there, a friend of mine for many years. We are very much alike, this man and I, in that he commands respect in his district, he is looked to as a leader. His position brought him to the attention of your government, but there was a difference between us. He did not want to take your money, to bow to your authority. I called him a fool, and I was right to do so, but I was also envious, because I admired his strength.

"Of course, it could not last. An American came to see him two months ago. He was young, like you." There was a brief, meaningful pause. "He offered my friend a hundred thousand U.S. dollars to switch sides, to give the government, *your* government, his support and the support of his men. My friend refused. His honor was worth more than any amount of money. At least, that is what he believed at the time."

Kassem watched Kealey for a reaction. When none appeared forthcoming, he continued. "That evening, your country dropped a bomb less than a hundred meters from the house in which he was sleeping. He survived the blast, and the following day, the American returned. This time he offered seventy thousand dollars. My friend accepted."

Kealey nodded absently. "It sounds like he made a smart decision."

The offhand comment was the last straw. Kassem's face twisted into a mask of rage, the hatred suddenly boiling to the surface. "You arrogant *fuck,*" he hissed. "Where do you think you are? Who are you to judge what is right for my people?"

Kealey didn't visibly react to the sudden outburst. His right hand, however, inched closer to the slight bulge beneath his shirt as the Iraqi continued, his voice rising with each passing syllable. "You come here with the belief that you are superior. What you cannot buy, you take. You stupidly believe that you are invincible, that you can survive anything. . . ."

Kassem abruptly half-stood, his body shaking in anger, and waved his arms around the tiny room. "This is *my* country!" he shouted. "Do you honestly believe that we are that weak? That we could not get rid of you if it suited us?"

The man's tirade confirmed what Kealey already knew: that at some point in his dealings with the Agency, Arshad Kassem had stepped over the line. Way over the line. "I know that we didn't have to drop a bomb next to *your* house," he said quietly. "That tells me more than all of your bullshit."

Kassem stopped moving. He stared at Kealey, openmouthed, for what seemed like an eternity. Finally, he sat back down, and when he spoke, his words were very soft.

"I think I'd like to be paid now."

CHAPTER 6

FALLUJAH

"What the hell is he doing?" Walland hissed, directing the question to Paul Owen over his MBITR handheld radio. Kealey's transmission was coming over the SINCGARS unit mounted to the dashboard; he could hear the rapidly deteriorating conversation through the sliding rear window of the Tacoma.

"I have no idea," was the Delta officer's strained reply. "It sounds like he's baiting him." There was a rush of static, then, "We're turning around. This looks like it's going to shit . . . I want to be able to get out of here in a hurry."

"I hear that. I'll cover the guards while you move."

"Roger that."

Walland resumed watching the two guards, his M4A1 across his chest, muzzle depressed. He couldn't point the rifle directly at the guards without starting an unnecessary gunfight. At the same time, his stance allowed him to bring the weapon to bear in an instant if the need arose.

It happened just as Kealey said it would. The guard on the right lifted a radio to his lips the moment Owen's vehicle started to roll, and it didn't fall to his side until the Tacoma had completed its three-point turn. The other pickup followed suit so that all three of the trucks were facing north, back toward the train station.

Walland lifted his handset. "Did you see that?"

"Yeah, I saw it. I'm squelching Kealey's radio. Let's hope he plays it smart."

The tension in the room was almost unbearable. For Kealey, the silence amplified everything else: the hatred in the eyes of Arshad Kassem, the particles of dust dancing in the hazy light, the nervous twitch of the one guard in his field of vision. The older man was staring at him expectantly.

"I want my money."

Kealey shook his head and said, "We're not through yet." With the guard watching his every movement, he slowly pulled a thin folder from the pack at his feet. At the same time, he checked to make sure that his radio was still transmitting. He tossed the file onto the table. "These are wire records, Arshad. *Your* records, traced back to the Allied Bank in Beirut. It looks like you're doing pretty well these days. Accounts in Luxembourg, Switzerland, and the Central Bank in the Dutch Antilles. What are you looking at, total? Five, six million dollars?"

Kealey's face grew suddenly hard. "Six *million*. Where the fuck did that money come from? We've paid you seven hundred thousand over two years."

"That is not your concern. It is a separate business arrangement . . . a separate client."

"A separate business arrangement?" Kealey's expression made it clear what he thought of this argument. "How does this 'client' feel about your dealings with the Central Intelligence Agency?"

The Iraqi smirked in response. This was not what Kealey had expected, but before he could recover, his radio emitted two short beeps.

Kassem didn't seem to notice. "You shouldn't have come here," he said quietly. He spread his hands over the table and stared hard at the younger man. "This was supposed to be simple. You have no idea what you're getting into. Now give me my money, and get the fuck out of my city."

Kealey met his cold, unflinching gaze for a long moment. Then he reached down for the pack, his eyes never leaving those of the Sunni warlord.

* * *

Walland was now watching the guards with greater interest. The more he heard of the conversation between Kealey and Kassem, the easier it became to think of the two men in front of the building as potential targets. He didn't know what Kealey was doing, but one thing was becoming increasingly obvious: Arshad Kassem did not have the best interests of the United States at heart.

It was the risk they took. To get things done in a place like Iraq, the Agency was forced to deal with some of the worst people on the planet. Not all of the bets turned out to be good, but Walland knew the meeting could still be salvaged. All Kealey had to do was stop talking and pay the man. They would pass the word on Kassem up the line, and then . . . well, it didn't really matter what then. Fortunately, those decisions were made by somebody much higher on the food chain.

He reached up and wiped a film of sweat from his face. The sun was barely over the horizon, but the temperature was already climbing rapidly. His eyes drifted over to the cooler. He remembered what Kealey had said. *I'm going to get some water. Just sit tight.*

Still cradling the M4 in the crook of his right arm, Walland leaned over and flipped off the lid. What he saw turned his spine to ice.

There was nothing to drink in the small compartment. All he saw was money. Stacks of hundred-dollar bills, neatly wrapped in plastic. Walland didn't know how much he was looking at, but he knew exactly where it was supposed to be. More importantly, he knew what Kealey was about to do.

He grabbed for the radio and pressed the *transmit* button. "Colonel, I think we have a serious problem here."

The guard Kassem had sent for the water had never reappeared. Kealey didn't know how many men might be waiting outside the door. He didn't know how Owen would react, and he didn't know if his plan, hastily composed at the last possible moment, had even the slightest chance of working. Somehow, he doubted it, but he was beyond caring.

His next movements were somewhat detached, almost mechanical in the precision with which they were carried out. Kealey reached down for the backpack, his hand slipping into the main compartment. He flipped a switch and lifted the bag, tossing it onto the table, counting the seconds in his head. At the same time, he used his left hand to grip the lower edge of his T-shirt. Arshad Kassem reached for the pack and pulled it across the table, his gaze fixed on the younger man. When he got to five, Kealey closed his eyes and threw himself to the floor.

The charge went off a split second later. Kassem and his bodyguard were instantly blinded by the flash of light, then deafened by the following concussion. The older man was blown out of his chair as Kealey struggled to his feet, ears ringing with the blast, pulling up on his shirt as his right hand wrapped around the butt of his Beretta 9mm pistol. The weapon came up an instant later. He had just enough time to meet the wide eyes of the guard over his front sights before he pulled the trigger. The man's head snapped back, and he crumpled to the floor in a lifeless heap.

Kealey couldn't hear the footsteps in the hall, but he knew they had to be coming. He scrambled for the dead guard's AK-47, jarring his fingers on the tile floor in the process. He lifted the weapon and squeezed the trigger as the door flew open. His rounds caught the advancing guard in the chest, propelling him back into the hallway. At the same time, Kealey flipped the metal table onto its side to put an obstacle between the door and his own body.

Kassem was splayed across the floor, his hands and face scorched by the magnesium powder in the improvised charge. He was howling in agony, hands pressed to his ravaged face. Trying to block out the screams of pain, Kealey listened for movement in the other parts of the building. He heard feet pounding overhead and then a shouted phrase in Arabic.

He wouldn't last long in this little room, he knew that much. Sliding the Beretta into his waistband, he leaned over and slammed a fist into Kassem's face. The man went instantly limp. Kealey crouched and grabbed him by the front of his shirt, lifting him up and onto his shoulders. It took all his strength; Kassem weighed at least 200 pounds. His radio was still transmitting. Tilting his head down to his hip, he shouted, "Paul, light up the second floor. *Now!*"

* * *

Walland wasn't sure what was happening, but when the sound of the explosion reached him, his training took over. The M4 snapped up in his arms, and he instantly found the guard on the left through his telescopic sight. He squeezed off a 3-round burst, then switched his aim to the next fighter as the first hit the ground. The man's AK was already coming up, his finger landing on the trigger as Walland's second burst tore through his chest. A wild spray of bullets ripped into the frame of the first Tacoma, shattering the glass in the driver's side door.

Owen flinched as cubes of safety glass exploded over his upper body. He turned to the left and tracked for targets with his rifle, but saw right away that Walland's shots had found their mark. The radio traffic was coming loud and fast; he heard Walland shouting something on the handheld and then Kealey calling for cover over the SINCGARS.

He immediately grabbed for the handset and shouted, "Gregg, Morales, that's you! Hit the second floor with everything you got!"

Kealey was moving as fast as he could through the dimly lit hallways, struggling to keep Kassem's body on his shoulders and his weapon up at the same time. The sound of a heavy machine gun thumped in his ears, growing louder as he pushed forward. He reached a corner and cut it wide, catching sight of an armed guard on a wooden staircase. He was about to fire when a volley of rounds ripped through the front of the building. Kealey saw a flash of red, saw the man's left leg collapse, and he went sideways, crashing through the banister to the floor below. The sound of the splintering wood was lost in another hail of automatic fire. Tipping his head back to the radio, Kealey said, "Owen, tell your guys to watch their fire. I'm coming out."

He burst into the sunlight a moment later, shards of cement from the building's façade crumbling beneath his feet. The Delta troopers in the first two trucks continued to pour rounds into the second floor as Kealey heaved Kassem into the back of the first Tacoma, then climbed in after him. He caught a jagged piece of metal on his way over the side, felt a sudden tearing pain, and looked down to see a bloody rent in his trousers, just above the left knee.

Owen was turned around in his seat, eyes wide in anger. He had to shout over the sound of gunfire. "What the fuck happened in there? And what the hell are you doing with him? There's no way we're taking him—"

"I can't explain it right now. Just drive." Kealey was fighting to stay calm, but when the Delta colonel didn't respond right away, he fixed him with a fierce look and screamed, "*Now*, Paul! Let's go!"

The other man seemed stunned by the expression on Kealey's face, but it pushed him into action. The truck accelerated rapidly a split second later, the other vehicles following suit. Soon they were racing back to the train yard. Owen called the other vehicles for a sit rep, breathing a long sigh of relief when the casualty count came back zero. Then he punched in the frequency for the Agency pilots on the dash-mounted SINCGARS radio. Once the call went through, he hurled the handset against the dash and turned to glare at Kealey through the open rear window of the truck cab.

"I hope you have a good fucking reason for this." There was a hard edge to his elevated voice. "One way or another, you owe me an explanation."

"I know." Looking down at Kassem's unconscious body, Kealey felt strangely numb. "And you'll get one, I promise. But for now, just get us out of here."

CHAPTER 7

SYRIA

With night slinking in, the sun slipped low to the west, red light bleeding over the sparse landscape, climbing over the limestone hills that surround the dead cities of the Byzantines before sliding south to touch the modest peak of Talat Musa on the Lebanese border. Far to the north, a lean figure wandered past the great earthen mound of the Aleppo Citadel, surrounded by humanity but, at a mere twenty-six years of age, lost to it already. No one cared to notice. They were occupied, as always, by the menial tasks that filled their waking hours. Had they looked closer, they might have thought the young man walked without haste, without purpose. These descriptions, however, were not applicable to any part of his life.

Rashid Amin al-Umari had been a driven man since the fall of the Baath regime. His drive was mired in hate, which was not unusual in this tumultuous region, though a rage of such rigidity is rarely forged by one incident, as was the case with this young man. Despite his youth, al-Umari often felt that he had nothing left to look forward to. All that remained to him were memories. Memories of the good years, the years before an American bomb stripped his world away.

He remembered that day with the kind of clarity that only enduring pain can provide. The Pentagon, of course, had called it an accident. Months later, unnamed U.S. government officials had, in a vague admission of sorts, described his mother and sister as "collateral damage," but the fact that they had been innocent bystanders was glaringly obvious; the most callous observer could not argue otherwise. On the other hand, even Rashid could concede that his father's activities had made him a valuable target. When the rubble was finally cleared, not enough of Karim al-Umari had remained to fill his grave, but the man's legacy lived on.

Karim al-Umari's rise to power had begun long before Rashid had the presence of mind to truly appreciate it. In later years, the elder al-Umari rarely indulged his only son when it came to the intricacies of the family business—or the politics of his country—but for Rashid, a naturally astute young man, it had not been difficult to piece it all together. The signs were hard to miss, the whispers easily overheard. By 1988, Karim al-Umari was known and feared as a dominant figure in the Baath Party, made prominent by the wealth his construction empire generated, made powerful by his connection to the chairman himself. It was the newly installed leader of the party who saw fit to provide the fledgling company with several lucrative contracts in the late 1970s, shortly after his own succession to the aging Ahmed Hassan al-Bakr. When it came to the expansion of the capital, it seemed as though the party's funds were limitless; even the prolonged, costly war with Iran had failed to lessen the regime's enthusiasm when it came to spending the people's money, and with each new government building that cropped up in the capital, the family empire continued to reap the benefits.

It was not, however, until 1985 that the elder al-Umari received his just reward. This prize came in the form of position, a chair on the Revolutionary Command Council, which carried with it control of the southern provinces of Muthanna and Qadisyah. It could scarcely have been a better gift. For Karim al-Umari, the oil-rich land offered an irresistible opportunity. He borrowed heavily against his company's assets to purchase several refineries, and as with all his business ventures, it proved to be a successful gamble. It was al-Umari who first adopted Western extraction techniques, and al-Umari who proposed the construction of a pipeline to the Red Sea port of Jeddah. When his plan was implemented in 1989, his newly created Iraqi Southern Oil Company saw an immediate 30 percent boost in profits. One year after Iraqi oil started winding its way across the Saudi Arabian desert, Karim al-Umari's personal net worth exceeded one billion U.S. dollars, and his position within the party was rivaled by only the chairman himself.

The al-Umari oil conglomerate endured the occasional setback, of course. The first gulf war was extremely costly; Rashid's father lost tens of millions over the course of the following decade, including the cost of repairing a bomb-shattered refinery south of Basra. In truth, though, Karim al-Umari barely noticed those losses; by the late 1990s, his considerable power was worth more to him than any amount of money. Unfortunately, that power also made him a target, and with the American invasion of 2003, it all came crumbling down.

In the thirty-six months since the bombing that claimed the lives of his mother, father, and twelve-year-old sister in the Iraqi capital, Rashid had worked to align himself with the insurgency. It was difficult, at first; it was a world he did not understand, and his connections were tenuous at best. Ironically, it was the demise of Karim al-Umari that provided his only son—the sole heir to the al-Umari oil empire—with the means to make contact. In those early days, Rashid's contributions were limited to his rather generous donations, most of which found their way to the Mahdi Army in Sadr City. Because of his ties to the former regime, the trust was hard won. He was forced to labor for months in the background, offering support from a distance, working his way into their confidence. The test, when it came, arrived in the form of information: the time and location of a meeting involving several high-level officials. When the empty building was not razed by a surgical airborne strike, it was believed that he was true to the cause, that he did not belong to the West, but to Moqtadr al-Sadr himself. With the trust came a place in the organization and the friendship of the most senior commanders. And then, on a frigid morning in late January, three days after he'd flown in from London via Amman, he'd been introduced to the German.

No one seemed to know exactly where Erich Kohl had come from. More uncertain still was his role in the organization, though the fact that he rarely left the sheik's side said much in itself. Some suggested that he'd been aligned with the Red Army Faction in the early nineties; others, that he had worked for the Stasi—the East German secret police—before the wall came down in '89, though al-Umari had quietly pointed out at the time that the German appeared too young to have taken part in those events.

In time, his interactions with the foreigner became more frequent. Their alliance was a strange one, born more out of their status as outsiders than anything else. Despite their respective ties to al-Sadr, Kohl remained an infidel, Rashid nothing more than the wealthy son of a Sunni power broker. Over the course of many conversations, al-Umari gradually revealed the depths of his frustration, the impotence he felt when the greatest victory they could claim was the lives of a few young soldiers on the road to Najaf. During these discussions, Rashid never noticed that the German's words were few and far between; al-Umari did the talking for both of them, but he was never dissuaded, never brushed aside.

Despite his rhetoric, the arrangement was largely satisfactory to Rashid al-Umari. He was doing his part, and in private moments, he could concede the truth: that no matter what he felt, that despite the terrible thoughts that drove him, he was content to speak with his money. He was a student of science, an academic . . . It was not in him to lift a weapon against his enemy, to find a man in his sights and squeeze the trigger. With this distinction in mind, the view from the periphery was enough to feed his inner rage; he felt no particular need to take the next logical step.

All of that began to change on a cool, still night in late May. It was Rashid's third trip to Sadr City in as many months, and although he took meticulously planned, circuitous routes out of London, he could not help but fear that Britain's Secret Intelligence Service—better known as MI6—would eventually take an interest in his movements. This concern had been expressed to Kohl in hushed tones, along with his displeasure at having to leave so early in the ongoing offensive, despite its undeniable lack of success. It was a familiar refrain, but the German did not offer his usual sympathetic ear. Instead, he spoke quietly of another path. He murmured of men in the north who were waiting to act, and the names he used were instantly recognizable to al-Umari. Some were dated names that went back to his childhood, while others could still be found on every watch list in

North America and Western Europe. Here, at last, was the possibility of a real victory. Rashid al-Umari listened intently for two hours and, the following morning, left Sadr City for the last time. He was not sorry to leave it behind.

Since then, his meetings with the foreigner had been extremely limited, their last conversation coming ten days earlier in a musty apartment on the west side of Baghdad's Jadriya district. In that meeting he'd been given the travel arrangements and the necessary papers, which might or might not have gotten him through an IPS checkpoint. Al-Umari was all too aware of the changing attitude in government service; the American-trained security forces could no longer be counted on to accept a generous bribe in return for safe passage, but as it turned out, he had not been forced to face that particular risk. In fact, the whole trip—including the border crossing south of the al-Maze military airport—had been astonishingly easy. The German had suggested that this might be the case, but that had not stopped him from delivering a seemingly endless litany of security precautions. The foreigner's words were still clear in his mind, but Rashid al-Umari was a young man with a young man's stubborn mentality, and the Old City of Aleppo was not without its charms.

The Aleppo souq, one of the oldest in the north and the best outside of Damascus, was somewhat crowded in the early evening. Old women and young wives, most wearing the traditional chador, others daringly clothed in Western attire, ventured out of their homes as the heat finally dropped to bearable levels. It was dark beneath thick canvas draped over stone archways, the individual stalls lit only by crude iron lanterns dangling precariously overhead. Rashid al-Umari turned left on Souq al-Zarb and began making his way through the city market, moving slowly in an attempt to take it all in.

It was truly a wondrous sight. It had been many years since he had seen such an array of goods; it seemed as though there was little one could wish for that could not be found in these crowded streets. Headscarves and *jalabiyyas*, the long robes worn by men and women alike, could be found in every size and color imaginable. He passed stalls bearing perfumes and spices, fresh meats and vegetables. He turned his head to gaze down one narrow *hara* and saw row after row of gleaming yellow metal. Another corridor was lined with stands heaped with antique silver jewelry. The sights of the bazaar battled only with the sounds; al-Umari was assaulted from every direction by the calls of Syrian vendors and the guarded replies of their potential customers. The steady sound of passing traffic to the east fought to drown out the tinny whine of an American pop song, which was emanating from a child's battered radio. It was, Rashid thought, completely chaotic, and yet, there was also something strangely controlled about the whole scene, for these were a people separated only by the worn counters over which they traded.

Certainly, it could not be compared to his own city. One could hardly turn around in Baghdad without seeing another American patrol. The superior smiles were always evident on those clean-shaven faces, despite the vast losses they had sustained. *How can they be so persistent?* Rashid wondered, the anger welling up as it always did. *Why can they not accept that they have failed?* It was incomprehensible to this young man that the Americans could be so ignorant of history. Had the British Empire not learned that the Iraqi people could not be ruled? The Europeans had certainly tried, of course, caught up in the New Imperialism which had dominated the last thirty years of the nineteenth century. Al-Umari smiled as he considered what Britain's greed for new territory in the Middle East had actually gotten them: disastrous losses in Afghanistan at the hands of Pashtun tribesmen, followed by two Anglo-Afghan wars, which resulted in the complete withdrawal of British forces by 1919. His own people had fought equally well the following year. That proud, bloody rebellion against colonial rule had earned the Iraqi people their independence in 1932.

Al-Umari mused over that point as he left the market on the west side and found a small coffee shop. Soon he was seated on a warm wooden bench outside, sipping from a small cup of *shai*, the hot, sweet tea favored by the Aleppines. Iraqis on both sides of the Sunni-Shia divide could point to the uprising in 1920 as one of the few times they had worked together in defense of their country, and *that* was something else to consider.

Despite his background, Rashid al-Umari did not believe that the Shiites should be denied a place in the new Iraq. What he had seen in

Sadr City, however, caused him to distrust the capabilities of the insurgency. It was reason enough to exclude the Mahdi Army, but there was something else: despite their ill-defined allegiances, al-Umari rightly suspected that they would not be able to get past the attempt on Nuri al-Maliki. It had been deemed necessary; the man was too closely aligned with the West. The fact that he had survived was not at all important. From all accounts, he was in no state to resume his duties, and with the prime minister out of the picture, the Americans were stripped of one of their most powerful allies in the region. It was only a start, of course. Their allies were many, including the oil companies, which had been so quick to prostitute themselves after the fall of Baghdad.

It was so typical, Rashid thought bitterly. History always repeated itself; the greatest of empires were also the greediest. After all, what really separated the current American government from the British imperialists of the twentieth century? The answer was simple: nothing. In the end, the only real objective was to enrich the invading country, and no matter what the Americans said, their intent was not benevolent. One only had to look at the Western contractors pouring into the region to see that.

But what of my ambition? Rashid Amin al-Umari lifted the cup to his lips once more as he considered that point. The plan they had set in motion, the laborious, dangerous weeks spent making contact, would benefit his people as a whole. Of that, he had no doubt. He was sincere in his desire to liberate the Iraqi people from their most recent oppressors, though his motivation was decidedly less pure in its origins.

Yes, he finally admitted, *I am almost as selfish as the Americans. Almost, but not quite.*

CHAPTER 8

LONDON

"This is going to take forever," Naomi finally said.

"Not forever," Liz Peterson replied. She shot the younger woman a teasing grin and said, "But close."

They were seated in identical chairs in a secure room on the fourth floor of the Ministry of Defence, a nondescript eight-story building faced in pale Portland stone. The room was cool, dim, and windowless, which didn't bother Naomi in the least, as the sight of rain drifting over the city for the third day in a row would not have improved her sour mood. They had been staring at the computer screen for nearly two hours now, and the young CIA analyst was beginning to think they were chasing a ghost.

As Peterson worked the keyboard, Kharmai studied the equipment laid out on the table. She was somewhat surprised at the quality of the MoD's spectrograph equipment, though she didn't know why this should be. If anyone could come close to matching America's bloated intelligence budget, it was the British. Some of the specific innovations were new to her, but she knew the process inside and out; after all, it was Bell Labs, her first employer, that had pioneered the use of voice-recognition technology back in the 1940s. Things had come a long way since then. Significant advances over the past few decades had done away with the cumbersome magnetic tape and photographic paper of the analog spectrograph. Digital signal processing, or DSP, had since taken its place, though in some ways, the new equipment was almost as tedious to use.

The British computer engineer caught her curiosity. "Have you guys replaced all that junk your contractors came up with in the sixties?" she asked, with a smile. Peterson knew about Naomi's years before the Agency.

"I couldn't really tell you," Kharmai replied honestly. "We obviously don't have anything as good over here, but I'm not sure about Langley. Last time I checked, they had a contract with Motorola in the works, but I'm not sure if they ever bought the gear."

"If your Admin Directorate had anything to do with it, they probably decided to look for something cheaper. Our budget people are the same way; they'd take the cost of this stuff out of our salaries if they thought they could get away with it."

Naomi smiled in agreement. Liz Peterson was the "man in mind" she'd mentioned to Emmett Mills the previous day. She had first met Peterson at an embassy function shortly after arriving in-country, and they had hit it off immediately, despite the fact that they were technically competitors. On the weekends they frequently met for drinks at the Dorchester Hotel, and while they genuinely enjoyed each other's company, both women habitually took those opportunities to dig for a little information. They both knew it was part of the job, and they took it all in stride. Naomi was well aware, for instance, that her access to Whitehall's database had been approved by somebody much higher on the pay scale than Liz Peterson, despite the informal nature of her request. She also knew that whatever they managed to turn up would soon land on the prime minister's desk, most likely within an hour of discovery. Sharing information with one's allies was the cost of doing business, but that wasn't much of a price to pay, especially when they managed to come up with something interesting.

Peterson sat up in her seat as the numbers paused on the monitor. Fixing her pale blue eyes on the screen, she brushed a strand of blond hair out of her face and brought up the relevant information.

"You have something?"

"Maybe," Peterson replied, a hint of excitement coming through. She leaned forward and traced the amplitude waves with her index finger. "Just going by the visual, that's a . . . sixteen-point match."

"Good enough for a probable," Naomi murmured. After purchasing their first analog spectrographs in the late 1970s, the CIA's Directorate of Science and Technology had adopted, for lack of a better system, the forensic standards used by U.S. law enforcement at the time. A "probable" identification was assigned to any match greater than fifteen but less than twenty points on a given spectrogram. In other words, there was an 80 percent chance that the voiceprint in the MoD's database matched the voice found on the tape in al-Umari's Knightsbridge home.

Peterson was still trailing her finger along the screen. On the monitor, the voiceprint resembled the cross section of a series of waves. "See here," she said, pointing to a large splotch of red in the left-hand corner of the graph. "That's a hard c, like in the word 'car.'" She moved over to the right-hand side of the graph, where the red was much less pronounced. "And this is a soft t, like in 'booth.' The fricatives you see here are really good news for us."

"Because of the language difference?"

"Right. You tend to find a lot of allophones in the Arabic language, and they sometimes lead to false negatives on a spectrogram, even after you convert from analog to digital and filter out the elec—"

"Hold on," Naomi said, a little exasperation creeping into her voice. "I understand the technology, Liz, but I have no idea what you just said."

"Allophones?" Kharmai nodded meekly, causing Peterson to smile. It wasn't often that her stubborn friend could concede when she was lost. "Well, a phone is a sound that has a definite shape as a sound wave, which is obviously really helpful when you're trying to match voiceprints. An allophone, on the other hand, is one of several phones in a phoneme. If you change one phoneme in any given word, you can produce another word entirely."

"So a phoneme is like . . . a syllable?" Naomi asked.

"Not really. More like the way in which syllables are put together. But as I was saying, the problem with allophones is that they can lead to false negatives. This happens for two reasons. First, the software is good, but it isn't *that* good. It can't always differentiate when two phones are that similar. Second, you're always going to have some electronic interference. Part of this occurs when the recording is actually made. In this case, we had to deal with distortion on the recording device *and* interference on the line itself."

"Also, you lose some of the source material when you convert from analog to digital, right?"

Peterson flashed Naomi the kind of smile a teacher reserves for her star pupil. "Exactly. We use filters to remove electronic noise outside of the desired frequency range, which helps, but you still lose some of the original conversation in the measurements."

Naomi shrugged. "Eighty percent is good enough for me. What's the background?"

The other woman minimized the spectrogram and double-clicked on the numerical file. Instantly, the screen filled with information.

"Voiceprint 243.55 belongs to . . . Abdul Rahman Yasin." Peterson sucked in her breath as her eyes scanned the screen. "God, this guy is right up there. Wanted on nine counts by the FBI. Involved with the PMOI in Iran in the early nineties, suspected collusion in the WTC bombing in '93 . . . He matches your profile, Naomi."

Kharmai leaned in to get a closer look. "Except for the languages. He doesn't speak German, and he learned Arabic in Tunisia. That's the Maghreb dialect, and we typed the voice on the tape as Gulf Arabic."

Peterson shot her a sideways glance.

"What?" Naomi asked.

"You didn't mention the German. Where did you get that?"

Kharmai winced. "Sorry. That came from the Babylon Hotel. We're pretty sure this guy Kohl is the second voice, but it's almost certainly an alias, because the Germans don't have any contractors by that name in the region."

"So he speaks Arabic and German. That should narrow it down." Peterson cleared the screen and began typing in the new parameters.

CHAPTER 9

ALEPPO · LONDON

From across the crowded asphalt road, Erich Kohl watched as the young man finished his tea and left the coffee shop, walking north on Souq Khan al-Harir. Kohl returned the copper pot he'd been examining to a disappointed shopkeeper and followed at a leisurely pace, the cuffs of his loose cotton pants gathering fine dust from the street. It wasn't difficult to trail the other man. Rashid al-Umari, he thought, still had a lot to learn about his new profession.

Kohl had arrived in the city two days earlier and had immediately taken up watch outside al-Umari's small room south of the Citadel. It was countersurveillance, really; he knew exactly where the Iraqi was supposed to be, for he had been the one to formulate the travel plans, and the young man was not imaginative enough to deviate from his instructions. At least, that was what Kohl had thought until earlier in the afternoon, when al-Umari had walked out after three days in seclusion, blinking his eyes like an animal emerging from a long hibernation, and had set out to explore the city.

At the time, he'd been angered by the Iraqi's inability to follow simple instructions. In retrospect, though, he could see that this was a positive turn of events. There were too many places around the hotel where security officers loyal to the West might have burrowed in. Had that been the case, even Kohl's practiced eyes might not have been enough to pick them out of the crowd. With Rashid on the move, a watcher was forced to risk exposing himself, which put him at a distinct disadvantage. Fortunately, it did not appear to be a concern in this case; Kohl had been trailing the Iraqi for several hours now, and nothing seemed out of the ordinary.

On reaching the intersection, al-Umari turned right on Sharia al-Jamaa al-Umawi, passing the north entrance to the Great Mosque a moment later. Devout Muslims carrying their prayer rugs were already congregating on the hard-packed dirt of the parking area, smoking and engaging in idle conversation. As al-Umari made his way through the small crowd, Kohl dropped back, preparing to break contact. The younger man was clearly heading back to the Citadel, but . . .

Something was wrong. Kohl slowed his stride and tried to take in the larger scene. The crowd was building by the minute. The muezzins started up far overhead—not the muffled recordings found in so many Middle Eastern cities, but individual singers perched high in the minarets, the stone towers attached to the mosques. The day's fourth call to prayer rippled over the city as the first singers were joined by hundreds more. With the mournful tones came the expected response; the crowd in the street continued to swell. His eyes passed over the scene: the wood-shuttered windows climbing above the pavement, the sand-stripped cars lining the curb, the faces sweeping past in the road. He was rifling his memory, searching for something, *someone* he had seen before. Nothing jumped out, but then he saw a dark head turning, tracking. He followed the gaze to al-Umari, who was just passing out of view, having found a shortcut through an alley framed by buildings of red stone. The man's feet followed the gaze, stepping into the street, pushing through the throngs. There was something wrong with this dark, unlined face, Kohl thought. It was the face of a boy not yet twenty, too young for intelligence work. But those eyes were so intent, so *focused*. . . .

Kohl considered quickly. There was nothing professional in the man's movements, though that could be intentional; he had seen it done before. One watcher was given away to draw a response, to distract the target, but he didn't think that was the case here. Syria's internal security apparatus was an ever-shifting maze of poorly funded agencies with overlapping missions. The internal squabbles prevented any one organization from becoming too powerful, and none had the ability to develop competent field men. It was, Kohl suspected, the way Assad wanted things; by limiting his subordinates' power, he robbed them of the authority they would need to displace him.

But there was something more. Through Kohl, al-Umari was tied in with the highest ranks of the Syrian government, and what he was prepared to fund would be greatly profitable to many people. These people, the parties of interest, would gain nothing by killing him.

Unless, of course, they were trying to cover their tracks, but it was too soon for that. They didn't have the money yet, and besides, Kohl had been running countersurveillance for two days, during which time nothing had piqued his interest. Which left just one alternative: a simple robbery, the worst kind of luck.

The boy was across the street now, 10 meters in front of him, stepping into the alley. Even at this sharp angle, Kohl could see that the space between the buildings was too dark and narrow to attract a shopkeeper's stand. Having lost sight of both men, he cursed under his breath and picked up the pace, brushing past a small group of bearded students before making the sharp right turn.

"Got something," Peterson announced.

Naomi glanced up from the folder she'd been reading. "What's that?"

"Nineteen-point match, ninety-five probability. It's your guy, Kharmai."

Naomi sat up in her chair abruptly. The file she'd been looking at slipped off her lap and scattered over the floor, but she was oblivious. "No way it's a mistake?"

"Not unless you forgot to tell me something else," was Peterson's sardonic reply. "This one matches all over the board. There's just one problem."

The younger woman groaned. "Please tell me you have the clearance. . . ."

"It's not that. The background file was purged from the system."

"What?" Naomi shook her head in confusion. "That doesn't make any sense. Why would you still have the voiceprint if the record was deleted?"

"It happens more than you'd think," Peterson confessed. "Remember, we intercept thousands of signals every week. We have a full-time staff whose only job is to compare the flagged intercepts with the records on file, but sometimes they make mistakes. It could be a clerical error. On the other hand, this record might have been deleted on purpose. If a known subject dies of causes natural or otherwise, the record is manually removed to save space in the servers, leaving only a couple of key identifiers, such as race, nationality, and languages. We don't usually bother with the voiceprints, because they're so small by comparison."

"So you're saying this guy is dead?"

"It's a possibility. I hate to let you down, but that's the truth."

Naomi sighed heavily. "I can't believe this," she said. "That recording was made less than three months ago."

Liz Peterson looked at her sharply. "How do you know that?"

"Because al-Umari—the known voice on the tape, I mean—wasn't . . . around when we found it." Kharmai silently chastened herself for nearly slipping up there; Peterson couldn't know where the tape was found. "There's no way he could have recorded it sooner, Liz."

Peterson thought about that for a second, then reached for the phone and punched in a number. Lifting the receiver to her ear, she turned to the younger woman and said, "You're right; none of this makes sense. We add new files to the database all the time, but extraneous files are only removed twice a year, and the last update was four months ago. If you're right about when this tape was made, he should still be in the system."

"So who are you calling?"

"The records section. We might have a hard copy, but they'll have to dig for it. I hope you have some time on your hands."

The alley was draped in shadow. Beneath his feet, damp stones worn slick by centuries of use. The smell of rotting fish rose to greet him as he moved past metal cans overflowing with garbage, past the rectangular black holes in the walls that passed for doorways. Somewhere, he heard running water. Up ahead, Kohl could see a hunched, fast-moving figure and, beyond, the familiar, rail-thin frame of Rashid al-Umari.

From there, things happened fast. Too fast. Kohl heard a voice, followed by a question—not nervous, exactly. The forced pleasantries of a man caught outside familiar terrain. A man who knows, too late, that he's in the wrong place. A guttural command, harsh words scraping the dirty walls, and then a panicked shout. A struggle up ahead, feet sliding on dark stone. Kohl closing quickly now, reaching out as a knife came up for the first time.

Al-Umari had hesitated, just for a moment, on entering the alley. Seeing the dark and the solitude, his inner caution had nearly won out, but he'd pushed forward, tired from the long walk, eager to save time. The regret came a few steps later, when he heard ungainly feet on the path to his rear. In this narrow space, Al-Umari was keenly aware of his slight stature and his privileged childhood. His hatred for the West was born of circumstance, backed up only by his native intelligence. It was his nature to develop, to fund, but never to execute. For this reason, he could not summon up the necessary indignation, which might have saved him when the hand came down on his arm.

He pulled away slightly, but it wasn't enough. He heard a harsh demand for money. Rashid al-Umari had a glimpse of dark eyes on the verge of panic. He felt a sudden surge of pride . . . Perhaps he could win this one. Before he could assert himself, though, a knife came out of nowhere. The right arm swinging around, the blade glinting in bright orange light . . .

The hand holding the knife was suddenly seized from behind, then snapped back at a strange angle. Rashid could only watch in disbelief as his assailant cried out in agony. In the confusion, he had not seen anyone approach. The knife clattered into the shadows, the boy's right leg buckling forward. He hit the ground hard, but still conscious, fighting for breath, groaning in pain.

Al-Umari took a few uncertain steps back, staring at the man who had come to his aid. In all his years he had never seen such speed of movement. There had been no hesitation . . . He was a student of science. His belief lay in consideration before action; it was the foundation on which he had built himself. Violence attached to such utter conviction was alien to him.

That he was prepared to do much worse—and on an infinitely larger scale—was, for the moment, lost on Rashid al-Umari.

The shock, still with its hold on his senses, delayed the connection. It took him a few seconds to reconcile the face he knew with the one he now saw, as the German's appearance had changed considerably. Hair that had once been reddish brown was now black and trimmed short, and watery blue eyes had given way to a dark shade of brown.

"What are you doing here?" Rashid demanded. "We're not scheduled to meet for another two days."

Kohl did not reply. Instead, he knelt by the wounded man and rapidly checked his pockets. Coming up with a thin leather billfold, he flipped it open and went through the contents: a frayed bus ticket, a few pounds in worn notes, and an expired identification card. This last item gave him a small measure of comfort. A trained intelligence officer might carry a forged card, but never an expired ID; it was the sort of thing to guarantee unwanted attention at a border checkpoint.

Rashid's assailant was starting to come around. He was still facedown, his left arm tucked under his body, his good hand clutching the fractured bones of his right wrist. Satisfied, Kohl placed his left knee in the small of the man's back. The weight brought another small groan, but the struggling ceased.

Kohl turned his attention to Rashid. The Iraqi was still talking, the words coming fast, his fear made plain in his pointed questions.

"What are you going to do? He's probably linked to Iraqi intelligence."

"He asked you for money."

"Yes," Rashid sputtered, "but they would have paid him to make it look like a robbery. They are not stupid, you know, and they still report to the Americans—"

"Go back to the hotel." Kohl spoke quietly, in fluid Arabic. "Stay in the streets on your way back, and don't go anywhere until I come for you. We have to move. I'll make the necessary calls."

Rashid nodded numbly. He tried to say something else but stopped and turned instead, walking fast to the end of the alley. He did not look back.

Once al-Umari was out of sight, Kohl turned his attention to the young man he had all but crippled. The boy was still writhing beneath his knee. A few distinct words came through on occasion, the surprisingly quiet, arrhythmic sounds of unbearable pain.

Al-Umari, as naïve as he was, had brought up a good point. The corruption born under the former regime was still rife in the region, and the CIA, after all but developing the Iraqi National Intelligence Service themselves, had resorted to recruiting men who had not been polluted by the old guard. For the most part, they were amateurs—too young to be truly effective. It was entirely possible, though unlikely, that this man was an Iraqi spy, but it didn't really matter; he had seen al-Umari's face. That was all the justification Kohl needed.

He fired a backward glance down the length of the alley. Seeing that he was alone, he slid his knee up between the man's shoulder blades. The shift in weight brought another muffled cry, but Kohl ignored the noise as he reached down and grabbed a handful of greasy hair with his left hand. Lifting up, he slid his right arm under the boy's head, tensed, then pulled back sharply.

He regretted the action a split second later, when the young man's vertebral column snapped in two places simultaneously. The sound was like a shot ringing off the damp stone walls. Aware of the uneasy silence that followed, Kohl paused only to pocket the boy's money and ID before tossing the billfold into the shadows. Seconds later he was back in the street, where the crowd took him in as one of their own. A startled cry rose up from behind, the body discovered too soon, but Erich Kohl was already gone.

The background file was hand-delivered less than ten minutes after Peterson placed the telephone call. As the other woman signed for the numbered folder, Naomi wondered at the speed with which the document had been produced. For a file that had been supposedly misplaced, it had reappeared rather quickly, and she couldn't help but think that it had been readily available all along.

The thought that this file might have been intentionally pulled out of circulation piqued Kharmai's interest, but the possibility seemed to have escaped Liz Peterson. The British computer engineer seemed almost bored as she closed the door and wandered back to their improvised work area, flipping the folder open and scanning the compact lines of text as she approached.

Her eyebrows rose as she dropped into her chair. "Wow, this is unbelievable."

Naomi was on the edge of her seat. "*What?* Come on, Liz. I'm dying here."

"He's an American. An ex-soldier, no less. You wouldn't have thought it, would you? I mean, his Arabic is nearly perfect, at least on tape—"

"Liz." Peterson looked up at her name and was surprised to find that Naomi's face had suddenly gone pale. "Who is he?"

Another glance at the file. "Umm, hold on a second. I hate the way they compile these damn reports. You can never find the most basic . . . Okay, here it is. Jason March."

Naomi felt like the ground had suddenly dropped out from under her. She caught her breath and struggled to think it through, looking for the rational explanation.

It had to be a mistake. Jason March was dead, killed in an airstrike on a Hamas training camp the previous year, less than a month after he had attempted—and failed—to assassinate three world leaders in the U.S. capital. The man's death had been verified through numerous sources and celebrated at the highest levels of U.S. intelligence. She had seen the after-action report; it had been leaked to the press. . . . She grabbed the edge of the desk to steady herself and held out her hand for the folder, knowing that the face she was about to see would be, *had* to be unfamiliar. But when she looked at the first page and saw the attached photograph, her worst fears were confirmed.

"Oh my God," she whispered.

CHAPTER 10

LANGLEY, VIRGINIA · IRAQ

When Harper stepped into the plush, seventh-floor office ten minutes late, he immediately registered the tension in the room. Director Robert Andrews, a large man draped in one of the Ralph Lauren Purple Label suits that he favored, was concluding a call in the meeting area. Sitting directly across from him was the deputy DCI. Rachel Ford was turned out in an ivory blouse of fine silk, which she'd paired with a form-fitting navy skirt. Her hair was perfectly arranged, for once, and her light make-up seemed freshly applied. Her anger, though, was almost palpable, and it hardened her features, somehow negating her aesthetic efforts.

Ford was the first to speak. "I'm glad you could make it, John. We seem to have quite a situation brewing here, in case you haven't noticed."

Jonathan Harper didn't respond to the sarcastic remark, instead moving forward to take a seat, glancing around in the process. The DCI's office was located close to his own and was similar in size and constitution. Harper's own space, however, was utilitarian at best: neat, sparsely furnished, and free of personal touches, save only for a small photograph of his wife. The director had gone the other way entirely, surrounding himself with inlaid mahogany and Italian leather. It was too much, but fitting. Harper had long ago noticed the not-so-subtle differences between career intelligence officers and outside appointees such as Robert Andrews. Still, Andrews was better than most, including the woman who was currently staring him down.

"Have you seen this?" Ford flicked a hand toward the television on the other side of the room. Even at a distance, Harper could make out the silent images of an Iraqi mob screaming their outrage into the cameras. Crude, hastily assembled posters of a cleric in full robes bobbed amongst the dark heads. The face on the banners was instantly recognizable to Harper as that of Arshad Kassem.

"CNN's been running it all day," Ford continued. Her voice was cold. "Some high-profile religious and political figures in Baghdad are accusing us—and by that, I mean *us*, not just the United States—of involvement in his kidnapping, and the press is all over it. Apparently, Kassem has some pretty important friends over there. Even worse, they know how to connect the dots. There's already speculation about how this might tie in to the bombing of the Babylon Hotel."

Harper nodded but remained silent. The DCI's face was equally neutral; for the moment, it seemed, he was content to let his subordinates have it out amongst themselves.

Finally, Ford raised her arms in exasperation. "So what's the situation?"

Harper shrugged. "I'm waiting on an update. Right now, I don't know any more than you do."

His apparent lack of concern was completely feigned. In truth, Harper was furious. He had never authorized Kassem's kidnapping, precisely because of what was unfolding on the screen before him. And this was only the beginning; despite the president's vague authorization, he knew that Kealey's actions would bring down some serious heat from the White House.

On the way back from their meeting with President Brenneman, Harper had briefed Ford on his plan, which was to put a lot of hard questions to the Agency's high-level informants in Iraq. Admittedly simple, perhaps, but it was a straightforward approach that had worked in the past. While signal intercepts and satellite photographs were popular with the politicians on the Hill, the DDO knew that HUMINT, or human intelligence, often proved the most reliable source of information. In time, they would have likely turned up a few names, people who might have had an interest in seeing the Iraqi prime minister dead, but it was now clear that Kealey had been the wrong man to pursue this task. The fact that he had been the president's first choice didn't matter in the least; politicians, Harper knew, had a limited memory span when it came to those kinds of conversations.

"I don't understand how you could have let this happen," Ford was saying. "To have a field man operating on his own, with no line of communication from our end, is just ridiculous. I mean, we can't even—"

"It works, Rachel." Harper was getting tired of this argument; he'd heard it too many times before. "We set up Special Activities for that specific reason: to avoid all the oversight. On this matter, I was personally briefed by Pete Hemming. He's the head of special operations over at Tyson's Corner, by the way." This was a reference to the National Counterterrorism Center, a state-of-the-art facility located in McLean, Virginia. "He assured me that the man they used on this is one of their best. If he took Kassem out of the city, it was done for a reason."

"You're telling me that you have *no* idea who this man is?" Ford asked skeptically.

"Unfortunately, no," Harper replied mildly.

"Even if we get some good intel out of it, nothing changes the fact that he broke every rule in the book. Unless I'm hugely mistaken, we don't have a presidential finding authorizing any of this. There has to be some accountability here."

"And there will be. You'll get a full report as soon as I do. Until then, we deny everything. Arshad Kassem may have a lot of friends, but he's got his share of enemies, too. We can play it off easily enough."

But Ford wasn't done. "I want the name of this operative," she said heatedly, "and I want him out of the Agency—"

"That's enough, Rachel." Ford's head spun around at the director's first words. Her cheeks flushed slightly at the mild rebuke, but she settled back in her seat, her angry gaze still fixed on Jonathan Harper.

"Inquiries will be made," the DCI continued. "But we have a more immediate issue to take care of. Jonathan?"

Harper nodded and cleared his throat, then went on to explain about Rashid al-Umari, Erich Kohl, and the tape found in al-Umari's London home. "Anyway," he concluded, "we received a lot of cooperation from the British on this, and the voice analysis seems to confirm that Jason March is still alive and working in conjunction with al-Umari."

Ford shook her head, her dark red hair flashing against pale skin. "I saw the after-action report on that. March was killed in an airstrike last December. . . ."

She trailed off when she saw that Andrews was already shaking his head. "First of all, Jason March is not his real name, and he didn't die in a Libyan training camp."

Perplexed, Ford said, "I don't understand."

The DCI gave Harper the nod, and the DDO turned to Rachel Ford, whose expression had softened in her confusion.

"Shortly after the Senate majority leader was assassinated last year, the president gave us carte blanche to hunt down the killer. We had a pretty good idea who was responsible, but the man you know as Jason March was—*is*, I should say—a former Special Forces soldier. As such, he was decidedly difficult to track, and everything pointed to something more.

"So we brought in a retired field man to hunt March down, somebody with, well, relevant experience. You see, our man was ex-army himself; in fact, he trained March in the late nineties. Then, while on deployment in Syria in 1997, Jason March went rogue. He shot five men in his detachment and nearly killed his commanding officer—our operative."

"And who is *he*?"

A subtle glance at Andrews brought another prompting nod. Reluctantly, Harper went on. "His name is Ryan Kealey. He's been with us for four years."

Ford made a mental note to pull the man's file. "And?"

"Once we had Kealey on board, we paired him with an analyst from the CTC, Naomi Kharmai. Together, they were able to learn March's true identity: William Paulin Vanderveen, a South African national. As it turned out, Vanderveen harbored some real hatred toward the United States, hatred that stemmed back to his father's death during apartheid. You'll have to read the briefing folders to get the whole story, but ultimately, the chase ended in Washington. What you may not know is that after the failed assassination attempt, Vanderveen turned the tables on Kealey and tracked him back to his home on the coast of Maine. There was a struggle—Kealey was nearly killed—but in the end, it was Vanderveen who went over the side and into the ocean.

"There was a storm, and it was a drop of about a hundred eighty feet. Basically, his death was a foregone conclusion."

"So you just *assumed* he was dead?" Rachel Ford was amazed, her anger forgotten. "That's pretty convenient."

"We helped the local authorities sniff around for a while—discreetly, of course. Even if Vanderveen had died in the fall, though, finding the body would have been nearly impossible."

"But why the cover-up?"

"Because Kealey was—and still is—one of our most successful operatives." The others were not surprised by Harper's choice of words. In the intelligence business, talent was never an issue; the end result—success—was all that mattered.

"We did our very best to bury this," Harper continued. "Not even Kharmai knows the truth. We couldn't afford to blow Kealey's cover, and he was considered a legitimate target at the time. It was done for his protection."

The deputy DCI considered these words for a moment. Then realization dawned on her face, a small smile touching her lips. Harper issued a silent inward curse; it was clear that she had made the connection between Arshad Kassem and the current topic. He briefly wondered what he had said to give it away, but Ford's next words cut his musings short.

"So where does this leave us?"

"We don't have a choice. We have to wait," was his simple reply. "Hopefully something comes in from Baghdad. All communications with respect to al-Maliki are being routed to the logistical hub in the embassy. If our man can't pull any information out of Kassem, we'll have to work our other sources and see what develops."

Rachel Ford snorted and seemed about to speak when her cell phone beeped. She glanced down at the number. "Gentlemen, I've been waiting on this call."

She was halfway to the door when she turned back to Harper and, in a strange monotone, said, "It seems to me that we need to engage in some serious damage control here. Needless to say, Kassem cannot be allowed to tell his story. I assume you agree."

Jonathan Harper was too surprised by the statement to respond immediately. Instead, he nodded once, and she walked out.

Once she was gone, the mood in the room seemed to lighten a little. Andrews glanced at his watch, stood up, and moved to a cupboard behind his desk. After a moment he returned with two half-filled glasses.

Harper gratefully accepted the generous measure of Glenlivet. The DCI regularly bent the rules by keeping alcohol in his office, but he was strict about its use. If a drink was offered, it was only after close of business, and while a second was consumed on occasion, a third was almost unheard of.

As Andrews sank wearily into his seat and loosened his tie, Harper brought up Ford's parting words, and the director nodded thoughtfully.

"I'm not sure about her yet," he mused. "It's hard to know where she stands. Did you know that she served on the House Permanent Select Committee on Intelligence?"

Harper nodded, not at all surprised by the turn the conversation had taken. Although Ford outranked him, Jonathan Harper had been with the Agency longer than Andrews and Ford combined, and the DCI had never been reluctant to take advantage of his subordinate's extensive experience. "I don't know that much about her—I don't get invited to the hearings—but I did see that in her bio when she was nominated."

"She also served as the vice-chair on the terrorism subcommittee."

Harper lifted an eyebrow. "I must have missed that part."

"She backed us up on quite a few things in that position, and that was before she got the nod from the president—before she was even considered, in fact. They had oversight on HUMINT and counter-intelligence as well. I *do* get called to those hearings, John. She could have made things hard for us more than once, especially after what happened last year, but she cut us some slack. That's why I went along so easily when she was nominated. When you get to the top, you have to pick your battles."

"I had wondered about that."

Andrews nodded again. "She's like me . . . still hitting her stride. This thing with Kealey . . . I think it bothers her because it could cause us some serious problems. She's not just being malicious, and she's right about Kassem. He can't be allowed to talk."

Harper's gaze drifted to the windows on the west side of the room. Weak light broke against heavy clouds, the melancholy end to a dreary day. "I'll give Ryan the word once he checks in," he finally said. "As for Ford . . . I'll try to cut her a break, but with Vanderveen active again, we can't afford to lose Kealey over internal dissent."

"I'll talk to her . . . She'll come around. Where do we go from here?"

"It's like I said; we have to wait and see if Kassem gives us anything useful. Kharmai's flying into Dulles tomorrow with a diplomatic courier. Once we have the tape, we'll get the voiceprint verified on our own equipment. Unfortunately, I think we'll find that the Brits were right."

"Wouldn't surprise me," Andrews said. "You know, I already briefed the president, John. He wants to keep Vanderveen's reappearance under wraps. Nobody gets to know, not even the Bureau."

"What about Kharmai's friend in the Ministry of Defence?"

"She had to be hushed up, of course. Brenneman placed a call to Ten Downing Street while I was in the room, and the prime minister agreed to keep it quiet."

"For how long?" Harper asked. "Until after the election, I should imagine."

Andrews addressed the obvious sarcasm. "John, it's all politics. You know that. The last thing the president needs right now is Vanderveen's face back in the spotlight. The public would go crazy. Of course, the escalating situation in Iraq isn't helping, either, so we'll have to see how it plays out."

The DCI fell silent for a moment as he finished his drink. "I noticed that you left something out when you told Rachel about what happened in Maine."

Harper shrugged. "She can read about it if she wants to; it's all on record. It doesn't really matter, anyway."

"It matters to Ryan. What do you think he'll do? I mean, when he finds out about Vanderveen . . ."

"I don't know," Harper brooded. He drained his glass and stared out at the flat sky. "I just don't know."

At that precise moment, Ryan Kealey was standing outside an abandoned, crumbling stone house three miles north of Amiriya, a small town situated on the northern banks of the Euphrates. It was a rural area; the closest house could be seen to the west, a gray smudge barely discernable in the dawn light. A rucksack containing a Raytheon AN/PSC-5 satellite radio rested on the ground a few feet away, next to a 20-liter can of kerosene. The radio was still packed away; he had not bothered to set up the collapsible dish, and the proper frequencies had not been loaded into the base unit. As a result, he was unaware of the decisions that had been made in Langley. He didn't know that what he was about to do had already been cleared, but in truth, he wouldn't have cared either way. In his mind, he had already decided that Arshad Kassem was going to die. The man had betrayed the Agency's trust, which, in itself, was not surprising—Kealey would have called it inevitable—but more than that, he had actively worked to procure weapons for the insurgency. Kealey had learned this and a good deal more over the last eighteen hours.

After his seemingly impromptu actions back in Fallujah, his return to the marine base east of the city had not been well received. Owen had vowed never to work with him again, and while Walland remained silent, the look on his face had said something similar. From there, things only got worse. On catching sight of the bound prisoner in the bed of the third Tacoma, the captain in charge of the guard had placed a hurried call to the office of Brigadier General Nathan Odom, commander of the 1st Marine Expeditionary Force. The vehicles were stopped just inside the fence, and Odom, a stocky, barrel-chested black man, arrived soon thereafter. He proceeded to ask three pointed questions, each of which Kealey answered honestly. After his response to the third question, the general had stared at him hard, as if gauging his sincerity. When Odom saw that the younger man meant every word, his orders were swift, short, and definitive.

Kealey did not try to argue with the general's decision. He didn't care if he couldn't conduct the interrogation inside the fence. In fact, he didn't care where it took place as long as he got the answers he needed. In the end, he simply asked permission to take his prisoner off-site, a request that was readily approved.

None of this bothered him. If he had told Owen exactly what he was up to before they'd gone into the Jolan district, the other man would never have provided him with the firepower needed to get Kassem out of the city. Even now, with time to reflect, Kealey felt no compunction about misleading his former commanding officer. He had done what was necessary, and he now had the information to prove it.

Kealey leaned back against the cool stone wall and rubbed his eyes, which were aching from lack of sleep. Seen from a distance, the marks on his hands might have been dirt stained red by the morning light. At this early hour, the pale orange sun was backed by a purple gold haze. The view was beautiful in a stark, desolate kind of way, but there was something strangely sinister in the sun's slow upheaval. The steady rise in the east promised a new day, but carried with it the constant memories, the weight of things he couldn't escape. The same old trials and tribulations, all that he had endured for the past ten months.

Still, he couldn't turn his eyes away; if he hadn't known the time, if he hadn't spent all night interrogating Kassem, he would have thought the sun was falling rather than rising. A sunset, at least to Kealey's way of thinking, would have been far more appropriate. For a long time now, he'd felt that he was coming to the end of things. He had reached a strange accommodation with this prospect; after all, he had lost too much to start anew.

He finally turned away from the scene. It was picture-perfect, too good for this place, and there was still work to be done.

From a holster on his right hip, he pulled his Beretta 92FS. Pulling the slide back a few centimeters, Kealey checked the chamber and saw the brassy glint of a single round. Letting the slide snap forward, he thumbed the safety into the fire position and walked back into the building, the light on his back, nothing but darkness ahead.

CHAPTER 11

LATTAKIA

They had been moving for two days. There had been no time to sleep off the endless stress, save for the three restless hours he'd caught on the cracked plastic seat of the bus to Lattakia. Now, as Kohl made his calls in the back of the squalid White Palace Café, Rashid al-Umari sat motionless at a corner table. He was hunched over the scratched aluminum, his head heaped on folded arms.

He was exhausted. It was new for him, this constant movement, but the movement meant they were close, that the danger was now real.

In the past there had always been warning. In the Iraqi capital, the streets leading into the Shia enclave were sealed with mounds of rotting garbage and the burnt-out, twisted remains of cars—the same cars that had once been loaded with explosives, then parked on one of the many roads patrolled by U.S. forces. When the raids came, the Americans were forced to endure the bitter task of moving these ruined vehicles before they could push into al-Sadr's nest. The process took time, and a child, once told of his importance, once given a meaningless title, could be relied upon to make the call in the early hours when the Bradleys rolled forward.

For this meeting, there would be no warning. If the Americans had advance knowledge of the time and location, and—more importantly—the guest list, they would respond from the air, and it would be over in the blink of an eye. It was this knowledge, al-Umari knew, that drove the German to such mind-numbing caution, but it was Rashid's offering that would draw them despite the risks. If they were willing to make an appearance, the plan would go forward.

It was all he wanted. He knew what would be asked of him, and he had come prepared.

Rashid lifted his head and rubbed his bleary eyes. Kohl was walking back to the table, a chipped mug of strong Arab coffee in hand. The previous day he had changed his appearance again, and from the way the new colors complemented his features, Rashid would have guessed that he had reverted to his natural state. The German slid into the opposite seat and turned his gaze to the window, absently gazing past the colorful lettering affixed to the clamorous street beyond.

A few minutes passed. The lunch crowd began filtering in. Soon animated conversations in Arabic and Farsi swirled around them, along with the harsh smell of cigarette smoke, flatulence, and the stench of unwashed bodies. The German's cup was half-empty when Rashid finally ran out of patience. "Well? What did they say?"

The other man did not reply and seemed unaware of Rashid's hardest stare. Through the grime of the storefront window, a small child bounced into view, his tousled black hair glistening in the midday sun. His right hand gripped a plain brown envelope, the thick paper lumping over what might have been the keys to a vehicle, a cell phone, or both. The boy slowed outside the entrance and peered in through the open door, as though searching for someone. His gaze quickly settled on the blond-haired, green-eyed man at the corner table.

Will Vanderveen turned to Rashid al-Umari and smiled.

Tartus, a small port on the Mediterranean, is the sort of place with a great deal of history and very little to show for it, a city much reviled by Western tourists and the guidebooks they travel with. As with all things, however, it remains a matter of perspective. For native Syrians, the rocky, litter-strewn beach overlooking the tiny island of Arwad is one of their country's better holiday destinations, and as close as most will ever come to the pristine sands and clear blue waters of Cannes or Mykonos.

It was still light when they drove into town on the coastal road, but thick violet clouds were tumbling in from the west, threatening rain. The car, a white, rattletrap Peugeot 504, had been waiting on Sharia Baghdad, the main street running through Lattakia. Now, at Kohl's direction, Rashid parked the small sedan on the western end of Sharia al-Wahda. Pushing open the car door, he was instantly overcome by the cold and the mingled scents of salt and broiling fish, an unsubtle invitation extended by the restaurants clustered around the harbor. The scents began to fade as they walked east on the wide boulevard, passing a number of cheap hotels, bakeries, and bathhouses.

A stiff wind swept in from the sea, a hint of the coming storm. Rashid al-Umari shivered beneath his quilted anorak. His wardrobe no longer reflected his wealth and his years in London, as it had in the past. Kohl had pointed out this mistake after the near disaster in Aleppo, and al-Umari's clothes—a T-shirt under the anorak, jeans, and running shoes—were now more in keeping with his surroundings. Kohl's outfit was similarly disreputable, but it had never been otherwise; indeed, the German seemed to go out of his way to maintain a disheveled appearance.

Rashid's nerves were stretched taut, adrenaline pumping through his veins. For nearly five years he had been waiting for this opportunity. A quick glance at the other man's face told him absolutely nothing; at this pivotal moment, Erich Kohl seemed to be made of stone. Rashid wondered if the man's calm could be attributed to his natural disposition or years of operational experience. He would have guessed that both factors played a role. Not for the first time, he had the uneasy feeling that the German was a much more important figure than he'd previously indicated.

His reverie was broken when Kohl seized his arm and pulled him abruptly into a narrow corridor. For a panicked instant, al-Umari feared that he had been lured into a trap, but he quickly realized how irrational that notion was. Nevertheless, he breathed easier when he saw that the other man was counting doors.

Kohl stopped at the fourth and rapped twice.

*   *   *

The foyer was dark, the only light emanating from the hallway beyond. Rashid had a brief impression of bare walls and scratched marble floors, but a bodyguard was already guiding him forward by the arm, Kohl trailing softly behind. They were not searched. From this, Rashid inferred that his host had not yet arrived, but the notion was quickly dispelled when he stepped into the next room.

A bare bulb hung over his head like an afterthought, spilling warm yellow light over painted doors, which were recessed in the plaster walls. In turn, the walls were further adorned with an excessive number of intricate tapestries, as if to draw one's attention away from the absence of windows. A marble floor was hidden beneath overlapping Persian rugs, the black-and-white mosaic revealed only in the far corners of the spacious room. A pair of overstuffed couches, conspicuous in their contemporary design, resided around a low wooden table.

For all the beauty of his surroundings, though, Rashid al-Umari's eyes were drawn first to the room's sole occupant, and in that moment, he knew that he had been right to come, that his work over the past several years had not been in vain.

Forewarned by their footsteps, the man glanced up. He was gaunt and surprisingly pale, but Rashid had expected as much, for he knew that this man, Izzat Ibrahim al-Douri, former vice president of Iraq, former deputy chairman of the Revolutionary Command Council (RCC), suffered from a long list of ailments that had plagued his health for years. It was widely speculated in the Western media that al-Douri, who was believed to be in his mid-sixties, had died of leukemia in November of 2005. The BBC had reported the story without verifying the source, but the U.S. State Department, unable to confirm reports of al-Douri's death, had kept its lines of inquiry open and to date still offered a reward of ten million dollars for his capture.

Strangely enough, Izzat al-Douri remained largely recognizable, despite his status as the most wanted man in Iraq, a position he'd claimed after al-Zarqawi's death in June of 2006. His sparse hair was slicked back, the eyes magnified by a pair of thick plastic spectacles. His mouth, pulled taut in a thin smile, was barely visible beneath a thick red moustache. He stood and appraised his visitor.

"Welcome, Rashid."

The younger man had trouble finding his voice. Rashid al-Umari had been fourteen years old the last time he had seen al-Douri. It had been a different time, a time when his own father had been at the height of his powers. Now, standing before this man, one of the few remaining symbols of the old regime, he was suddenly seized by emotion. "Comrade," he managed to choke out. "A privilege . . ."

He was instantly appalled by his own display, but al-Douri smiled reassuringly and stepped forward, grasping Rashid's shoulders with skeletal hands. The younger man was surprised by the strength in the grip and deeply touched by the gesture.

"No, my friend," al-Douri said gently. "The privilege is mine." He released al-Umari and gestured to the seating area. "Please sit. You must be tired. How was your journey?"

They took their seats, the bodyguard moving forward to murmur in the older man's ear. Al-Douri nodded once, and the guard withdrew.

"The journey was excellent, comrade. Long, of course, but well worth the trial."

"Good." There was a brief pause, and the smile faded. "I was sorry to learn of your loss. You have my sympathies and those of your countrymen. This war has taken something from all of us, I think."

"Yes."

"Your father was a great man. I was honored to know him."

"Thank you."

"And your mother." Izzat al-Douri's voice had dropped to a whisper. His pale hazel eyes, unblinking, were fixed on the younger man. "Your sister . . . a tragedy."

Al-Umari did not trust himself to respond. Once more he was standing on the hard-packed dirt of the al-Kharkh cemetery, fists balled by his sides, watching in silent, helpless rage as they lowered the bodies . . . He could scarcely breathe and his eyes burned, but he would not shed tears in this man's presence. He would not humiliate himself any further.

Al-Douri seemed to sense his distress and remained silent as Rashid composed himself. Neither man noticed when the guard slipped into the room and deposited a silver tray bearing tea.

"Tell me, my friend. Why have you come? What do you hope to achieve?"

The words came out in a torrent; he could not control himself. "I want them to learn that the world is not their playground. They cannot take what is ours. They must learn humility. They must learn that they do *not* know what is best for the Iraqi people, that it is *not* their right to decide. . . ."

"This is what you want?"

"It is what I seek."

"And revenge." It was not a question. "You seek revenge for your family."

Al-Umari looked into the other man's eyes. "Yes," he finally murmured. "And revenge for my family."

Al-Douri nodded slowly. He poured the tea. Behind them, Will Vanderveen paced aimlessly in the darkness of the room, his feet beating a slow, soft rhythm on the Persian rugs.

"It is possible for me to help you, but it will not be easy. The Americans have great influence. They have the best and most of everything: money, technology, weaponry. . . ."

Rashid's jaw tightened at this last point. He had been in London on the day his family was killed, but he had later seen what a single laser-guided bomb had done to his father's estate.

"They are connected as well. A word from their State Department brings banks across the world in line. They have the power to freeze accounts, to seize funds. . . ."

"Not my funds."

Al-Douri's eyes gleamed beneath the raw light. "Your funds as well, Rashid. You are not immune."

"It has not happened yet. I would have been told."

"By your accountants, perhaps, but not by the British, and certainly not by the Americans. Still, you need not be concerned. Your accounts are still fluid."

Al-Umari's eyes opened wide. "How can you know . . . ?"

The other man waved the question away. "It is not important. What *is* important is that we find ourselves in a unique situation. At this critical time, my young friend, we are in a position to help *each other*."

Izzat al-Douri leaned forward. "For five years, Rashid, I have eluded capture. I have done what I could to strengthen the mujahideen, to unite our brothers against the Zionist invaders. I would like to think that I've made a difference."

"How could you think otherwise?" al-Umari demanded.

The older man nodded once, acknowledging the compliment. "Still," he continued, "the war hurts most those who are willing to fight it. You know this as well as I."

The statement, carefully calculated, seemed to cause Rashid al-Umari physical pain.

"They have taken everything from us, my friend, but we have not backed down," al-Douri continued. "As we speak, two of my own sons are in Samarra, rallying our forces. Our funds have been seized, and still, we rail against the invaders."

Al-Douri's eyes were fixed on his prey. "I would not believe," he murmured, "that a man of your great wealth, Rashid, would turn his back on his brothers in their hour of need. I do not believe that after enduring so much, you would not fully dedicate yourself to those who require your assistance. The faithful rely on those who are willing to fight. Iraq is rightfully theirs, but they cannot take it themselves. They rely on the strong. Their sons and daughters rely on the strong. Would you deny them?"

"Never." Rashid rasped the single word.

"Will you help us?"

"Yes. I will do what I can, gladly."

"I had no doubt of it." Al-Douri settled back in his chair and lifted his cup. A long moment passed. "I assume Kohl told you what was required."

It seemed strange to talk about the man as if he were not present. The footsteps had ceased, but al-Umari could hear quiet breathing in the background. "Yes."

"And you are ready to do your duty?"

"I am. I have come prepared."

At this, al-Douri smiled, and for a split second, relief flashed in his eyes. He nodded to Vanderveen, almost imperceptibly, and the younger man left the room. A moment later he returned, the body-guard trailing, phone in hand.

It was easily done; al-Umari had made most of the arrangements in person several days before the bombing of the Babylon Hotel. It had not been easy to get away at that critical time, but the Industrial Development Bank in Jordan had produced the necessary paper-work with consummate speed. As always, their cooperation stemmed from Rashid's extensive holdings with their corporate division.

Once he had his account officer on the phone, he spoke some prearranged code words and turned to al-Douri. "I'll need the account and routing numbers."

The older man nodded to his bodyguard, who stepped forward with a sheet of paper. Al-Umari read from the list, verified the instructions, and concluded the call.

In the space of twelve minutes, ten million U.S. dollars had been wired from the IDB in Amman to the Banque du Bosphore in Paris. From there, it would carve an impossible trail over much of Western Europe, as would a further sixty million over the course of the next few hours. Each successive wire transfer would be wiped clean of electronic surveillance by passing through the Ghariban Islamic Bank, a shell bank established just three months earlier by Farouk Haddad, an Iraqi who'd lost his wife and child to American artillery fire in the winter of 2004. The Ghariban had correspondent accounts with Citibank in France, which gave it access to the U.S. banking system. While Congress had recently passed laws to limit the risk, the financial centers in other countries were not always as diligent when it came to verifying the location, size, and customer base of the banks with which they did business. The Ghariban was one such bank; it had no corporate offices, no employees, and very few account holders, but it was still a legitimate financial institution with the ability to hold and move funds.

Al-Umari handed the phone to the bodyguard and turned to his host. The stress of the past few days was etched into his face. "The transfer has started." He paused. "Comrade, if I could do more . . ."

Al-Douri stepped forward and embraced the younger man for a long moment. When he finally let go, there were tears in Rashid's eyes.

"You have done a great thing for your people, my friend. Your work here is finished. You must leave at dawn, but now you should rest. Ahmed will show you to your room."

Al-Umari nodded wearily and followed the bodyguard out the door. After a few seconds, their footsteps faded away entirely.

Izzat al-Douri and Vanderveen were left alone in the cavernous space on the ground floor. The younger man was still concealed in the shadows.

The Iraqi leaned back in his seat and lifted his eyes to the gilded ceiling. "How much does he know?"

"Very little. He believes our efforts are aimed at the military."

"Good."

"The Americans will learn of this, you know. They are interested in Rashid. It was a mistake to use him in Baghdad. And when they learn . . ."

"They may suspect, my friend, but they will never learn. Remember, everything lies on misdirection. We have worked hard to plant the seeds of uncertainty."

Vanderveen nodded absently. "And Kassem?"

"You believe the reports?"

"Of course. Who else but the West would take him?"

"Perhaps you are right." There was a brief, uncertain pause. "Can he hurt us?"

"No," Vanderveen replied. "I've already made the call to Washington. An operation has been in the works there for some time, and my contact is now in a position to finish the job. Most of the links have already been severed. Just one remains, and when he dies, there will be nothing left to tie us to Kassem."

"Good."

"Did he know of your involvement?"

"No, I always used intermediaries." Al-Douri deliberated for a long moment. "Arshad is not a true believer. He was always in it for the money. He insisted on thieving from the Americans, even after I warned him against it. I should have taken care of that problem a long time ago. Still, if your man in Washington is as efficient as you say, there is no cause for concern."

Vanderveen did not reply. He was not surprised by the other man's assumption that his U.S. contact was male; like most Islamic extremists, Izzat al-Douri would never believe a woman capable of carrying out such a crucial task.

"Then we are set to proceed."

"Indeed." A terrible smile eased its way across the Iraqi's face. "Ahmed? Bring him in."

The bodyguard slipped from the room and returned with a second man. Will Vanderveen, still lost in the shadows, carefully appraised the new arrival. He was dressed in a neat double-breasted charcoal suit, which served to conceal his heavy frame. The face was fleshed out, the dark hair fading to gray, but the man's eyes were his most noticeable feature. They were coal black, and they radiated authority. Vanderveen immediately thought, *Internal security, intelligence at the outside.*

His intuition was rewarded a moment later, when al-Douri said, "Mr. Kohl, this is Jalil al-Tikriti. We've worked together for many years. Jalil was . . . shall we say, a *prominent* figure in the RCC."

Vanderveen's right arm swept into the light. He shook the proffered hand of Tahir Jalil Habbush al-Tikriti, former director of the Iraqi Intelligence Service, currently number sixteen on the U.S. most wanted list. It began to click into place; under al-Tikriti, the IIS had been charged with the creation of front companies in the mid-nineties, the purpose of which was to acquire missile technology from neighboring states. Now, those same companies—or others like them—could be used to hide incoming funds for the insurgency.

But there was something more; Vanderveen understood why the older man was reluctant to reveal al-Tikriti's true capacity in the Baath regime. Years earlier, it had been reported that the former director of the IIS, in conjunction with the Palestinian terrorist Abu Nidal, had taken part in the training of 9/11 hijackers during the summer of 2001. Nidal was later found dead in the Iraqi capital, and a great deal of speculation had cropped up regarding Tahir al-Tikriti's role in the whole scenario. Regardless of the truth, the Americans would be very interested in hearing what the former Iraqi intelligence director had to say on the matter. However, al-Douri's caution—if that's what it was—was clearly misplaced. To these men, William Vanderveen *was* Erich Kohl, and if Kohl had wanted to betray them, they would already be dead.

"Comrade Jalil," al-Douri continued, "was instrumental in the development of the al-Quraysh Hotel in Mosul. As it happens, young Rashid is the new owner."

"A wise investment," Vanderveen said. The other men smiled. "And what has al-Umari actually purchased with this money?"

Izzat al-Douri flicked his gaze to the shadows, peering into the darkness. "Come into the light, my friend. Men should look into each other's faces when discussing such matters."

"I prefer the view from here. I'll repeat the question. What happens to the money?"

The elder Iraqi's eyes narrowed; he was finding it difficult to restrain his temper in the face of such arrogance. "The money," he began tersely, "will be divided as follows. Ten million goes to our politicians on the governing council. They are few, but they are powerful, and they are prepared to support our return to power in exchange for offshore accounts and the continued well-being of their families. Five million goes to the Iranian; he is already laying the groundwork in Washington. Another five million goes to the Syrian defense minister, who has agreed to make his contacts with Hezbollah, Hamas, and the Popular Front for the Liberation of Palestine available to us. As you undoubtedly know, all three groups have offices and substantial support in Damascus. A further thirty million has been set aside to entice them into crossing the border when the time comes. It is the most costly part of the operation . . . We have never enjoyed good relations with the Syrians, or the groups they sponsor, for that matter. Our freedom here has come at a steep price."

"And the rest?"

A tight smile appeared on the elder Iraqi's face. "The rest goes to you, my friend. Twenty million U.S. dollars, as agreed. However, I have yet to see justification for such an outrageous sum. Let us not forget that you failed in Baghdad."

"The main goal was achieved," Vanderveen reminded him quietly.

"Al-Maliki is no longer in a position to challenge you. Besides, that was done to establish my credentials. You incurred no cost."

"And the Iranians?" al-Douri asked. The smile had turned smug. "Is it not true that you failed them as well?"

Will Vanderveen felt a sliver of cold running down his spine. His face, however, remained impassive.

Al-Tikriti said, "We know who you are, Mr. Vanderveen. A former U.S. soldier, a traitor to your own people. Surely, a man of your intelligence can see the point . . . What is to stop you from turning on *us*?"

"If you know who I am, then you'll know that they are not my people. What the West has done to me makes your suffering pale in comparison."

Izzat al-Douri's face tightened in fury, but before he could lash out, Vanderveen continued in a calm, measured voice. "Gentlemen, I have seen copies of the watch lists going back three months, and my name does not appear on any of them. U.S. intelligence believes I am dead, which gives me the ability to move and operate. You, on the other hand, remain two of the most wanted men in Iraq. I failed in Washington because the Iranians insisted on interfering. That will not happen again. I know what needs to be done, and I need no further assistance."

Al-Tikriti considered this for a moment, tenting his fingers beneath his chin in a strangely pontifical gesture. "As you know," he finally said, "this plan is not in its infancy. Arrangements have already been made in Paris . . . arrangements that could make your work much easier." He paused. "Of course, the final decision is yours to make."

Vanderveen hesitated, then said, "Go on."

The former intelligence chief spoke for twenty minutes. When he was done, Vanderveen nodded his agreement, impressed in spite of himself. It was easy to see how al-Tikriti had earned his post; the older man was not bound by the usual limitations of Islamic extremism. In particular, his views on the fairer sex seemed to be far more progressive than those of his peers.

"I'll need a point of contact," Vanderveen said. He proceeded to recite a lengthy string of digits as well as an access code. "You can leave and pick up messages on that line. Obviously, face-to-face meetings will no longer be possible once we've set things in motion."

Tahir al-Tikriti nodded once. "I'll provide you with the number before you leave. Since we're on the subject, the Jordanian's successor has offered the use of his people."

"I don't need them. I'll use the woman, but I'll arrange everything else myself."

"And documents? We can provide—"

"I have those as well. Let me make myself clear. Anything that connects us is dangerous. The fewer the links, the better off we are." He paused. "There is one other thing. I understand the need to move immediately, but I expect the first ten million to be deposited in two days' time. The rest should be delivered once the job is completed in New York. If the plans for the meeting are changed or cancelled completely, I'll reserve the right to end things there. Agreed?"

"Agreed. You understand what we are looking for. The goal is to—"

"The goal is to eliminate the targets you've drawn up in the prescribed manner. A simple task—provided the meeting at the UN goes forward."

"It will go forward," al-Tikriti intoned. "I have no doubt of it."

"Then our business here is concluded," al-Douri said. He stood, and though he was looking into the blackness of the room, his pale eyes seemed to be fixed on Vanderveen's. "With one exception."

"Yes," the younger man said. "With one exception."

Rashid al-Umari turned restlessly in a bare room on the second floor. He had not been able to sleep, despite his exhaustion. The skies had opened just after midnight, and though the window was shut and the curtains drawn, the room was filled with the sound of rushing water and the occasional peal of distant thunder.

A sudden noise drew his gaze to the door. He saw a black silhouette against the light in the hall. Rashid blinked the sleep from his eyes and sat up on the foldout cot. He was not alarmed in the least. In this place, he was on safe ground; he was amongst brothers. "What is it? Kohl . . . ?"

He saw the gun come up, but it wasn't real. He recognized the extended barrel of a suppressed weapon, but it *couldn't* be real, not after what he had done for them. Mired in disbelief, he didn't react, but it wouldn't have mattered.

The muzzle flashed twice, and Rashid al-Umari tumbled back into permanent night.

CHAPTER 12

WASHINGTON, D.C. • VIRGINIA

A premature winter wind whipped over the tarmac at Dulles International Airport as a Dassault Falcon executive jet taxied in on the 12/30 runway, the same plane having landed less than a minute earlier. Jonathan Harper, leaning against the rear fender of a black GMC Suburban—the only vehicle parked on the apron—brushed a few drops of rain from the sleeves of his Burberry overcoat and watched as the sleek jet rolled to a stop, the twin Pratt & Whitney engines winding down to a gradual halt. The cabin door swung out to the left a few moments later, the stairs came down, and the Falcon's only passenger appeared in the doorway.

Harper instantly saw that Ryan Kealey was in rough shape. The lower half of his face was still covered in the thick, matted beard, and lank hair hung past the line of his jaw, further obscuring his features. His lean frame was covered by a pair of tattered khakis and a gray Nike sweatshirt, his rugged Columbia hiking boots still bearing clumps of red brown Iraqi mud. A large military rucksack was thrown over his right shoulder. He didn't seem to be straining under the load, but there was something about the empty expression on his face that worried the DDO; it was a look that spoke of more than physical exhaustion.

As Kealey started across the windblown tarmac, Harper considered the events of the previous day. He had personally brought Kealey up to speed when the younger man finally called in, but it had been difficult to gauge his reaction over the static-filled line. If appearances were any indication, though, Kealey was having trouble with the revelation that Vanderveen had finally resurfaced, after almost a year of not knowing whether the man was dead or alive.

Crossing the last few feet of cement, Kealey shook Harper's extended hand and offered something approaching a smile.

"Good to see you, John. I didn't expect to be met by a man of your stature."

"A lot's been happening. I thought I would fill you in on the ride."

Kealey nodded to the vehicle. "I guess your driver is cleared for it."

"He's cleared as high as you are."

"Sounds good." Kealey opened the rear doors and tossed his pack into the cargo area, then made his way to the backseat. Harper went to the passenger side and climbed in front, as was his habit. Once both doors were shut, the driver put the truck into gear.

Harper handed Kealey a carryout cup of steaming black coffee over the back of the seat. "I thought you could use this," he said.

"Thanks. I didn't get any sleep on the plane."

"I can tell. You look like shit."

"I'm aware of that," was the wry response. "I need a shower."

"And a haircut," Harper noted. "You'll get all of that soon enough. I've got you set up at the Hotel Washington."

Kealey raised an eyebrow, and Harper caught the gesture. "Yeah, I know. Admittedly, it's much nicer than what you'd usually get, but I pulled some strings for you. After six months in the desert, I thought you could use some dependable air-conditioning and a comfortable bed. Oh, and Kharmai's there as well. She's already checked in."

"Naomi," Kealey said in a flat voice. "What's she doing here?"

"We brought her back to work on al-Umari's finances, among other things. It's been less than twenty-four hours, but she's already managed to dig up some interesting information. I'll let her brief you herself."

"Is that where we're going? The hotel?"

Harper nodded without turning around, then changed tack. "Anyway, here's where we stand. As soon as you called in, we started running the names you got from Kassem. Two of them, unfortunately, belong to the recently deceased. Interestingly enough, both men were killed during the same raid on the Syrian border."

A skeptical expression came over the younger man's face. "I suppose that came from—"

"No." The DDO had anticipated the response. "That came from the Pentagon, not the Iraqis. It's been confirmed."

Kealey leaned back in his seat and rubbed a hand over his eyes. He couldn't believe he'd wasted all that time for nothing, but Harper had only accounted for two. . . . "What about the third?"

"Well, that's the thing. The third man on your list, Anthony Mason, is located here."

"Here as in the U.S.?"

"Here as in Washington."

Kealey leaned forward in his seat, suddenly interested. "Well, that's great. Have we picked him up?"

"No. As soon as the name went into the system, bells started ringing in Landrieu's office at the NCTC."

Kealey grimaced involuntarily. He harbored a strong dislike for Patrick Landrieu, the director of the National Counterterrorism Center, and the feeling was decidedly mutual. They'd had a run-in the previous year, but for Kealey, a petty disagreement was not the issue. He was far more concerned by the fact that the other man had managed to keep his job after a series of major terrorist attacks in the nation's capital.

"The problem," Harper continued, "is that we're not the only ones with an interest in Mason. For the last three months, he's been the subject of a joint investigation being run by the Bureau and the ATF. That's how we knew his location."

"You're kidding me." Kealey thought back to what Kassem had told him. "They want him for arms trafficking?"

"Something to that effect. I didn't get the full picture, but here's the interesting part. The Bureau's stepped up their surveillance over the past week, and they already have a warrant."

"When are they going in?"

"Today."

Kealey stared at the other man in disbelief. "Please tell me you're joking."

Harper shook his head grimly. "I'm afraid not."

"They're doing it *today?* That's not interesting, John. That's . . . disastrous." *And also far too coincidental*, he didn't say. "If they're forced to shoot him, we'll be shit out of luck."

"I realize that, but it's out of our hands. When the senior FBI rep at Tyson's Corner heard we were sniffing around, he told Landrieu in no uncertain terms that this was a very large, very expensive Bureau op, and that any interference would not be tolerated. So Landrieu, of course, made the call to Langley. Andrews nearly handed me my ass when he heard . . . We're already in hot water for that little stunt you pulled in Fallujah. The heat isn't just coming down from the White House, either. The Pentagon was distinctly unhappy with the way you misled Owen. According to the director, the last thing we can afford to do is interfere with a DOJ investigation on domestic soil. That's a direct quote, by the way."

"That fucker Landrieu." Kealey couldn't restrain his anger. "The guy spent twenty years in the Agency, and he still stabs us in the back every chance he gets."

"I hear you, but like I said, it's out of our hands. We just have to hope that the Bureau brings Mason in alive, and that, at some point, we get an opportunity to talk to him."

Kealey sat back in his seat and sipped the coffee, thinking about it. Of the three names Kassem had given him, Mason was the one he really wanted to talk to. The men who'd been killed on the Syrian border were Iraqi nationals, but Mason held American citizenship. Setting up secure lines of communication between Iraq and the United States would have been extremely difficult, which made it a good bet that Mason was involved at a much higher level.

And that brought him to something else. It was something that he'd tried to push out of his mind for the last twenty-four hours, but with this development, he could no longer ignore Will Vanderveen's return to the ranks of the living. Vanderveen had joined the U.S. Army under false pretenses and had posed successfully as an American for years. Both Mason and Vanderveen had ties to Iraq, the latter man through Rashid al-Umari. Kealey knew it was entirely possible that the two men were connected by more than just circumstance.

He made a decision. "John, forget the hotel. I want to go out to the site."

"Why?"

"I want to talk to whoever's running things. At the very least, they'll be able to tell us more about Mason than we can get on paper. Moreover, we might be able to convey how important it is that they take him alive. I mean, you said Brenneman wanted answers. You'd be surprised at what happens when you drop the president's name."

Harper considered the request at length. "Okay," he finally said. "As it happens, I talked to one of the lead investigators in McLean this morning."

This made sense to the younger man; McLean was just another reference to the NCTC, which was staffed by members of fourteen different government agencies, including the FBI and the CIA. It was one of the very few places where information was collated and disseminated within the U.S. intelligence community, though Kealey had never bought into the rhetoric. Based on what he had seen, the NCTC was no more effective than its predecessor, the Terrorist Threat Integration Center, at minimizing interagency competition while maximizing output.

"She seemed willing to talk," Harper continued, "so we might have an in. Just don't push too hard, Ryan. Remember, this is their operation and their turf. They don't have to cooperate."

"I'll keep it in mind."

CHAPTER 13

ALEXANDRIA, VIRGINIA

They arrived at the staging area thirty minutes after leaving the runway at Dulles. Harper had spent half the trip on the phone, trying to get the location of the command post, as the Bureau rep at the NCTC just hadn't seen the benefit in giving the CIA access to one of its ongoing operations. In the end, though, it was the use of the president's name—as Kealey had anticipated—that settled the argument.

They were passed through following a brief examination of their credentials. The Suburban bounced over a concrete lip and into the parking area, where the driver pulled in next to a fleet of Bureau Crown Vics. Several agents in blue FBI windbreakers were standing around the vehicles, smoking and sipping from steaming Styrofoam cups, engaged in low conversation. Kealey got out and went to the rear cargo doors, where he opened his ruck sack and replaced his sweatshirt with a corduroy barn jacket. Then he tucked his Beretta into the waistband of his khakis, where the grip of the weapon was neatly concealed by the wrinkled folds of his coat. A few of the Bureau agents were shooting him curious looks.

Harper waved him over. "Remember what I said, Ryan. They didn't have to let us in."

The younger man caught the drift immediately: *keep your mouth shut and your eyes open*. He'd heard the words often enough that they weren't really necessary; by now, the accompanying look was enough.

The command post itself was based on the second floor of a two-story walk-up. The room was overheated, despite the fact that someone was coming in or out every few seconds, and filled with agents and communication equipment. Clear plastic draped over the unused gear served as protection against the leaky ceiling, but nothing could be done about the sagging floors, which looked ready to give. A series of monitors on one wall provided numerous angles of the target building, which was located a block to the east. It was almost impossible to tell who was in charge, but Harper was already cutting a confident path through the crowd. Kealey trailed at a distance, swearing under his breath when he tripped over one of the numerous extension cords snaking across the scuffed wooden floor.

Harper stopped at a functional steel desk in the back of the room. Standing behind it was a young woman—mid twenties, Kealey guessed—dressed in a pale purple pullover and faded jeans. A black DeSantis holster containing a 10mm pistol was clipped to her belt, the shirt pulled behind the grip to allow easy access to the weapon. Her soft blond hair was not her own—a trace of light brown could be seen at the roots—but it was done well, and the color suited her brown eyes and lightly tanned skin. Her ears were adorned with small diamond studs, and she wore a thin silver chain at her neck, the bottom half of which slipped under her shirt. Kealey couldn't help but notice how bright she was in the otherwise somber, dark-suited crowd. She clutched a manila folder in both hands but seemed to be more interested in the phone that was pinched between her right shoulder and cheek.

"Yes, I told you that, Tom," she was saying, her voice carrying over the din. "I *did* call HQ, but they wouldn't put me through to Judd, and he has to approve it. As it stands, we just don't have enough bodies. . . ."

Harper leaned in to explain. "They were supposed to go in with the D.C. SWAT team and an ATF contingent. It sounds like she's trying to beef up the numbers."

"Who's Judd?"

"Harry Judd, the deputy executive director. He's the only one who can authorize the use of the HRT."

Kealey nodded. He knew that the Bureau's Hostage Rescue Team—frequently without any hostages to save—often served as an elite SWAT unit and was renowned for its low subject fatality rate. For this reason alone, he hoped the team would get the nod, but judging by the agent's obvious frustration, it didn't look good.

The woman finally tossed aside the file she was holding to more efficiently slam down the receiver. She clearly wasn't in the mood for conversation, but Harper pressed forward. "Agent Crane, this is Ryan Kealey. Ryan, Special Agent Samantha Crane."

Crane was nearly as tall as he was. She sized him up with a sweeping glance and offered a small, disapproving frown. Kealey couldn't really blame her; he knew how he looked. Finally, she stuck out her hand and said, "Nice to meet you."

Her grip was surprisingly strong, her voice hinting at a regional accent he couldn't quite place. He was still trying to figure it out when she turned her attention back to Jonathan Harper. "No offense, Mr. Harper, but I have no idea how you were even cleared to this site. This is a domestic operation, a *Bureau* operation, and I've been working this case for three months. So unless you have something to contribute, I'm—"

"Agent Crane, I understand how you feel, and I'm sorry for the intrusion," Harper said, moving fast to appease her. "Trust me when I say that we're not here to interfere. That said, we *would* like to talk to Mason once you have him in custody."

She frowned again. "That might be arranged, but not through me. He'll have to be arraigned first, and—"

"What are you charging him with?"

Crane turned back to Kealey, clearly annoyed by the interruption. "The U.S. attorney files charges, Mr. Kealey, not the FBI."

"So how did you get the warrant?" Kealey shot back.

She sighed impatiently. "Anthony Mason was served up to us by a cooperating witness three months ago. Based on his testimony and supporting documents, we can link Mason to the distribution of more than two hundred thousand dollars in various Class III weapons over the past two years. We know he's responsible for much more, but that's what we can prove. Everything's in the affidavits we filed with the D.C. Superior Court." She pointed to the folder on the desk and said, "That's Mason's file, by the way. You can check it out for yourself."

"Where's your witness now?" Harper asked.

"Federal custody."

"Why don't you use him?" Kealey asked. "You could send him in with undercover agents to make a buy. That would save the need for all of"—he waved his arms around the crowded room—"this."

"Because Mason knows we're holding him," she replied. "They picked him up on a high-profile bust, a joint DEA-ATF operation. As usual, they held a press conference and started celebrating before they knew what they had, so Mason was tipped off before his buddy had the chance to give him up. Obviously, the trail went cold until this week." She paused as though thinking it through. "Besides, the witness was kind of shaky to begin with."

"So let me get this straight," Kealey said. "Mason's been at the top of your list for months, during which time you had shit. Now, by some miracle, you've suddenly managed to stumble onto him. Is that right?"

A cold look settled over her face at the tone of the question.

"How did it happen?" he asked.

"We received some unexpected information, an anonymous tip. I'm not going to tell you anything more than that."

Kealey gave her a hard stare. *Anonymous tip?* That was clearly bullshit. "Can't you at least wait to get him outside the building? If he sees you coming, he'll barricade himself inside. Besides, who knows how many—"

"Mr. Kealey, I don't have to explain myself to you." She set her feet and folded her arms. "But I will say this: It really isn't up to me. I have my orders as well, and at the Bureau, we *always* follow orders."

She didn't expand on this last statement, but Kealey caught her meaning instantly: things didn't work the same at the CIA. It wasn't a compliment.

"Now is that it?" she asked sarcastically. "Or do you have any more questions?"

"Just one. If your witness is that shaky, how can you trust what he's been telling you?"

"Because everything he told us before checked out." It was a new voice. Kealey turned toward the person who had approached unannounced, and Crane reluctantly made the introductions. Matt Foster looked to be about a year out the Academy and was dressed the part in a well-cut gray flannel suit, which struck Kealey as somewhat strange; for some reason, he'd always associated gray flannel with men in their forties or fifties. With his broad shoulders and dark, neatly combed hair, Foster could have been handpicked by Hoover himself; the young agent's attire, impeccable posture, and poorly restrained confidence could have come straight out of a manual, and probably had. Kealey disliked him on sight.

Foster was still talking. "We missed Mason back in September, but we *were* able to get hold of some of his documents, which he left at a warehouse in Chicago. Careless, but understandable. . . . He had to leave in a hurry. Incidentally, that place was also located on the waterfront. Anyway, we were able to track payments in excess of $1.2 million to an account at Citibank. Before that, the money was wired out of the Gulf Union Bank in the Caymans. They weren't as forthcoming, but we only got that far because of the witness, so we know he's being straight with us."

"Maybe so, but since he's in custody, there's no way he can tell you what's in that building," Kealey said, pointing across the room to the wall of monitors. He wasn't sure of the power differential here, but he assumed Crane was in charge, so he aimed his next words in her direction. "The truth is that you have no idea what Mason's stockpiling, right? Isn't that why you wanted the HRT?"

She looked uncertain, and he knew that he'd gotten it right. "Listen, you have to call this off. If you send men in without knowing what they're up against, you're—"

"I already told you there's nothing I can do," Crane snapped defensively. "Besides, what makes you such an expert? How do you know so much about my case?"

"Because I found the link between Mason and Arshad Kassem," Kealey shot back in a low voice. Recognition sparked in her eyes; Harper had clearly briefed her earlier. "Agent Crane, Mason didn't receive that kind of money for small arms. The insurgency has all the assault rifles it can carry, and it would have been costly *and* dangerous to set up an international link. The only reason to take the risk would be to get something better than what they had, and what they had was pretty damned good. I'm talking about RPGs, prepackaged explosives, and heavy machine guns." He paused to let that sink in. "I'm telling you, this raid is a bad idea."

"We never found a link between Mason and the Iraqis," Foster protested. "In fact . . ."

He trailed off when Samantha Crane shot him a stern look. She turned back to Kealey and said, "I understand your concern, but it's out of my hands. Like I said, we've been on this guy for three months with nothing to show for it. When this fell into our laps, Headquarters saw it as a chance to make up for lost time." She dropped her defiant pose, letting her arms fall to her sides. Suddenly, she looked overwhelmed. "Besides, our provisional warrants expire tomorrow. We have to move now or show cause to get them renewed."

"So get them renewed. It's better than getting your people killed."

Crane shrugged helplessly, catching the eye of another agent, who was frantically gesturing in her direction. "Like I said, it's out of my hands." She moved off a moment later, Foster trailing a few steps behind like an obedient pet.

"She knows this is wrong," Kealey said quietly. "I can't believe they're going forward with it."

"It's a mistake," Harper agreed. "You'd think they would have learned after Ruby Ridge and Waco, especially since the ATF has a hand in it."

"Apparently not." Agents were already beginning to cluster around the wall of monitors, and the room had grown quiet. "It looks like it's about to start."

CHAPTER 14

ALEXANDRIA, VIRGINIA

Inside the warehouse on Duke Street, Anthony Mason stood off to the side and studied the scene with rising impatience. The other two men were struggling to move one of the black plastic cases scattered over the concrete floor. At 3½ feet in length and 2½ feet in width, each case was not particularly bulky, but at more than 100 pounds each, they did become difficult to move after a while. The men were loading the cases onto flat wooden pallets, after which they were strapped down for the two-hour drive to Richmond. The vehicle that would be used to move them, a twenty-foot Isuzu NPR box truck, was parked a dozen feet away. Also parked on the first floor was a small Gerlinger forklift, which was sitting next to the metal stairwell. Although the Isuzu was equipped with a hydraulic lift, the pallets, once loaded, were too heavy to shift with a hand truck, making the forklift a necessity.

Mason glanced at his watch for the fourth time in as many minutes. The container ship was scheduled to depart at 8 PM, and they were running late. "How many is that, Ronnie?"

The other man paused to wipe the sweat from his face, glancing round in the process. "Thirty. That's thirty fully prepped, once we strap this down."

"Well, hurry the fuck up, will you? We've got to get moving."

Ronnie Powell instantly picked up the pace, as did Lewis Barnes, although the younger man had not been addressed. Mason noticed this with a hint of a smile. It was the smile of a man who was used to getting his way, the smile of a man who, when he took the time to size up his own accomplishments, was inclined to indulge just a little too much.

Mason knew how far he had come since the early eighties, when his activities had been largely confined to the Lower Manhattan area. He'd done well for himself in those early years, selling recreational drugs to bored, wealthy students at Marymount and Columbia. By the end of the decade, his customer base began to spread into the neighboring boroughs, leading to conflict with some of the city's more established dealers. Despite repeated threats, Mason refused to back down. The standoff came to a head outside a Staten Island nightclub in 1991, when he was confronted by one of his leading rivals. The man accused him of encroaching on his territory. The argument reached the boiling point; shots were exchanged, the rival was killed, and Mason was arrested a few hours later, caught trying to sneak into his girlfriend's apartment on West Fifty-seventh Street.

Unfortunately, there were a number of witnesses to the incident outside the club. The trial moved forward rapidly, and the jury returned the expected verdict. Convicted of second-degree murder, Mason was sentenced to thirty years in the Attica Correctional Facility in upstate New York. Despite the overwhelming evidence against him, he immediately appealed the conviction and set to work. In the end, it was remarkably easy; he bribed two guards to smuggle in a cell phone and charger. Then he began to spread the word. When the hearing took place at the New York Court of Appeals the following spring, three of the witnesses for the prosecution recanted their testimony. Mason was immediately accused of using his contacts in the city to intimidate them, but no proof could be found to support that claim. Furthermore, the weapon used in the murder had since disappeared from a police evidence room. The conviction was overturned, and a new trial ordered, but a second arraignment never took place; by the following year, the DA had moved on to easier targets. Anthony Mason was a free man.

Unfortunately, the entire affair earned him a certain notoriety, which resulted in round-the-clock police surveillance. Eventually, the pressure caught up to him. A second conviction in 1993—this one for assaulting a police officer—sent him back to Attica for a three-year stint. After his first month inside, Mason swore that he'd never again return to prison. By 1973, New York's Rockefeller laws had imposed lengthy sentences for even minor drug-related offenses. Mason had lost his desire to test the limits of those laws, even though he'd never actually been charged under them. By the time he was released in '96—two months early for good behavior—he had turned his attention to a booming new business with less risk and plenty of room for expansion: the black-market sale of Class III weapons.

Anthony Mason fell easily into this new enterprise. He had plenty of capital stashed away, tens of thousands in offshore accounts, and numerous contacts throughout the city. His operation expanded at a frenetic pace during the explosion of U.S. gang violence in the early nineties, but for a number of reasons, he never quite made it into the international markets. He knew what was out there: unlimited access to the tons of small arms and ammunition moving out of Ukraine following the collapse of the Soviet Union, the demand for Eastern bloc weapons in Sierra Leone and other parts of Africa, as well as the insatiable appetites of the Middle East's various terrorist groups, the most prominent of which was the PFLP—the Popular Front for the Liberation of Palestine. But for Mason, all of that remained just out of reach. He just didn't have the necessary connections to step into the world arena.

All of that had changed just six months earlier. His link to the Iraqis had been arranged through Robert Boderon, a shadowy international figure Mason knew only by reputation. At Boderon's request, a meeting was set up through a mutual contact. The offer put forth at that first meeting was simple but very enticing: movement of not less than $150,000 worth of weapons a month, with Mason receiving 50 percent of the profits for transportation alone. Boderon was responsible for acquiring the weapons themselves.

He had been reluctant at first: it seemed too good to be true, and the bargain required that he take a more hands-on approach, which was dangerous for obvious reasons. Eventually, though, his greed overcame his concerns. Now, as he stared at the rows of matte black plastic, he thought about what this one transaction would mean for his reputation as well as his bank account: more than $450,000 in profit alone, once Boderon took his cut. Some of that would be needed to set up a new base of operations—he'd been moving weapons out of this particular warehouse for nearly a month, and he knew it was time to move—but even after expenses, he'd still walk away with plenty of purchasing power. Boderon had access to some new weaponry that the Arabs would love to get their hands on, and Mason was more than willing to meet their needs—as long as they continued to meet his price.

Ronnie Powell interrupted his reverie. "Tony, I can't find the keys to the forklift."

Annoyed, Mason walked over and checked the ignition, which was empty. "Fuckin' . . . They're probably up in the office."

"I'll get 'em," the other man intoned.

"Don't worry about it. Just finish this shit," Mason replied, pointing to the unsecured cases. "I'll get 'em myself."

Powell shrugged and reached for his end of another case as Mason started up the stairs to the second floor, the iron steps heaving beneath his heavy frame.

Inside the CP, Ryan Kealey was holding a warm Coke and staring at the wall opposite the bank of monitors. Taped to the peeling wallpaper were blurry blueprints for the warehouse on Duke Street, as well as hand-drawn maps indicating possible insertion points for the D.C. SWAT teams. As he went over the diagrams, Kealey thought that raiding the building was, at best, a risky proposition. Normally, he would have accounted for the fact that he had only arrived a few minutes earlier, but in this case, the assault teams were no better off. They'd only been pulling surveillance for two days, and though they were set up in the garage on the ground floor, Kealey didn't think they would have had time to go through the usual exhaustive preparations. In other words, the raiders were hardly prepared for what lay ahead.

According to the blueprints, the exterior walls of the warehouse were constructed of reinforced cement, and the doors were steel, two inches thick, embedded in stout frames of the same material. Besides the roll-up vehicular entrance, there were only two points of entry on the south side of the building, which opened up onto Duke

Street, and no way in from the back. To make matters worse, the assaulters would have to cross fifty feet of open ground before they could even get to the doors, which would have to be breached with explosives, causing yet another dangerous delay. The place was a veritable fortress, ideally equipped for a defensive stand.

Kealey turned away from the diagram and surveyed the cramped room. Harper was standing a few feet away, talking to someone on his cell phone, as was Samantha Crane. Matt Foster, drifting nearby, caught Kealey's eye and walked over. He had removed his suit jacket, revealing a starched white shirt and a hand-tooled leather shoulder holster. The grip of his service weapon poked out from beneath his left arm.

Foster nodded toward the blueprints and said, "It's a nightmare, isn't it?"

Kealey started, surprised to hear the other man say what he had just been thinking. "Yeah, as a matter of fact. I don't know how you plan on pulling it off."

"Well, it's not really up to us, you know. We had some concerns as well, but Sam was overruled."

Sam? What was the deal between these two? "I thought she was in charge."

"It kind of looks that way," Foster agreed. "See that guy over there?"

Kealey followed the other man's gaze to a slight, balding man in an off-the-rack, lightweight linen suit. The older man was sandwiched between two subordinates, both of whom were taller, better dressed, and far more representative of the typical agent.

"That's Craig Harrington, the assistant director in charge for the Washington field office," Foster explained. "Technically, he's the guy running things, but he's got a lot on his plate, so he handed it off to Sam. The WFO called her in a few days ago, when they first got a line on Mason. She was running the investigation down in New York, and she's done some good work with the JTTF in Dallas, so they figured she was best equipped to deal with it."

JTTF stood for Joint Terrorist Task Force. The acronym referred to a handful of agents in each of the Bureau's fifty-six national field offices who worked with local law enforcement, as well as nearby ATF and DEA offices, to combat terrorist activity. Kealey wasn't at all surprised that Crane had been called up from New York to organize the arrest, as the Bureau was much more flexible than local law enforcement when it came to matters of jurisdiction. After the Oklahoma City bombing in 1995, agents from half a dozen field offices around the country had been brought in to assist with the investigation. The same thing had transpired at Ruby Ridge, though just about everyone at the Bureau would prefer to forget all about that particular incident.

"So how do you fit in?"

Foster grinned, suddenly looking all of twelve. "Sam needed a gopher, so she asked me to tag along. That about sums up my role in this little drama."

Kealey nodded again, deciding that he might have judged this young agent a little harshly. Apart from the overly casual references to Samantha Crane, he seemed to know his place. Belatedly, Kealey realized that he might have an ally here.

"Listen, Agent Foster. I'm going to tell you something in the hopes that you'll pass it along. See this open area here?" He pointed on the diagram to the parking area just south of the warehouse. "The brick wall running next to the road might shield their vehicles on the approach, but once they dismount, the assault teams are going to be completely exposed for at least fifty feet. I'm sure you have sniper support, but—"

Kealey stopped in mid-speech when he saw that the other man was shaking his head. "They're not going in that way," Foster explained. He pointed to spots on the map just east and west of the warehouse. "You can't see it from this layout, but there are chain-link fences just outside the building. The boys from D.C. SWAT cut gaps in the fence last night . . . All they have to do is push through and hug the face of the building. That way, the shooters across the street can cover the assault teams *and* the warehouse. Mason has cameras, of course, but we've arranged to cut power just before our guys go in. They've already set up a hard perimeter, so we should have it covered."

Kealey nodded. The plan didn't sound like much, especially coming from Foster, but it was better than the alternative. Still, he knew that the raid carried a great number of risks. First and foremost—at least in *his* mind—was the danger that Mason might not survive. He was the only link between Arshad Kassem and the Iraqi insurgency, and Kealey wanted to know where the weapons were coming from. The file he'd read a few minutes earlier had cast some serious aspersions on Anthony Mason's ability to run a successful criminal enterprise, and Kealey was no longer sure that the trail stopped with the American-born arms broker.

Looking around the room once more, his gaze fell on Samantha Crane, whose eyes were fixed on the bank of monitors. She was anxiously chewing on a fingernail, her left arm wrapped around her waist in a curious way.

"Is she going to be all right?"

Foster glanced across the room. "Yeah, she's good under pressure."

Kealey nodded again but noticed that the other man's words didn't carry the same weight of confidence as they had during the first half of the conversation.

CHAPTER 15

PARIS • ALEXANDRIA, VIRGINIA

It was just after 8:00 PM as the last of the 82 passengers on Lufthansa Flight 1822 trudged into the glass and concrete expanse of Terminal 2F, weighed down by the standard mélange of discarded coats, carry-on bags, and sleeping infants. For the most part, the travelers moving toward the main building looked as tired as they felt, which was not surprising, as most had merely connected in Frankfurt. Essentially, their journey had begun eight hours earlier in Istanbul's Ataturk International, only to end here, on the northeastern fringe of the French capital. As one of two main hubs in the Paris area, Charles de Gaulle International was sometimes referred to as "Roissy Airport" by the abrupt locals, although the second part of this title was occasionally dropped altogether.

The last passenger to step out of the Jetway moved with a studied ease and appeared remarkably well rested, which was ironic, as his journey had been considerably longer than that of the other passengers. After leaving Tartus, Will Vanderveen had driven a Peugeot back to Lattakia, where he'd dumped the vehicle and caught the Qadmous bus to Aleppo, essentially retracing his steps. From there, he'd purchased a bus ticket to Istanbul. While the ticket was remarkably inexpensive, the equivalent of twenty dollars, the modest sum was not the reason for his circuitous route. Of far more importance was the fact that the bus crossed into Turkey via the Bab al-Hawa border station, the most congested—and, therefore, the least demanding in terms of security—of all four border checkpoints. His French pass-port had been expertly crafted two months earlier by an embittered former department head with the DGSE, the French external secu-rity service. The gold-embossed burgundy booklet—which contained the appropriate entry stamp acquired at Damascus Airport—had been enough to satisfy the overworked Turkish officials. From Istan-bul, the passport and 1,400 Turkish lira had bought him a seat on Alitalia Flight 386 to Frankfurt, and from there, it was another hour in the air to Paris.

The only luggage he carried was a black Coach messenger bag, which contained a change of clothes and basic toiletries. His numer-ous false passports were concealed on his person. Stepping into a bathroom, Vanderveen relieved himself and stopped to wash his hands. Looking into the mirror, he was pleased with the face he saw, although it was not his own. As Nicolas Valéry, senior lecturer in Greek studies at the Sorbonne, his brown hair was cut short and streaked with gray, as was his three-day growth of stubble. His eyes were still green but were subdued by a pair of clear-vision contacts. He wore a pair of fashionable wire-rimmed spectacles as well as a fawn-colored corduroy sport coat, vintage jeans, and frayed suede loafers. The completed ensemble gave him the air of an aging acade-mic, which suited him fine. His current persona was not entirely ran-dom; Vanderveen could discuss the trials of Heracles and Homer's *Iliad* for hours if the need arose, although he did not expect that it would.

After passing through the main building, he stepped out into the cool air and joined the taxi queue. He didn't have to wait long, but he cursed his luck as soon as he climbed into the backseat of the Re-nault wagon. The driver stank of liquor. As Vanderveen shrugged off his sport coat and set it aside, he caught a quick glimpse of the man's glassy eyes in the rearview mirror. The vehicle rolled away from the curb, and soon they were streaking south on the A1 toward the city center.

Ten minutes passed in strained silence. Despite the fact that traffic was light, they were driving much too fast, tires squealing on the slightest curves in the road. Glancing at the mirror once more, Van-derveen saw beads of sweat pooling on the driver's broad forehead, a nose full of broken capillaries over unkempt facial hair . . . all the telltale signs of a raging, lifelong alcoholic. He thought about the thick bundle of notes tucked into the pages of his false passport, glanced at his watch, and made a decision.

"Monsieur Grenet?"

"Yes?" The man's bloodshot eyes moved up to the mirror, appraising his passenger. There was a brief, uncertain pause. "How do you . . . ?"

"*Il est sur le tableau de bord,*" Vanderveen said, responding to the unasked question.

"Yes, of course," the driver muttered. He glanced down at the dash, where his name was prominently displayed, along with his license number. "I'm sorry. You had a question . . . ?"

"When does your shift end?"

"It just began." The driver swept a filthy sleeve over his damp face. "I have until six in the morning."

He made it sound like a death sentence, an interminably long period of time. Vanderveen leaned forward, close enough to inhale the man's rank odor. "Undoubtedly, there are things you'd rather be doing," he murmured. "There are several good bars just north of the Pont Neuf. I'm sure you know them well."

The driver hesitated, unsure of where this was going, unwilling to disagree. There was something about this passenger that frightened him more than the thought of another ten hours without a drink. The man's observations were blatantly offensive; he knew he should say something to that effect, but he couldn't quite summon up the courage to object.

"Grenet, I have a proposition for you."

In the CP on Duke Street in Alexandria, the tension was mounting slowly but steadily. Most of the junior agents had been sent outside to keep the radio chatter audible, but dozens of tense conversations still clouded the air. As an outsider whose presence was barely tolerated, Ryan Kealey had been pushed to the back of the group, along with Jonathan Harper. Although he was clearly removed from the proceedings, Kealey didn't mind in the least; he was fairly sure he wanted no part of what was about to happen.

From where he was standing, his view was limited to the shiny bald dome of Dennis Quinn, the D.C. SWAT commander. At this point, the man's job was all but finished; once the teams crossed "phase line yellow," the last point of cover and concealment, all commands from that point on would be relayed by the assault team leaders, the ranking men on the ground.

"Control, this is Alpha One. We're in position, requesting permission to advance, over."

All noise in the CP abruptly ceased. Quinn keyed his radio and said, "Alpha One, this is Control. I copy you five by five . . . Bravo One, what's your status?"

A brief hiss of static, then, "Control, this is Bravo One. We're ready to roll, over."

"Roger that. Standby."

Quinn ran an uncertain hand over his glistening scalp, then turned and scanned the crowd. "Schettini, where do we stand?"

The young woman broke off from her cell. "The techs are on channel nine, sir. Wilson's running the show. He's waiting to hear from you."

Quinn punched in the appropriate frequency and repeated the question.

The disembodied voice came back right away, reedy and high. "We're good to go, sir. Power is off the board."

The SWAT commander confirmed the report, then switched channels once more. "Team leaders, this is Control. You are clear to advance."

Kealey suddenly pictured ragged sections of chain-link fence being torn aside, the assaulters moving fast through the narrow gaps. As if reading his mind, the first of several black-clad men appeared on the first monitor, which provided a view of the west side of the warehouse.

"There they are," someone murmured. Moments later, the second team appeared on the third screen, five men spaced in even intervals, cutting a straight path toward the target building.

The office was unusually large in comparison to the overall size of the building, enclosed by four-foot cement walls, which were topped by panes of glass. The exposed concrete of the west wall was lined by a pair of cheap wooden foldout tables, which bowed under the weight of six monitors and a computer tower. Pausing in the open doorway, Mason cursed under his breath as he studied the makeshift desks, which were strewn with heaps of paperwork and fast-food debris. The search for the keys could take some time, he knew. The office doubled as his living space and was littered with his personal effects. He'd purchased the building three months earlier through an Illinois-based holding company, which in turn was owned and managed by a half-dozen fictitious individuals.

Mason spent most of his waking hours inside the warehouse. It was one of the few places he felt comfortable, as he had no reason to doubt its security. Very few of his clients had the time or desire to track down his base of operations, and he had little cause to distrust them; after all, he was doing more for them than they could ever do in return.

Pushing a stack of paperwork off the desk, Mason began his search, then stopped when the overhead lights went off. He instantly looked up at the bank of monitors and froze in disbelief.

The FBI techs had done their job as instructed. The power to the building had been cut, but what the technicians hadn't known—what no one knew—was that Mason's security system was run by a PoE (Power over Ethernet) connection. The eyes of the system consisted of twelve IP cameras, all of which monitored the exterior of the building. The cameras were connected by Ethernet cable to a twelve-port midspan, which was similar in function to a server. The midspan, in turn, was linked to a switch, which ran directly to the tower. The computer was set to automatically switch to a backup battery in the event of a power disruption. The battery wouldn't last more than a few minutes, as it was supporting too many end terminals, but it did provide a crucial window during which time the system would stay online. As Mason stared at the screens with escalating panic, another team moved in from the east, making its way to the second steel door.

Swearing viciously, he turned and took a few quick steps to his foldout cot, where he pulled back the coarse woolen blanket to reveal a Dell laptop computer and a Heckler & Koch G36 assault rifle. A

30-round magazine was already in place, the first round chambered. After grabbing two spare, fully loaded magazines, Mason ran out of the office and back to the stairwell.

Benjamin Tate, the lead assaulter on the team moving in from the west, was a wiry eight-year veteran who'd spent half his career serving on SWAT teams in numerous cities, including Houston, Atlanta, and New York. During that time he had served dozens of high-risk arrest warrants, many of which had involved this same type of tactical entry. But that was the smallest part of his job; he was also a fraud investigator with an MBA from Cornell and a heavy caseload. As such, he'd been among the first to suggest that the HRT take over in Alexandria. When his request had been shot down, however, he'd left it at that; over the course of his career with the Bureau, Tate had learned that you could make the suggestion once, but then, regardless of the result, you did as you were told. Complaining just wasn't an option.

Reaching his destination, he crouched and motioned for his breacher to move forward. The other man began prepping the door with strips of Primacord, then inserted the detonator and stepped away. Moving back to the MSD—minimum safe distance—Tate keyed his mic and said, "Bravo, this is Alpha One. We are ready to breach, over."

"Copy that, Alpha One. You have the lead, over."

"Roger that." Tate signaled his men, two of whom stepped forward, flash-bangs loose in their free hands, pins out. "Entry in five, four—"

Ronnie Powell had guessed something was wrong as soon as the lights cut out on the first floor, but he *knew* when he heard more than saw Mason's form on the stairwell, unsteady feet on rickety steps. The other man was barely visible in the weak light streaming through the high windows.

"What's happening?" Powell asked. Then he saw the outline of the G36, and his stomach balled into a knot. "Feds?"

Mason nodded sharply, throat constricted, unable to speak as he crossed the last few feet.

"*Shit.*" Powell was already reaching for one of the unsecured cases. "Where are they?"

"Both doors." Mason pointed and managed to choke out the necessary words. "Two teams, five or six men each. Heavily armed." This last part was wholly unnecessary. Powell had seen firsthand on numerous occasions how such assaults were carried out. In his experience, the government always brought two things to a federal raid: overwhelming force and firepower.

Barnes, the youngest of the three and the only one who'd never served time, seemed to catch on too late, but when Powell popped the latches and came up with an olive green tube, his mouth went slack. Backing up, he held up his hands and said, "No, no, we gotta talk to them—"

Mason didn't hesitate; if the man wasn't going to contribute, he would only be in the way. Lifting the G36 to his shoulder, he fired a single round, catching Barnes in the base of the throat. The younger man stumbled back over one of the cases and hit the floor hard, his head bouncing on the cement with a wet, sickening crack.

Mason looked to the man left standing. Ronnie Powell had the gaunt, strained features of a man who'd started life with little and had gone downhill from there, the kind of career criminal who could describe—in intricate detail—the accommodations offered by at least five state penitentiaries. They'd once discussed what they would do in this kind of situation and had reached an agreement of sorts. Neither was prepared to finish out his days in a concrete box. "You ready?"

Powell lifted the fiberglass-wrapped tube to his right shoulder, his face tight with resignation and resolve. "Yeah."

"All units, this is Bravo One. *Compromise.* I repeat, *compromise.* We have gunfire inside the building, over."

Tate immediately looked to his breacher, saw the other man grimace and nod quickly, then keyed his mic and said, "Roger, we're going now—"

He was instantly cut off as the wall next to his men exploded outward, slinging concrete and the torn remains of four assaulters into the parking area, Tate included. The two surviving agents instinctively ran out to assist the fallen men and were promptly cut down by a hail of automatic fire.

In the CP, all eyes watched in disbelief as the bright flash appeared on the first monitor.

"What the hell was that?" Harrington shouted, inadvertently cutting off part of the next transmission.

"*Bravo One! We have agents down! I repeat, we have—*"

A second flash on the screen cut off the call, the blast engulfing most of the second team. Grainy black figures could be seen lying amidst the piles of rubble; the two members of Bravo left standing appeared to be running back toward the fence. The chaos seemed to bleed from the screens and into the room; everyone Kealey could see was moving and yelling. Despite the confusion, Dennis Quinn seemed remarkably composed as he tried to gain control of the situation, though he was having a hard time fighting his way through the frantic radio traffic.

"Snipers, Control. What do you got?"

The calls came back in rapid succession. "Control, Sierra One. No shot."

"This is Sierra Two, no shot."

"Sierra Three, no shot . . ."

A sudden movement caught Kealey's eye, and he turned to see Samantha Crane pushing her way across the room. Harrington was yelling something after her, but she ignored him and kept running forward, stumbling once, then breaking free from the crowd. Flinging open the door, she banged her way down the iron stairs at a dangerous speed, Matt Foster close on her heels.

"Ryan, what are you—"

Kealey didn't hear the rest as he pulled away from Harper and burst out of the building, hitting the street a moment later. Cars were screeching to a halt behind him on Columbia Street, which had not been closed to through traffic, as people jumped out of their vehicles to get a better look at the rising plume of smoke a block to the east. Turning left, Kealey saw Crane, 40 feet away and gaining ground, her hair streaming behind her in the westbound wind. She was sprinting toward the ongoing battle, Foster running a few feet behind.

Screams behind him as shots rang out. Kealey moved after the agents, doing his best to close the distance.

What the hell is she doing? The question kept pounding away at Kealey's mind. None of it made sense, but one fact cut through the confusion: unless Mason had wired the doors in advance, he must have had access to some type of launcher, and Crane would be hard pressed to compete with the dinky 10mm clipped to her belt.

Of course, Kealey wasn't faring any better himself in that department. He reached back under his coat, awkwardly because he was still running, and came up with his Beretta. Knowing what he was heading into, the weapon didn't inspire a lot of confidence, but it would have to do.

He kept running hard.

Inside the warehouse, Anthony Mason turned away from the ragged holes in the south wall, choking on the dust and smoke that the twin explosions had thrown into the air. He was completely focused, despite the small, intensely painful hole in his right thigh. Someone had gotten off a lucky shot, but that didn't matter. He had done more damage than he would have thought possible, and it was all because the Bureau had jumped the gun before discovering what was stored inside the building: a total of 136 M136 man-portable launchers, four to a case.

Better known as the AT4, the shoulder-fired launcher had been readily adopted by the U.S. military in the mid-1980s, and for good reason: the weapon was light, easy to use, and devastatingly effective. The 84mm High Explosive (HE) round it fired was capable of penetrating 14 inches of armor or, as Mason had just discovered, more than 12 inches of reinforced cement. Although each launcher cost just $1,500 to produce, they could easily go for five times that amount on the international market. Although he had moved the AT4 before, this would have been his first sale of this particular weapon in more than two years. While he'd never complete the transaction, there was some satisfaction to be had in the fact that he'd been able to put the launchers to some good use.

Powell was already dead. He'd been standing too close to the south wall when he fired his launcher and was torn apart by the resulting shrapnel. Dropping his own empty tube to the ground, Mason touched the grip of the G36, which was still slung across his chest, then turned and started back up to the second floor, counting on the smoke and confusion to block the snipers' line of sight. It was a reasonable assumption, as the front of the building was, in fact, partially obscured. When he reached the top of the stairwell, though, he was plainly visible through a south-facing window, and although he appeared for less than two seconds, that was all it took.

On the second floor of the brownstone across the street, Special Agent Kyle Sheppard leaned into the fiberglass stock of his SSG 3000 Sig Sauer rifle, his right eye positioned 2 inches behind a Nikon Tactical mil-dot scope. He was completely focused on his area of responsibility, despite the numerous distractions: the spotter crouched by his side, peering through a tripod-mounted Schmidt-Cassegrain scope; the calls coming loud and fast over the radio; the flash of purple cotton and blond hair in the parking area below.

The radio sputtered. "Sierra teams, I repeat, agents are moving through your fields of fire. Provide cover if necessary."

The spotter picked up the handset. "Control, Sierra Two. Copy last—"

Sheppard never heard the rest. Finding a target, he squeezed the two-stage trigger much faster than he would have liked. The rifle's report was impossibly loud in the small room, the .308 match-grade round well on its way before the spotter could even say, "Subject scoped."

Mason was turning right at the top of the stairwell when he felt something slam into his left shoulder. Vaguely aware of tinkling glass, he fell to the ground and scurried for cover, which he found behind a series of stacked metal containers. It was only then that he realized he'd been shot a second time, but this was different. When the pain came a split second later, it was intense, unreal—unlike anything he'd ever felt. The bullet had passed through the glenohumeral joint, sending jagged shards of bone tearing through the fragile tendons of the rotator cuff before coming to an abrupt halt in the left side of his clavicle. But he didn't know any of that. All he knew was that it *hurt*, and when he tried to lift his arm, he let out a choked scream and nearly passed out from the pain. He looked around wildly, trying to find some way to level the field.

The cameras. He had to get back to the screens, to see what was happening. Rising on unsteady feet, he moved toward the office, which was not visible from the exterior of the building. Stumbling through the doorway, he made it to the makeshift desk just after Ryan Kealey, the last person running into the warehouse, moved out of the cameras' line of sight.

The first floor was neat and mostly intact, a marked difference from the rubble-strewn parking area, except for the motionless form of Lewis Barnes and the scattered remains of Ronnie Powell. Samantha Crane still had a sizable lead, Foster falling back and breathing hard. Kealey had closed the distance to 15 feet, but it seemed like miles as Crane hit the stairwell. She reached the second floor just as Kealey got close enough to hear her yell, "FBI! Drop the weapon!"

A long burst of automatic fire and crashing glass, followed by a series of sharper, shorter reports. Kealey reached the top of the stairs to see Foster on one knee behind a pile of metal containers. Samantha Crane was beyond him and out in the open, her gun up in her right hand, her left fumbling for another magazine. Mason was still in the office, a dark stain on his chest, working desperately to clear a jam in his weapon. Fixing the problem, he steadied the rifle against his hip with his one good arm. He was wearing a strange expression, something Kealey couldn't place, but he didn't have time to think about it.

Sprinting forward, he hit Crane with a flying tackle as Mason's G36 raked the wall behind them, the last round angling down, tearing the air past Kealey's face. Crane hit the ground hard, her breath coming out in an audible rush, and Kealey moved forward to cover her body as Foster came up from behind the containers and opened fire. Mason's weapon fell silent a second later.

"Stop shooting!" Kealey shouted the command, but Foster kept squeezing the trigger. "Stop fucking *shooting!*"

The FBI agent finally complied, or maybe he just ran out of ammo; Kealey couldn't tell. He got to his feet and, ignoring Crane, who was still lying prone, stepped forward to the office, swearing viciously when he saw what awaited him.

Anthony Mason was on his back, surrounded by shattered glass, eyes wide and unseeing. He'd taken several rounds in the chest as well as both legs, and blood was already beginning to pool beneath his inert form. Kealey saw it was hopeless but moved forward anyway, kicking away the G36 and kneeling to search for a pulse. Finding none, he pulled his fingers away, and Mason's head lolled to the left.

Matt Foster was standing in the doorway, a Glock .40 up in his right hand. He was still breathing hard, but did not look particularly distressed by the sight of the man he had just killed. "He's dead?"

"Yeah." Kealey got to his feet and looked through the wooden frames where the glass had been. Crane was sitting up now, her back propped against the metal containers. She was checking herself for injuries, finding nothing at first, but Kealey saw it all unfold, saw the stain on her left shoulder even before she did, and when she found it and pulled her hand away, dark red streaks on her fingers, her eyes went wide and she said, "Oh, shit. I'm shot."

Still in the doorway, Foster turned and stupidly said, "What?"

"I'm shot. I'm . . . *shot*." She started to get to her feet, and Foster said, "No, DON'T MOVE," and ran out of the office. Seconds later he was on his knees by her side, checking the wound, talking low to keep her calm even as she struggled to see for herself, twisting her head at a sharp angle, eyes wide and locked to the left.

Kealey could already hear voices moving up from the stairwell. He knew he didn't have long; they would remove him as soon as they got the chance. Fighting the urge to rush, he looked around the office, eyes skipping and dismissing all at once, searching for some way to salvage the situation. He paused on the papers strewn about the desk, but that was too obvious. Then something caught his attention: an attaché case propped against the side of the desk and partially hidden from view. The retaining wall was high enough that when he crouched down, he couldn't be seen by the people swarming up to the second floor. Grabbing the case and trying the latches, he was surprised when they instantly popped open. Inside, nothing but more loose paperwork.

He swore again and looked around. Something caught his eye on the cot, poking out from beneath the blanket. Pulling it back he saw a laptop.

The voices in the stairwell were now accompanied by the sound of fast-moving feet. Samantha Crane was saying something, sounding angry and scared. Kealey caught, "Bastard *tackled* me . . . ," and then her voice was lost in the background. He looked round the room, searching, finding a backpack. Staying low, he dumped out the contents, stuffed in the laptop, and removed his coat. The footsteps coming closer, the backpack on, the coat going over . . .

Foster was in the open doorway with another agent, a questioning look on his face. Getting back to his feet, Kealey pointed to Mason's still form and said something inane as he moved forward, trying to distract them from the lump beneath his jacket. Foster reached out for his arm in a hesitant way, sensing something was wrong, but Kealey pretended not to notice and brushed past. Crane was still sitting up as another agent checked out her arm. She shot him a furious look as he walked past. Then he was next to the stairwell, half expecting a hand to come down on his shoulder, a raised voice ordering him to stop. . . .

He moved against the tide on the stairs, holding his CIA credentials up at arm's length, knowing they wouldn't help, but doing it anyway. The first floor was rapidly filling with frantic agents, some of whom wore suits or casual attire, others the black Nomex and bulletproof vests that marked them as SWAT assaulters. Kealey forced his way through the throngs, relieved when no one gave him a second look. He stepped out into the destruction of the parking area a few seconds later.

Vehicles bearing government plates were already lined up on Duke Street, parked off to the sides to make room for the police cars and ambulances racing toward the scene. Kealey could hear the discordant sirens working against each other, growing closer as he jogged across the rubble-strewn cement. The pack was bouncing against his back beneath the coat as he scanned the cars for something familiar.

He finally spotted Jonathan Harper standing next to the rear cargo doors of the black Suburban. Breathing a sigh of relief, Kealey abruptly changed course. Someone called out from behind him. It might have been Crane, but he didn't turn to look, and reached the road a moment later. Harper started to say something, but Kealey cut him off in a hurry.

"No time, John. We've gotta move."

The other man nodded and opened the front passenger door. Kealey climbed in back, and the Suburban squealed away from the curb. Seconds later, the vehicle swung a hard left onto Union Street and disappeared from view.

CHAPTER 16

PARIS · LANGLEY

Midday in a busy part of the 8th Arrondissement, people ambling in and out of cafés, searching for a late and leisurely lunch in the Parisian tradition. It was, perhaps, the least appropriate time of year for the City of Lights, the well-known moniker reinforced only by the natural sheen slipping over the blue slate roofs of time-worn, half-timbered homes and shops.

Sitting in the driver's seat of the Renault taxi he'd temporarily procured for the exorbitant price of four hundred euros, Will Vanderveen watched the scene unfold through the windshield—the same scene, in most respects, rolling over and over again, with just slight variations on a common design. A series of popular shops climbed the gentle slope of the street, making their way up in price and prestige to the Place de la Concorde, the largest square in the city and the heart of the Right Bank. On this road just north of the famed Champs-Elysées, there was much to catch one's attention, especially for a tourist whose entire experience, at least in the long run, was mired in images. That particular point of view was lost on Vanderveen—he knew the city inside and out—but he could imagine the sight through the eyes of the typical guest: charmingly dilapidated buildings towering over the worn cement, flower boxes filled with dark soil and bright flowers, and tiny compacts fighting for room with the colorfully clad bicyclists making their way up and down the precarious street.

For the most part, the city's natural charms were lost on him. The only thing that concerned him was the solitary café halfway up the rue de la Paix. The exterior tables were sparsely occupied, as the weather was surprisingly cold for September. In fact, only two people were presently braving the crisp autumn air: an elderly man with a grizzled white beard, a worn flannel cap perched over his forehead, and a young woman with flowing dark hair, her lithe body draped in a white woolen cardigan. She had one elbow propped over a thick novel, a steaming cup of café au lait at her right hand.

Vanderveen had been watching her for the better part of the last forty minutes. He could not help but admire her tradecraft; she'd kept her head down the entire time, seemingly lost in the book, except for the few brief occasions when she'd raised her eyes to take in her surroundings.

There was something that didn't quite fit, though. She was almost too casual . . . A woman of this reputation would not put herself in such a vulnerable spot. He knew this instinctively, and yet everything he saw—her easy demeanor, the indifferent people hustling by on the street—made perfect sense.

He was reluctant to rush to judgment. When it came to tasks like this, he was painfully aware of his own shortcomings. He'd joined the U.S. Army in 1984, at the age of eighteen, starting out as a private with the 25th Infantry Division (Light) before completing airborne training, Ranger School, and Explosives Ordnance Disposal. After that came Special Forces Assessment and Selection, followed by the Q Course at Bragg. By 1993, he was assigned to the 3rd Group as a staff sergeant, soon after which he received his sixth and final promotion.

As a relatively young E-7, Jason March had completed nearly every advanced school the army had to offer. He learned how to hit a man-sized target from distances up to 700 yards with 90 percent accuracy; to jump from a plane at 30,000 feet, landing within 30 feet of his target destination; and to kill another human being using everything from a rifle down to his bare hands. However, the tradecraft required for intelligence work was simply not part of the curriculum; such training was reserved for people on a very separate career path. Even those who were "sheep-dipped"—borrowed by the CIA and other U.S. intelligence agencies for covert paramilitary operations—were only allowed a very brief glimpse into the world of government-funded "black" operations. Once he'd taken everything he needed from the army, though, such information became invaluable to the newly reborn Vanderveen, and so he sought to educate himself in the camps along the Pakistani border. He quickly discovered that the guerilla groups he was involved with had no idea what they were doing, and the archaic manuals and Russian instructors on which they relied were all but useless.

The truth was that he was out of his element here, but he was fairly sure of one thing: the woman had slipped up. The most experienced professional could make mistakes, but mistakes of this severity were extremely rare and hard to forgive. If what he was seeing was correct, she'd left herself open to a secondhand contact, which meant that she trusted her handlers much more than she should have. Unless . . .

He pulled out the pay-and-go phone he'd purchased earlier and dialed the number by heart. As expected, he saw the woman glance down at her side, then come up with a phone in her right hand, her face twisted away from the road—away from him. It was this last gesture that caught his attention, the first real sign that something was wrong.

"Yes?"

"It's Monterré," he said in fluent French, using the prearranged code. "I missed you at the restaurant last night." *I'm ready to meet.*

"Yes, I'm sorry about that. We should set something up." *As soon as possible.*

"How about Le Bouclard at four p.m.?"

No response. "Le Bouclard," he repeated, "at—"

A rap on his window stopped him in mid-sentence. He froze, then lowered the phone in a casual movement and turned his head to the right, his stomach sinking. He had no weapon, no means of defense. His hands were useless in this confined space. If the Iraqis had grown tired of him, if they had lost faith in his abilities, it would all end here.

He lowered the window. The woman staring in at him was clutching a cell phone in one hand, the other pushed deep beneath the folds of her coat.

"Keep your hands where I can see them," she said. He did as he was instructed, eyes riveted to the bump beneath her dark coat, calculating distance and opportunity. "Can you leave this car?"

"Yes."

"Then get out and follow me." She seemed to sense his thoughts. "You should not be concerned. We're on the same side . . . I'm only taking the proper precautions."

Relaxing slightly, Vanderveen nodded once. "Fair enough. Lead the way."

"This could be a problem."

"Could be," Harper agreed.

They were seated in the director's palatial office, the last light of day drifting through the west-facing windows. After leaving the chaotic scene on Duke Street, Harper had ordered his driver straight back to Langley as Kealey filled him in. Less than two minutes after clearing the turnstiles in the Old Headquarters Building, Harper had been called up to the seventh floor. While he'd fully expected this development, the urgent summons to the director's office wasn't made any more palatable by his foresight. To make matters worse, Rachel Ford was seated next to the DCI, her lips turned up in a smile of self-satisfaction. Their chairs faced his and were arranged in a distinctly confrontational manner.

"I just got a call from Harry Judd," Andrews continued, shaking his head in semi-disbelief. "He was extremely pissed, John, and I didn't get the impression he's going to let it rest. According to him, you went behind his back to get access to the staging area, and then—and this is the part that really gets me—Kealey went into the building and engaged the subject? Is that right?"

The DDO frowned and said, "No, that's not accurate. He never fired his weapon."

"You're sure?" Ford asked skeptically. "It doesn't seem to me that you have much control over this man."

"I'm sure," Harper replied, an edge to his voice. "Kealey was the only person I saw who was even slightly concerned about taking Mason alive. He wouldn't have fired unless it was absolutely necessary."

"I hope to God you're right," Andrews said. "Where is he?"

"Getting cleaned up. He didn't get a chance before he flew out."

"And the laptop? What's the story on that?"

"It's hard to say. I turned it over to Science and Technology, but it could take a while. Mason probably deleted most of the relevant files. I'm not holding my breath."

The DCI began tapping the end of a cheap ballpoint pen against the edge of his desk, lips pursed in thought. "I don't see why we need to be involved in this," he finally said. "We were tasked with identifying and tracking down the people who bombed the Babylon Hotel. We managed to do the first part in record time—without Kealey's help, I might add."

"Bob, we knew that Kassem was—"

"In fact," Andrews said, raising his voice a little, "all he's done is cause problems. That shit he pulled in Fallujah put us on shaky ground with the military, and now he's interfered in a Bureau investigation on U.S. soil. How does any of this help us, John?"

Harper caught Ford nodding in agreement as he turned his gaze to the windows. Not for the first time, he was struck by the fleeting nature of gratitude. Nearly a year earlier, Ryan Kealey had saved at least 500 lives and possibly many more. Included in the list of potential casualties was at least one head of state—David Brenneman, the president of the United States. Now the Agency was ready to dump him for what would amount to a small embarrassment, and even that was an unlikely scenario. The failed raid on Duke Street was already beginning to generate serious fallout, and bringing charges against Kealey would only result in more press coverage, making matters worse. None of that would appeal to the Bureau's leadership. They would be more likely to hold on to the chit for a time of real crisis, for a time when the Agency had dirt on something the Bureau would rather keep quiet. Such events were not as rare as the public perceived.

"Look, John," the director continued, his voice dropping a notch. "You and Kealey go way back. I can understand that, and I know what he's done for us. Believe me, I do. But things have changed, and right now, he's doing more harm than good. Perhaps it would be best for everyone—including him—if he just stepped down. Christ knows he's been through enough."

Ford's smug expression disappeared, and she turned toward Andrews in surprise. Clearly, she'd been expecting him to take a much harder line.

"I can't ask him to do that." The other man frowned, and Harper's anger boiled over. "Jesus, did you ever think about what would have happened if Vanderveen had succeeded last year? What if he'd gotten all three—Brenneman, Chirac, and Berlusconi? How would that have reflected on us?"

"I hear you, but—"

"I know exactly how it would have played out, Bob. The dollars would have skyrocketed, but we wouldn't have seen a dime. Everything would have gone to Homeland Security or the NCTC, and rightfully so. The oversight committees would have been screaming for blood." *And you would have been out of a job*, Harper didn't add.

He paused and looked away, trying to rein in his emotions. "Kealey is the only reason we managed to avoid all of that. He didn't ask for a damn thing in return, except for a full-time place in the Agency. I'm not inclined to take that away from him because of a minor spat with the FBI, and I don't give a shit about what they're saying on al-Jazeera. The man deserves our support."

"I don't think you can discount the Bureau's position that easily," Ford began heatedly. "They have a right to—"

"No," Andrews said, cutting her off. "John's right on this." Realizing she was on the losing end of this argument, Ford sat back in her chair and glared at her subordinate.

"Kealey does deserve our support," the DCI continued. "Still, I think you know that something's wrong with him, John. He wanted to stay busy after what happened last year. He wanted back in, and I signed off on it. Against my better judgment, I might add. Your recommendation had a lot to do with that."

"It was the right thing to do."

"That's debatable, but irrelevant. In any case, it boils down to a simple question. Is he operating at the necessary level?"

The DCI paused to let the rhetorical question sink in. Somewhere along the line, Harper reflected, Andrews had mastered the art of making his words—however inflammatory—seem reasonable. "You've known him a long time, John. What is it now? Seven years? Eight? I have a hard time believing he could have lasted that long in his current state."

Harper pinched the bridge of his nose and nodded reluctantly, deciding it was best to defuse the situation. "I'll talk to him."

Temporarily satisfied, Andrews gave a little nod and exhaled slowly, as though relieved.

"And the laptop?" Harper asked.

Andrews waved his hand dismissively. "I'll talk to Davidson myself to get the ball rolling, but I'd be surprised if it comes to anything. More importantly, I'd be very reluctant to let Kealey take the lead on any new information. But we'll cross that bridge when we come to it."

The DCI lifted his heavy frame out of the chair, ending the meeting with an abrupt handshake. Ford didn't move from her seat. There was no Glenlivet on offer this time, Harper noted wryly as he stepped toward the door, and he definitely could have used the drink.

"She's got it in for you in a big way."

Kealey had used the time at Headquarters to shower and find some clean clothes. He'd also removed his thick beard. The result shaved years off his appearance, though it also revealed his hollowed-out cheeks, a clear indication of the weight he'd lost in recent months. The Suburban they were riding in was currently mired in traffic, stuck on the Key Bridge. Harper had used the time to fill him in on what had gone down at the meeting.

"I don't get it with this woman," Kealey replied, a hint of anger coming through. "Where is she coming from?"

Harper shrugged. "Ford was confirmed while you were in the field. Her connections got her the job, but she's an outsider. She has this idea that the operations directorate is slowly but steadily destroying the whole organization. She pounces on our every mistake. Unfortunately, now she seems to be focusing on you."

"For what? I've never even met her, for Christ's sake."

"Come on, Ryan. You can only milk your previous successes for so long." Harper paused and looked away. The words felt wrong, but they would help Kealey in the end. That was how he rationalized it; that was how he justified his callous tone. "That crap you pulled in Fallujah was completely against protocol, and what you did in Alexandria won't help. By straying outside the lines, you're just giving her what she needs to bring you down."

The younger man flared. "I had to do something, John. If I hadn't intervened, we would have lost our only lead. Hell, we probably still did. Doesn't it all seem a little too convenient for you?"

"Yeah, as a matter of fact, it does. But that won't work as an excuse if the Bureau decides to make it an issue."

Kealey fell silent, knowing that the other man was right. He didn't bring up the thing that bothered him most: the look he'd seen on Mason's face just before Foster's rounds punched into his chest. It had been a look of pure recognition, Kealey thought, but if he was right, it brought up an interesting question: who had Mason been looking at? If Foster really was nothing more than a gopher—and he was too young to be anything else—then it had to be Crane.

It didn't necessarily mean anything. Perhaps she'd been involved in one of his prior arrests. Maybe Kealey had misinterpreted the look altogether. Still, it bothered him, as did the timing of the raid itself.

The traffic had started to clear. The driver merged onto US-29 North, then took a slight right onto K Street. From there, it was just a few minutes to Harper's brownstone on Q Street, just off Dupont Circle. As the heavy truck pulled up to the curb, Harper gave instructions to his driver, pushed open the door, and stepped out. Then he turned back to Kealey. "I'll see you tomorrow. Talk to Kharmai if you find time. And Ryan?"

"Yeah?"

"Try to keep your head down, okay? For one night, at least."

*   *   *

Rachel Ford sat behind her rosewood desk, head down. Her elbows were propped on the polished surface, her fingers, with their short, functional nails, doing little spirals at her temples. The room was dark except for the weak light of a freestanding lamp in the corner. She had just taken a double dose of Maxalt and was anxiously waiting for the medication to kick in; hopefully, it would relieve what felt like the first pounding beats of an earth-shattering migraine. She was tired and annoyed, and sorry that she, of all people, appeared to be the only person on the seventh floor with any balls whatsoever. The director had caved under Harper's intense defense of his protégé. She knew she should have expected it, but she was furious nonetheless. She winced as her head thumped, the pain drilling up from the base of her neck, and wondered what else she could do to convince Andrews that Ryan Kealey was nothing more than a hindrance to the Agency.

There was a time when she wouldn't have interfered. During her two terms as the ranking member on the House Permanent Select Committee on Intelligence, Ford, along with twenty of her peers, had been responsible for overseeing seventeen of the nation's most visible entities, including the Departments of State and Defense, the National Security Agency, and, of course, the CIA. During her tenure, she had rarely been given the entire picture by the officials who were called to testify before her panel. She had pushed on occasion, when she thought it was necessary, but for the most part, she had cut those officials a great deal of slack. Because of her prominent position on the committee, her leniency had set the tone for many of those proceedings.

The reason for her latitude was simple; first and foremost, Rachel Ford considered herself to be a patriot, and as such, she regarded the various U.S. intelligence agencies as the nation's first line of defense. Admittedly, it put her in an awkward position; personally, she wanted to give them the leeway needed to get the job done, but at the same time, she was responsible for setting and enforcing limits on what those agencies could and could not do. It was an unusual dilemma, but somehow, she had managed to balance her conflicting interests.

In recent months, however, her views had changed dramatically.

Since her nomination to the second-highest post in the CIA, she had witnessed, with growing concern, the apathy and ineptitude of the Agency's rank and file. She could almost understand the apathy; the CIA *was* by and large a bureaucracy, after all. On the lowest rungs of the ladder, even a certain degree of ineptitude was forgivable. What she could not abide was the astonishing lack of operational discipline in places like Iraq and Afghanistan.

In an effort to bring herself up to speed, she had pored over any document she could find that related to the Special Activities Division. Everything she read was a revelation; she had almost no previous knowledge of the group's "activities." During the course of her research, she was shocked to learn just how many hastily trained paramilitary specialists were given access to huge sums of government money, then turned loose in the field with little or no oversight. When these so-called "specialists" screwed up, which they seemed to do on a fairly regular basis, the Agency suffered on every level. Relations with other nations were frequently damaged, sometimes beyond repair, and while these incidents were never good, they were especially damning when it came time to submit the yearly secret budget to Congress. It was why she had suggested the removal of Arshad Kassem: not to protect Ryan Kealey, but rather, to insulate the Agency itself from further harm.

Kealey. Ford lowered her arms to the desk and flipped open the file, an involuntary scowl spreading over her face. Despite her misgivings, she had to admit that the man's record was remarkable. He had separated from the army as a major in 2001, but not before being awarded a Bronze Star, then repeating the feat twice more. He had also earned a pair of Purple Hearts, the Legion of Merit with one Oak Leaf Cluster, and a Distinguished Service Cross, one of the highest commendations a soldier could receive. What really caught her attention, however, were the awards conferred by the CIA. Kealey had been awarded the Intelligence Star in a secret ceremony three years earlier, but even that was secondary. For his subsequent role in preventing the assassination of President David Brenneman, he had received the Distinguished Intelligence Cross—the Agency's most prestigious and coveted award.

He was educated, as well. He'd done his undergraduate work at the University of Chicago before earning an MBA from Duke in 1994. By that time, he was already a first lieutenant fresh out of Special Forces Assessment and Selection. Kealey's extensive academic credentials did not surprise her in the least; she knew that many officers in the U.S. military held advanced degrees in their respective fields. It was a moot point, though, because Kealey was no longer a soldier. Now he was just an undisciplined, uncontrollable field operative. The directorate of operations was full of them. Nearly all of the Agency's public disasters could be attributed to the DO, and for this, she held Jonathan Harper personally responsible.

Ford let out a sharp breath through pursed lips and closed the file. The meeting had not gone as expected. She had been whispering in the director's ear ever since she'd learned of Kealey's involvement in the kidnapping of Arshad Kassem, but she had yet to completely sway his opinion. Apparently, Andrews thought quite highly of the young operative. Ford would get rid of them all if she could, Jonathan Harper being first on her list. To her way of thinking, his entire directorate was a thing of the past. Men on the ground were useful to a point, but the future lay in technology, satellite reconnaissance, and signal intercepts. Harper, in particular, was nothing more than a relic, an antiquated symbol of everything the Agency *used* to be. Unfortunately, he was also well connected. It would be nearly impossible to unseat him, but Ford was willing to try. In fact, she was almost relishing the challenge.

Kealey was another matter entirely. Thinking about it, she suddenly realized that she might be working too hard. Given time, it was very possible that he'd do something to ensure his own demise, something so unforgivable that not even his record could save him. Even as she acknowledged this possibility, her impatience carried more weight than her logic. If the man didn't self-destruct soon, Ford decided she would have to step things up a notch. It wouldn't be hard; Kealey was well beneath her on the food chain, and that, she knew, made all the difference.

As she left her office and slid her key into the director's elevator, two concurrent thoughts cut into her pain-addled mind. *Things are going to change around here.*

And I'm going to change them.

CHAPTER 17

PARIS

The woman's vehicle was a silver Mercedes ML500, parked 100 meters behind his own, facing north. Vanderveen looked for a rental sticker as they approached from the rear and, not seeing one, decided that the SUV had probably been provided by her local contacts. It could also be hers, in which case she was probably based out of the city. Paris was as good a place as any to hide, he thought as he moved to the passenger-side door. The city was home to a rapidly expanding Muslim population, as was the rest of Western Europe, where the number of Arab Muslims had more than doubled over the past two decades. The person sitting next to him would blend right in.

She introduced herself as soon as they pulled into traffic, apparently unaware that he'd already been given the basics. Yasmin Raseen was about forty, not that it was easy to tell; only the fine lines around her eyes and the slight crease on either side of her strong nose prevented her from passing as a much younger woman. Her mouth was wide and perfectly shaped, and her face was slightly squared off, the full cheekbones framed by an unruly mass of black-brown hair. She was perhaps five feet four, judging from the way she'd stood next to the car, and about 130 pounds, her healthy curves concealed by snug slacks and a loose-fitting blouse.

She could feel his attention—that much was obvious. Her discomfort could be seen in her iron grip on the steering wheel and the way her dark eyes flickered between him and the road, as well as the rearview mirror. He made no attempt to avert his gaze, pleased to see that his presence disturbed her. Perhaps Raseen had been told a thing or two about him as well, but he was annoyed with himself, and that was why he didn't mind watching her squirm. She had easily outmaneuvered him at the café, and that had never happened before. Mindful of the lack of concealment in the area, he'd gone out of the way to acquire the taxi for the afternoon. He might have been just another driver on his afternoon break, and yet she'd seen right through the ruse.

Her appearance could be a problem; he could see that much already. She was beautiful—far too alluring for this line of work. Her skin was surprisingly pale, not much darker than the average Westerner's summer tan, and bore no distinguishing marks that he could see. But that didn't matter, because all it would take was one picture, one current photograph sent out through Interpol, and her face would be fixed in the mind of every male law-enforcement officer in the world. He was reminded of what he'd been told in Tartus. Before he'd left, Tahir al-Tikriti had filled him in on Raseen's background— not too much, just a tease, just enough to establish her value. What had really caught Vanderveen's attention, however, was the reverence and care with which the intelligence chief had chosen his words.

She is known to the West. Not her name, of course, and certainly not her face, but her existence is not a secret. It is a rare thing, you understand, to encounter a woman capable of such terrible things. A woman like this defies the cultural norms in most countries, but especially in the United States. As you well know, the Americans are taught their roles from birth, inundated with the idea of what a woman should be. I can tell you now, Yasmin Raseen fits very few of their criteria. For Raseen, killing is a simple task, as natural as drawing breath. In this respect, she is far ahead of our time. Ahead of yours, even . . .

Her resume was short but very encouraging. In particular, her connections to the Parisian underground had proved extremely useful. According to the former head of the IIS, she'd been based in the city for the past several weeks, arranging the details. If she'd done even half of what al-Tikriti had promised, he would have to find a way to use her in New York, assuming the meet went forward. He would know in the next few days, but there was plenty to do in that time frame.

After thirty minutes of seemingly random turns, the woman abruptly pulled in to the curb, expertly nestling the small SUV between a Honda motorcycle and a black Citroën. She got out first and motioned with a curled forefinger for Vanderveen to follow, gliding through the afternoon crowds with practiced ease, making her way toward a small boulangerie. They'd done a complete circle, he saw; they were back in the 8th Arrondissement, not far from where he'd left the Renault.

The bakery was cramped, too warm after the frigid street, the air laced with the scents of sugar and yeast. Vanderveen was starting to wonder what they were doing there when he caught sight of the woman behind the counter. Dark hair, white cardigan . . . the same woman he'd seen at the café.

Raseen turned and followed his gaze, then smiled. "She's a friend," she whispered in heavily accented French. "Not to me, exactly. A friend to *us*."

Vanderveen nodded and followed her up a narrow flight of wooden stairs, the sense of unease growing worse. He was completely out of his element here, despite his intricate knowledge of the city and the language. He didn't know the people he was dealing with, and that put him at a distinct disadvantage. They passed through an open door, the sounds of the busy shop fading as they climbed yet another staircase, emerging on the third floor.

"Close the door," Raseen commanded. He obliged as she walked over to shut the sole window, blocking out the steady rumble of afternoon traffic on the rue Tronchet. She turned and crossed to an intricately carved armoire. Opening the heavy oak door, she ducked down and leaned into the cavernous opening, her body disappearing from the waist up.

As she gathered her materials, Vanderveen looked around. It was set up as a loft-style apartment, a chipped Formica table occupying the center, cabinets and a sink against the west wall, a white wooden door leading into a tiny bathroom. The bed was away from the window, tucked against the back of the armoire. Stepping into the kitchen, he ran his hand over the counter, leaving marks in the dust. He opened the fridge and saw that it contained only the necessities. It was clear that the room was used infrequently, which was a good thing. Different faces tramping through every week would be more likely to raise suspicion than a new face every few months.

Raseen emerged from the stand-alone closet, easing the door shut with her foot, a stack of papers and photographs in her hands. She placed the pile on the table and gestured toward a chair.

"Take a seat, Mr. Vanderveen, please. We have a lot of work ahead of us."

He looked at her for a very long moment. With the use of his name, she was making it clear that al-Tikriti had passed information in both directions. More importantly, though, the discomfort she'd shown in the car had vanished without a trace. She met his even gaze without a hint of anxiety. He was oddly pleased; her new behavior meshed with what he'd been told, but he sensed something more, something that appealed to him on many levels: her true nature. Vanderveen guessed that she was much more capable—and dangerous—than her masters knew.

"If we're going to work together," he said, "we'll have to get past the formalities." He smiled at her, wondering just how much she really knew. "Call me Will."

She gazed back at him, intractable, unshakable. She didn't return the smile, but the corner of her mouth twitched, and her eyes flickered with amusement. She knew; he could read it in her little gestures. She knew exactly what he was, and it didn't bother her in the least.

"Very well," she said, acknowledging his offer. "Now please, sit down. We have little time, Will, and there is much to do."

They worked for two hours straight. Raseen had taken meticulous notes, but didn't seem to need them. She relayed the information in a low but confident voice, everything from the target's personal habits to his schedule and security measures. From his discussion with al-Tikriti in Tartus, Vanderveen knew the information had come from a highly placed source in the Iraqi legislature.

She also told him about the men who would carry out the actual assassination. It was Vanderveen's greatest concern, so he listened intently as she skimmed over their backgrounds. They had the requisite nationalities and a shared history of violence, but their operational experience was all but nonexistent, limited to a few shootings and the bombing of a Shiite mosque in Basra. According to Raseen, they were part of the swell of foreign insurgents that had crossed the border into Iraq shortly after the fall of the regime. They had cut their teeth taking potshots at American soldiers on the streets of Kirkuk; for some inexplicable reason, they assumed this gave them the necessary skills to move into freelance work.

"Where did you find them?"

"Argenteuil. I had many to choose from. Unfortunately, few were qualified."

Vanderveen nodded, not in the least surprised. Argenteuil, a crumbling housing estate located south of the city, was a hotbed of antigovernment sentiment. The vast majority of the suburb's residents were impoverished Muslims, and as such, they harbored considerable disdain for French authority, a near-tangible hostility that extended to the security forces. For Iranians who'd entered the country illegally, Argenteuil would be the perfect place to seek shelter.

"I assume they agreed to your plan," he said.

Raseen nodded abruptly. "Obviously, they didn't have access to my information, so they were forced to let me pick the time and place. It did not matter to them; money was their only concern, and they've been well paid. I supplied the weapons as well. The fourth stop on the schedule offers the best line of sight, which is why I selected it. I hope you agree."

He nodded once. The assassination would take place on the Right Bank, a short distance from the Champs-Elysées, just outside Le Meridien Etoile. In twelve hours time, the hotel was scheduled to begin hosting a two-day economic development conference, sponsored by the International Chamber of Commerce. Some of the world's most prominent economists would be in attendance, as would a number of foreign business leaders and politicians. Representing Iraq's National Assembly was Dr. Nasir al-Din Tabrizi, a prominent Sunni politician and a man who was respected on both sides of the Sunni-Shia divide. His efforts to unify the Iraqi government had not gone unnoticed by the U.S. president. Unfortunately for the London-trained physician, his work had not gone unnoticed by Izzat al-Douri, either.

"What time is he scheduled to leave the conference?" Vanderveen asked.

"Seven o'clock in the evening. He has a meeting right after that at the Palais des Congrès, which is directly across the street. It works very well for us. Based on my surveillance, traffic will be heavy enough at that time to slow the police response, but not so heavy as to prevent our escape. The second vehicle will be parked three minutes away. I've driven the route a number of times, and that's the average: three minutes."

"Tell me about the location of the second vehicle."

"It will be parked in an underground garage on the rue Guersant. It's used primarily by the staff of a financial group across the street. They arrive early and leave late, so with any luck, the garage will be empty when we arrive. More importantly, there are no cameras. The woman from the café will leave the second vehicle by herself."

Vanderveen shifted uneasily; it was yet another complication. "I assume you trust her."

"With my life," Raseen replied evenly. "She has served us well. I only hope she will not be implicated when it's over."

Vanderveen shook his head absently, thinking it through. What he had to accomplish the next day was the only thing on his mind; the safety of the woman downstairs was the very least of his concerns.

He pushed back from the table and stood abruptly. "Grab your keys."

Raseen looked up from her notes. "Why?"

"I want to look at the hotel and get a feel for the area. I also want you to show me where the backup car will be parked." He glanced at his watch. "Then we're going to take a drive."

A small, unreadable furrow appeared between her eyes. "Where are we going?"

His gaze moved to the black plastic case at the foot of the bed. "We're going hiking."

CHAPTER 18

WASHINGTON, D.C.

The trip from Harper's home on Q Street to the hotel passed relatively quickly, for which Kealey was grateful. He had considered stopping in for a drink or two, and he knew that he would have been more than welcome. Julie Harper was, after all, as much a friend to him as Jonathan was, but he knew where the conversation would lead, and he was too tired—both emotionally and physically—to deal with the past. After an exhausting ten-hour flight and the raid on Duke Street, he wanted nothing more than to get some sleep.

The driver dropped him at 15th and Pennsylvania, a stone's throw from the White House. As he entered the eleven-story building and walked through the newly renovated lobby, Kealey could not help but admire the beautifully appointed interior of the Hotel Washington. It could not have been more different from the surroundings he'd grown accustomed to over the past six months, and it was definitely an improvement.

Harper had given him a key card in advance, so there was no need to check in. He reached the elevators and punched a button for the fifth floor. As he was waiting, a familiar voice called out from behind.

He turned to find Naomi Kharmai standing a few feet away. She was watching him with a strange expression, almost as if she didn't recognize the man standing before her.

"Hey," he said, breaking the strained silence. "It's good to see you."

"You, too," she replied, crossing the distance between them. "How have you been?"

"Not bad."

For her part, Naomi could see that this wasn't true. For one thing, he'd lost weight, a good deal of weight. His face was gaunt, the cheekbones razor sharp beneath tanned, taut skin, and his eyes were smudged with dark circles. His hair was far too long, and he looked incredibly tired, as though he hadn't slept in months. It was a shocking transformation from the man she remembered, but despite the obvious changes, her attention was fixed on a much smaller detail: the fact that he wasn't wearing a wedding band.

Naomi wasn't sure what to make of the missing ring, but she did think it strange that he hadn't gone through with it. She knew all too well how much he cared about the other woman, and Ryan didn't seem like the type to draw an engagement out over the months and years. From the way he had once described it, it sounded as if they had the perfect relationship, and Naomi couldn't help but wonder what might have happened to change all that.

The question kept popping up in her mind, but she didn't have time to consider it further, as he was saying something, returning her inquiry.

"Oh, I've been okay, I guess." Trying to conceal her initial reaction, she smiled and tilted her head. "You don't seem surprised to see me."

He looked her over quickly. Her glossy black hair was cut short, falling just to her shoulders, and she was wearing a featherweight sweater the color of raspberries, low-slung jeans, and blocky heels. He'd forgotten how young she looked, like a teenaged girl who'd been pushed kicking and screaming into womanhood. It was hard to believe she was in her thirties.

"Harper told me you were here."

"Oh." She paused uncomfortably, then nodded toward a pair of double doors in carved walnut. "I was going to get a drink. Want to join me?"

Kealey could barely keep his eyes open, but not wanting to hurt her feelings, he nodded and they went inside. The Two Continents Lobby Restaurant was large and warmly lit, Charlie Parker's "April in

Paris" playing softly over hidden speakers. Despite the relatively early hour, the room was nearly empty. An elderly couple sat at the end of the polished bar, sipping martinis, and a young woman with squinty eyes and silky brown hair was slumped over the counter a few seats down, her body all but consumed by an oversized sweatshirt. Taking in the slightly pathetic scene, Kealey was struck by an absurd desire to laugh; he'd nearly been killed a few hours earlier, and now he was standing in a bar and listening to jazz as though nothing had happened. Strangely enough, it actually felt that way; it was almost as if his mind had already filed away the day's events, along with the relevant emotions.

They took their drinks to a corner table and sat across from each other in awkward silence, Naomi intricately involved in the task of picking a loose cotton thread from the sleeve of her sweater.

"So," he finally began. "I heard you're working on al-Umari's bank accounts."

Naomi couldn't help but feel a slight pang of disappointment; they hadn't seen each other in nearly a year, and the first thing out of his mouth was work related.

She sighed and said, "That's right. It's tough going, though. Most of the banks stand to lose a great deal of business by cooperating, so the first thing I did was place a call to the FATF. They have a way of getting things done, but it still takes some time."

Kealey nodded and lifted his glass. The Financial Action Task Force was widely respected for its unique ability to extract information from banks and government agencies alike. Although it consisted of less than a dozen people working out of a Paris apartment, the small group had reliable ties to more than twenty-eight countries, including the United States, a charter member.

"Anyway," she continued, "we've already come up with something interesting. Rashid al-Umari recently sold off the Muthanna Division of the Southern Iraqi Oil Company, which includes a small refinery just east of Samawah."

"Who did he sell it to?"

"That's the interesting part." She leaned forward in her seat, her green eyes sparkling. "How much do you know about real estate transactions in Iraq?"

His blank expression made the answer clear.

"Well, to break it down for you, buying real estate in Iraq is very, very difficult," she said, pausing to take a sip of wine. "Everything is run out of the Real Estate Registration Department, which is part of the Ministry of Justice. When an agreement is reached between buyer and seller, both parties are required to make an appearance at the local RERD office, where their identities are verified, as well as their nationalities. Currently, only Iraqi-born citizens can legally purchase land in Iraq."

"To avoid forgery, right? I heard that people were making their own title deeds during the war."

"That's right." She seemed impressed, and Kealey felt vaguely insulted. He may not have known the specifics, but he did know a little something about the country in which he'd spent the last six months.

"Anyway," she continued, "as it turns out, the Muthanna refinery was sold to a conglomerate of twenty-five Iraqi Sunnis, all of whom are active in mosques that have come to our attention for one reason or another, mostly for suspected recruitment of suicide bombers. Six have connections to known terrorist organizations, including Ansar al-Islam, but listen to this: at least three of those men can be directly tied to Mahmoud Ahmadinejad."

Kealey was stunned by the reference to the Iranian president. "How the hell was that approved? I mean, if they had to turn up at the RERD—"

"We don't think they did," Naomi said. "It's starting to look as if some money might have changed hands to, well, *expedite* the process. You see, the first appearance is just the start of it. If an application for sale is cleared by the RERD, it's forwarded to the Civil Affairs Department. There, the identities of both parties are double-checked, after which the Monitoring Committee is brought in to confirm both the type and value of the property being sold. Finally, the sale has to be approved by the General Taxes Department, after which the application is filed at the PRER, the Permanent Real Estate Registry. It's very complicated, and as you said, it never would have been approved if it had gone through the proper channels. A bribe to certain high-level officials would also explain why we didn't pick up on this earlier . . . Once the paperwork is filed away, it pretty much disappears."

"But we know that the sale was illegal under Iraqi law, right? Doesn't that negate the transaction?"

She shook her head and traced the rim of her wineglass with a slender forefinger. "It's just a suspicion, Ryan. We can't prove it, but even if we could, we'd have to turn over our findings to the Ministry of Justice. It would be up to them to act on it, and there's no guarantee when it comes to someone like Rashid al-Umari. I mean, he's connected to everyone, and he has the money to make things happen."

"So in other words, twenty-five Islamic extremists legally purchased an oil refinery in southern Iraq, and we can't do a damn thing about it."

"Well, we don't know for a fact that they're all extremists, but it's starting to look that way. And there's something else. According to records, the refinery and the land were valued at more than one hundred forty *million* dollars, but only sold for half that amount."

Kealey thought about that for a second. "I'm guessing al-Umari needed cash in a hurry. Most of his net worth is probably tied up in land and infrastructure."

She nodded her agreement. "That would make sense. Anyway, we're still working with the FATF to track those funds. Of course, the Agency is playing a more direct role in the hunt for the man himself."

"I take it you haven't found a connection between Kassem and al-Umari."

"Not yet, but it's still early."

"There's something there," Kealey muttered. "I'd stake my life on it."

Unfortunately, Harper wasn't going to allocate resources based on a hunch, which left them with just one lead: Anthony Mason's laptop. Kealey told her about it, as well as about what had transpired in Alexandria.

Her eyes were wide when he finished the story. "You're right. That *is* a huge coincidence. How did the Bureau suddenly get his location? And why were they so eager to storm the building?"

"I don't know," Kealey answered, "but I plan on finding out." He drank a little more of his beer and sat quietly for a moment, his gaze drifting around the room. The old couple had left, their empty glasses lined up in a neat row. The bartender appeared to have lost all interest. The young woman in the oversized sweatshirt was working on a huge glass of clear liquid that couldn't possibly be vodka, though she *was* starting to look a little unsteady. . . .

He turned back to Kharmai. "Listen, where did they put you?"

She shrugged. "Nowhere in particular, but I was planning on working out of the CTC tomorrow."

"Davidson has the laptop," Kealey said, referring to the head analyst at the DST. "Do me a favor and check it out, will you? I really need to know if anything's on there."

"Sure. I'll look at it first thing in the morning."

"Thanks," he said distractedly. He looked at his beer and seemed surprised to find it had hardly been touched. Watching this, Naomi couldn't help but wonder again what was going on with him. He was the same in so many ways—the same neat movements, the same slightly distant personality that others might mistake for arrogance—but something was definitely wrong. Whatever it was, she didn't have long to figure it out. Her curiosity wouldn't allow her to wait another day for the answer, but he was clearly exhausted and ready to call it a night.

"So . . . what else have you been up to?" she asked.

He seemed to hesitate, then cast her a wary glance. "How much did Harper tell you?"

"Everything."

With her one-word response, some of the tension dropped from his face, as though they had narrowly avoided some dangerous topic. Still, she noticed that he remained on edge, as though he expected her to say something more. Once again, she felt herself wondering. . . .

"What's it like over there?"

"Iraq?" He shrugged in a way that suggested he didn't want to discuss it. "It's kind of hard to explain."

"Do you have to go back?"

"I don't know. Probably not." Kealey didn't expand on this, but the truth was that a return to Iraq would be extremely dangerous for him. If the leaders of the insurgency were to learn of his involvement in the kidnapping of Arshad Kassem, they would stop at nothing to get their hands on him. From a broader perspective, things could much worse; if it ever came out that the CIA had been directly involved in the death of a leading Sunni cleric, Kassem would suddenly look like a saint on both sides of the Atlantic.

"So," Kealey said, trying to shift the burden of conversation. "What about you? How do you like living in England?"

She went on for a short while, warmed by the wine, talking about Liz Peterson and the other people she'd grown close to in London, as well as the resurrection of old friendships. It became clear after a few minutes that, despite her love of the city, she was desperate to get back to the States on a more permanent basis. He followed the more interesting things she had to say, nodding along on occasion, nursing his beer in the process.

After a while his attention wandered, his eyes roving around the bar. Naomi took the opportunity to shoot another quick glance at his bare left hand. Once more she forced the question down, but it kept coming up. She knew it would be completely inappropriate to ask, but she had to know, and there was only one way to find out. . . .

"So, how's Katie?"

She tried to pass it off as a casual question and began to look away, as if the answer was only mildly interesting, but his reaction caught her completely off-guard. His head whipped around, his dark gray eyes finding hers with the first real look he'd given her all night. Taken aback, she only caught part of what happened next: he started to hunch over slightly, as if he'd been kicked in the stomach, and his face contorted in a way that defied the rules of human expression. Belatedly, Naomi realized that she'd missed something important.

"Ryan, what is it?" Her voice was high and panicked, not her own. "What's wrong?"

He didn't answer as he got to his feet in one jerky movement, his knee catching the edge of the table. The glasses crashed to the floor, wine and beer spilling everywhere. Naomi was standing a split second later, but rooted in place. She called out after him, but he didn't respond, and all she could do was watch as he walked away.

Once he disappeared from view, Naomi looked around in helpless confusion, trying to draw some insight from her spare surroundings. The bartender looked annoyed at the mess, but she barely noticed and cared less, shocked to her core by what had just transpired. Still not seeing it, she reached into her purse and pulled out her cell phone, then punched in the DDO's direct line. She knew that Harper wouldn't want to give her any answers over the phone, but she didn't intend to give him a choice.

Kealey had only made it as far as the men's room. The room was otherwise empty as he hunched over the sink, eyes squeezed shut, his hands gripping the sides of the basin. He was trying his best to force down another wave of nausea and failing badly.

He had managed to keep it locked away for so long. Maybe too long. Even after he'd learned that Vanderveen was still alive, he had somehow managed to block out that terrible night, mostly by focusing on the task at hand. None of that mattered, though, because in the end, all it had taken was one innocent question to bring everything crashing back to the surface.

He straightened slightly and shook his head unconsciously, refusing his own conclusions. None of that was true; he was making excuses, and it wasn't Naomi's fault. The truth was that he was tired of fighting it. He was tired of trying to hold it all back, and now, for the first time in weeks, he allowed himself to think of Katie Donovan.

Her features sprang to mind on a whim, but they were all peripheral: the way her golden brown hair framed her face, her teasing grin, the way her nose scrunched up when she laughed. It was the way he wanted to remember her, the way she deserved to be seen, but it couldn't last. The image dissolved without warning, replaced by something else entirely: the expression she'd worn in her last fleeting seconds of life. She had not been able to talk in those final moments, but the look in her panicked blue eyes had said everything. She had begged him for help, begged him to somehow undo what had happened, but he had been helpless. By catching him off-guard, by finding his one true weakness, Will Vanderveen had stripped away everything Kealey had ever cared about: the chance to break free of the things he had seen and done—the chance of a new life with the woman he loved.

He took a deep, unsteady breath and looked up, staring into his own haunted eyes. For a split second, he was tempted to put a fist through his own reflection. He might have done just that a year earlier, but the rage had started to slip in recent months, replaced by the guilt and despair that comes with prolonged grief and the passage of time.

He was suddenly aware of a second face in the mirror. Naomi could have been standing there for hours on end; he wouldn't have known either way. She looked to be on the verge of tears, and for a brief, bitter instant, he wondered if they would be tears of sympathy or embarrassment. Neither would have surprised him.

"Ryan, I'm so sorry." She was fumbling for words, her voice little more than a whisper. "Harper just told me. I didn't know, I swear. . . ."

"That's what you said before, Naomi. You said that he told you everything."

She hesitated; his voice was too calm. "That's not what I . . . I mean—"

"Don't worry about it." He turned unexpectedly, and suddenly he was like a different person, his face assuming a tight but neutral expression. "I'm fine, okay? Listen, I'll see you tomorrow."

She paused again. "Ryan, I'm here. If you want to talk—"

"I don't." He met her gaze; the message was clearly conveyed. "I'll see you tomorrow."

Finally, she left reluctantly, the door easing shut behind her, and Kealey returned his gaze to the sink.

CHAPTER 19

DORDOGNE, FRANCE

The Loire Valley passed by in a colorful blur, the scenery enhanced by the onset of fall. The sky was cold and contradictory, a flat, gunmetal gray, but the air inside the Mercedes was almost too warm, the heater going full blast.

Vanderveen stifled a yawn and lowered the window a few inches, trying to ignore the ache in his back. Only now was he beginning to feel the effects of the constant travel and stress over the past few weeks. He was grateful that the woman's SUV had comfortable seats and plenty of leg room. Turning his head, he could see that she was still staring absently out the passenger-side window, just as she'd been doing for the last several hours. They had passed through Rocamadour, the cathedral city of Tours, and Sarlat, a town that had scarcely changed in the eight hundred years since its inception. The views were impressive, but Yasmin Raseen had failed to remark on any of it.

After leaving the bakery in the 8th Arrondissement, they'd paid a short but informative visit to the boulevard Gouvion Saint-Cyr, a narrow, tree-lined road that ran directly past the main entrance of Le Meridien Etoile. Right away, he could see that she'd chosen well; the sight lines were nearly perfect. From there, a quick stop at an Internet café did much to ease Vanderveen's concerns; he learned that, besides the central police station, there were only two UPQs (District Police Units) in the 17th Arrondissement, both of which were located on the northeast side. The closest was more than 7 kilometers away from the hotel, and as they drove to the parking garage, he noticed for the first time how light the police presence actually was in the southern half of the district. They stopped for supplies, after which he navigated his way through a warren of narrow streets, finding the D50 a few minutes later. Soon they were out of the city, streaking south into rural France.

During each stop in the city, the woman had quietly reiterated all the information she had gathered over the past week. The repetition didn't bother him in the least; in fact, he was reassured by her meticulous nature. There was one thing that kept him on edge. The simple truth was that the men she had hired were complete amateurs. What was required of them wasn't much, but should they fail, security around the target would become impregnable. Still, he had to admit that Yasmin Raseen had performed exceptionally well. She had acquired everything he needed, from the gunmen to the necessary intelligence to the simple black case that was hidden away in the back of the vehicle.

Soon after they crossed the swollen, frigid waters of the Dordogne River, an eighteen-century stone farmhouse appeared on the left, set several hundred feet back from the pitted road. It was a familiar landmark, and Vanderveen slowed the vehicle, turning onto an asphalt track lined on either side by towering maple and poplar trees. The track had obviously been cleared earlier, and was bordered by piles of icy slush and sodden brown leaves. After another few hundred feet, he pulled over and brought the Mercedes to a stop next to a worn wooden fence.

As they climbed out of the vehicle, Raseen looked around doubtfully. "Are you sure it's secluded enough?"

Vanderveen had opened the cargo door and was retrieving the case. "It should be," he replied. "I've used this place before, and I didn't have any trouble."

Shouldering the second bag, a small backpack, he climbed the fence and trekked into the woods, Raseen trailing awkwardly in the hiking boots she had purchased earlier that day. A hard rain the previous night, combined with the unusually low temperatures, had whipped the ground into a lake of mud. After getting her foot stuck for the third time in a row, she looked up and saw that he was watching her with a small smile of amusement.

"I'm not used to this," she said self-consciously. It was a trivial, unavoidable shortcoming, but she was embarrassed nonetheless.

"We're almost there," he assured her. "Just another few minutes."

They kept walking. The trees began to thin out a little, giving way to a flat field on the left. A small copse of pines provided some natural protection from the weather, the leaf cover less pronounced, patches of brown soil visible in places. Vanderveen stopped and looked around. Raseen had folded her arms tightly across her chest and was shivering visibly.

He dropped the pack from his shoulders and tossed it to her. She unfolded her arms in time to catch one of the straps.

"There are some gloves, a jacket, and a thermos of coffee inside," he said. "Try to keep warm. This will take a little while."

She nodded and opened the pack, hurriedly pulling on the nylon jacket, then the black knit gloves. Turning his attention back to the case, Vanderveen flipped the latches and began removing the components of a FAMAS G2 assault rifle.

First developed in 1967 by GIAT Industries, an unprofitable corporation owned by the French government, the FAMAS F1 was designed to replace the aging MAT-49 submachine gun, which had been in use in the military and police forces for nearly sixty years. Like its predecessor, the G2 featured a bullpup design. The magazine well was located behind the grip and trigger guard, and its design allowed for ambidextrous use. Over the years it had proved a most reliable weapon, easy to maintain and highly accurate out to 500 yards. For this reason, the FAMAS G2 was still in use with most of the French law-enforcement community, including the CRS, the general reserve of the national police. Not coincidentally, it was this last group that was tasked with the protection of Dr. Nasir Tabrizi in Paris.

The weapon that Vanderveen was putting together now, however, was slightly different from that used by the CRS in that it had been converted for use by police snipers. The barrel was 25.5 inches in length, a little more than 5 inches longer than a standard G2, and the carrying handle had been replaced by an integrated telescopic mount. The barrel modification extended the rifle's range to about

650 yards, but also made the weapon more accurate at shorter distances.

Earlier in the day, he had used a range finder to check the distance over which he would actually be firing. It came out to 230 yards, a relatively easy shot by most standards, a walk in the park for a graduate of the U.S. Army's Sniper School. Nevertheless, a number of factors played into that range; for one thing, Vanderveen would be shooting from the backseat of a car. That meant cramped quarters, which would lead to muscular strain and irregular breathing, both of which could throw off his aim. Second, he would be firing through glass, an iffy proposition in most cases, but especially when using a rifle chambered for anything less powerful than .308 match-grade ammunition. If that wasn't enough, he would only have about five seconds of confusion for cover, and it was imperative that his targets did not survive the initial engagement. There was a strong possibility that the French security officers on the scene would incapacitate at least one of the assassins, but he couldn't count on that to transpire. So in the space of a few seconds, he would have to watch, decide, and act accordingly.

Yasmin Raseen was leaning against a moss-covered tree, watching with obvious interest as he finished putting the rifle together. He had to admit that it was an intimidating weapon, despite its rather ugly design. The standard flash suppressor had been removed, the barrel threaded externally in two places to accommodate a sound suppressor. As he turned the cylindrical can into place, Vanderveen was pleased to see that the machinist had used left-hand threads. It was rare, but meant that the suppressor would not loosen, but rather tighten with each successive shot. The two-point mount would also help ensure the suppressor's stability.

Finally, he attached the telescopic sight, a Leupold Mark 4, which locked easily onto the standard NATO mount. Walking over to Raseen, he handed her the weapon and, unzipping the pack once more, pulled out a heavy-duty stapler and a single paper target. The bull's-eye design was conventional in size and form, with a 1-inch background grid for easy elevation changes. Leaving the G2 with Raseen, he used his Leica range finder to pick a tree 25 yards away from his shooting position. Walking out, he stapled the target to the tree, the trunk of which was wide enough to accommodate the full scale of the target, then came back and retrieved his weapon.

A thin shooting mat was rolled up inside the backpack. Vanderveen pulled it out and unrolled it before placing the pack on the end. Lying down on the mat, he propped his left forearm over the pack and settled in behind the makeshift support, tucking the butt of the rifle into his right shoulder. Peering through the scope, he found the paper target immediately. After centering the crosshairs, he released the air from his lungs and squeezed the trigger.

Pierre Besson brought his tractor to a rumbling halt and stared down at the vehicle on the rutted road. He'd just finished his work for the afternoon and was looking forward to a hot meal and a leisurely nap in his converted farmhouse 2 kilometers up the road. It wasn't much of a respite, but Besson took great pleasure in minor comforts, as befitting the humble existence of a dairy farmer in rural France. Besson had inherited the family business the previous spring, and the ensuing months had changed the way he defined work. So far he had found it to be a lonely, secluded existence, and it definitely wasn't where he had seen his life going one year earlier. It was then that he'd completed the agricultural program at the Institute Supérieur d'Agriculture in Lille. He had been leaning toward research in the months leading up to graduation, dreaming of someplace sunny, but the natural course of events had brought him back to the life he had always known.

He had to admit that it wasn't all bad; according to his solicitor, the property was worth upwards of 1.3 million Euros. If he ever grew tired of the lifestyle, he knew he could sell it all and live out his days in idle luxury. It was a tempting proposition for the twenty-six-year-old Besson, but his name was too attached to the land for him to seriously consider that option. Despite his youth, his roots were grounded in tradition. More than 200 acres of the French countryside had been in his family for nearly seventy-five years, including this narrow lane, where the offending vehicle was parked.

Setting the brake, Besson climbed down from his tractor and walked up to the SUV. The late-model Mercedes was obviously empty, its owner nowhere in sight. The hood wasn't up; there was nothing to indicate engine trouble. And yet, why would anyone stop here? It was a long walk to the river, so it couldn't be fishermen. Besides, what kind of fisherman would drive a vehicle such as this? It didn't make sense at all.

There were tracks, he suddenly noticed. Tracks in the mud, twin trails moving away from the vehicle, leading up to the fence and beyond.

Besson gazed into the woods for a moment, deciding. He didn't really feel like walking out there, and if it was just locals, it probably wasn't a problem. He'd made it clear that they were free to hike or even hunt on his land, assuming they had his verbal permission in the latter case. On the other hand, poaching was common in this part of the country, and it was something that Besson had been forced to deal with on several occasions. Like most serious hunters, he despised poachers. It sickened him to see the way they perverted a noble sport, and he certainly didn't want them anywhere near his land.

Walking back to his tractor, Besson dug behind the seat and retrieved a shotgun, an old double-barreled Winchester, as well as a handful of shells. Sliding two into the breech, he pocketed the rest, retrieved his keys, and walked backed to the fence. Climbing over, he cautiously followed the twin trails into the trees.

Holding the rifle in the crook of his arm, Vanderveen crossed the last 20 yards and examined his target, pleased by what he saw. After shooting half-inch groups from the initial distance, he'd moved it out to 100 yards. The Federal 69-grain rounds he was loading would allow for better penetration when the time came, but they also prevented the suppressor from realizing its full potential, the heavier rounds producing an audible "crack" as they passed through the air. Unfortunately, it was a trade-off he was obliged to make; 5.56mm subsonic ammunition was notoriously unreliable, and he had to make every round count.

He'd noted the position of his elevation and windage turrets, having made only minor changes to achieve his zero. To finish up, he'd fired an eight-shot group at 200 yards. As he looked at the paper, he could see that his efforts had been rewarded with a single ragged hole in the black, in what looked like a 1-inch group.

Satisfied, he pulled down the target and began walking back to his original position. He'd crossed about 100 yards when he saw something that caused him to freeze in his tracks.

A man had emerged from the woods. His face was contorted in confusion, or anger maybe; it was difficult to tell at that distance. Either way, the shotgun he was holding was clearly pointed toward Yasmin Raseen. Vanderveen was tempted to raise the rifle, to get a clear view through the scope, but that would only complicate matters. Instead, he quickly unscrewed the suppressor and slipped it into his pocket, then walked forward at a rapid but casual pace, an easy smile spreading over his face.

"What are you doing here?" Besson demanded. It was something of a rhetorical question; he could see the spent brass to the right of the shooting mat, and he'd already caught sight of the man in the near distance.

"I'm awfully sorry," the woman babbled in fluent French. She looked frightened, her eyes repeatedly darting down to the shotgun. "We didn't know this was private land. My boyfriend just came out to test his new hunting rifle, and, well . . ."

The boyfriend was rapidly crossing the ground between them, but that was no hunting rifle. Besson had been visiting his aunt in Paris in October 2005, when riots broke out. He'd seen groups of black-clad *gendarmes mobiles* patrolling the streets, as well as the regular riot police. Their presence was such that he couldn't help but notice the weapons they carried, and what this man was holding looked vaguely familiar. He was slightly relieved when the approaching figure slung the weapon over his back, but Besson refused to drop his guard. Instead, he tightened his grip on the Winchester and took a few cautious steps to the rear. It suddenly occurred to him that he had not heard any shots during his hike into the woods.

"Hello," the man said, stepping into the clearing. "I'm an American. Uh, *parlez . . . parlez-vous Anglais?*"

The man's French was atrocious, but it wasn't a barrier. Besson had studied with a number of American exchange students in Lille, and they had been just as ignorant. "Yes," he replied warily. "I speak English. What are you doing here?"

"Just sighting in. Is this your land?"

Besson straightened and looked around, as though deciding. "Yes, it is. And I don't recall giving you . . ." He stumbled on the word *permission*. "I don't remember letting you use it."

The man cracked an apologetic smile. He didn't seem to be aware of the shotgun, the muzzle of which was now hovering over his chest. "Sorry about that. I didn't know where to ask. I'm Scott, by the way, Scott Kessler, from Houston, and this is Marie. We're traveling with my gun club. We had a meet set up for this afternoon, but the damned range in Vercors was shut down on account of the rain . . . Listen, what's your name?"

The American moved closer and held out a hand, the dumb smile plastered over his face. Besson's good manners took over. Relaxing slightly, he instinctively transferred the shotgun to his weak hand and reached out with his right.

A blur of movement followed, and Besson felt two things happen at once. His left arm was swiftly knocked away from his body as something hard drove into his upper abdomen, crushing his solar plexus with one brutal blow. His forefinger tightened on the trigger reflexively, the Winchester booming once as the air rushed out of his lungs. He collapsed to the ground and curled into a protective ball, gasping for air.

Vanderveen took a step forward and picked up the shotgun, breaking the action. One round remained, the first having sprayed harmlessly into the woods, peppering a number of trees along the way. Satisfied, he closed the action and handed the weapon to Raseen, whose icy composure had settled back into place.

Vanderveen kicked the man in the side. "Get up."

Besson rose to his feet unsteadily, using his hands to protect his bruised ribs. "What do you want?" he blurted in French. "Please, just leave. I won't tell anyone what you were doing here—"

"How did you get here?" Vanderveen asked. He adopted the man's language once more, but now his French was remarkably fluent. "You have a car? Who's with you?"

"Nobody," Besson sputtered, overwhelmed by the sudden turn of events. "I . . . I have a tractor parked on the road. Nobody else is out here. It's just me. I followed your tracks. . . ."

Vanderveen stared at him for a long beat before nodding thoughtfully. "I believe you." After another moment of feigned deliberation, he gestured toward the field and said, "Go on, get out of here. Run."

"You're letting him go?" Raseen was astonished.

Besson looked at the field in confusion, then back to his assailant. The rifle was still slung over his back.

"Run," Vanderveen repeated. "Right now."

Besson took a few uncertain steps, then turned and broke into a brisk trot. After twenty paces, he opened his stride and began to sprint for the opposite tree line, red winter wheat whipping around his flailing legs.

"You have to stop him!" Raseen cried in Arabic, forgetting herself. "He saw the car! He saw *us*!" She began to lift the shotgun, but Vanderveen grabbed the barrel before she could level the weapon.

"Relax. I'm not letting him go. Besides, you'll never hit him at this range." Moving calmly but quickly, Vanderveen lifted the rifle over his head and detached the sling from the rear. Fashioning the loose end into a noose, he looped it over his left arm, then tightened the sling around his bicep. When he brought the rifle up to his right shoulder, the loose material pulled taut, producing a stabilizing effect. In its entirety, the process took twelve seconds.

Dropping into a crouch, he propped his supporting elbow forward of his left knee and peered through the scope. Once in position, he began running through a familiar mental checklist. He was virtually level with the field, negating the need for up/down compensation. From there, he moved to the target lead charts he'd memorized twelve years earlier, cutting the values in half because the Frenchman was running east at an oblique angle—he knew that based on the position of the man's opposite arm. It was hooked up and partially visible, moving back and forth in a natural runner's stride.

"He's almost there," Raseen said urgently. "It's his land; he knows where he's going. *Shoot him.*"

Vanderveen did not respond, still working through the formulas. Standing next to him, the Frenchman had been about an inch taller, which put him at exactly 72 inches. Through the scope, the man now measured 8 mils, which placed him at a distance of . . . 250 yards.

He hesitated. Movement changed everything, but at that distance, a flat-out run made a first-round hit all but impossible. Vanderveen's right thumb hovered over the selector switch, but in the end, he left it unchanged on single shot.

A light rain was beginning to fall, the fine drops drifting east on a 2 mph wind. Giving the Frenchman a 5 mil lead to start—five marks on the horizontal wire in his scope—Vanderveen took a deep breath, then exhaled slowly, settling into his stance as the air was completely expelled from his lungs. The distant figure had just moved into the trap at 3½ mils when he fully depressed the trigger.

Besson's own lungs were burning, his legs like rubber as he stumbled into a drainage ditch on the far side of the field, feet sliding in the mud as he sought to regain his footing. He looked back, and his heart nearly stopped. The American was there on one knee, the rifle up at his shoulder. Besson knew exactly what was going to happen. Something in the back of his mind told him that he had to move faster, but his body refused to cooperate with his brain's urgent commands, his energy sapped by a dangerous combination of fear and adrenaline.

He somehow managed to emerge on the other side of the ditch and kept running hard, his arms clawing the air in a desperate attempt to pull his body forward. He was close now, the trees less than 15 yards in front of him.

Relief poured into his veins. The trees were too close, and there was still plenty of foliage; at this distance, there was no way the shooter could—

He never heard the sound of the shot. Nor did he feel the impact. Instead, his thoughts simply stopped with the flick of a switch, the lights going out once and for all.

"Incredible," Raseen breathed. Her lips parted slightly in amazement. "You hit him with one shot."

Vanderveen remained motionless. He'd seen a puff of red, heard the slap as the round drilled into the man's head. The Frenchman had gone straight down, but even with two indications of a fatal wound, it was too early to tell for sure. He'd seen people defy the odds and not only survive, but walk away from similar injuries, the most memorable of which, at least in his experience, involved a shot taken eight years earlier on a Syrian hilltop. The target in that case had been his commanding officer, Ryan Kealey. It should have been a fatal wound, a clean shot straight to the chest from 437 yards, but Kealey had somehow pulled through. Given the man's subsequent interference in his own personal agenda, Vanderveen privately ranked that shot as the worst of his life.

He had made up for it, though, at least to some degree. While Kealey's actions the previous year had cost him dearly, Vanderveen had exacted a fitting revenge. Even now, he could remember that night so clearly. The look of utter despair on Kealey's face had been priceless, but as satisfying as that was, it had lacked the physical force of the woman's reaction. That had been the best part, the way she'd trembled in his arms like a frightened rabbit, the way she'd stiffened in shock when the knife went in. . . .

"Why are you smiling?"

Raseen's voice snapped him out of his reverie. The smile faded, but the memory remained. "No reason."

"What are we going to do about him?" she asked, nodding toward the still form in the distance.

Vanderveen cleared his mind and considered the question. "We don't have a lot of options. We can't risk moving the body. I checked the weather report before we left Paris; it's supposed to rain fairly hard for most of the night. Hopefully, the tracks will wash away in a few hours. We'll collect the brass and the targets. By the time the locals start their investigation, we'll be finished and out of the country."

She lifted an eyebrow. "We?"

"I could use your help, but it's up to you. After tomorrow you've done your part; you're under no obligation. If you have to make some calls, or if you'd prefer not to go . . ."

She considered briefly before nodding her agreement. "My instructions are to assist you in any way possible, so yes, I'll go if you need me. I have a place in the city where I keep my passports. I'll have to stop to collect them." She paused. "You know, it would be better if this looked like a mistake."

"An accident, you mean?"

"Yes. The authorities will learn the truth, of course, but it might buy us some time if we run into problems."

He nodded slowly. "I see your point. Here, hand me that shotgun."

"No, I'll do it." She showed him her hands. "You don't have gloves."

"You're sure?"

She took the weapon out of his hands, then walked off without responding. Vanderveen watched as she marched across the field, holding the Winchester low in a two-handed grip. He waited for some sign of regret, for a hitch in her stride, but it never came.

She reached the body and kneeled, presumably checking for signs of life. From 250 yards, it was difficult to see exactly what was happening, but Vanderveen checked off the list in his head, unaware that she was doing the same as she went through the motions: searching the man's pockets for shells, removing the first empty cartridge, then lifting the body into a sitting position, a considerable chore for a woman of her slight stature. Once she'd elevated the body, just one task remained. She took four paces away from the half-slumped form, then turned and lifted the weapon.

Vanderveen saw what was left of the Frenchman's head explode through the falling rain. The sound of the shotgun followed instantly, a hollow boom spreading over the field, the noise lifting dozens of birds in a flurry of feathers. Then he watched in fascination as Raseen began to adjust the body's position. She was clearly taking her time in getting it right, stopping occasionally to view the scene from a number of angles. When she was finally satisfied, she carefully placed the shotgun several feet from the corpse and tramped back over the field.

Vanderveen studied her face as she approached. She'd been too close for the last part; the right side of her white nylon jacket was covered in a fine red mist, which was running down with the rain. If she'd noticed, though, it didn't register in her even expression. When she reached him, she handed over the empty cartridge. The cold air had lent a pink glow to her cheeks, but her face was otherwise unreadable.

They pulled down the shredded targets and collected the brass from the FAMAS, stuffing it all into the backpack, along with Raseen's soiled jacket. On the return trip, they stopped in Castillon-la-Bataille, on the stone bridge over the Dordogne. After weighing the pack down with an armful of abandoned bricks, Vanderveen dropped it into the water and watched as it spiraled into the murky depths.

They reached Paris just after midnight.

CHAPTER 20

WASHINGTON, D.C.

Kealey's eyes cracked open against their will, fighting the gray, drizzling dawn that was pushing its way through the half-closed drapes. Over a cluster of rumpled sheets, he could see through the window overlooking Pennsylvania Avenue. A constant hiss was coming from somewhere, and it confused him until his brain cut through the haze and connected his eyes and ears; it was just a light rain beating against the glass.

He rolled over and put his face in the pillow, conscious of the empty bottles strewn across the floor. He'd raided the minibar the night before. He didn't need to see the evidence to know it; he felt his mistake in the pounding headache that was just beginning to ruin his morning as well as the foul taste in his mouth. And then, wondering what had brought this on, he was struck by the memory of what Naomi had said, and all that accompanied those misspoken words.

Abruptly pushing the thought out of his mind, he rose and made his way unsteadily to the bathroom, his right foot banging painfully against a half-empty bottle of Jameson's. Looking down, he briefly wondered where the full-size bottle had come from; as far as he knew, the small refrigerator in the corner contained only miniatures. He filled a plastic cup with tap water and knocked it back, then repeated the process. He was filling it up for a third time when someone began pounding on the door to his room.

"Go away," he yelled. The banging resumed, and he repeated the phrase, only louder.

"Kealey, is that you?" More banging. "Open the door!"

He paused, trying to place the voice. When it came to him, he muttered a low curse and crossed to the door.

Samantha Crane was standing there when he pulled it open, hands on her hips, an angry expression spread over her face. She was dressed in baggy gray warm-ups, New Balance running shoes, and a navy Penn State sweatshirt, which, if she'd been born and raised in that state, might have explained the slight accent he'd noticed before. Her long blond hair was dripping wet, errant strands plastered against her cheeks. She'd clearly been caught in the rain on the way over.

He gestured to her outfit and said, "Were you out running, or is this pretty much standard attire for FBI agents these days?"

The question caught her off-guard, but she collected herself and snapped, "That's none of your business. I want the . . ."

She momentarily lost track of her words as her gaze moved down to his lean, muscular torso, her brown eyes widening slightly. Kealey was suddenly conscious of the prominent scar on his lower abdomen, as well as the older scar on the left side of his chest. He wished he'd thought to pull on a T-shirt.

"I want the computer," she hurriedly finished, snapping her steely gaze back to his face. "Mason kept a personal laptop at the warehouse. You took it, and I want it back. Right now."

"How did you find me? The room isn't registered under my name—"

"That's not important!" Her voice was too loud; she was nearly shouting. "Now where is it? You gave it to Langley, didn't you?"

He held up his hands and said, "Back up a minute. What makes you think he had a computer?"

She sighed in exasperation; clearly, she wasn't buying his act. "We picked that up from the witness I told you about. The laptop was first on our list, so we sealed off the warehouse and sent in an Evidence Recovery Team. Obviously, they came up empty," she added sarcastically. "Then we had the techs check the tower in Mason's office. It didn't take them long to decide that it was only used to display the feeds from the security cameras."

"So?"

"So that doesn't add up, because he would have needed some way to keep track of clients and shipments. He did that using a laptop computer, the laptop you *stole* from my crime scene. I want it back, Ryan, and in case you haven't noticed, I'm running out of patience."

He shrugged and said, "I don't know what you're talking about, Sam." He caught himself reciprocating, using her first name to draw a response. Then he wondered why he had done it, deciding it was probably the combination of his pounding hangover and her goading, elevated tone.

Whatever the reason, it worked. Her face darkened, and she poked a finger into his chest. "Don't fuck with me. If you don't start cooperating, I'm going to go and talk to the assistant director at the WFO and have him call the attorney general. The oversight committee will be tearing you and your employer apart by the end of the workday. That's how long I'm giving you to hand it over. After that, all bets are off."

Kealey just looked her square in the eye and said, "When were you going to get round to thanking me?"

Her mouth dropped open as she stared at him in disbelief. "*Thanking* you? For what?"

"For saving your life. Last I saw, Mason had the drop on you."

"Until you tackled me, you mean?" She scowled and rubbed her left arm, as though the pain accompanied the memory. "That really hurt, by the way, and it's not like it did any good. Your little college flashback didn't stop him from shooting me."

Something about what she'd just said struck a chord with him, but he stored it away and said, "It couldn't have been that bad. You're walking around, aren't you?"

"It was just a nick, but that's not really the point, is it?" She looked at him suspiciously. "Why didn't you just shoot him, anyway?"

"That would have been bad for both of us," Kealey pointed out. "Besides, I told you I needed to talk to him. I would have been able to do that if you'd just taken my advice in the first place. Not to mention the fact that seven of your fellow agents would still be alive."

That seemed to get to her. She fell silent and averted her gaze.

"Listen," Kealey continued, "I didn't take the laptop. I can't give you something I don't have."

Her eyes flashed, and she straightened her shoulders. "Then I guess I'll be making some calls," she snapped. "You should probably start thinking about a new career, Kealey. Like maybe in fast food, because that's all you'll be qualified for by the time I'm through with you."

And with that, she spun on her heels and stormed off down the hall, her damp sneakers squishing over the expensive carpet.

Kealey closed the door and moved into the room, considering her words as he glanced at the digital clock on the nightstand. Despite what she'd said, he knew that Crane's offer was less than sincere. If he were to hand over the laptop, she would probably hit him with charges of tampering with evidence and obstruction of justice. However, her unexpected appearance did serve one purpose: she had tipped her hand, and Kealey knew he didn't have long to gather the necessary information.

Scooping his jeans off the floor, he searched the pockets for the secure cell that Harper had given him. Once he found it, he called Naomi, who answered sleepily. After bringing her up to speed, he placed a second quick call to Harper. Then he cut the connection and headed back to the bathroom, where he showered quickly and brushed his teeth. As Kealey finished getting dressed twenty minutes later, he was still thinking about Samantha Crane. Something about that woman just didn't fit.

CHAPTER 21

FAIRFAX COUNTY, VIRGINIA

The Liberty Crossing Building in McLean, Virginia, serves as the logistical hub of the NCTC, which was founded in August of 2004 under Executive Order 13354. The main floor is cubicle free and littered with pale, wood-topped modular desks bearing flat-screen monitors, while the second floor is home to glass-enclosed offices, from which supervisors representing fourteen different agencies are able to keep a watchful eye on the worker bees below. Just after 11:00 in the morning, Naomi Kharmai was working at a free desk on the lower level, surrounded by forty fellow analysts, when she saw Kealey push through the glass doors on the other side of the room.

Remembering her careless words of the previous night, she was tempted to crawl under her borrowed desk and hide. Instead, she just swung her gaze back to the screen and pretended to be engrossed in her work as he started across the floor toward her.

Naomi had lain awake nearly all night thinking about what Harper had told her over the phone. It explained everything, from Ryan's drastic change in appearance to his reluctance to talk about the past ten months. Her first reaction had been anger. She couldn't believe that Harper had sent her into that situation without giving her all the facts. Moreover, she now had a pretty good idea of why she'd been transferred to London in the first place. After all, she had played a major role in the events of the past year, and the senior leadership couldn't very well have her sitting around asking questions about something they were trying to cover up.

The fact that they had pushed her aside was infuriating, but at the same time, Naomi knew her place. Stubborn as she was, she wasn't about to go off on the CIA's deputy director of operations, and since their brief conversation the night before, her anger had faded considerably. Instead, her thoughts had turned to Ryan. All she could think about was what he must have felt that night and what he had endured since.

It was clear that he had been damaged by the whole affair, but Naomi could not have said to what extent. He was one of those men whose training and inherent nature caused them to keep it all inside, but all that did was delay the inevitable. Eventually, no matter how strong the individual, the combination of rage, pain, and guilt always found an outlet; it was simply unavoidable, the end result of any similar tragedy. The harsh truth of this was evident in the escalating suicide rate among soldiers who'd seen combat in the Middle East. Naomi just couldn't see Ryan breaking to that extent, but the relatives of those dead soldiers might well have said the same thing in the weeks and months leading up to their loss.

Naomi had been exposed to her fair share of pain and suffering in her short career, but she had never experienced that kind of guilt or sorrow, and now, as she thought about what Ryan had endured, she prayed that she never would.

She shook off her morbid thoughts as Kealey crossed the last few feet. He gave her a little nod and said, "Hey."

"Hi," she replied, attempting a hesitant smile. "You're late."

"Well, I didn't expect you to have something this fast." She'd called him at Langley thirty minutes earlier. "I drove straight over."

"I didn't think Director Landrieu would let you get past security." Kealey scowled at the man's name. "Is he around?"

"I haven't seen him." The smile faltered, and she looked away. "Listen, Ryan, I know you don't want to talk about it, but I just want to apologize for what I said last night. Harper let me walk in there without any—"

"It's fine, Naomi." She looked at his face quickly, but there wasn't a trace of what she had seen the night before.

"Really, it's not your fault," he continued, "and I'm sorry for snapping at you. You couldn't have known, but let's just drop it, okay?"

"Okay." She blew out the breath she'd been holding and turned to business, tapping a few keys on her keyboard. A list of names and dates instantly appeared on her screen. "The contents of Anthony Mason's hard drive, as requested."

Kealey was stunned. "How did you do this?" he asked.

"Simple, really. I booted from a standard Windows XP CD and used this to create a new administrator password." She held up a 3.5-inch disk between her fingers. "The software was developed at Stanford a few years ago. Basically, it takes advantage of an existing loophole by disguising decryption code as a driver. Once installed, it allows the user to bypass the SYSKEY utility in the SAM."

Kealey shook his head slowly. "I have no idea what that means."

"SAM stands for Security Accounts Manager," she explained. "It's a database in the registry where user passwords are stored in Windows NT."

"I thought you said he was running XP."

Naomi waved her hand dismissively. "XP is just a commercialized version of NT 4.0. But as I was saying, the SAM is fairly difficult to crack because passwords in NT are protected with a hash function. A hash is an algorithm that rewrites data as a series of apparently random numbers and letters. The hash is complicated enough, but you can't even begin to contend with that until you break through SYSKEY, which encrypts the hash in turn. It's like a firewall on top of a firewall."

"Sounds complicated," was all Kealey could think to say.

"It is," she agreed, "but that's not all. Mason also used EFS, which stands for Encrypting File System. It's notoriously difficult to circumvent because it uses four different keys, both public and private. Fortunately, that's where he finally slipped up."

"How?"

She smiled and said, "I'm glad you asked. You see, when you use EFS to encrypt an entire folder, every file created in that folder is automatically protected, but it works differently when you encrypt files *individually*, which is what Mason did. In that case, EFS creates a plaintext backup before encryption. Once the encrypted file is saved on the disk, the backup is automatically deleted."

"But if it deletes the backup, how can you—"

"Deleting a file doesn't necessarily make it disappear, Ryan. They have to be overwritten before they're wiped off the tape. Older files are overwritten first, so I was able to salvage parts of the recently deleted manifests using a disk-editing tool. It's not a complete list, mind you, but it's the best I could do."

"I'm surprised he didn't try to erase the whole drive."

"Why would he?" Naomi asked. "According to what you said last night, it didn't sound like he expected to survive the raid. In light of what happened, I'm surprised he went as far as he did in protecting his files."

"I guess you're right," Kealey conceded. He leaned over her shoulder and surveyed the screen. "So what did we get?"

She continued to scroll through the list. "I haven't had the chance to go through everything yet, but so far, I've been focusing on shipments departing the U.S. I haven't found a client list yet, but see these names here? I think they indicate container ships. On the left side, we have manifests. Unfortunately, Mason's containers are not specified. The shipments didn't go out on any regular basis, but they all seem to have found their way to a limited number of destinations. Only I can't tell if these are the final destinations or just stopping points. Tarabulus, Banghazi, Tubruq, Port Said East . . . pretty exotic. Do any of them sound familiar?"

He looked at the names first, but nothing popped out. He agreed with Naomi; they sounded like vessels. Then he turned his attention to the cargo manifests. "What do you think?"

"Well, Tarabulus is a port city in Libya. That's the only one I recognize."

"My guess is they're all ports," Kealey said, eyeing the screen closely. "But that doesn't help us. I already know most of the weapons traveled overland once they came off the boats. Kassem arranged the transportation, but he didn't do much apart from that. He definitely wasn't kept in the loop. What we need are arrivals. Lists of shipments that didn't originate with Mason. I want to know who was supplying him."

She shot him a quick look. "Ryan, where are you going with this? Nothing connects Kassem and al-Umari, or Kassem and Vanderveen, for that matter, and that's what we're supposed to be focusing on."

Ignoring her question, he gestured toward the consignments on the left side of the screen. "Look at that list, Naomi. That's a huge and varied quantity of weapons. Now, how many of those have been picked off dead insurgents in the last few months?"

The question caught her off-guard, but she saw his point. "Umm, none?"

"Exactly. None. So where are they going?"

She considered briefly. "They could be building up to something. Trying to take out the prime minister was pretty audacious, but maybe that was just an opening play."

"It's possible, but who was behind it? We know Vanderveen was involved in the bombing of the Babylon Hotel, but who's funding him?"

"Maybe it was a one-off. Al-Umari might have hired him personally."

"Then why did Rashid make the tape? Why did he sell that refinery? If he only needed Vanderveen to take out al-Maliki, it wouldn't have taken that kind of money."

Pointing back to the screen, he said, "It seems like at least some of this stuff would have shown up by now. More to the point, I can't see the insurgency being patient enough to sit on these kinds of arms for an extended period of time, and some of the shipments go back five months."

She was a little confused. "Are you saying the insurgency wasn't responsible?"

He shook his head. "No, there's definitely a clear link between Mason and Kassem, and Kassem was working with the insurgency. But we do have some contradictory evidence. Look at what you told me last night. The guys that bought the refinery from al-Umari are connected to the Iranian president. I'm still trying to understand how that fits in."

She nodded. "Me, too."

"I just don't see Mason being able to carry this off alone, Naomi. Brokers who move this kind of equipment usually have the protection of at least one major government. They *don't* operate out of a warehouse on U.S. soil. I mean, he was definitely the most visible part of the whole operation."

"Maybe so, but you picked up on Kassem first."

"I knew Kassem was screwing the Agency, but I thought he was just skimming off the top. I had no idea he was importing arms . . . That was just a lucky break. If anyone was going down first, it should have been Mason."

"He wasn't *that* ignorant," she protested. "I read the file. He was smart enough to get himself out of prison, wasn't he?"

"He was stupid enough to go in the first place. Look, he shot some guy in front of a handful of witnesses, then got himself busted for assaulting a police officer. Granted, he was younger then, but does that sound like a guy who could set himself up with the Iraqi insurgency?"

Naomi remained quiet for a moment. "Not really, and that reminds me of something else. According to his file, Mason didn't have any languages apart from English and a little bit of Russian. It makes you wonder how he was negotiating deals in all these countries, especially in the Middle East."

"Exactly. It doesn't add up."

She hesitated before continuing her thought. "I'm inclined to agree with you, Ryan. I mean, it doesn't feel right, but feeling alone isn't going to convince the seventh floor. Besides, if Mason *was* meant to take the fall, his employers are going to know what happened by now. They're probably already on the move."

"That's why we need to start generating leads." He paused and ran a hand through his thick black hair before releasing a sharp breath of frustration. "Look, you're right about Vanderveen and al-Umari. We have nothing on them right now, so let's go with what we *do* have." He pointed to the screen and said, "Will you print me off a copy of that?"

"Sure."

As she carried out his request, he looked over her desk and was struck by a sudden realization. "Where *is* the laptop, anyway?"

"You said you weren't supposed to have it, right?" The printer finished its work, and she handed over the pages. "Well, I knew this place would be crawling with Bureau reps, so I did the decryption at Langley and put what I found on a disk. The computer is still with Davidson."

He looked at her for a long moment, a strange expression sliding over his face. It was something she couldn't quite place. Admiration, maybe? Or was it something more?

It looked like he was about to offer some praise, but instead he just said, "You might want to run the names you found through the NCIC, but make sure you attach them to another query. I want to keep the Bureau out of this as long as possible."

"Sure." The National Crime Information Center housed an FBI database that collected and stored a vast amount of info on known fugitives, everything from physical descriptions to last known locations. It was an invaluable tool to a number of government agencies, including the CIA. "I'll send it out through Interpol as well."

"Thanks." He straightened and said, "You can get me on my cell if you need me."

"Where are you going?" she asked.

"Back to Langley." He took a few steps toward the door before remembering something. Turning back, he pointed to the 3.5-inch disk she'd used to break into Mason's computer. "You said the code on that was developed at Stanford, right?"

"Yep."

"Didn't you go to Stanford?"

She looked up from her screen, and a little smile spread over her face. "Yep."

CHAPTER 22

WASHINGTON, D.C. • PARIS

Jonathan Harper's personal vehicle was a '98 Explorer, hunter green, with 120,000 miles on the clock. The SUV had been dropped at the hotel that morning, the keys left at the front desk. After leaving the NCTC, Kealey drove the vehicle south on the G. W. Parkway, then crossed the Key Bridge and made his way into downtown D.C. He had not been honest with Kharmai. He wasn't going back to Langley, but she didn't need to know that. She probably would have wanted to join him, and he needed some time to himself. He had already endured two awkward apologies that morning: one from Naomi and the other from Harper, over the phone. He wasn't in the mood for another similar conversation.

He found a parking spot at Judiciary Square, then got out and locked the door. A light rain had drifted over the city for most of the morning, but the skies had opened substantially over the last hour. He turned up the collar of his jacket and headed south along 3rd Street, skirting the D.C. Courthouse before entering John Marshall Park on the north side.

On account of the weather and the time of day, the park was sparsely occupied. A few truant teenagers cycled by, leaving puddles of muddy water rippling in their wake. They were followed by an elderly woman wielding an umbrella that could have covered her tiny frame four times over. A homeless man lay on a bench, his back to the footpath, his right arm wrapped loosely around a bulky, threadbare pack. Colorful wet leaves blew across the path, trailing a battered aluminum can, but Kealey saw none of it. He was lost in thought, consumed by the events of the past week.

Before long he found himself on Pennsylvania Avenue, drifting past the pale, unpolished marble of the Canadian Embassy. The National Gallery of Art appeared on his left through intermittent squalls of rain. He kept walking until he reached the eastern edge of the Federal Trade Commission, then stopped and stared across the road.

The Capital Grille didn't look like much from the outside. The façade was rough red brick, brass lanterns hanging from either side of the wide wooden door. A pair of stone lions stood guard beneath a black canvas awning, as though warning indifferent diners away, prolonging their search for inelegant fare. The building itself was not why Kealey had come; it was just another overpriced D.C. restaurant. At the same time, this place meant something to him, something he could not have explained to anyone else; it was the closest he had been to Katie Donovan, or at least the lingering footprints she had left in the world, in nearly a year.

As he stood there in the rain, staring across the street, he was seized by a sudden realization. For the first time, he knew why he had actively sought the Iraqi posting six months earlier: the desert was as far removed from civilization as one could get. The sparse surroundings had done nothing to dredge up the memories, giving him a reprieve, however temporary, from the aching guilt that was buried inside. From the moment he'd landed at Dulles, everything he saw seemed to remind him of her: the brownstone on Q Street, where they had once shared a meal with Jonathan Harper and his wife, Julie; and the restaurant he was looking at now, where she had drunk too much wine and nearly gotten them kicked out in a fit of unprovoked laughter. Even the Hotel Washington reminded him of the Hay-Adams, another D.C. landmark, and a snowy night the previous November, when they had made love with the windows open, the snow swirling into the room, her soft, sensual cries spilling out over Lafayette Park.

None of it reminded him of the night she had died at Vanderveen's hand, but that didn't matter. It always came back in the end. It was the one thing from which he could not shake free.

After another few minutes, Kealey crossed the street and started up 6th, heading toward Chinatown. His thoughts were ever shifting, as were his feelings, but he could admit this: he had no desire to shake free. He needed the pain, and he needed the guilt. They served as constant reminders. Reminders of what he had done, what he had failed to do, and what he had lost.

He deserved nothing less.

The conference room on the eighth floor of Le Meridien Etoile was filled with a dull roar, which was perhaps inevitable when 250 of the world's most prominent business leaders were pushed into the same confined space. From his seat on the left side of the room, Dr. Nasir al-Din Tabrizi could see a few familiar faces scattered throughout the crowd: the chief financial officer of Dow Chemical, a plump deputy chairman of Barclays Bank, and the new CEO of Lockheed-Martin, a petite, polished blonde who had graced the covers of both *Fortune* and *Forbes* the previous month.

Tabrizi smiled as he lifted a glass of water to his lips. He enjoyed these conferences, not only because they generated enormous opportunities, but because his country was finally in a position to *profit* from those opportunities. Iraq had floundered for so long; it was only fitting that she now had the chance to prosper. The worst had come after 1990, when the UN-imposed sanctions had devastated what was left of the country's economy. Tabrizi had been in England when the Gulf War began, teaching at the London School of Economics, but he'd closely followed the news from home. Like many prominent Iraqis in London, he had been a member of the Iraqi National Congress, the leading opposition group outside Iraq. The only difference was that Tabrizi had been one of the very few Sunni Muslims involved with the organization.

The group was founded after the war and secretly funded for years by the CIA. Following the American invasion in 2003, many long-standing members of the INC had sought out leadership positions in the interim government, Tabrizi included. In this respect, his close association with Ahmed Chalabi, a presidential hopeful and one of the group's leading members, had proved invaluable. In January of 2004, Tabrizi was awarded a modest position with the Iraqi

Governing Council, the first government set up by the Coalition Provisional Authority. Since then, he'd hung on through a number of interim administrations, resulting in his recent appointment to the lofty post of foreign minister.

Nasir Tabrizi was deep in thought as the secretary-general of the International Chamber of Commerce made his way to the podium. Tubrizi's feelings toward the United States were decidedly mixed. During his years in London, the INC's murky relationship with the U.S. government had made him extremely uncomfortable. At the same time, that relationship was largely responsible for his current position. His country was even more divided than he was. A recent poll had suggested that more than 80 percent of Iraqis wanted American troops out of the country. Tabrizi understood the sentiment, but he knew that a rapid withdrawal would likely cause the new government to break down completely. At the moment, the only thing holding it together was international pressure for results, and as one would expect, most of that pressure was coming from the United States. The troops were a highly visible reminder of the U.S. commitment to the region, and while the nature of that commitment was cause for constant debate, no one could deny that the Americans were in for the long haul.

Of course, the current situation left much to be desired. The attempted assassination of Nuri al-Maliki had led to numerous outbreaks of violence over the past two weeks, particularly between Sunni insurgents and followers of the Shiite cleric Moqtadr al-Sadr. Since that failed attempt, 30 American soldiers had died in Baghdad alone. Tabrizi knew that the U.S. president's approval ratings were at an all-time low, hovering around 40 percent. Richard Fiske, the Democratic challenger, had promised a rapid withdrawal of troops as part of his election campaign, and the American people seemed to be responding to that platform. Tabrizi worried constantly about what the results of that election might mean for his country, but unfortunately, all he could do was watch from the sidelines.

A noise behind him caused him to turn. A French security officer tapped the face of his watch and whispered so as not to interfere with the speech being given at the front of the room. "Ten minutes, Dr. Tabrizi."

"Thank you." He nodded cordially, and the man retreated. After arriving in Paris two days earlier with the Iraqi delegation, he'd been surprised to find that three CRS men had been assigned to his security detail. Like all senior officials in Iraq, he was provided with an armed escort whenever he left the Green Zone, but that kind of protection was rarely afforded by other nations, even during official visits. Knowing they could count on Tabrizi's voice in the legislature, the Americans had most likely slipped a quiet word to the French. At least, that was what he assumed had happened. Despite the attack in Baghdad, he didn't think the security was particularly necessary. Still, the presence of his young guardians was somewhat reassuring, even in a city as civilized as Paris.

The secretary-general concluded his remarks, and the room filled with applause. Rising from his seat, Tabrizi shook a few extended hands and exchanged some pleasantries, then turned to the CRS man. "The next meeting will not take long. I assume the car is outside?"

A brief nod. "Yes, sir. The convention center is right across the street. I'll walk with you that far, and the car will take you on to your hotel afterward."

"Wonderful." The Iraqi physician smiled and gestured toward the door. "Lead the way."

CHAPTER 23

WASHINGTON, D.C. • VIRGINIA • PARIS

The restaurant was located on the 700 block of 6th Street, just across from the recently renamed Verizon Center. It was hard to spot from the street, and Kealey walked past it several times before he finally inquired in a video shop, which happened to bear the correct address. The sullen clerk on duty wordlessly guided him out to the road and pointed toward the entrance, a covered staircase running up the side of the building. Making his way up to the second floor, he was greeted at the door by a pretty Chinese woman in a red silk dress. He followed her through the busy dining room to one of several smaller rooms in the back.

He found Jonathan Harper digging into a plate of chicken curry, a cup of steaming amber tea at his right hand. The woman handed Kealey a menu and departed, softly closing the door behind her. It was quiet inside the little alcove, the only sounds the clanking of plates from the adjacent dining area, low snatches of conversation, and the rain beating against a small frosted window.

Harper pointed to a chair and said, "What kept you? Christ, you're soaked."

"I felt like walking."

"From where? McLean?"

Kealey poured some of the tea and looked down at his damp clothes. "I got caught in the downpour."

There was a slight tap at the door, and the woman reappeared.

She smiled demurely and handed him a towel. He was surprised but accepted it gratefully. Harper murmured a few words in Chinese, and the woman departed.

"This is a nice place," Kealey remarked, working the towel through his hair. "How did you find it?"

"I know the owner. He's Burmese, a former diplomat. I worked with him when I was attached to the State Department back in '94. He liked the city so much he decided to stay. He bought this place when he retired. I don't come here that often, but they seem to remember me."

"So you weren't just speaking Chinese?"

Harper shook his head and laughed. "I hope we never need you for anything over there. You'd be dead in a week, with those language skills."

Kealey offered a slight smile. The DDO set down his fork and bent down to a case by his feet, then straightened and slid two manila folders over the patterned tablecloth. The younger man pulled them across and opened the first. It contained what he'd requested from Harper that very morning: black-and-white photocopies of Samantha Crane's personnel file. He instantly began flipping through the pages.

"Interesting stuff," Harper said, digging back into his meal. "I got the files through a friend at the Bureau, my old roommate at Boston College. He's pretty high up now, a section chief at the Los Angeles field office, and he owed me a favor."

"Some favor," Kealey said.

"Yeah, well, he knows about this woman firsthand. Samantha Crane has a reputation of sorts, and it's not the good kind. She was sworn in as a special agent six years ago. Since then, she's killed eight people in the line of duty and wounded a dozen more."

Kealey looked up. "Jesus."

Harper nodded. "Amazingly, all of the shootings were cleared by the Office of Professional Responsibility, but as you can imagine, it left a bad taste in the Bureau's mouth. They don't like that kind of publicity. Fortunately for Crane, she has a guardian angel."

The waitress returned, bearing more food. As she began unloading the dishes, both men fell silent, but Kealey continued to flip through the file. Samantha Evelyn Crane was born on June 8th, 1978, in Scranton, Pennsylvania. She'd earned a degree in criminal justice from Penn State in 1999, but not before attending the Windward School in Los Angeles from '90 to '93.

"She was only a kid when she went to this Windward place. What's that about?"

"It's a private school and very prestigious," Harper replied. "It turns out a lot of promising young actors; in fact, Crane did a fair amount of commercial work as a teenager. You won't find this in the file, but she was in her second year at the school when she lost her parents. Her father was a full colonel, an army Apache pilot, heavily decorated. He was shot down behind Iraqi lines in '91, but they never found the body. He's still listed as MIA."

"And the mother?"

Harper looked uneasy. "She killed herself. Slit her wrists two months after she was notified of her husband's disappearance. I had some people check it out, though . . . Apparently, she was going downhill prior to the incident. Drugs, alcohol abuse, that kind of thing."

Kealey turned his attention back to the paperwork, but Harper could tell his mind was somewhere else. He knew they were both thinking the same thing: that Samantha Crane's childhood bore a remarkable similarity to that of William Vanderveen. Major General Francis Vanderveen had also been a heavily decorated officer, only with the South African Defence Force instead of the U.S. military. The elder Vanderveen was killed during the South African invasion of Angola in 1975, and shortly thereafter, his wife, Julienne, committed suicide, leaving Will Vanderveen an orphan at the age of nine. According to the file, Crane had not been much older when she'd endured the same.

The second folder contained info on Matt Foster, the agent who'd fired the shots that killed Anthony Mason. Foster was twenty-five years old, a graduate of Amherst College and Phillips Exeter Academy. Interestingly, he'd never been involved in an on-duty shooting until the raid in Alexandria. Apart from that piece of info, there was little to go on. Disappointed, Kealey set the folders aside and started in on a plate of egg noodles. He wasn't particularly hungry, but he hoped the food might settle his queasy stomach.

Picking up the thread, Kealey said, "So what about Crane? Who's looking out for her?"

Harper leaned forward, inadvertently shifting the tablecloth. "You're never going to believe it, Ryan, but as it turns out, her aunt is none other than Rachel Ford."

Kealey set down his fork and stared across the table. "As in *our* Rachel Ford? The deputy DCI?"

"One and the same."

Kealey exhaled slowly, taking it in. "That's incredible."

"I know. I couldn't believe it either."

"It makes sense, though."

"What do you mean?"

Kealey told him about the confrontation at the hotel that morning. "She said something strange, John. She was talking about the raid in Alexandria, and the way I knocked her to the ground to get her out of the line of fire. I guess I was a little rough. Anyway, she said, 'Your little college flashback didn't stop him from shooting me.'"

"So?"

"So I played cornerback at the University of Chicago. Just two seasons, and I didn't start, but how the hell could she have known that unless she was checking up on me?"

Harper nodded slowly. "That makes sense. And the only way she could do that is with help from someone high up in the Agency. Someone like Ford."

"That's probably how she found out I had the laptop as well." Kealey's face tightened in anger. "This Ford woman is really starting to piss me off. Why is she going after me, and why in this way?"

"The accusation carries more weight if it comes from another agency, Ryan. And I already told you why she's after you—because you keep making it easy for her, and because you're part of my directorate. It doesn't matter, though; you're in the clear on the laptop."

"Really? How did that happen?"

"The attorney general received a call from Harry Judd this morning. Basically, Judd accused us of interfering in a Bureau investigation and tampering with evidence. He was calling to ask about the possibility of filing charges."

Kealey closed his eyes and shook his head. Crane must have set things in motion right after she left his room.

"Anyway," Harper was saying, "the attorney general advised the president of the situation."

"That probably wasn't a good idea."

"It wasn't," Harper agreed. "Brenneman already has too much on his plate. The election is coming up. He needs to be campaigning, but instead, he's dealing with this shit in Iraq. More U.S. soldiers have died in the past week than in the past two months combined. A pissing contest between the Bureau and the CIA is the last thing he needs right now."

"So he sent word to the respective directors to work it out themselves," Kealey guessed. "Or face the consequences."

"I know Andrews got the call, but I can't say for sure what happened at the Hoover Building. Anyway, you said that Crane instigated this. My guess is that word trickled down from the director's office. Someone probably told her she was lucky not to have gone the way of the ADIC and to keep her mouth shut."

Kealey nodded. Craig Harrington, the assistant director in charge of the WFO, had already been placed on administrative leave. The Judiciary Oversight Committee was looking for someone to take the fall for the disastrous raid on Mason's warehouse, and Harrington was emerging as the most likely candidate.

"The Bureau will still want the computer, though," Kealey pointed out.

Harper nodded. Having cleared his plate, he set his fork aside and said, "Andrews advised me we are obliged to turn over the laptop within twenty-four hours. I guess he struck some kind of deal with Judd. Either way, I can't postpone it forever, Ryan. I hope Naomi is working fast."

At that moment, Kharmai was hurrying back to her temporary desk in McLean, holding a half-empty can of Sprite. Over the past two hours, she'd done everything she could think of to generate leads on Mason's files. She'd entered every name she could find into the NCIC, but so far, no flags had been raised. She'd struck out with Interpol as well. In a final act of desperation, she had placed calls to a number of CIA stations, all of which were located in countries with ports on Mason's list. She was hoping something might come of her last-ditch effort, but she wasn't holding her breath. Her phone started to ring when she was halfway across the floor, and she immediately increased her pace.

Sprinting the last few feet, she snatched it up. "Kharmai."

"Naomi, it's Bill Staibler."

Her heart thumped with anticipation. Staibler was a veteran case officer operating out of Cairo. She'd first gotten through to him two hours earlier. During that brief conversation, he'd intimated that his network of agents included a number of dockworkers on the Egyptian coast. That little tidbit made him a star on her sad little list of prospects. "Hi, sir. Thanks for getting back to me."

"No problem." He sounded tired. Naomi remembered the time difference and glanced at her watch. It was nearly 7:00 PM in Cairo; Staibler must have been coming off a long day.

"According to your information," he was saying, "this guy Mason had a container on the *Kustatan*, a Panamanian vessel which docked in Port Said East on the eighteenth of August. Unfortunately, you don't have a container number. Is that correct?"

"That's right. The info I have is fragmented at best."

"Okay, well, here's what I can do for you. I can give you a list of all the containers off-loaded that day, as well as the names of the people who collected them. It's all documented. One of my assets came through for me, but I have to warn you: if Mason's container was transferred to another ship, you're shit out of luck. As for what came off the boat, I can tell you what is *supposed* to be in those containers. That information is listed on the manifests, but as you know, they don't count for much. You can run the names I'm giving you through the system at Langley, of course, but I'd be surprised if anything comes back."

He paused, perhaps sensing her disappointment. "I'm sorry, Kharmai, but this is the best I can do."

She let out a little sigh of frustration before catching herself. She hoped he hadn't heard it over the line. "I understand, Mr. Staibler. Anyway, thanks for trying. I'd still like to see the log, though, if you don't mind sending it over."

"You have a secure fax number?"

She gave it to him and ended the call, then walked over to a bank of fax machines on the east side of the room. A minute later, one of them started to whir. The machine spit out three sheets of paper. Naomi snatched them up and walked back to her desk, where she slumped into her seat and began to read.

Two minutes later, she straightened and her eyes opened wide. Placing the loose pages on her lap, she rapidly brought Mason's files up on her screen, then scrolled down until she found the appropriate dates. Picking up the phone, she quickly got Staibler back on the line. He sounded slightly annoyed at this second demand on his time, but not unwilling to help.

"Sir, I think I have something here. Is there any way your asset can get me the collection logs from Port Said for two other dates?"

"Possibly. What are they?"

"June twenty-first and July seventeenth." She continued to read from her screen. "On the date in June, I'm looking for a vessel registered in Italy, the *Cala Levante*. The vessel that docked in July is Honduran, the *Belladonna*. I want to know who collected the containers from both of those vessels. A complete list if possible. And, Mr. Staibler, I need this ASAP."

"You got it. Give me an hour."

For the next thirty minutes, Kharmai paced steadily behind her desk, the other analysts shooting her little looks of concern or annoyance, depending on their personal inclinations. Lost in thought, she was blind to the attention she was receiving, but eventually, she forced herself to sit down, take a deep breath, and concentrate.

Her feet were aching, so she slipped off her pumps and slid her feet under the desk, massaging one bare foot with the other, then reversing the process. She found this little quirk of hers to be immensely helpful when thinking things through.

First, she considered what she'd found on the collection log from the Egyptian port. Potentially, it was a very important piece of information, but it wasn't a breakthrough. Even if Staibler could produce verification, it wasn't going to bring them any closer to finding William Vanderveen, or Rashid al-Umari, for that matter. She needed a workable lead, but where could she find it? The names on the documents in Mason's computer had seemed so promising, but none had panned out. There had been partially composed letters, faxes, even an invoice or two. She'd run everything through the NCIC and the Pentagon's database, but nothing had matched. It just didn't make sense.

Her head snapped up as she realized something. She had never checked the list of vessels through the system, and some of them didn't sound like ships at all. In fact, some of them sounded very much like first and last names. It might be nothing, she thought, but at this point, anything was worth a try.

The Mercedes was parked perpendicular to the boulevard Gouvion Saint-Cyr. From the backseat, Vanderveen had a clear line of sight down the length of the road. The façade of Le Meridien Etoile, glowing amber in the light of the fading sun, could be seen rising above the boulevard, and in front, a number of hired cars and taxis were lined up to accept and discharge passengers.

Raseen had pointed out the unmarked Peugeot 406 shortly after they'd moved into position. The rear window was heavily tinted, but Vanderveen could make out the vague outlines of two occupants. According to Raseen, both were CRS officers assigned to Tabrizi. The men were almost certainly trained in close-quarter protection. He knew they would react instantly when the first shots were fired; for this reason, his own shots had to be perfectly placed.

As Vanderveen watched through a pair of binoculars, the passenger lifted a phone to his right ear and held it there for approximately fifteen seconds. A number of conference attendees were already beginning to stream out through the steel-and-glass doors, though most were still upstairs, presumably mulling over business opportunities with their peers.

"What's happening?" Raseen asked impatiently. She was fidgeting behind the wheel, her fingers tapping out a nervous, irregular beat on her thighs.

"It looks like somebody just called one of those officers. I think he's coming out."

Raseen looked at the clock in the dashboard, then lifted her phone and speed-dialed a number. When the call was answered on the other end, she simply said, "It's time. Get moving."

She kept the phone to her ear, tucked under her hair, as Vanderveen studied the sidewalk outside the hotel. Finally, the target stepped into view, a third bodyguard trailing a half step behind. "I've got him. Charcoal suit, yellow tie. Third from the left."

Raseen repeated the information over the line. As the last word left her mouth, a black Ford sedan pulled up alongside them, then swung a hard left onto the boulevard, tires squealing.

"Idiots," Vanderveen hissed. "They're going too fast."

Raseen was still relaying rapid instructions as she lowered the rear window from her console, each word running into the next. "You have him crossing the road, third from the left, *third from the left.* . . ."

Vanderveen had the G2 ready, the barrel stabilized on a large pack level with the open window. Cars passing by could see into the Mercedes, could see the rifle, but it couldn't be helped. He found the notch for his cheek and positioned his right eye behind the Leupold scope.

Alerted by the fast-moving vehicle, the bodyguard walking with Tabrizi began pulling his principal back toward the hotel. The Ford squealed to a halt in the middle of the road, smoke rising up from the tires. A long burst of automatic fire erupted from the passenger-side window. The first volley was off, tearing into a line of parked cars, then over the sidewalk and into the glass doors of the hotel. A number of people were on the ground, blood spattered over the pavement, screams rising up as panic ensued. Tabrizi was only a few steps from safety when Vanderveen saw him stumble. Then his arms splayed out, his body jerking violently as a number of rounds ripped into his back. The physician dropped to the ground in a lifeless heap. The bodyguard collapsed next to him, but managed to crawl a few feet before being hit with a final burst, his life blitzed away in an instant.

The Ford was already squealing away as the first officer exited the Peugeot and brought his FAMAS to bear. He released a long burst of automatic fire after the departing vehicle, the rear windshield shattering instantly.

Despite the frantic scene unfolding before him, Vanderveen had been breathing slowly and steadily from the moment the Ford first accelerated down the boulevard. Now he found the gaping hole in the rear windshield. Through the scope, he could see that the passenger was slumped over the center console, the driver clearly fighting for control of the car. He centered the crosshairs on the back of the headrest, released the air from his lungs, and squeezed the trigger.

The suppressor dulled the report and the muzzle flash, but even at 270 yards, the effect of the 3-round burst was obvious. The headrest on the driver's side exploded in a puff of white cotton filler, and the Ford lurched from the road, swiping a number of vehicles before grinding to a halt. The CRS man stopped firing and moved forward cautiously, his back to the Mercedes, as the third officer—one of the two left standing—ran out to assist the wounded, having already called for an ambulance. Apparently, Vanderveen's shots had gone unnoticed.

"Go!" he said to Raseen, placing the rifle down by his feet. "Move!"

He punched the button and the window came up as she started the engine and pulled into traffic. Cars were fishtailing to a halt behind them, but the road ahead appeared to be clear. "Did they get him?" she was saying excitedly. "Was he hit? Was he hit?"

Vanderveen turned to look out the rear window. He could hear distant two-tone sirens but didn't see anyone following as the Mercedes swung onto the rue Guersant, slipping into the busy traffic. "Slow it down. There's nobody behind us."

"Did they get him?"

He thought of Tabrizi's body crumpling, hitting the pavement. He visualized the second volley punching up his legs and into his back.

"Yeah, they got him. He's gone."

CHAPTER 24

WASHINGTON, D.C. • VIRGINIA

It was just after two in the afternoon when they left the restaurant. The Suburban was waiting at the curb, but Harper crossed to the passenger-side window, leaned in, and dismissed his driver, preferring to walk for a while. The rain had moved on, and the air was beginning to warm, steam rising up from the damp pavement. Overhead, the sun poked out from behind thick gray clouds. They walked south on 6th, skirting a small knot of tourists before taking a left on E Street. As they strolled, Kealey quietly brought Harper up to date on what was happening at the NCTC.

When he was finished, Harper said, "Do you think it'll come to anything?"

"As a matter of fact, I do." Kealey paused. "Naomi keeps surprising me, John. I don't remember her being this capable."

Harper flicked a sideways glance at the younger man, wondering where this was going. "I don't know why you would say that, Ryan. Every fitness report she's ever received has been stellar. Emmett Mills, for one, can't say enough about her. He desperately wants her back, but I think it's time to give her a starring role at the CTC. She's more valuable here than she is in London."

Kealey nodded and was about to comment when his cell phone rang. He pulled it out, looked at the number, and flipped it open. "Yeah?"

It was Kharmai. "Ryan, I've got something." Her voice was tinged with excitement, but there was a crackle of static. "Can you hear me?"

"Yeah, I've got you. What did you find?"

She explained about the calls she'd made to the various CIA stations, and then told him about Staibler's contact in Port Said East. "This guy has access to everything, including collection logs. In other words, he can tell us exactly who arrived at the port to collect containers on a given date. Over a three-month period, the same man signed for containers coming off vessels that Mason was using. I can't guarantee they're the *same* containers, of course, but—"

"Naomi, what was the name?" Kealey asked impatiently.

"Erich Kohl." She paused for effect. "It's Vanderveen, Ryan. He was in Egypt on those three dates, collecting consignments. We found the link."

He stopped in his tracks, and Harper looked at him, questioning. His head was buzzing, but he didn't know why; when it came to the movement of arms through Anthony Mason, Kealey had suspected that Vanderveen was playing a key role all along.

Still, they had no idea where the man was, and Rashid al-Umari was proving equally elusive. As if reading his thoughts, Naomi continued. "There's something else. I had a hunch about the vessels Mason was using, so I checked them out, and some never docked on the dates he specified. In fact, some of them don't exist at all."

"What does that mean?"

"Well, I ran the names through the NCIC, and as it turns out, his contacts were listed under the container ships heading. That's why we couldn't find them anywhere else . . . I guess listing them that way was just one of his little security measures. Unfortunately, most of them are black holes. I've already contacted MI5, Interpol, Mossad, and come up with nothing. Some are in prison, some have fallen off the radar completely, but one jumped right off the screen. The *R.B. Boderon* out of Honduras."

"Why would you run container ships through the NCIC? The database doesn't—"

"Ryan, just listen, would you?" It was her turn to lose patience. "That ship *doesn't exist*. Boderon is an alias used in the past by a man

named Thomas Rühmann. He's an Austrian industrialist and suspected arms broker. He's quite influential, apparently, but there's
more to it than that. For one thing, he used to work for the UN. As a
weapons inspector. In *Iraq*."

Kealey paused to take that in. "And where is Rühmann now?"

"Well, that's the thing. He's . . ."

The silence went on. "Naomi? What's wrong?"

"Hold on. Something's happening here."

Inside the Liberty Crossing Building, a strange tension in the air
had caught her attention. Naomi stood up from behind her desk and
unconsciously pressed the phone to her chest as she surveyed the
room. Everyone on the ground floor was wearing an animated expression, and most were typing furiously, while others were relaying
urgent messages over the phone. Some were juggling both tasks
with varying success.

Her eyes moved up to the second floor, where supervisors were
hurriedly walking from room to room, presumably looking for updates. Naomi finally found her answer in the most obvious location,
the 70-inch protection screen that hung from the second-floor walkway. The images that confronted her were horrific, bodies strewn
across the street in front of a large, pale building with hundreds of
windows, dozens of which were shattered. Sitting back down at her
desk, she brought up the feed on her screen, then turned up the volume to hear the voice-over:

"*. . . attack occurred at 7:03 PM Paris time. This video was shot by
a tourist outside Le Meridien Etoile, the site of a two-day economic
conference being held by the International Chamber of Commerce.
According to witnesses, a number of conference attendees were exiting the hotel when a black Ford sedan sped down the boulevard,
then braked to a halt in front of the main entrance. Automatic gunfire was leveled at the crowd from the passenger-side window. Although French police have yet to release a statement, the attack is
believed to have claimed the lives of . . .*"

Naomi listened for thirty seconds more before remembering that
Ryan was still on the line. She lifted the phone back to her ear and, in
a shaking voice, explained what she'd just heard.

*   *   *

On E Street, Kealey lowered the cell and looked at Jonathan Harper, who was methodically beating his pockets, obviously wondering where his own phone had gone.

Giving up the search, Harper turned to the younger man and said, "Tell me."

"Two men just attacked a hotel in Paris. At least eight people are dead, including Nasir al-Din Tabrizi, the Iraqi foreign minister."

"Oh, Christ," Harper muttered. "This can't get worse."

CHAPTER 25

WASHINGTON, D.C.

Naomi Kharmai had never been more nervous; at least, not in the absence of imminent physical danger. Her hands were shaking, and her breath—when she could breathe at all—was coming in quick, short spurts. For the third time in a row, she stood and walked on shaky legs to the room's only mirror. She checked her reflection with overly critical eyes, smoothing her hair and examining her suit. It was a Donna Karan two-piece in burgundy wool, the best she owned. Oblivious to the admiring gaze of the Secret Service agent standing nearby, she adjusted her skirt and turned to Kealey, who was slumped in a chair next to the door. He was wearing an ill-fitting Brooks Brothers suit he had borrowed from Harper. "Ryan, are you sure I—"

"Naomi, you look fine, okay? Try to relax."

She turned back to the mirror in exasperation. He hadn't even looked. She wondered how he could be so calm; as far as she knew, he had never met the president, either, or even been to the White House.

They were waiting in a dimly lit lobby on the first floor of the West Wing. Brenneman was in a meeting with the DCI, Jonathan Harper, and a number of FBI officials, including Harry Judd. Several hours earlier, Naomi had brought Kealey and the DDO up to speed on everything she had learned since the assassination in Paris. Afterward, Harper had talked to Andrews, asking that Kharmai be allowed to brief the president herself. Naomi had tried to flatly refuse, but Harper had insisted and assuaged her fears. Or at least he had made the effort; now, waiting to be called in, she was once again seized with terror. It didn't make sense, and she was frustrated with her inexplicable lack of control. She was a professional, and she believed in what she had to say. At the same time, she had never even briefed the DCI, let alone the president of the United States, and she knew she only had one chance to make a convincing argument. She was determined to do so.

Naomi had been working feverishly ever since the attack. Through her contacts at the DGSE, she had learned the identities of the two gunmen. Both were Iranian, which, unfortunately, did not help the case she was about to make to the president. Tehran had yet to make an official statement, though she was confident that the regime would deny having played a part in the incident. For the most part, everything she had managed to dig up pointed in one direction: the Iraqi insurgency. Now, all she had to do was convince the president that she was right. In that respect, she rated her chances as good. What she was going to propose afterwards, however, might not be received as well, even though the DDO and the DCI had both agreed with her assessment.

She heard a door open behind her, and she swung on her heels, her heart leaping into her throat. The aide nodded to her and then to Kealey, who was still seated.

"Ms. Kharmai? Mr. Kealey? They're ready for you. Follow me, please."

Naomi stepped past the aide and entered the Roosevelt Room first, her leather briefing folder tucked tightly under her right arm. Kealey followed a few steps behind. Jonathan Harper, the only other person in the room, was waiting for them. He was standing before the fireplace, examining the Nobel Prize on the mantle. Naomi recalled that Theodore Roosevelt had won the prize for his work in ending the Russo-Japanese War, though she couldn't remember the year. When the door closed behind them, Harper turned and crossed the beige Berber carpet. She immediately saw that his face was set in a grim expression, which didn't help her nerves at all.

"The director stepped out to make a call," Harper informed them. "The man himself is about to walk in here, so I'll make this quick. Judd just railroaded us."

"What are you talking about?" Kealey asked.

"Apparently, the Bureau has a source with strong ties to the Iranian government. This man predicted the attempt on al-Maliki, as well as the assassination of Nasir Tabrizi. They've been feeding this information to the National Security Council for weeks."

Naomi shook her head, trying to see all the angles. "If they knew, why didn't they pass the warnings along? Why did the attacks still take place?"

"The information *was* passed along. The Iraqis just didn't act on it in time. Both attacks occurred earlier than anticipated, and in different places."

"Is the president buying this?" Kealey asked doubtfully. "We don't have much to implicate the Iranians."

"He wants to. He's been looking for an excuse to hit Iran ever since Senator Levy was killed last October."

Both Kharmai and Kealey considered that for a moment. The previous year, the United States had formed an alliance with France and Italy to limit European oil exploration in Iran, the goal being to curtail the funds working their way into the regime's weapons program. In response, the Iranians had formed a partnership with al-Qaeda to destroy the nascent alliance. They had started by targeting Senator Daniel Levy, the Senate majority leader and Iran's most vocal opponent on the Hill. Levy had been a close friend of the president and one of his most ardent supporters. While the Iranian regime was never concretely linked with that attack—or those that followed—it was widely believed that the new hard-line regime had played a decisive role.

"So where do we stand?" Naomi asked. "Am I still doing the briefing?"

Harper opened his mouth to answer the question, but never got the chance. The door to the right of the fireplace swung open, and Director Andrews walked in, followed immediately by President David Brenneman.

* * *

The president walked over to Kealey first and extended a hand. "Ryan, it's good to see you again. I wish it could be under better circumstances."

"I feel the same way, sir, but we'll find who was responsible."

"Yes, I don't doubt that we will."

Listening to this strangely familiar exchange, Naomi was stunned. Here was yet another surprise: Ryan had met the president at least once before. But when? Her mind began ticking off the possibilities, but David Brenneman was already crossing the carpet toward her. He looked older in person, she thought, although it might just have been the strain of the past few weeks. He was tall—at least six feet four—and trim, with neat silver-brown hair and strong, handsome features. Despite the anger clouding his face, he looked *presidential*. She felt her mouth go dry as he offered a hand. She accepted it, painfully aware of how damp her own palms were.

"Naomi, I'm pleased to meet you. It should have happened before now . . . I know you played an important role in last year's events. The country owes you a debt of gratitude, young lady."

"Thank you, sir," she managed. "It's nice to be appreciated."

She instantly wished she'd limited her response to a polite nod, but the president didn't seem to notice her embarrassment. He gestured to the table and said, "Let's get started, shall we?" They all took the appropriate seats, Brenneman at the head of the table. "Ms. Kharmai, I understand you've stumbled onto . . . excuse me, *discovered*, some interesting information regarding today's attack in Paris."

"Yes, sir." She started to rise, but Brenneman waved her back into the seat.

"Unless you need the screen, we can do this in comfort," he said. "Please proceed."

"Of course, Mr. President." Naomi flipped open her briefing folder, took a deep breath, and did her best to steady her jangling nerves. "Sir, let me start from the beginning. You see, the story does not begin with the bombing of the Babylon Hotel, but rather with the shipment of weapons through Anthony Mason to ports in the Middle East, where they were collected by none other than Will Vanderveen. At that time, he was using the name Erich Kohl. Over the next six months . . ."

*   *   *

She spoke for twenty minutes, detailing the links between Rashid al-Umari, Arshad Kassem, Anthony Mason, and Vanderveen. She also addressed the possible Iranian connection. Watching her from across the table, Kealey could not help but admire her poise and the way she managed to tie everything together. It was strange to listen to her speak to this audience; for the first time, he was acutely aware of her East Midlands accent, which had never seemed more out of place than it did in this room.

Naomi concluded by referencing Thomas Rühmann. "He's actually an Austrian national, but accommodations have been made for him by some of his friends in the German federal cabinet. Though he's listed on the boards of some of Germany's most reputable companies, we've long suspected him of dealing arms to a number of governments and rebel groups. Needless to say, most of his customers are not people we want to see armed. The German government lets him get away with it because he's done some work for them as well, but he's also something of an embarrassment. They keep a close eye on him."

Brenneman nodded and said, "What do you mean by that? They protect him directly?"

"In a way, sir. Let me give you an example. Three years ago, the State Department discovered that Rühmann was involved in the sale of two hundred Starburst man-portable missiles to Adnan al-Ghoul, a senior Hamas official. Incidentally, al-Ghoul has since been killed. Shortly after the sale came to light, State requested a formal audience through the appropriate channels. They expected full cooperation from the Germans, but the door was slammed shut in their faces. And that was then. Apparently, Rühmann has since enlarged his circle of influential friends, which makes getting access to him even more difficult."

"Why the wall? Why would they go to that length to protect him, and what did you mean about him being an embarrassment?"

Kealey straightened in his seat and fielded the president's questions. "Sir, do you remember the incident at Al Qaqaa in 2003?"

Brenneman considered for a moment. "Vaguely. Refresh my memory."

"Al Qaqaa is a weapons storage facility located about twenty miles south of Baghdad. In 2003, it was reported that more than three hundred eighty tons of explosives, including HMX and RDX, had gone missing from the stockpile. That amounts to about forty truckloads. The *New York Times* was the first to break the story. Predictably, everyone started pointing fingers. The IAEA said that the material was accounted for in January of that year, and that U.S. troops were responsible for safeguarding the facility. The Pentagon turned the accusation around, but no one ever really took the blame. Some of the explosives later turned up, used in attacks on our troops, but most of it simply vanished. There was a lot of dispute afterward about what else might have been stored at Al Qaqaa."

"How does Rühmann fit in?"

"Thomas Rühmann was in Iraq at the time, sir," Naomi said. "In fact, he was the UN representative in charge of the last inspection at Al Qaqaa. That is, the last inspection before the explosives disappeared. Questions were asked, of course, but he resigned his post with the UN before his name came up, and his connections have since kept him out of the spotlight. Frankly, the Germans just want to forget the whole thing."

"Okay," the president said. "So to summarize, Rühmann can be linked, at least indirectly, to al-Umari and Vanderveen, both of whom were responsible for the attempted assassination of the Iraqi prime minister."

"That's correct," Naomi confirmed.

"But none of this can be tied to the assassination of Nasir Tabrizi in Paris, right?"

"Not yet," she agreed reluctantly. "We're still looking at that angle, sir."

"And this is the only lead we have? Apart from the Iranian connection?"

"Unfortunately, that's all we have at this time."

"I could call Chancellor Merkel directly," Brenneman pointed out. "She can hardly refuse the request if I make it myself."

"Actually, sir, she might very well do just that," Andrews put in. "At best, she'll stall, and time is a factor here. The meeting at the UN is scheduled to take place on September sixteenth, coinciding with the opening of the General Assembly's annual session. As you know, Prime Minister al-Maliki was the only member of the core Shiite group *not* scheduled to attend, the core being thirty-five key members of the United Iraqi Alliance. Nasir Tabrizi was on the other side, of course, but a moderating factor, nonetheless. From the Agency's point of view, the fact that these men were specifically targeted is very troubling, and perhaps indicative of a larger attack here on U.S. soil. If the alliance is being targeted, we may be looking at more to come."

Kealey instantly shot Harper a questioning look that said, *What meeting?* He didn't notice that Kharmai had done the same thing, but Harper ignored both of them and turned to the president. "Sir, here is what it comes down to. I understand the Bureau has told you otherwise, but the Iranians have only been loosely implicated in the information we've gathered. Everything from our end points to an Iraqi mastermind. We need to talk to Rühmann, but we have no idea where he is. Nor do we know what name he's using, and we've already checked the obvious."

"So you need to find him without going through diplomatic channels. I assume you've come up with a way to do that," Brenneman said. He did not need to voice his displeasure that two of the country's key agencies were at odds over who was responsible for Baghdad and Paris; the look on his face said that much and more.

Naomi cleared her throat gently. "Sir, we know that Rühmann was stationed here in Washington for two years, beginning in '98. He worked out of the German Embassy, commuting to the UN when necessary. It's likely they have a record on him at the embassy, including a point of contact. It would be classified, of course, but we have a way around that little problem."

"And how do you propose to get this information?" Brenneman asked. His voice was dangerously quiet, as though he were daring them on.

A hush fell over the room. Finally, Naomi took a deep breath and took the plunge.

"We steal it, sir. We break into the German Embassy and steal it."

CHAPTER 26

CALAIS · WASHINGTON, D.C.

The drive from Paris to Calais took just under four hours, delayed by an overturned tractor-trailer on the A26. The second car, a maroon Audi with a slippery clutch, had been waiting in the parking garage on the rue Tronchet, as expected. After collecting it and wiping down the Mercedes, they followed the aptly named boulevard Périphérique around Paris to the A1, which became the A26 near Lille. They pulled off the main road just south of Amiens, following a rural road through a thick forest of black pine. The detour added twenty minutes and five brief stops to the trip, but gave Vanderveen the time needed to break up the G2 assault rifle and hurl the components deep into the trees.

After producing the keys to the Audi in the garage, Raseen had climbed into the driver's seat without a word. Vanderveen had nearly offered to take the wheel, worried that she was too tightly wound to handle the car with the necessary skill, but one look at her face told him that she needed the activity. She began flicking through the channels as soon as she started the engine, but the first report did not come through until they were twenty minutes outside of the city. The facts were sparse at best, but the Iraqi foreign minister was confirmed dead at the scene, along with a veteran CRS officer and two unidentified gunmen. Unsatisfied, she continued to scan the news channels. They were 40 kilometers outside of Paris when the story took on new depth, stoked by the rising body count and the death of a prominent American businessman.

"Twelve dead?" Raseen seemed strangely unnerved by the possibility, as if realizing for the first time the scope of what they had started. "Is it possible?"

"It's possible," Vanderveen conceded. The fact that 12 people—including 4 Americans—had died in the attack did not bother him in the least. In fact, it was a positive turn of events. American casualties would only serve to cloud the president's judgment, provoking him into an emotional response when the assassins were identified as Iranian nationals. That much may have happened already; in a case such as this, enormous pressure would be placed on the French security service to come up with quick answers.

Of course, the fact that the killers were Iranian would only lead to suspicion, nothing more. It was al-Douri's asset in New York who would support the idea that Tehran was working behind the scenes to destroy the nascent Iraqi government and undermine U.S. policy in the Middle East. Once the accusation became public, the Iranian president would undoubtedly incriminate himself by veiling his denial of wrongdoing with his usual rhetoric. The inflammatory comments he had made in the past would only increase suspicion and remove any lingering doubts.

Killing al-Maliki and Tabrizi was designed to do two things: first, to eliminate the most prominent supporters of the U.S. presence in Iraq, thereby weakening the Shiite-dominated parliament, and second, to fan the flames between radicals on both sides of the Shia-Sunni divide. The second goal had already been largely achieved, despite the fact that al-Maliki had survived the bombing in Baghdad.

Everything they had done so far, however, served only to set the stage; success hinged entirely on the upcoming meeting at the UN. With the assassination of the core leaders of the Shiite alliance in New York, the National Assembly—the Iraqi parliament—would lose all credibility, and the country would fall into complete disrepair, giving al-Douri the perfect opportunity to snake his way back into power. Promises had already been made, money exchanged. The attack on U.S. soil would be immediately followed by an unprecedented wave of violence in Iraq, propagated by Syrian insurgents sweeping into the western half of the country. The violence would lead to desperation; that much was inevitable, and with the fear would come the search for established leadership, the search for a steady hand. A well-known Sunni candidate had already been earmarked for advancement, and with his ascension, al-Douri would return to the seat of power. He would be forced to wield his authority behind the scenes, of course, but it would be his nonetheless, and few would dare to oppose him. Memories were long in the Middle East, and the men who now represented U.S. interests would quickly fall back into line once the Baathists returned to the beleaguered capital.

This much had been explained to Vanderveen days earlier, whispered while al-Umari's body was cooling on the second floor of the house in Tartus. It was hugely ambitious, and the plan was strewn with obvious flaws. If the U.S. government took the bait and held Iran responsible, it could very well lead to open conflict. Troops would be pulled out of Iraq to support the offensive, but ultimately, the United States would gain yet another foothold in the region, however precarious. When Vanderveen had pointed this out, the Iraqi had waved it away with mild irritation.

"How can things be any worse?" he had argued. "The Americans have already taken all that was ours. Let the Iranians suffer as well. That is their concern. *Our* opportunity is here and now, and it must be seized, whatever the consequences."

During this speech, Vanderveen revealed none of his doubts, which were as real as al-Douri's monstrous ego. The former vice president was as irrational and narrow-minded as his peers, but he was not a man to cross. With al-Umari's final contribution, al-Douri now had the financial ability to track him to the ends of the earth, and Vanderveen had no desire to spend the rest of his life looking over his shoulder. None of that really mattered, though, because he *wanted* to go through with it. He had taken the money, but that was not a mitigating factor, and it did nothing to secure his allegiance; Izzat al-Douri had made him a wealthy man, but Vanderveen was no more indebted to the Iraqi than he was to the country that had trained him to kill. What pushed him on was not what he could buy with the money, but what he could accomplish with it.

A total of twenty million dollars. He had not had much time to think about it since the agreement was struck, but now, as the Audi swept toward the lights of Calais, the sum rattled around in his head, pinging off the possibilities, illuminating the darkest corners of his mind. As the road narrowed and the buildings grew large around him, he was engaged in what had once been dreams. His dreams were as ambitious as any man's, but they were not of the luxuries that the millions could buy. Instead, what consumed him was the memory of a warm September morning in 2001, and the knowledge of what one man had done with nothing more than time, desire, and a fraction of the sum that would soon be sitting in his numbered Zurich account.

"Well, that could have gone better," Harper said.

They were strolling through the National Mall, which was strangely deserted in early evening. The tourists had retired to their hotels, but the city's homeless had yet to emerge from the shadows. Kealey felt conspicuous in the borrowed gray suit, and his feet were cramped in black leather loafers that were a size too small. Still, the air felt good after the claustrophobic atmosphere of the White House, cool with a slight breeze coming in from the east. They'd left the executive mansion through the southwest pedestrian gate, making their way down Pennsylvania, past his hotel. Naomi had disappeared without warning; but Kealey had seen Harper murmur a few words in her ear before her sudden departure. He briefly wondered what they had talked about, but now was not the time to bring it up. There were other things on his mind.

The president had received Kharmai's proposal with a healthy dose of skepticism, but to his credit, had listened carefully as she explained the need to break into the German Embassy, as well as how such a risky maneuver could be successfully pulled off. She had made a convincing case, but in the end, Brenneman had referred once more to the Bureau's conflicting information, and announced his intention to contact the German chancellor on unofficial terms the following day. It was exactly what they'd hoped to avoid.

"Do you think she'll cooperate?" Kealy finally asked.

"Chancellor Merkel? I doubt it. She has nothing to gain by investing herself in this mess. Rühmann will probably get a call from someone in the German cabinet sometime tomorrow afternoon, and he'll be out of the country in a few hours' time. Going to Brenneman with this was probably a mistake, but it had to be done. We both know that."

"Maybe so, but we need to stall," Kealey said quietly, more to himself than anything else. "Once he makes that call tomorrow, it's out of our hands. Rühmann is our only lead, John. If anyone knows what Vanderveen's planning, it's him."

"I agree, but I don't see a way out of this little hole we've dug for ourselves. Judd paid us back in spades for that stunt you pulled in Alexandria. I mean, he has a source in the Iranian government, for Christ's sake. Who would have thought it?"

"It sounds like bullshit. This supposed informant knows a little too much if you ask me. What I don't understand is why the FBI can't see that. Nobody has access to that kind of intelligence without being somehow involved." Kealey paused. "John, we really need to know who this guy is. More to the point, we need to know who he's talking to in the Bureau. Maybe we can get some kind of access."

"I'll look into it," Harper said, surreptitiously wiping a drop of clear fluid from his nose. He pulled a wad of tissue from his pocket and blew into it sharply. "Damn cold . . . It's been creeping up for days. They come like clockwork twice a year, always in March and September. I'll have to start scheduling my vacations accordingly."

Mired in thought, Kealey let that comment slide. Something had been gnawing at the base of his brain ever since they'd left the White House, but he didn't know how the other man would respond. He needed to broach the subject carefully, but he also needed to get his point across.

"John, if the president had signed off on the embassy break-in, we could have pulled it off, right?"

"Absolutely." Harper rammed his hands into the pockets of his Burberry as a swift, sudden wind swept the gravel footpath. "You know about ORACLE . . . That was all we needed. Well, that and a man with the skills to get inside. It would have worked."

An uncomfortable silence ensued. ORACLE was the CIA code name for a long-term operation that had started back in 1983, shortly before the FBI and the National Security Agency embarked on a highly ambitious joint operation of their own, the construction of a tunnel below the new Soviet Embassy in Washington, D.C. The tunnel cost hundreds of millions of dollars to build and maintain, and although it was manned round the clock by NSA technicians with eavesdropping equipment, the project was only a modest success, garnering nothing more than low-grade intelligence. Years later, the Bureau would learn that the tunnel had been compromised shortly after its completion by the infamous Robert Hanssen, a Bureau agent who had spied for the GRU, the KGB's military counterpart, from 1979 up until his arrest in 2001. Even at the height of the project's output, the top minds at the Agency had recognized just how inefficient the tunnel actually was, and they began searching for ways to gain maximum output with minimal cost.

The result was ORACLE, an operation designed to gain embassy blueprints, access to secure computer systems, and the names of intelligence officers concealed within the diplomatic community. Embassies were a natural starting point, as they serve as jumping-off points for nearly every intelligence officer brought into a host country. Recruitment was the most difficult part, but once that was accomplished, it was a simple cash-for-information exchange. Defection was clearly not an option, as the disappearance of a member of the embassy staff would simply result in immediate changes in security. Ironically, the CIA was initiating measures already in use with both the KGB and the GRU. It was the latter agency that purchased from Hanssen the details of the tunnel—a multimillion-dollar project—for less than $30,000 in cash and diamonds.

Over the next two decades, ORACLE expanded exponentially, the Agency cultivating sources in embassies representing forty-eight countries, including Germany. As required by the Agency's charter, all of the embassies were located overseas, but many agents—having served in the United States—were able to relay information regarding embassy security on domestic soil as well. Such was the case with the chancery, the German Embassy's office building on the western edge of Georgetown. The CIA's operations directorate had access to passwords, blueprints, and the specific security measures—both human and electronic—that served to protect the building from intruders. All they were lacking was authorization.

They crossed 7th, heading east, the dome of the Capitol Building shining in artificial white light, the waters of the reflecting pool lapping silver in the distance. They strolled silently for a while, their feet crunching on the gravel, until Kealey finally took the plunge.

"If somebody broke into the chancery tonight, John, what would it mean for you?"

Harper glanced over and frowned, but to the younger man, it looked more like concern than disapproval. "I think I'd probably be finished. They wouldn't kick me out on my ass, not after what we pulled off last November, and not this close to the election, but my options would certainly be limited. They would squeeze me out by the end of the year."

"Maybe not," Kealey countered. "You have a lot of friends at State and Justice. If enough of them landed on your side, the president might—"

"Don't kid yourself, Ryan. If I go against the president, I'm done at the Agency. It's that simple."

A short silence ensued, and Kealey feared that he might have pushed it too far. The DDO was only forty-two years old, and retirement was a long ways off. They approached a bench on the left, partially illuminated beneath a white sodium lamp. Harper took a seat unexpectedly, emitting a weary sigh in the process. Kealey joined him.

"I want to go in, John. I want to do it tonight, but I need your help. You know it needs to be done. I saw it on your face while Brenneman was searching for ways to say no."

"That's true," Harper replied. "It *does* need to be done. Rühmann might be able to give us Vanderveen, but it's more than that. This meeting at the UN could be a coup for Brenneman, but that also makes it a prime target. They went after the prime minister first, and now Tabrizi. Tabrizi was a Sunni, but definitely a moderating factor. Nuri al-Maliki, on the other hand, was—and still is—the recognized leader of the United Iraqi Alliance, and the UIA counts for two-thirds of the National Assembly. If Vanderveen is going after that particular group, he'll have the perfect opportunity in New York. It would totally destroy the Iraqi government, take away all credibility. The country would plunge into civil war."

"With our troops caught in the middle," Kealey muttered.

"Exactly."

"This meeting on the sixteenth . . . Why did Brenneman keep it so close to the vest?"

"He's afraid of leaks, I imagine. Like I said, this could be big for him. If the UIA throws its support behind him and his plan for bringing the troops home, it could have a dramatic effect on the polls. People are tired of the situation over there. They want rapid withdrawals, but that could easily destroy the little we've managed to accomplish over the past five years. Needless to say, Brenneman can't make that kind of statement himself; it just doesn't resonate. Hearing it from the leading members of Iraq's National Assembly, on the other hand, might change some minds. After all, their support is the only way we can accomplish anything over there. It's a risky play, and it's late in the game, but it's all he has if he wants another four years."

Kealey looked down at the gravel, thinking about it. "If I'm going in, it has to be tonight. Once Brenneman makes that call to the German chancellor, we're dead in the water."

"It's impossible, Ryan. Even with the access codes and the security layout, you'd need at least a week to set it up."

"We don't have a week." Kealey paused, looking over the grass. The National Air and Space Museum could be seen in the near distance, the towering windows reflecting the night sky in shimmering shades of blue and black. "I'm not asking the president, John," he continued quietly. "I'm asking *you*. I'll be finished as well. I know that. They won't give me a glowing send-off, either. I'm willing to pay the price, but I can't make that decision for someone else, and I certainly can't make it for you. If you want me to look for another way, that's the way it'll be."

Harper nodded silently to himself, and his chin drifted down to his chest. Kealey briefly wondered if he was dozing off, but then his head rose. "I've known you for eight years, Ryan. I think you forget that sometimes."

"What are you getting at?"

"I knew you'd ask for the chance, regardless of what Brenneman decided, so I pulled everything together in advance. I gave Naomi instructions before we left the White House."

The younger man was not particularly surprised; Kharmai's hasty departure had seemed a little unusual. "And?"

"She'll bring the relevant material to your room at ten tonight. Take all the time you need with it, but be sure to give it back to her before you leave the hotel. If they catch you in the act, you can't have anything on you."

That much was obvious, but Kealey nodded anyway. Something lifted from his shoulders, and his vision seemed suddenly sharper: he was back in the hunt. "I understand. If—"

He fell silent as Harper grabbed his arm forcefully, something he'd never done before. "I hope you *do* understand, Ryan. If you're caught, you're on your own. I can't lift a finger to help you. And Naomi is not to have a part in this. She'll give you the file, but her involvement ends there. I don't care how much she complains, you leave her out of it. I have a feeling that she'd do just about anything for you, but bear in mind that we're talking about her career, okay? And make that clear to her as well."

Harper released his arm and reached again for the Kleenex, erupting in a short series of hacking coughs. Kealey rose to his feet. "Ten PM?"

"Yeah, you'd better hurry."

He took a few quick steps back down the path, then slowed, stopped, and turned. Harper was still sitting on the bench, shoulders hunched with fatigue. Watching him, Kealey felt a sudden rush of emotion. There was barely ten years between them, but Harper had been the closest thing to a mentor he'd ever had, and now the man was putting his career on the line for him. For Kealey, it had nothing to do with Thomas Rühmann or the upcoming meeting in New York. It was all about finding Vanderveen. In the end, that was all that mattered, at least in his mind. He suspected Harper knew this much and probably more.

But none of that needed to be said; they had known each other too long. Instead, Kealey simply turned and walked away.

CHAPTER 27

WASHINGTON, D.C.

Kealey had been back in his room at the Hotel Washington for less than ten minutes when the knock came at the door. He'd had just enough time to shower and change into a pair of dark gray utility pants, running shoes, and a North Face zip-neck fleece. Crossing the room, he pulled open the door and Kharmai stepped inside immediately.

She brushed past him and stopped, staring around as if picking out the differences between their respective rooms. Then she walked past the bed, tossed a folder onto the small table, and turned to face him. "I guess Harper told you—"

"Yeah, he did."

"Quite a risk on his part, I would have thought."

She was eyeing him steadily, but he turned away and picked up the phone. "I was going to order up some coffee. You want anything?"

"Tea would be great."

He nodded and dialed room service. After the order was placed, he walked over and joined her at the small wooden table, pushing aside the hotel stationery and a complimentary guide to the city. Naomi began describing the embassy's external security measures as soon as he eased into the seat, but something was wrong, and he picked up on it right away. She was talking too fast, as if trying to ward off an impending argument, and she refused to meet his gaze. Finally, she stopped and looked up to catch him staring at her.

"What?" she asked.

"Why are you dressed like that?"

She looked down at her clothes. It wasn't the outfit itself that had caught his attention; there was nothing conspicuous about her loose-fitting hoodie, tracksuit bottoms, and sneakers. But the fact that she was dressed entirely in black, given the situation, could only mean one thing.

She took a deep breath, lifted her chin, and looked him square in the eye. "I'm coming with you."

"No," he replied instantly. "You're not. There's no way I'm going to—"

"Ryan, just think about this for a second, okay?" The words came out in a torrent, as if by talking faster, she could overwhelm him with the force of her argument. She leaned forward and slapped a hand on top of the bulky file, which was still closed. "Even if we hold off as long as possible, we only have a few hours to go over this. There's just too much to learn, and you have to remember it all under pressure. I'm not talking about going into the building with you, but you need someone to walk you through. Otherwise, it just won't work . . . One mistake will alert security, and we can't allow that to happen. Remember, I have just as much invested in this as you do."

She didn't realize what she'd said until Ryan looked away, pain flickering over his face. Remembering just how much he had lost to the man they were now chasing, Kharmai winced and opened her mouth to apologize, but he went on before she could get the words out.

"Naomi, even if we get what we need on Rühmann, I'm going to lose my job over this. Do you understand that? It only has to happen to one of us, and it won't be you. There is no way you're coming along."

"Well, you're going to have a hard time getting into the embassy computers without the administrator password," she said, leaning back and adopting her best poker face. "I seem to have misplaced it."

"That's unfortunate."

"Yep." She gave him a meaningful look. "Makes your job a lot harder, anyway. On the other hand, I might be able to track it down with a little effort."

He shook his head, but he had to smile. "That's bullshit, Naomi. I know you better than that. There's no way you would let me go in there without the right information."

She tried to keep her face blank, but it couldn't last, and she finally looked away in defeat. "Ryan, I just want to help," she said softly. "If it wasn't for me, you wouldn't even have gotten this far. Believe me, I know what I'm doing. I also know the odds, and there is no way you can pull this off alone."

A shadow crossed his face, and she went on before he could object. "Think about what you're risking, will you? This is our only link to Rühmann, and that makes it our only link to Vanderveen. Knowing that, are you still willing to take the chance? Any chance at all?"

He hesitated, and she felt a weight lift; she had finally gotten through to him.

"What are you suggesting?"

She tapped the folder again. "When I went to pick this up at Langley, I stopped by to visit an old friend in the DST. He gave me the use of some radios. They're not encrypted, unfortunately, but they *are* pretty powerful. I'll wait in the car with the layout and walk you through. That way you can focus on what you're doing in there. Security's light, especially on the grounds, and the building itself will be all but empty."

"Isn't that normal, given the time of day?"

"Yes, but tonight the ambassador is holding a reception at the residence, so most of the staff will be tied up with that. It's perfect for us."

Kealey nodded absently. He wasn't pleased that Naomi had talked him into giving her a more active role, but he couldn't fault her logic. It occurred to him that she had changed his mind with amazing speed, and he couldn't help but wonder about the way she had brought Vanderveen into the equation. *I have just as much invested in this as you.* Had she dredged up the past intentionally? If so, she was a promising actress, judging by the embarrassment that had crossed her face once the words were out. She was difficult to read, but he had always thought as much; she appeared to wear her emotions on her sleeve, but knowing how intelligent she actually was,

Kealey could never be sure how much was real and how much was feigned. Methods aside, she seemed happy enough to have gotten her way; her eyes were bright as she opened the folder and began leafing through the pages with obvious enthusiasm.

Kealey knew how much those pages meant; everything hinged on the accuracy of the file's contents. If the source recruited through ORACLE had given them good information, their chances were vastly improved, but Harper was right; under normal circumstances, an operation such as this, with the potential for enormous fallout if they were caught in the act, would be planned out weeks in advance and rehearsed extensively. This worrisome fact plucked at his confidence, but he'd made the decision, and he wasn't about to back out now.

Room service arrived a moment later, and Kealey got up to collect the tray. When they were settled back in, Naomi said, "So, where should we start?"

He turned some of the documents so he could see them better, then selected a stack of paper. "Entry points. I have to get in fast and out of sight. If I can't do that, nothing else will matter."

"That makes sense. When are we going in?"

He looked at her sharply. "*I'm* going in at four AM. That gives us five hours, allowing for time to test the radios."

"Right." When their eyes met, she offered a neutral smile instead of a broad grin. She had already gotten her way, and she knew rubbing it in wouldn't help. "Well, there's a lot of ground to cover, so let's get started."

The Hotel Victoria, located just off the Quai du Commerce, was a charmless, two-story structure of grey stone situated in the heart of Calais. The fourteen-room hotel was marked only by two small, flickering signs in bright blue and orange; otherwise, it could have been any other building on the block, and no better for it.

It was this very anonymity that had pulled Vanderveen in when they arrived in town late that evening, nearly four hours after Tabrizi's death in Paris. They were met at the door by a bleary-eyed woman in her late fifties, who managed to greet them graciously, despite the late hour. They presented their passports and signed the registry as she searched for a free room. Handing over the keys, she smiled again and sent them up to the second floor.

The accommodations were adequate at best; the carpet was frayed, the furnishings scratched from years of use and lack of polish. The tile in the bathroom was cracked and stained, the wallpaper above the sink speckled with some unknown substance. The smell of antiseptic was overpowering. None of it mattered to Vanderveen; he had spent months, even years on end in places far worse. After pulling the curtains closed, he went into the bathroom and stripped down, then showered quickly. When he emerged ten minutes later, the room was dark, but he could see Raseen's still form on the bed. She was still fully clothed, curled into a tight ball on top of the covers, her right side rising and falling with each shallow breath. He studied her for a minute, dispassionately picking out what was visible in the low light: the line of her square jaw, the gentle curve of her right shoulder, and the slope of her slender neck, which led up to a tangled nest of black-brown hair.

Watching her, he was reminded of her demonstration in the field near Dordogne, as well as the remarkable poise she had shown outside the hotel in Paris. She had witnessed and participated in a number of atrocities over the past few days, and yet she slept without stirring, her face serene in a sliver of moonlight. He thought this trait—the ability to sleep soundly after what she had seen and done—said more about her nature than any words he had been offered in Tartus. In this respect, he knew, they were much the same. With this realization, this *acknowledgment*, he felt something he had not felt in many years: affection for another human being. It was a strange, unnerving sensation, and for a moment, it left him confused and vaguely annoyed.

Shrugging off the momentary lapse, he closed the drapes with a swift tug, the clean white light blinking out in an instant; then he crossed to the door and slipped out quietly. He went down the narrow, musty flight of stairs and stepped into the street a moment later. Then he turned left and began walking south on the rue de Madrid.

*   *   *

Calais, a town of approximately 80,000, is located on the northern coast of France, overlooking the choppy gray waters of the English Channel. On a clear day, the white chalk cliffs of Dover can be seen from the shore with the naked eye; closer still is the fleet of ferries and commercial vessels that make the daily crossing. Although it has its charms, 90 percent of the town's infrastructure was destroyed during World War II. As a result, there is little history to be found in the narrow streets of Calais, and even fewer architectural achievements. In fact, Calais is nothing more than a stopping point for most of the tourists entering France, as evidenced by the vast array of transportation options at hand. Vanderveen knew the Eurotunnel Terminal was located just southwest of the town, and there were a number of bus stations scattered about in convenient locations. Those facilities would become useful soon enough, but for now, Calais would suffice. It was as good a place as any to drop off the radar for a few days before moving again.

The pale quarter-moon slid behind a bank of clouds as he crossed the rue Mollien, making his way past the ornate redbrick façade of the train station. He entered the Parc Saint-Pierre a few minutes later, the Town Hall lit up to his left. The building's 75-foot belfry towered over the trees and Auguste Rodin's famous bronze, *The Burghers of Calais*.

Vanderveen stopped and appraised the work. He was well aware of its history. Completed in 1888, the sculpture was commissioned to commemorate an event that occurred during the Hundred Years' War. According to documents dating from that period, the burghers were recognized as the city's leaders, and, as such, were responsible for the defense of Calais. When Edward III laid siege to the city in 1347, Phillip VI of France commanded them to hold out indefinitely. When support failed to arrive, however, they were eventually forced to surrender, trading their lives and the keys to the city in exchange for the lives of the city's inhabitants. Although the burghers were eventually spared by the English, it was this image of them—leaving the gates of Calais in utter defeat, each with a noose tied round his neck—that Rodin had immortalized in bronze more than a hundred years earlier.

Vanderveen stood before the figures for several minutes, listening intently, then walked in a wide circle to view the sculpture from a number of angles. While his interest in the piece was genuine—there was something about those pained expressions that he found intensely appealing—he was far more concerned with what was happening across the boulevard Jacquard. He'd passed the Church of Notre Dame nearly fifteen minutes earlier, and ever since then he'd felt uneasy. It was nothing he could see, which meant it was almost certainly his imagination, but he couldn't shake the feeling that he was being watched.

The footpath wound its way through the park, bordered on both sides by misshapen trees, black silhouettes in the low ambient light. Vanderveen crossed the boulevard and continued on, making his way past a wartime telephone exchange. At some point, the unremarkable concrete structure had been converted to a museum; twin flagpoles stood outside the single entrance, the trees giving way to rows of dark green hedges. A sudden noise to his left caught his attention: the bray of a young man's drunken laughter, followed immediately by a burst of profanity and a shouted rebuke.

Vanderveen felt a sudden spark of concern. He knew about the darker side of Calais, the side that could not be found in any guidebook, no matter how honest the author. Because of its proximity to England, the city was a gathering place for asylum seekers from all over the Near and Middle East, including some of the globe's most troublesome regions: Sudan, Afghanistan, and the Palestinian territories. The hopeful masses had once congregated in the sweeping square next to the Parc Richelieu but moved around constantly to avoid the gendarmes, the local police. Vanderveen knew that by and large, the locals thought of these "asylum seekers" as nothing more than human waste, criminals forced from their native lands. Ironically, most of the criminal activity that stemmed from the immigrants' presence was propagated by French nationals, blue-collar men who were quick to exhibit their frustration over the ongoing problem.

In his current persona, Vanderveen could hardly be mistaken for one of the refugees, but that was a small comfort. Ethnicity aside, he had no desire to confront a nationalistic dockworker on the tail end of a daylong drinking binge. Pushing his right hand into his jacket pocket, he felt for the handle of the 4-inch Benchmade knife he was carrying. He had no doubt that he could extricate himself from any situation, but he would prefer to stay on in Calais until it was time to move. An unexpected confrontation could quickly ruin his plans, especially if he was forced to leave a body behind.

By skirting the shadows, it was easy enough to avoid the source of the laughter, and soon after leaving the park, he found what he was looking for on the rue Aristide Briand. He'd passed half a dozen public telephones since leaving the hotel, but he'd wanted to walk, craving the exercise after the lengthy drive north from Paris. It had little to do with spotting surveillance; if they were being watched, the authorities would have moved in by now, but the tingling sensation at the back of his neck was only getting worse. Still, he had to make the call. He'd put it off for too long already.

He'd purchased a French Telecom smart card shortly after arriving in Paris. Slipping it into the card reader, he punched in a thirteen-digit number and lifted the phone to his ear.

"Yes?"

"It's Taylor," Vanderveen said, using the prearranged code. "What do you have for me?"

When the response came, the soft, familiar voice was tight with irritation and concern. "I was expecting your call yesterday. There's a problem. The meeting did not go as planned."

"Explain."

"We had a couple of uninvited guests show up in Alexandria. They were both from the Agency, and one of them managed to get hold of our friend's laptop after he died. There was some politics involved—some sparring on the top floors—but we should have it back in a matter of hours. Unfortunately, we don't know what's on it. The man in the north may be compromised."

Rühmann. Vanderveen's grip on the phone was firm, but his words were calm and measured. "When will you know for sure?"

A slight hesitation, then, "Twenty-four hours, max."

"That's too long. He has to go if they're onto him."

"He has to go either way. You need to understand, there is no way I can bury this . . . If the hard drive contains usable information, the Bureau will find it and act on it. I can only control so much."

"I understand," was Vanderveen's terse reply. "I'll take care of it."

"Has the package changed hands?"

"Not yet. There are a few details to work out, but I'll finish the transaction soon enough."

"When exactly?"

The brief, uneasy silence that followed the question was answer enough, but Vanderveen voiced the words anyway. "That is not your concern. Just keep me updated. I need to know what's on the computer. Mason may have known more than we thought."

"Fine. Is there anything else?"

He was about to respond in the negative, but something sparked in the back of his mind. "The men from the Agency . . . I don't suppose you caught their names?"

"The senior man called himself Jonathan Harper. He showed up at the NCTC earlier in the day, looking for information. His ID said he was with the Office of General Counsel, but something about it didn't seem right to me. For one thing, I've never heard of an Agency lawyer showing up at a Bureau raid. There was no reason for an OGC rep to be there."

Vanderveen considered for a moment, then said, "I want to know more about him. Do you have access to that kind of information? It could prove useful."

"Possibly."

"Good. Do what you can. What about the subordinate? He's the one who took the laptop, right?"

"Yes. His name is Kealey, Ryan Kealey."

Vanderveen closed his eyes and replaced the receiver. He remained in that position for nearly a full minute, then opened his eyes slowly and lifted the phone once more. This time, the number he dialed put him through to a very different part of the world.

When the receiver was picked up on the other end, he simply said, "It's me. I'm afraid we may have a small problem."

CHAPTER 28

CALAIS

After concluding the second call, Vanderveen left the glass booth and walked back toward the path leading into the park. Sounds emerged from a brightly lit restaurant across the avenue: the tinkle of a woman's laughter, the clinking of glasses, and dozens of meshed conversations in a multitude of languages. The rich smells wafting out of the open doors served as a stabbing reminder that he hadn't eaten in nearly a day, but for the most part, his mind was consumed by what he had just learned.

Kealey. Vanderveen shook his head in delayed disbelief. At the same time, he wondered why he was so surprised. The man's involvement was all but inevitable; he was, after all, one of the Agency's most experienced field men, particularly when it came to the Middle East. Still, the unfortunate development raised uncomfortable doubts, forcing him to question some of his earlier choices. It seemed as though the shot he had taken on that sweltering Syrian hilltop eight years earlier had haunted him ever since. Rightly, Ryan Kealey should have died that day. Vanderveen could understand the need for revenge after that kind of betrayal, but the truth was that the man's motivations ran far beyond the near-fatal wound he had suffered in Syria, far beyond the loss of his fellow soldiers. With this personal admission, Vanderveen once again found himself wondering: Had killing the woman in Maine been a mistake?

Yes, said the insistent voice inside, the same voice that had guided him since adolescence. He had been asking himself that specific question for months on end, and now he had his answer. It *was* a mistake, an act carried out in a moment of black rage. Better to have killed the man and been done with it. By sparing Kealey and taking his woman instead, Vanderveen had given him all the motivation he would ever need to track her killer to the end of the earth.

Despite the recriminations, despite the uncomfortable examination of his past decisions, Vanderveen was comforted by one truth he had learned over the years, which was this: opportunities are rarely lost, only delayed. The trick lay in recognizing a second chance when it presented itself, and it went both ways. After all, fate had given Ryan Kealey his fair share of opportunities, all of which he had squandered. He had missed his target in Syria after losing nearly half of his detachment to Vanderveen's aimed fire, and he'd failed to finish the job on that frigid night in Maine nearly one year earlier, counting instead on nature's fury to finish the work he had started.

Now the tables were turned once more, and this time, Vanderveen knew he could not fail. In fact, he suddenly realized there might be an opportunity here, a chance to remedy two problems at once. There was no doubt in his mind that Kealey would do everything in his power to track down Thomas Rühmann. In this respect, Vanderveen had the advantage, as he already knew exactly where the Austrian arms broker was holed up. All he had to do was get there first. He would also need the proper materials.

A frown crossed his face with this realization. The second person he'd called had promised to fill Vanderveen's order, but he was reluctant to place his faith in the distant voice. His own contacts, while abundant in the Middle East, were extremely limited in Western Europe. On the other hand, if the insurgency's agent in England failed to come through, there was a chance—a good chance, even—that Yasmin Raseen could get hold of the right people. According to al-Tikriti's veiled speech, she had operated extensively on European soil, a fact she had already demonstrated with consummate skill during their time in France.

As Vanderveen made his way through the park, the lights of the belfry drawing ever closer, he was pulled from his thoughts by the sound of a woman's scream. The indignant cry was cut off in the middle, as though a hand had suddenly clamped over an open mouth. In the intense silence that followed, a burst of drunken laughter cut through the trees, followed immediately by a sound he could not quite place, a shuffling, grunting noise, which carried clearly in the brisk night air.

He did not hesitate; his stride was unbroken. In fact, he quickened his pace, hoping to get clear of the park before the police were alerted. The station was nearby, he knew, on the eastern side of the Town Hall. Whatever was happening—a rape, a robbery—was not his concern. His continued freedom precluded his intervention in such matters, but it was his utter indifference that sealed the decision to walk away, which was made unconsciously. The next sound he heard, however, caused him to freeze in his tracks and breathe a soft curse.

The woman had cried out again, apparently breaking free of the hand that silenced her. This time, the scream was accompanied by a flurry of pointed obscenities, which were not uttered in French, but in Arabic.

The park beyond the footpath was reasonably open, which worked both for and against him. The grass beneath his feet was close clipped, damp from the earlier rain, and the trees and hedges were neatly pruned, giving him a clear view of what lay ahead, or at least as much as the diffused light would reveal. Fortunately, the vegetation surrounding the war museum was less well kept, as though the men and women who maintained the exhibits had no time or concern for the aesthetics of the building itself.

It was from that copse of tangled trees that the woman's scream had originated, and now, drawing closer, he heard yet another muffled cry. There was no doubt in his mind that the woman was Yasmin Raseen; what he didn't understand was why she had followed him. He was struck by a sudden flash of anger; he had watched his trail carefully, and yet she'd somehow managed to track him for nearly an hour without giving herself away. She had operated in this capacity for much longer than he had, he knew, but knowing her capabilities didn't slow the rising anger, which threatened to overwhelm him.

Taking a deep, calming breath, he forced himself to clear his mind and focus on the approach. He moved in a crouch, his weight perfectly balanced on the balls of his feet. Judging by the drunken sound of the laughter he'd heard a moment ago, Raseen's assailants were in no state to offer a serious challenge. For this reason, Vanderveen left the knife in his pocket. Whatever happened next, he was determined to keep things simple, and that meant leaving them alive if at all possible.

There. The trees gave way, and he took in the scene with a practiced eye: two bodies were intertwined, grappling on the ground, the larger figure on top. There was a second shape several feet to the right, a still form on a bed of crushed leaves. The figure was lying on its back, not moving, arms outstretched.

For a split second, he considered leaving her. It would be better if he did not have to explain her death, but some things couldn't be helped. On the other hand, Vanderveen realized that she could be carrying some kind of identification. If so, she would quickly be traced back to the hotel on the rue de Madrid. Once the police learned that Raseen had not checked in alone, they would seek out her traveling companion for questioning. Once the companion failed to materialize, he would become the prime suspect. To complicate matters, the woman at the desk still had his passport, which he'd been asked to leave when they checked in. The passport contained a false name, and his appearance was subtly altered in the photograph, but it was still evidence. He had no desire to leave it behind.

Turning his attention back to the struggle, he focused on the man astride the smaller figure. Having made his decision, he moved forward and snaked his right arm around the thick neck in front of him, then pulled back sharply, placing his left hand on the side of the head for leverage. Hands instantly sprung up to wrap round his arms, trying to loosen the grip. The man was strong; for a moment, Vanderveen's right arm began to give way, and then he felt something hot and wet spraying against the thin fabric of his long-sleeve shirt. The man seemed to jerk spasmodically, then fell forward, crashing onto the smaller figure. Surprised, Vanderveen stepped back. Raseen's assailant began to choke as she pushed him off with a huge effort. She rolled away and tried to sit up, gasping for breath. Beneath her open coat, her blouse was visibly torn in several places. There were leaves in her hair and a wet streak over her left eye—

blood, Vanderveen realized—but there was nothing in her expression to indicate fear, panic, or even relief that he had come to her aid.

The larger man was bleeding out; that much was obvious. She must have nicked the artery before he arrived in the clearing. Ignoring the dying man, Vanderveen went to the other body and checked for a pulse. Not finding one, he looked at the face. It was obscenely white in the dark, eyes wide in surprise. The throat was intact, but there was a dark spot on the shirt, indicating a puncture wound placed neatly between the fourth and fifth ribs.

He turned back to Raseen, who was still breathing heavily. Her eyes flicked down to the bodies, and something changed in her face; she seemed not pleased, but oddly satisfied with what she had done, as though she had confirmed some long-held belief in her own capabilities. He wondered if she had ever killed before, despite what he'd been told in Tartus. The knife was still in her hand, a slim shard of steel, the blade glistening wet in the moonlight.

Vanderveen met her gaze, his face tightening. She seemed to sense his thoughts, as she clambered to her feet and took a fast step back, her eyes fixed on his. Strangely enough, she seemed wary, but not afraid. He could tell the difference; he was all too familiar with the nuances of joyless expressions.

Kill her, said the voice inside.

He took a slow step forward; for the moment, his body was as irrational as his mind, his limbs trembling with rage. She moved the knife in front of her body, as if to remind him that she still had it. Still, her expression did not change. Her face was cool but not distant; she was entirely engaged in the moment.

She's too much of a risk . . . Just look at the mess she's left you. Kill her now.

He took another step forward, which she countered with another step back. She opened her mouth to say something, then changed her mind and clamped it shut. They were separated by 2 feet at most; if he moved quickly and got hold of the knife hand, he could crush her trachea in a matter of seconds. He just needed the slightest distraction. . . .

Feet in the underbrush, branches whipping around an advancing form. Vanderveen stepped into the shadows instinctively, and the woman froze in place.

"Hello?" a gruff, cautious voice, asked with authority. "Police. Is anyone there?"

Raseen's gaze skipped to the shadows, questioning. Vanderveen moved carefully forward, nodded once, then stepped back. He was now completely reliant on her, and it occurred to him how quickly the tables had turned; in other circumstances, it would have been almost amusing.

Raseen dropped down to the wet grass, simultaneously wiping her hand over the cut near her left eye. Smearing the blood over her face, she positioned herself next to one of the bodies and cried out in faltering French. "I'm over here! Please, help me! Please . . ."

The noise through the brush grew louder, leaves sliding under fast, heavy feet, branches snapping. A portly figure burst into view. Even in the dark, Vanderveen could make out the patrol uniform and the radio hooked to the right side of the man's belt. The officer took in the scene, murmuring an obscenity. Then he dropped to his knees next to Raseen. *"Mademoiselle? Mademoiselle, êtes-vous blessé?" Are you hurt?*

In one swift motion, Raseen grabbed the policeman's hands and pulled him over her body, lifting him off his feet. At the same time, Vanderveen approached from behind, the Benchmade knife coming out of his pocket. He flipped his thumb and the serrated, 4-inch blade sprang free, clicking into place.

The policeman shouted a warning to no one in particular and started to rise, struggling to find a foothold in the slick grass. He was clambering to his feet, fumbling for the radio, when Vanderveen knocked off his cap with his left hand. At the same time, he gripped a handful of hair, pulled the man's head to the left, and thrust the knife up under the right ear. The police officer shuddered and emitted a strange sound, something between a cough and a scream. Then he went still. Vanderveen jiggled the blade back and forth a few times before pulling it out and releasing his grip. The dead man fell to the ground with a muffled thump.

Yasmin Raseen was already moving. Her coat was soaked in blood; pulling it off, she rubbed the cloth liner over the damp grass, then used it to wipe her face. Then she placed the knife inside the coat and wrapped it into a bundle, arranging the material under her left arm so that none of the stains were visible.

For the moment, she was unarmed. She glanced at the knife in Vanderveen's hand, but a quick look at her face told him that nothing had changed; she remained unafraid.

She could not have known what her indifference meant; she had no way of knowing that it was this—her complete lack of fear—that had saved her life. If she had shown an ounce of panic, a moment of indecision, or a trace of dependence on him, he would have killed her instantly. Instead, he wiped down his knife and carefully dropped the weapon next to one of the bodies. Then he took Raseen's free arm and guided her out of the park.

The lights of the hotel were all but extinguished by the time they returned. Vanderveen pulled open the front door and led her past the drooping, disinterested eyes of the girl at the desk, past the wilting plants in the shabby stairwell. They climbed the dark stairs. In the room on the second floor, Raseen felt her way into the bathroom and flipped on the light, then closed the door behind her. Vanderveen heard tap water running in the sink as he went to the window. Cracking the drapes slightly, he stared down at the road. There was no sign of anything amiss, though he could hear distant sirens through the glass.

They had dropped their bloodied coats into a pair of trash cans on the way back, reaching the hotel clothed only in jeans and T-shirts. The brisk walk back from the park had taken less than twenty minutes, but that was more than enough time for his rage to climb to impossible heights. The woman had compromised everything to satisfy her idle curiosity. She had overstepped her bounds, exceeded any authority her connections afforded her. By the time she emerged from the bathroom, his fury had pushed him past any semblance of rationality; now, he was willing to endure any consequence to see her dead. He would leave her body in the room if he had to. At least, that was how he felt until the door swung open and she appeared before him, backlit by the bulbs over the sink. Then it all fell away, and he could not help but stare in frank admiration.

Her beauty was evident in any light, but there was something about the dark that brought out what lay within, perversely illuminating her darkest desires. Raseen had stripped off the T-shirt and stood before him in worn jeans and a black lace bra. The light from behind made her curves stand out in sharp relief, but it was not her physical attributes that pulled him in. There was something else that he found inexplicably unique and appealing, something about her utter indifference that stripped him of all self-control; he felt as though he would do anything to elicit some kind of reaction, something beyond the enigmatic crease between her eyebrows. He wanted to know who she really was, what had driven her into the life she was leading. What had created her? Who—if anyone—had turned her into a killer?

And then it all came back: the rage, the frustration, the desire to simplify what had become too confusing. Vanderveen could recognize his sudden changes in mood, but he could not control them, just as he could not control the circumstances that had shaped his youth. He was on her in an instant, his left hand like a vise around her throat. He pinned her to the wall, grabbing her right hand with his, and crossing it over her body to control both arms. He was surprised when she refused to struggle. Even as a minute passed and her face turned scarlet from lack of air, she refused to lash out with her feet, to cry out with the last of her breath.

"You stupid bitch." He hissed the words, his face not more than an inch from hers. The fact that she wouldn't fight only enraged him more. "You should have stayed in the room. You brought this on yourself. Why did you follow me? What were you trying to prove?"

She didn't try to reply, not that she could have. Instead, as he tightened his grip, trying to squeeze the last breath from her lungs, she rolled her head back against the wall. At the same time, her eyes closed and her lips parted in an unmistakably sensual way. Surprised and confused, he began to open his hand. Using all the movement left to her, she slid her left hand over his right and squeezed softly.

He could not help what happened next: his grip continued to falter, and she was allowed a deep, shuddering breath, her throat expanding beneath his hand. He took an uncertain step back, ready to strike again, but instead of collapsing or stumbling away, she leaned over for several seconds, gasping for air.

Then she straightened and stepped into his arms, her mouth fastening over his.

He was too stunned to react right away; her fingers were fast in his hair, then sliding down the taut muscles of his back. His first thought was to pry them loose, but she seemed to sense his thoughts; before he could stop her, she had moved her mouth to his ear. She whispered a few breathless words of encouragement, urging him on. At the same time, she pulled off his shirt in one fast movement and pressed her body to his, her full breasts lifting and falling against his bare chest.

He did not have time to consider this strange turn of events. She began pulling him back toward the bed, her movements soft but insistent. In that moment, he knew, with abrupt and complete certainty, that he would never get the truth from her. He would never know what had produced her, what pushed her forward; her mind and her past were equally inaccessible. But as trying as that knowledge was, for the moment, it didn't matter at all.

Her hands slipped behind her back, and her bra fell to the floor. Vanderveen pressed her down to the covers and lowered his head to her bare skin.

When he woke, it seemed as though hours had passed, but a quick glance at the bedside clock told him he'd been asleep for less than an hour. He lay back for several minutes, letting his eyes adjust to the dark. Then he sat up quietly and looked around the room. Raseen was sitting next to the window, a threadbare blanket wrapped round her bare shoulders. She'd pulled the curtains back; as a car passed in the street below, the headlights flickered over her strong features, momentarily brightening her dark brown eyes. Sensing his attention, she half-turned to smile in his direction.

"You're awake."

Vanderveen sat up and leaned against the headboard, running a hand over his eyes. "Yes."

She stood and walked back to the bed. She curled up next to him and rested her head on his shoulder, still wrapped in the blanket, as though guarding her virtue. He wrapped his left arm around her and pulled her close.

"Can't you sleep?" he asked.

"No."

Strange, but the single word was answer enough. They sat in silence for minutes on end. He wondered if she ever experienced remorse for her actions, but he could not ask the question. Nor would he have trusted her answer. Finally, she pressed her lips to his ear and said, "I saw you on the phone, you know. Who were you talking to?"

He hesitated, and she locked on to it immediately. "We're in this together, Will. You must learn to trust me if we are to succeed."

Trust. It was a hell of a thing to expect, considering what she had just done. Still, she had a point. He had asked her to join him, not the other way round. If he couldn't trust her, she had already outlived her usefulness. And yet, for all of her skills, she was beyond his experience and, therefore, beyond his control. It was the one fact he could not set aside. He thought about it for a few minutes more, weighing the options. She remained silent, awaiting his decision. Finally, he began to talk softly.

He told her everything. He started with that day on the Syrian coast, all the way through to his work for Iran and al-Qaeda. He told her about the failed assassination of the U.S. president one year prior. Finally, he told her about Kealey and the threat that the man now posed.

"I brought it on myself," he said when he was finished. "I killed five of his soldiers, five men he was responsible for. Five of his friends. Then, seven years later, I killed his woman right in front of him. He has every reason to want me dead."

She shifted against him, trying to find a more comfortable position. "Perhaps so, but that's in the past and can't be helped. The question is, what will you do now?"

Vanderveen smiled into the dark. "He's close to Rühmann. Once he tracks him down, Kealey will come to Europe himself; he won't trust anyone else with something of this importance."

"And we'll be waiting," Raseen said.

"Yes," Vanderveen replied. "We'll be waiting."

"And in the meantime?"

"We meet the man our employers have sent. He arrives in London tomorrow afternoon."

CHAPTER 29

WASHINGTON, D.C.

The streets of Washington, D.C., were not as empty as Naomi would have expected at 4:00 AM. They had passed a number of vehicles en route to the Palisades, a wealthy residential area that stood out in the city, even amidst the redbrick opulence of Georgetown. Their route had taken them past the closed roads surrounding the White House, through Foggy Bottom and the river mist hanging over the Potomac. Shortly after they entered Arlington County, the lights of the States Naval Observatory appeared in the distance, glistening eerily in the damp morning air.

Naomi took M Street off Pennsylvania, then swung a right onto Wisconsin Avenue, the wheel shimmying slightly beneath her fingers. The car was dark blue, a late-model Taurus with tinted windows, new tires, and Virginia plates. The vehicle looked modest enough, right down to the surface rust, but things were not as they seemed. A standard check through the DMV would lead the police to a crumbling brownstone in downtown Richmond, and the engine compartment contained a block that was far more powerful than the standard 3.0 liter V6.

The car, which had been discreetly pulled from the Agency's motor pool, was Harper's final—and most dangerous—contribution to their unauthorized task. With enough work, Kharmai felt sure that the paper pushers at Langley could trace the car back to the DDO, but she was hoping it wouldn't come to that. With any luck, they'd have it back in the pool before the workday began. She lowered the window slightly and checked the clock in the dashboard, wondering how long they had before sunrise. She was guessing it was at least three hours, which was more than enough time, assuming everything went according to plan. And that, she thought wryly, was a very large assumption.

Kealey had been checking his equipment and murmuring directions since they'd left the hotel. She didn't need his help, but she was too keyed up, too involved in her own thoughts, to point this out. Her nervousness was a source of lingering irritation, and it didn't make sense; she'd felt fine when they were poring over the embassy blueprints. Of course, that had been in the safety of a warm, brightly lit hotel room. Now reality was starting to sink in, and for the first time, she realized how much she was actually risking. If anything went wrong, her career at the Agency would almost certainly be over. The thought made her stomach contract into a tight, queasy ball, but she shook her head unconsciously and steeled herself. She'd made her decision, knew it was right, and she'd stand by her choice, regardless of the consequences.

Kealey looked up from what he was doing to issue instructions, but she beat him to it, swinging a sharp left onto Reservoir Road. The Taurus coasted along for a few minutes more, gliding into the suburb of Senate Heights. Naomi pulled off to the side of the road and doused the headlights. The car was completely dark inside; Kealey had already removed the interior bulb.

He opened the door as soon as the vehicle stopped, swinging his legs out to the pavement. At the same time, he hooked the earpiece into its proper position. They'd tested the radios at the hotel earlier. Naomi had driven the Taurus east on Pennsylvania, transmitting periodically back to Kealey's room on the fifth floor. The Motorola XTS 2500 operated in the same high-frequency range as television and FM radio broadcasts; as a result, she grew tired of driving around the city long before noticing a meaningful drop in the audio quality. She had programmed the radios herself and felt sure they would perform as expected.

Kealey turned back to her as she was slipping her earpiece into position. She met his unflinching gaze and resisted the urge to look away.

"Naomi, this is your last chance. Are you sure you want to do this?"

She was annoyed that he felt it necessary to question her commitment again, but she pushed it down. "I'm sure. Just . . ."

"What?"

"Just be careful, okay?"

He nodded once and clambered out to the pavement, closing the door softly behind him. She watched through the passenger-side window as he walked down the darkened street at a brisk pace, his hands jammed into his pockets. She followed him with anxious eyes until the night closed in behind him. Then she started the engine and drove on.

The German chancery, the brainchild of famed architect Egon Eiermann, had clearly been designed with diplomacy in mind. Located far from the tumultuous rhythm of downtown Washington, the building was a true aesthetic achievement, a six-story amalgamation of glass, delicate wooden sunshades, and tubular steel support beams. The grounds, which encompassed 9 acres of prime real estate, were as unobtrusive as the building itself, marked only by the occasional poplar or oak. It was this very lack of vegetation that was troubling Kealey as he turned right on Foxhall Road and followed it north, adjacent to the chancery grounds. Garden lights were strewn about the grass, but from where he was standing, the narrow building was nothing more than a dark haze against the blue-black sky. To reach his objective, he would be forced to cross a great deal of open ground.

Kealey turned away from the fence, adjusted the straps of his backpack, and continued walking. A small SUV swept past on the indistinct road, followed by a D.C. Metro police car. At the sight of the cruiser, Kealey made an effort not to visibly react. The vehicle slowed but continued on. Once it faded from view, he breathed an audible sigh of relief. On foot he was vulnerable. His dark clothes and pack, combined with the early hour, made him stand out in this affluent neighborhood, where the heavy police presence was designed to intimidate people just like him, or at least what he appeared to be: a transient of dubious means. He was extremely fortunate the officer had not stopped to investigate further, but given what was at stake, he couldn't count on that kind of luck; he had to get off the street as soon as possible.

The black-iron fence was waist high and did not present much of a challenge. He scaled it quickly and began making his way through the grounds. He had crossed several hundred feet when his earpiece came to life, and Naomi's voice sounded clear. "Ryan, I'm in position. Where are you?"

He keyed his mic and said, "I'm in the grounds, approaching from the northeast."

"How far are you from the building?"

"About two hundred fifty meters."

"Okay. Hold on a second."

From the front seat of the Taurus, Naomi found the appropriate document and spread it across her lap, trying to pinpoint his location. The satellite photographs that supplemented the ORACLE file were shot with half-meter resolution, which made it easy to determine distance and spot specific landmarks. She had parked the car beneath a streetlamp on Hoban Road, directly opposite the embassy grounds, but the light was weak—weak enough to make her task more difficult than it should have been. Squinting into the semidark, she finally managed to pick out his approximate location on the creased paper.

"Ryan, you should see a group of trees to the west, about thirty meters from your position."

A brief pause, then, "I see them."

"Stay on your side of those trees, and follow them southwest. They give way to a hedge that will lead you right up to the building." She grabbed for another sheet of paper and scanned it quickly. "The cameras are beneath the first balcony, above the door. The second balcony extends from the edge of the building to the spot right over the cameras, so that's your point of access, the northwestern corner."

"Got it."

"Remember, the cameras can pick you up from fifty meters out, so make sure you stay below the hedgeline."

"Right. I'll get back to you when I'm in position."

She nodded to herself and took her thumb off the PTT (PRESS TO TALK) switch, then began leafing through the hefty manila file, searching for the diagram of the chancery's ground-floor interior layout. All of it, except for the satellite photographs, had been supplied by the source recruited through ORACLE. The source—a senior assistant to the third secretary, responsible for administration—had been promoted and moved to the embassy in France nearly two months earlier. Unfortunately, he had been killed in a car accident less than a week after arriving in-country, a fact that Naomi had confirmed just five hours earlier. If he had still been in place, he would have had complete access to the information they were after. The second option, of course, was to cultivate a new agent within the embassy, but convincing foreign diplomats to switch sides was a sensitive business, and not something that could be accomplished in the space of twenty-four hours.

Not for the first time, Naomi's eyes flickered up to the rearview mirror. She was parked in a residential neighborhood and knew that she would look extremely suspicious to anyone who happened to glance out their windows. It couldn't be helped, though, and they needed less than an hour, perhaps as little as forty minutes. All she could do was hope that their luck would hold.

Come on, Ryan, she thought, anxiously fingering the radio hooked to her belt. *Hurry.*

After scaling the fence, Kealey had paused to pull down his black balaclava. Now, leaning against the exterior wall, just out of sight of the cameras, he looked down at his dark clothes. They were soaked through from the morning dew, which covered every square inch of the manicured lawn. He had crawled the last 70 meters to reach the building, and as he shrugged off the backpack, he tried to shake off the exhaustion that threatened to overtake him. He had not slept in nearly twenty-four hours, and while he had carried out dozens of missions under similar duress during his military career, he knew that what he was about to do would require all of his strength, both mental and physical. He could not afford to lose focus for even a second.

The Radionics V1160N cameras were just around the corner, mounted 8 feet over the concrete walkway. From there, they were wired to a multiplexer in the control room, which split the monitor into four screens, representing these cameras and two others. The multiplexer, in turn, was routed to a Bosch VMD01, and from there to the tower. Despite its modest appearance, the VMD01 represented the cutting edge of motion-sensing technology. It was capable of adjusting automatically to changing environmental conditions, as well as correcting for camera vibration, thereby reducing false alarms. From head-on, the system was almost impossible to beat.

Kealey thought back to the file that he'd studied for hours on end. Naomi had been the one to point out the obvious problems. For one thing, the cameras were too high to reach without a ladder of some type, which was clearly impractical, considering the distance from the fence to the building. If he was compromised or otherwise forced to leave in a hurry, he could not be slowed by unnecessary weight. Besides, the local insomniacs would be quick to pick out a person carrying a ladder around the neighborhood at 4:00 a.m.

With decreasing enthusiasm, she had also pointed out that the cameras had overlapping detection envelopes. Due to the VMD01 they could not only detect, but *analyze* motion in an arc of 180 degrees, which encompassed the only possible angles of horizontal approach.

And that, Kealey had realized, was the key word: *horizontal*. The cameras could not be defeated from ground level; to take them out of the equation, he'd have to go in from above.

Placing the pack on the ground, he opened the main compartment and pulled out the first of two ½-inch climbing ropes. It took several attempts, but he managed to sling the free end over the railing of the second balcony. Then he played out the rope until he had both ends back in his hands, after which he tied a hitch knot with an adjustable grip, something he recalled from his days at the Air Assault School in Fort Campbell, Kentucky. By pulling on the base line, he was able to work the knot up to the railing. He took a moment to listen to the environment. There was the distant sound of a siren, but it seemed to be moving away. Otherwise, there was nothing.

He zipped up and shouldered the pack once more, then began to climb. Once he reached the second balcony, he climbed over the railing and pulled up the rope, then untied it and slung it over his shoulder. Walking to the other end of the balcony, he peered over the side, carefully examining the next challenge. The cameras were directly beneath him, about 20 feet down, level with each other and spaced a foot apart. The service door, in turn, was located beneath the cameras.

Straightening, he turned to his right and checked out the windows. It was as he expected: the windows opened only from inside the building. If he tried to force one, there was a good chance the pane would give way. Clearly, the door below was the best option, although that wasn't saying much.

Dropping the rope from his shoulder, he tied a knot at one end to prevent him from sliding all the way to the ground. The other end of the rope was secured to the railing with an anchor bend, which, once pulled taut, was almost impossible to untie. Loosely coiling the free end of the rope, he dropped it onto the floor of the balcony and opened the pack, pulling out a handful of nonlocking caribiners. He was already wearing a Petzl rappelling harness, which was nothing more than a waist strap attached to fabric loops that encircled the thighs. Kealey hooked a few caribiners to the gear loops on either side of the harness, then selected another object from the pack. The small metal device was known as a shunt. Once clamped around the rope and linked—with the help of a caribiner—to the main attachment point on the harness, the shunt could be used to arrest an uncontrolled rappel. More importantly, it could be locked at any point, giving him free use of both hands.

Finding the gear had been a challenge in itself. It had taken a number of calls, but he'd finally managed to get through to an instructor at Camp Peary, otherwise known as The Farm, the CIA's main training facility, near Williamsburg, Virginia. By chance, the instructor had left most of the necessary equipment at Langley a week earlier. Kealey had made the drive to headquarters just after midnight, stopping along the way at a twenty-four-hour Wal-Mart. There, he had collected the rest of what was needed: a battery-operated screwdriver, a Mini Maglite with an assortment of colored filters, and a pair of thick leather gloves. He'd also picked up a Gerber multi-tool. Favored by military personnel, the Gerber was similar to a Swiss Army knife in form and function. The Maglite remained in the pack, which he left on the balcony. The screwdriver was hooked to his harness, dangling from one of the gear loops, as was the Gerber.

Having secured the shunt to the rope and his harness in turn, he pulled on the pair of thick leather gloves, adjusted his lip mic slightly, and said, "Naomi, I'm about to take care of the cameras. Ready on your end?"

"Yes. I'm making the call now."

In the Taurus, Kharmai pulled out her cell phone and speed-dialed a number. The other end was picked up after the first ring. A brisk voice announced, "German Embassy."

"Yes, hello?" She was nearly shouting into the phone. "I can hardly . . . I can't hear you. Hello?"

"Yes, this is the German Embassy. How can I help you?"

"I'm looking for Gunter. Is he . . . Is he there? Sorry, can you hear me? This phone is . . ."

She allowed herself to trail off and held her breath, waiting for the reply.

"Yes, he's right here. One moment please . . ."

Naomi hung up immediately. The file contained the names and positions of nearly everyone who worked at the chancery, including the guards on the night shift. Anything could have changed over the past couple of months, but their luck seemed to be holding. She wasn't sure if the guard on the phone had bought her act, but it didn't really matter. There were only two men on duty from 8:00 p.m. to 6:00 a.m., and she'd just verified their locations. Both were in the security booth, which was on the other end of the building. Ryan would not get a better chance.

She keyed her mic and said, "They're in the booth. You're free to move."

234   Andrew Britton

On the second-floor balcony, Kealey acknowledged her transmission and started to move. First, he slipped the rope over the side of the railing and began lowering it carefully. It was going to go too far, he realized; if he descended, he'd overshoot his target and end up in full view of the cameras. Pulling the rope back up, he looped it around the railing a few times, tied a second knot, and lowered it once more. This time, the rope stopped right where he wanted it to.

He performed a quick check of his clothing, looking for anything loose, something that might snare in the shunt's pulley. Satisfied with his preparations, he climbed over the railing and stood with his heels between the bars, facing out into space.

Inverted rappelling basically amounted to descending a rope face-first. It was a dangerous proposition under the best of circumstances, but here in the dark, with the bare minimum of equipment, it was nearly suicidal. Kealey knew this as well as anyone, but he was completely calm as he leaned forward and loosened his grip on the rope. It all came down to timing.

Kneeling, he dropped forward over the railing. He fell with startling speed for the first 10 feet before pulling the rope hard over his chest. At the same time, he pinched the trailing end between his feet. Although he was using every ounce of strength he possessed to slow his fall, he was unable to stop in time. His hands bounced over the knot in the end of the rope, and he slammed to a halt a split second later. Looking up at his harness, he could see that the shunt was jammed into the anchor knot; it was the only thing that had stopped him from tumbling headfirst to the cement footpath.

The heart-stopping descent had left him shaken, but there was no time to waste. Stripping off his gloves, he examined the cameras, both of which were in arm's reach. Each was covered by a weather-proof plastic housing. The housings were screwed into place; four screws on each, he could see, and beneath that, another four screws to remove the access panels.

He hooked his leg around the rope to stabilize his body, then felt back to his side for the screwdriver, unhooking it from the caribiner. He moved slowly; if he dropped the screwdriver, he would have no choice but to abort. Once the cameras went off-line, one of the guards would surely come to investigate. If he were to find a screw-driver beneath the disabled units, the embassy would be locked down immediately, and reinforcements called in. If, on the other hand, the cameras did not appear to be tampered with, the security guard might simply ensure the door was locked, head back to finish his shift, and report the incident in the morning. Kealey was not sure of any of this, but given the situation, there was no other alternative.

He managed to get both housings off in less than a minute, prop-ping them on the mounts drilled into the walls. The access panels came next. Although the cameras were set to ignore a certain amount of vibration, he was careful to avoid bumping them. He felt sure that the slight vibration generated by the screwdriver would set off the alarm. If that happened, he would not know until the door was opened below; the alarm wired to the cameras was only audible in-side the security booth. The process was nerve-wracking, and by the time he was down to the last two screws, his face was bathed in sweat, despite the cool air.

The last one came free. He pinched it between his fingers, but it slipped free, rattling off the front of the camera.

Shit. Kealey looked down to the cement. The screw was clearly vis-ible, impossibly bright in the weak light. There was no way the guard would miss it when he came to investigate. No way.

He swore under his breath, shaking his head. There was nothing he could do now; he just had to carry on in the hope that the guard was too tired or ignorant to notice. Snapping the screwdriver's fabric loop back into the caribiner, he reached next for the Gerber. Unfold-ing the wire cutters, he found the appropriate bundle of wires in the exposed circuitry of the first camera. He would have preferred to simply short out the cameras, thereby creating the illusion of an elec-tronic malfunction, but he couldn't be sure of success. Cutting the wires was the only way to guarantee the feed would go down. He snipped the wires quickly, then did the same to the second unit. The cameras were off-line.

Now there was not a moment to lose; the guard would arrive in less than a minute. Most of the embassy's security measures were ex-ternal. Inside the building, the doors were secured by cipher locks, each of which could be opened with a simple four-digit code. The guard would have access to every door on the ground floor, and it wouldn't take him long to reach the back of the chancery.

Kealey hooked the Gerber back to the harness and retrieved the screwdriver. Ten seconds had elapsed. Moving fast, he slipped the metal covers back into place, covering the access panels, then began screwing them down. Thirty seconds gone.

He reached for the weatherproof housings. One came free right away, but the other started to slide off the opposite side of the mount. Lunging out with his left hand, he caught it at the last possible second, the plastic material pinched between his thumb and forefinger. Breathing hard, he set the housings over the cameras and checked his watch for the third time, lighting up the digital face: forty-five seconds.

No time to screw in the housings. Unhooking his leg, he shifted so his body was horizontal with the ground, then reached for the rope and started to climb. The shunt, still jammed into the knot at the end of the rope, followed him up. Naomi's voice was loud in his ear, but he couldn't make sense of her words; all he could hear was his own ragged breath and the sound of his blood, which was hissing in his ears.

Five feet to go. He was climbing fast, hand over hand, the coarse rope stripping his fingers bare. Beneath him, he heard the door snap open, and his heart nearly stopped; he was in plain view. If the guard looked up, it would all be over, and how could he not? The cameras were right there, right in the line of sight. There was no choice. Kealey kept climbing and flung himself over the railing, willing the iron to absorb the sound of his falling body. At the same time, he yanked the wires out of the radio, unsure if Kharmai's transmission could be heard on the ground.

He lay still for a long moment, trying to silence his breathing. Below, he could hear cautious feet on cement as the guard moved around. It sounded like one man, which meant that the other guard was probably still in the booth. He was tempted to look over the side of the railing, but common sense kept him in place; there was nothing to gain by exposing himself. If the guard had spotted the screw on the footpath—or if he'd seen some other sign that things were amiss—Kealey would know soon enough.

Finally, a short phrase drifted up to the balcony. It carried a note of finality, but the words made no sense to him. Kealey was fluent in four languages, but German, unfortunately, was not among them. The door slammed shut a moment later, and everything was quiet again.

As carefully as possible, he slid over the iron and looked down to the chancery grounds. The security guard was nowhere in sight. Plugging the earpiece back into the radio, he reached Kharmai and repeated the phrase he had heard to the best of his ability. When he was done, there were a few seconds of silence while she translated.

"I think you heard him correctly," she said. "He told the other guard there was no sign of tampering. They think one of the boards went bad, that it was just a nuisance alarm. It sounds like you're in the clear."

"Good. I'll let you know once I'm inside the building."

"You remember the code?"

"Yeah, I got it."

Less than a minute later, Kealey was back on the ground, standing in front of the service door. He had changed his shoes to avoid trailing mud through the building. He had also stripped off the Petzl harness, replacing it with a waist holster containing his Beretta 9mm. There was no way he could use the gun, but he was not used to working without it. Just having it on him made him feel better about the whole scenario. The climbing rope was back in the pack, along with the rest of his equipment. He'd taken care of the cameras, but the pressure was still on. It should have been easier. Thanks to the ORACLE source, they had the computer passwords, cipher lock combinations, alarm codes—even the names of the guards on duty. Everything but the key to this door.

He examined the lock carefully. It was just as the file promised, a Schlage pin tumbler housed within a Securitron dual alarm/door unit. He was not surprised to see a small red light protruding from the steel plate, which indicated the system was armed. This was perhaps the riskiest part, as the cylinder had to be picked twice: once, to deactivate the alarm, and again to unlock the solenoid bolt. Unfortunately, there was no way of knowing how the switches were wired.

He might turn the cylinder clockwise to unlock the door and end up triggering the alarm. Normally, he would just remove the cover to get a look at the wiring, but in this case, the plate was held in place by tamper-proof screws. He had no choice but to pick the lock and hope for the best. The odds of getting it right the first time were fifty-fifty, which didn't inspire a great deal of confidence.

The red filter was already in place, covering the lens of the Maglite. Holding the light in place, Kealey looked at the keyway. For most pin tumbler locks, a lock-pick gun was the most expedient choice. Unfortunately, it was also the noisiest method, and in this case, the Securitron switch precluded its use. Besides, having already drawn attention to this door by disabling the cameras, Kealey was unwilling to further provoke the guards. Shrugging off the pack once more, he reached inside and withdrew a small nylon case. Inside were a number of picks and rakes, all of which had been legally acquired through ESP Lock Products, a company based out of Leominster, Massachusetts.

Selecting a standard diamond pick and a dual-tension wrench, he clamped the Maglite between his teeth and set to work on the lock, applying torque with the wrench as he felt for the pins, manipulating the pick with his thumb and forefinger. After a short while, he'd pushed all of the pins past the shear line, allowing the cylinder to turn to the right. Moving the wrench to the opposite side, he repeated the process, and the cylinder turned to the left. Holding his breath, he pulled open the door. Nothing happened. Stepping inside, he found the backup alarm, a keypad placed next to the door. He punched in the four-digit code, praying it would work, knowing it probably wouldn't. The source had been out of the picture for months. During that time, people had been hired, fired, promoted, sent back to Europe . . . The code would not be the same.

But it was. The alarm stopped beeping, and he moved forward into the building.

CHAPTER 30

WASHINGTON, D.C.

For Ryan Kealey, embassies were not a place of sanctuary. At no time in the past had that fact been more apparent. During his years with the Agency, he could count on the fingers of one hand the number of times he'd operated with official cover, which would have afforded him the safety net of diplomatic immunity. He had, however, visited dozens of embassies over the course of his short career. As such, he would have had a good idea of what he was walking into, even without the ORACLE source. Owing to their relatively small size, most U.S. embassies and consulates were monitored from a single room, known as Post One, which could usually be found right inside the front door, for the purpose of intimidating the few guests whose intentions were less than honorable. It was from this small space that the entire building was monitored, everything from the grounds to the fire doors to the CCTV cameras and the exterior lighting. In U.S. embassies, Post One was manned during the workday by a specially trained team of marine security guards, while after-hours exterior security, in an oft-overlooked display of diplomacy, was usually provided by contract guards from the host country.

In this building, exterior security was limited to the gatehouse on Reservoir Road. Post One was represented by the security booth on the south side of the chancery, staffed at this early hour by just two men. The guards were not capable of monitoring the whole building, at least not effectively, but Kealey still felt on edge as he moved through the darkened halls, following Naomi's instructions over the radio. He had already realized that her help was invaluable; without her guidance, his progress would have been slowed substantially. She directed him through a maze of offices and conference rooms on the ground floor, keeping him as far from the booth as possible. Soon he was in the stairwell, making his way up to the third floor, the home of the administrative department.

The passenger seat of the Taurus was strewn with paper and diagrams depicting the chancery's layout. Naomi was doing her best to arrange the unruly pile when Kealey's next transmission came over the radio. She pressed her earpiece more firmly into position, but she wasn't quite fast enough, and she missed part of the message.

"Sorry, I didn't catch that. Say it again."

"I need to get through a cipher lock. Room 304."

She grabbed a handful of paper and flipped through it as quickly as possible. She wasn't expecting a miracle, but when a page slipped out of her hands and fell to the floor, she snatched it up and saw it was the right one. "It's on the list. The code is seven, four, one, three."

"Okay." There was a pause as he punched it in. "I'm in."

"Right, the next thing you'll need is the administrator password." She was rifling through the loose pages. "If you'll give me a second, I have it right here—"

"I remember it," he said, cutting her off. She heard distant tapping over the line, then, "Okay, I just logged on. I'm bringing up the file now."

She waited as long as she could, but the silence was too much. "Ryan, did it work? What came up?"

"Just a minute . . . Yeah, it worked. Everything's here. Fitness reports, commendations, reprimands, even a forwarding address. He's in Germany, Naomi. The bastard's in Berlin."

She breathed a prolonged sigh of relief. She was slightly amazed it had worked. Raiding the chancery had been a long shot from the very start, but now, against all odds, they had what they needed. "Okay, let me know when you . . . oh, my God."

There was a short, uncertain pause, then, "Naomi? Naomi, what happened? What's wrong?"

She couldn't respond; she couldn't even breathe. Her heart was in her throat, her eyes wide and locked to the rearview mirror.

A D.C. Metro police car had slowed to a stop directly behind her vehicle. As she watched with rising panic, the officer behind the wheel stepped out of the cruiser, adjusted his belt, and started toward the Taurus.

On the third floor of the chancery, Kealey had seated himself at one of the desks and was working the keys as fast as he could. He was struck by how easy everything had turned out once he was inside the building. The computer had readily accepted the password contained in the ORACLE file, giving him access to the entire database. There was a wealth of information at his fingertips. Normally, he would have taken the time to copy everything to a high-capacity zip disk, but given the circumstances, he wasn't interested in learning which members of the German diplomatic community were actually professional intelligence officers. All he cared about was finding Thomas Rühmann.

Using an integrated search engine, he narrowed the parameters to the two years that the Austrian arms broker had worked at the embassy. He was waiting for the computer to kick up the results when Naomi's faint voice came over the radio. It was clear she was speaking to herself, but the edge to her voice was unmistakable.

At first, he thought she had come across something unusual in the file, but when the radio stayed silent, he knew something was wrong. He immediately pressed the TRANSMIT button and asked her what was happening.

"Ryan . . ." The single word was nearly inaudible, arriving as a strained wheeze over the line. She sounded like she was in the throes of an asthma attack. "There's a police car behind me. I can see the officer through the windshield. I think he's running the tags right now."

"What?" His mind raced to find a solution, but he was stuck on the fact that she had the ORACLE file in the car. No matter what happened, they could not let that folder out of their hands. "You have to get out of there. Right now. You can't let him—"

"Where am I supposed to go?" she asked frantically. "I can't lose him. It's too early. There's no traffic. Oh, shit, he's getting out of the car. What do I do? Ryan, *what do I do?*"

"Naomi, listen to me. You have to . . . Naomi? Naomi!"

She was gone. He couldn't hear anything over the radio. Even static would have been preferable to that terrible silence.

Breathing a soft curse, he exited the program with a few keystrokes, then deleted the history. Standing, he reached for his pack, slung it over his shoulders, and turned toward the door. Only then did he realize he was not alone in the room. Two men were blocking his path. Both were wearing the austere blue uniform of the embassy security detail, and both had 9mm pistols leveled at his chest.

CHAPTER 31

WASHINGTON, D.C.

"2054, D.C. I need you to run a tag for me."

Officer First Class Steve Lowe ran a hand over his fleshy, clean-shaven face and peered through the windshield, eyes locked to the car parked in front of his cruiser. The call had come in a few minutes earlier, and as one of just 8 beat officers in PSA (Police Service Area) 205 in the 2nd District, he'd had little choice but to respond. Two of the other cars were responding to an 11-6—shots fired—which left Lowe to deal with this minor incident.

Suspicious vehicle reported in Senate Heights . . . He shook his head wearily. Like 90 percent of these calls, it was probably nothing: somebody locked out and waiting for spare keys to arrive, or a spurned lover parked outside her ex's house, hoping to beg for a second chance. Everyone had a story, of course, but over the years, Lowe had learned how to tell the truth from the bullshit. He'd also learned how to interpret a scene on sight. The car he was looking at now—a late-model Ford Taurus—was not setting off his internal alarm. From what he could see, there was just one person inside, and it looked like a woman, as the call had suggested. This was something he could handle alone, which was a good thing. His partner was out sick, along with half of the force. Normally he would have picked up a spare man for the shift, but the flu had decimated the department's ranks. Lowe didn't mind in the least. Frankly, he preferred to ride alone. He despised his partner, and the feeling was mutual. In fact, he was barely on speaking terms with just about every officer in the 2nd District.

It had started a year earlier. The first whispers cropped up when several officers in his squad had been called into the lieutenant's office to answer for minor infractions. Lowe had been present when each incident took place, which made him the only possible source of the leaks. The rumors had never been verified, but they had earned him the worst kind of reputation a cop could have: that of a man willing to narc out his fellow officers. Worse still, it appeared he was willing to betray them for nothing more than a chance to advance his career. The irony was that he had been angling for assignment to Internal Affairs all along. His aspirations were well known within the department, and they only reinforced the prevailing rumors.

Lowe didn't care what they thought of him; he had the right pedigree, the right education, and the right connections, all of it hard earned. Nothing else mattered: not the disgusted look on the face of the lieutenant, which she'd worn even as she'd mouthed the appropriate words, commending him for doing the right thing; not the rejection of the so-called blue brotherhood, that supposedly upstanding group of ignorant, narrow-minded assholes; and certainly not this bitch of a dispatcher, who seemed to have made it her life's mission to send his calls to the bottom of the list.

Irritated by the delay, he snatched up his radio and repeated the call. "2054, D.C. Can you run these tags or what?"

The woman's voice, completely neutral, came back after a lengthy pause. "Go ahead, 2054."

"I'm on Hoban Road in Senate Heights, just off the two thousand block of Reservoir Road. The car is a blue Ford Taurus, Virginia tag, Victor-Paul-David 7376."

Half a minute passed, then, "2054, that vehicle comes back to James Dobson. It's registered to an address in Richmond. No 29."

Lowe nodded to himself. "No 29" meant that the vehicle had not been reported stolen. It was another reassuring sign. A woman alone in a car . . . She was probably just lost. This would be easy to handle. "D.C., I'm going to check it out."

He got out of his car and adjusted his belt, tucking it under his paunch. Then he checked to make sure his radio was on the primary channel. As he started toward the Taurus, he heard the officers responding to the 11-6 clearing the call. He briefly considered requesting a second unit—"contact and cover," which required two people, was SOP when approaching a vehicle—but decided against it. They would take forever to show up anyway. From where he was standing, he could see the woman's face in the side mirror. She looked a little nervous, but that wasn't unusual. Maybe she'd never been approached by a police officer. Lowe smirked to himself. He knew that some people couldn't differentiate between being approached and being arrested. Maybe she thought she was going to jail for no reason at all.

He reached the driver's side window and tapped the glass. The car wasn't running, but the window slid down, so the key was in the ignition. He took note of that fact as the driver offered a strained smile and said, "Hi, Officer. What can I do for you?"

Lowe caught the accent right away. That voice was something all by itself, but she was a good-looking woman, too: in her midtwenties, he guessed, with shoulder-length black hair, green eyes, and a cute little nose. He unconsciously smoothed his thinning blond hair and smiled broadly, revealing crooked teeth and more than a scrap of his evening meal.

"Good evening, ma'am. Or morning, I should say."

She looked at her watch and laughed, but there was something forced about it. "Yes, I suppose you could say that."

"Can I ask what you're doing out here?"

"My car clunked out on me," she said, sounding exasperated. "As luck would have it, I just lapsed on my AAA, too." She shrugged her shoulders and laughed again. "Just one of those days, I guess."

"Where are you coming from?"

"Richmond," she replied, without hesitation. "I'm going to visit my mother. Or at least I was."

"Did you manage to get hold of a tow truck?"

"Yes, I did. Mike's Towing. I got the name from directory assistance. They should be here shortly."

Lowe nodded politely. "And where does your mother live, if you don't mind my asking?"

". . . Baltimore. Just outside of Baltimore, I mean."

He couldn't help but take note of the pause. It could be the truth, but it seemed a little strange; even the least capable traveler could hardly stray this far off course, engine trouble or not. He checked the woman's hands for the second time; they were still in her lap, one clasped over the other. *Good.* Scanning the passenger seat, he saw a hooded pullover resting on the cushion. He couldn't see what might be beneath the article of clothing, but he remembered seeing a blur of motion when he'd first flashed his lights, and he couldn't help but wonder what the sweater might be covering. His curiosity was piqued by the loose papers scattered over the floor. All of a sudden, he had the feeling that something wasn't right here.

"Well, I'm sure she'll be happy to see you, ma'am," he said tonelessly. "May I see your license and registration, please?"

She didn't reply right away, her mouth working silently. "Is that really necessary? I mean, I was just sitting here—"

"I'm afraid it is. You see, we received a complaint about your vehicle, so we have to be thorough."

"Well, I don't have it on me, actually. In fact, I don't have any ID at all."

"What about the registration?"

"I, umm . . ." She made a show of looking in the glove compartment. "I don't have that either. Listen, Officer, I—"

"Whose car is this?"

"It belongs to my boyfriend."

"Ma'am, I'm going to need you to step out of the car. You can take the keys with you."

"Officer, I really don't think—"

"Step out of the car, please. Right now."

He'd added a note of authority that time, and she complied right away, pushing the door out toward him. He stepped back to let her out, then said, "Move to the front of the vehicle, please, and put your hands on the hood. Are you carrying anything I need to know about? A weapon of any kind, needles, anything like that?"

"No, of course not." She was indignant but complied readily, leaning against the fender and opening her stance. He took a long moment to admire the view. "Are you even allowed to do this?" she asked. "I haven't done anything wrong."

Lowe ignored the question. He patted her down slowly, using the backs of his hands as regulations required, but not without a tinge of regret. Technically speaking, he was feeling for anything solid, anything lumping beneath the dark, loose-fitting clothes. That was another thing, the way she was dressed . . . not suspicious in itself, but something to file away.

She didn't appear to be armed. Satisfied, he stepped back. "Ma'am, I'd like to search your vehicle. Do you mind?"

"Do I . . . ? Yes, I do mind." She raised her level of indignation, knowing he would only expect it if she truly had nothing to hide. "That's completely uncalled for."

He nodded slowly, wondering how far he wanted to take this. In truth, the woman's story made perfect sense: she had engine trouble; she was waiting for help. She knew the name of a local tow company, and her tags had checked out. Still, he couldn't ignore his instincts, and they were telling him that something was wrong with this whole situation. His radio stuttered to life. He listened for anything interesting, but it was just another unit clearing a call.

Lowe gripped her right arm just above the elbow and steered her toward his cruiser. She stiffened under his grasp, but didn't try to resist. "I'm going to have you sit in my car for a few minutes while we sort this out."

"But why?" she asked, her voice beginning to climb. "This is ridiculous. I haven't done anything wrong!"

"Then you won't mind answering a few questions." He moved to open the rear door, but before he could, she caught his eye and spoke again in a more reasonable tone.

"Officer, do I really need to sit in the back?" She gave him a pleading look. "I mean, it's not like I'm under arrest, right?"

He looked at her, then back at the car. It was true; she hadn't really done anything wrong, and he didn't want to invite a harassment charge at a later date. Besides, he'd rather have her up front, anyway. At the very least, it would give him something to look at for the next thirty minutes or so.

"Fine," he said, guiding her round to the passenger side. He opened the front door, and she reluctantly got in. "Just wait here," he ordered. "I'll be back in a minute."

*   *   *

Once the door was closed, Naomi quickly composed herself and watched intently as the officer walked to the front of his car, unhooking his shoulder mic. As he turned away and faced the embassy grounds, she sat up and checked out the cruiser. She didn't bother trying the door, as there was nowhere to go. Looking down to her left, she examined the radio mounted between the seats. The chatter was audible, and the green LED light showed a "1," which she assumed was the primary channel. She listened for the officer's voice, which was nasally, unpleasant, and easy to catch, but heard nothing she recognized. She quickly decided he must be transmitting on a secondary channel.

She nearly pressed her ear to the window in an attempt to hear what was happening, but stopped herself in time, realizing how futile the gesture would be. He could be double-checking the tags on the Taurus, or he could be calling his patrol supervisor. Her panic was starting to get the best of her. She had done her best to seem disadvantaged but not incapable. After all, she needed him to leave; it wouldn't do to have him sitting around, waiting for a tow truck that would never arrive. Unfortunately, he hadn't bought her act, and now, the only thing working in her favor was that she had talked herself out of the backseat, where she would have been completely vulnerable, stripped of all her options.

She swore under her breath, second-guessing her actions, wondering how else she could have handled it. It might have been better to just hand over her real ID, but the officer might have detained her anyway, and she couldn't risk being listed on a police report. It would be too easy to link her to the embassy break-in at a later date, as she was parked so close to the building. Ideally, she would have had a false ID to satisfy a casual inspection, but even if Harper had been willing to go that far out on a limb, there just hadn't been time to get one forged. Besides, forging an ID for a mid-level analyst would have raised a lot of questions. It also would have meant bringing too many people into the loop, and in this case, that simply wasn't an option.

Things were not looking good right now, but they had the potential to get much worse. If a detective was called down to take over the questioning, she would never get rid of them in time. Ryan would be making his way through the grounds; from his last transmission, she knew he had found what they needed. All he had to do now was get out of the building and back to the car.

Maybe he'll spot the cruiser and walk away, she thought. Naomi didn't think he would leave her, but given the situation, it might be the best thing. She couldn't be arrested; she hadn't done anything wrong. They might hold her for questioning, but if she stuck to her story, they would have no choice but to let her go. On the other hand, if they managed to dig up probable cause—or at least enough to convince a magistrate—they could get a warrant to search the Taurus. And if that happened, one of the first things they would find was the file on the front seat.

With this thought, she felt suddenly sick. The ORACLE file contained enough damaging information to drag the Agency through the mud for the next five years. Needless to say, its public disclosure would also completely destroy her career. Letting them search the car was not an option.

She looked through the windshield. From where she was sitting, the chancery was barely visible, a black smudge over the treetops. She peered into the darkness, searching in vain for the smallest sign of movement.

Come on, Ryan. Where are you?

CHAPTER 32

WASHINGTON, D.C.

O n the third floor of the chancery, Kealey sprung into action. He reached out for the gun in the hand of the closest guard, shouting at the top of his lungs to distract them. He had been in this kind of situation before and knew almost nothing would work in his favor. One man was easy to handle—even easier to outwit—but two was a different proposition altogether. Even with the bare minimum of training, the guards would be hard-pressed to miss him at this range. At the same time, he guessed they would be reluctant to fire. As German nationals, they would have endured the compulsory nine months of military or civil service, but embassy duty did not typically draw the best and the brightest. They might be covering each other properly, but they would be slow to pull the trigger, fearing the inevitable fallout. His only chance was to play on that hesitation, using the one point in his favor for all it was worth.

As it turned out, he was wrong; the gun went off as Kealey closed his left hand around the guard's wrist, his right coming down in a hammer blow on the radial nerve. The 9mm slipped from the guard's limp hand and fell to the floor. The man near the door was screaming something in German, but Kealey ignored him, turning the incapacitated guard around and drawing his Beretta at the same time.

He wrapped his left arm around the throat of his hostage and jammed the muzzle into his lower back, then crouched behind the

German, trying to make himself as small a target as possible. He could feel something burning in his left side and knew he was hit; the guard's single round had found its target. It was a sickening realization; until he looked, he had no way of knowing how bad the wound actually was. It could be a scratch, or it could be life-threatening. The pain had not yet realized its full potential, but that would change in a matter of seconds.

The guard near the door was still shouting commands in his native language. He was clearly out of control; his eyes were like blue saucers, wide and irrational. The gun was moving all over the place; obviously, he did not have a shot from that angle, but was desperately trying to find one. Kealey had time here, but only a little. Naomi needed his help; that much was clear, but until he got past these two guards, he could not do a thing for her. He only hoped that she had the good sense to stall.

Raising his head by a tiny fraction, he spoke quietly into the ear of his hostage. "What's your name?"

"My . . . ?"

"*Your name*," Kealey hissed, adding a menacing edge to his tone.

"Klein. My name is Gunter Klein. Please, I have a daughter in Bonn. . . ."

"Relax, Gunter." He winced; the pain was getting worse. If it was only a flesh wound, it was a bad one. "I want you to tell your friend to drop his weapon. Do it now."

He knew the man near the door spoke English; it was an unwritten rule for embassy postings in Washington. But Kealey also knew the instruction would carry more weight if it came from his own countryman. Klein, clearly terrified, stumbled over the few necessary words. The man at the door replied with a short verbal barrage, but didn't release the gun.

"He won't do it. He says you'll kill us both."

"I won't. . . ." Kealey swore under his breath and made a decision. There was no convincing them, and this was taking too long. The bite in his side was nearly intolerable, and he could feel something warm running over his hip; it wouldn't be long before the wound started to slow him down. *Fuck it.*

He straightened and pushed Klein aside, exposing his body for the briefest of moments. Then he leveled his weapon and squeezed the trigger.

The bullet tore into the guard's right arm, just above the elbow, shattering bone. He screamed and the gun jumped out of his hand, clattering across the ceramic tile. A split second later, Kealey stepped to the left and slammed a fist into Klein's face, sending him staggering into a nearby desk. A chair flipped over, and papers scattered across the floor. The other guard was reaching down for his gun with his good arm, his left hand wrapping around the grip. Crossing the few feet between them, Kealey kicked it out of his hand at the last possible second. Then he administered two judicious blows to the face. The man fell back to the floor and stopped moving.

Kealey looked back at Gunter Klein. He was clearly unconscious, his body immobile. Kealey quickly retrieved their weapons, as well as their radios. They would have already made the call, but should they wake before he was clear of the building, there was no point in giving them the opportunity to provide more information. Nor did he want to catch a bullet in the back on his way out.

He ejected the magazines on both of the weapons and shucked the rounds out of the chambers. Then he pulled the batteries out of one of the radios. The second radio he put in his pocket, along with the batteries, rounds, and the spare magazines, both of which could be used with his own Beretta. He left the guns and the spare radio, now useless, on one of the desks, then moved toward the door, shooting a quick glance at the guards. Neither had moved. Only when he was out in the hall did he remember the backpack; he could have simply dumped all of the gear inside and saved himself some time, but that couldn't be helped now.

He kept moving forward, jogging toward the stairwell. Soon he was out of the building, making his way through the darkened grounds, heading north. Again he heard a wail in the distance, but this time the sirens were drawing closer, and there were many more of them. It was just as he feared: the chancery guards had made the call before confronting him. He couldn't help but wonder how they had learned he was in the building, but he knew it was no longer important. All that mattered now was getting back to Naomi.

Behind him, an alarm started to sound, lights coming up in the chancery. At the same time, hidden security lamps flickered up from the grass; it was as if the earth itself was conspiring against him.

He was gasping for air, the pain like a hacksaw blade digging into his side. He ignored it and ran harder.

"You know, I don't think this is legal. You can't hold me unless you have a reason."

"Actually, I can," Lowe replied in a bored tone. He had tried to ingratiate himself, but the woman had yet to respond to his mild flirtations, and he was beginning to lose interest. "Listen, ma'am, you should have just answered my questions. We could have saved ourselves a lot of trouble."

"I *did* answer your questions, and I answered them truthfully. I don't understand the need for this."

"And I don't understand why you're still waiting for a tow truck at this hour of the morning. What time did you place the call again?"

Naomi took a deep, stalling breath and looked down at her hands. It was becoming more and more difficult to evade the officer's inquiries. He had climbed back into the car a few minutes earlier, and he'd been peppering her with questions ever since.

"Officer Lowe, I already explained this to you. My engine started to make this strange noise on I-95, so I got off to look for a hotel. I thought I'd just find a mechanic in the morning. But then I got turned around and ended up here, which is when the engine died completely. So I called for a tow truck, and that's when you showed up. You knocked on my window a second later . . . literally." She allowed a note of indignation to creep into her voice. "If anything in there constitutes a crime, I'd like to know what it is."

"No," he replied patiently, "nothing you've done is a crime. But I do find it interesting that you decided to take an eight-hour trip starting so late in the day. More to the point, you left Richmond without ID or the registration to your car. Most people remember those kinds of things."

"It was stupid, I know. But it doesn't really matter, does it? It's not like I can go anywhere. Once the tow truck shows up, I'll catch a taxi to a hotel. Believe me, Officer, the first thing I'll do is call my boyfriend and get him to send me my license. Or maybe I'll have him drive up and give it to me. Either way, this problem is easily solved."

"You'd think so," Lowe said, shifting his weight in his seat. "But I'm afraid I can't leave you here, Ms. Brown."

Naomi did not react; after debating the risks, she'd decided it was better to give him a false name rather than nothing at all.

"I've already called my sergeant," Lowe continued. "As soon as he gets down here, he's going to have a little talk with you, but either way, you're going to have to stay in the city tonight. You're welcome to use the phone at the station . . . Maybe your boyfriend can overnight your license, as you suggested. With a little bit of luck, you'll be on your way to Baltimore first thing tomorrow morning."

Naomi felt a stab of panic, her throat constricting. She quickly looked out the window to hide her reaction. It was what she had feared all along. He must have made the call when he was out of the car. In doing so, he had sealed her fate; there was absolutely no way she could get out of this.

Commanding herself to relax, she tried to think of anything she might have missed. There had to be a solution. As her mind raced to find one, the radio sputtered to life.

"All units in PSA 205, this is D.C. 10-95 reported at the German Embassy on Reservoir Road. Shots fired, repeat, shots fired. All available units respond."

Naomi froze, aware of the intense silence that followed the call. She couldn't bring herself to face him, but she knew exactly what the officer had to be thinking; she was parked right next to the embassy, and she had refused to let him search her vehicle. It wouldn't take a genius to connect the dots.

Lowe grabbed for the radio. "2054, D.C. I'm still in the area. I, uh, may have a subject of interest with respect to that call—"

He was cut off by a sudden flurry of activity outside the car. Their heads snapped forward simultaneously as lights exploded on the other side of the black-iron fence. At the same time, a distant alarm began to scream. It was piercingly loud, even inside the cruiser. Neither of them really had time to react; a few seconds later, a dark figure crossed the fence in the distance and began jogging in their direction.

* * *

From the moment Kealey crossed the fence and stepped into Fox-hall Road, everything inside the car started to move much faster. Muttering something under his breath, Lowe reached for his gun, his left hand moving to open the door. It was clear he had made the con-nection between the call and what he was seeing. As his hand moved down to the right side of his belt, Naomi knew she had to do some-thing, anything, to stop him from getting out of the car and drawing the weapon on Ryan. Without thinking, she reached over and grabbed Lowe's right hand with both of hers just as the gun came out of the holster. Shocked by this unexpected assault, he shouted for her to stop and pulled his arm up violently, trying to break her grasp. Naomi held on desperately, even as her elbow smashed painfully against the dash in the struggle.

She had picked a fight she couldn't win; that much was immedi-ately obvious. He was much stronger than her to begin with, and she didn't have any leverage. To make matters worse, there were a num-ber of obstacles in her way, including the radio and the dash-mounted laptop. Still, she held on with all her strength, struggling to keep his gun hand immobilized. Through the windshield, she saw Ryan run-ning hard toward the cruiser, though something about his stride seemed a little bit off. . . .

Without warning, Naomi was blinded by a sudden flash of light. Momentarily stunned by the muzzle blast and the deafening noise, she released her grip and raised her hands instinctively. For a brief, terrifying instant, she thought she'd been shot in the face, but the pain never came. A split second later, the driver's side door was yanked open. Lowe swung in his seat to counter this new threat as Kealey reached inside, grabbed him by the hair, and pulled him out of the car. Lowe was still screaming as his feet left the cruiser, firing his weapon without regard for his aim. One round missed Naomi's right side by less than an inch, slamming into the passenger-side door; another whined past her ear and punched a hole in the roof. The next four drilled into the dash, the fifth exiting the windshield.

As the sound of gunfire faded into the night, replaced by the scream of approaching sirens, Naomi thought she heard a pair of sharp, brutal blows. She couldn't be sure; for the moment, she was completely disoriented, her ears ringing, her head thumping. She found herself wedged against the door, trying to make herself as small a target as possible. She couldn't see what was happening, and she wondered why, before realizing that her eyes were still squeezed tightly shut. Just as she found the courage to open them, the passenger-side door was pulled open, and a familiar hand reached in for hers.

Naomi could see he was hurt from the moment her feet touched the pavement. He was favoring his left side, and as she pulled him into the light, she could see that his face was drawn, pale, and shining with sweat. There was blood on his hands and a large wet stain on his shirt, barely discernable against the dark material.

"Oh, God, what *happened?*" she asked anxiously. She moved to examine the wound, but Kealey waved her away.

"Don't worry about it. Are you hit?"

She looked down and performed a quick visual check. She didn't see any blood, and nothing seemed to hurt except for her elbow, which was still throbbing painfully. "No, I'm fine."

"Good." Still holding his side, Kealey pointed toward the unconscious officer. "Take his radio." The words were pinched off at the end; clearly, he was in considerable pain. "Get rid of it, and cuff his hands. He'll have the keys in his pocket. Make sure you get them, too. Hurry."

She was already moving. Kneeling, she stripped off the officer's shoulder mic, following the wires to the radio itself, which she pulled off the belt. Wrapping it all into an untidy ball, she tossed it into a bush near the sidewalk. Then she turned over the body, pulled the limp arms back to the rear, and snapped the cuffs into place. After a second of rummaging, she found the handcuff keys in a spare magazine pouch and slipped them into her pocket. "Done."

Kealey was leaning against the front of the cruiser. Wincing, he straightened and started toward the passenger side of the Taurus. "We have to move. The responding units will be here in less than a minute. You have the car keys?"

"Got 'em." She hesitated. "Ryan, you have to get to a hospital."

He shook his head in the negative. "I already checked it out. Trust me, it's not as bad as it looks."

"But—"

"Naomi, we don't have time to argue. Get in the car."

She did as he asked. Starting the engine, she put the Taurus into drive, accelerated quickly, and swung a hard right onto Reservoir Road. As the screeching alarm started to fade, it all seemed to catch up with her. The adrenaline dissipated quickly enough, but even as her breathing returned to normal, her hands just wouldn't stop shaking. As she struggled to regain control, she turned in her seat and said, "So where are we going?"

Kealey looked down at his side and grimaced. The options were few. A hospital was clearly out; the police would be monitoring emergency-room activity, watching for someone to be admitted with a gunshot wound. At the same time, he knew he needed immediate medical attention. The truth was staring him right in the face. He had shot a man in the German chancery, and he had brutally assaulted a police officer. There was only one place to seek refuge, just one place beyond the reach of the D.C. Metro Police Department.

"Langley," he said through gritted teeth. "We're going to Langley."

CHAPTER 33

LONDON

Mid-afternoon in the heart of the West End. The skies above were gray and fatigued, the sort of overcast weather that promised rain, but would never deliver. They were sitting outside the Embankment Café, which was surrounded by bright green grass, towering hedges, and trees wielding their colorful autumn leaves. Beyond the trees and a dirty brick wall, the River Thames curved on a gentle, slow-moving arc to the south, Waterloo Bridge to the east.

Vanderveen had ordered a full English breakfast of eggs, bacon, chips, and beans, but Raseen had settled on black tea. As she sipped from the steaming cup, she kept shooting him little glances across the dingy plastic table. Vanderveen was guessing they were based partly on what had happened the night before and partly on how he looked now, which was considerably different. He had decided to switch passports shortly after they checked out of the hotel in Calais, which naturally meant a change in appearance. Now he was traveling as Russell Davies, a British national. The dark hair was gone, as were the beard and the tinted contacts. As with Tartus, he had returned to his natural state, although his blond hair and green eyes were much better suited to the streets of London than they were to a dusty Syrian souq.

Raseen had changed her persona as well, but her features were much less malleable, and her various passports reflected this fact. Anything other than her original hair color would look highly unusual, only increasing her visibility in a crowd. As a result, she had wisely stayed close to her natural look in all the photographs that accompanied her forged documents. The French passport she was using now—which had passed Vanderveen's careful inspection—bore the name Nina Sebbar.

She had suggested they check out of the hotel the night before, but he had refused, knowing it would look more suspicious to leave in the middle of the night than it would to wait for morning. At the same time, he had not gotten much sleep, as part of him had been waiting for the police to kick down the door. The raid had never come, but the restless night meant an early morning. They made the first ferry from Calais to Dover, endured the standard customs check on arrival, then caught a National Express bus to London. From Waterloo Station, it was a short taxi ride to the Embankment. They had arrived with an hour to spare, which was enough time to partake in a leisurely meal and watch for lingering eyes.

Embankment Café at noon. A man will sit outside, gray suit, green paisley tie. He'll be carrying a black attaché case and a copy of the Times. *Follow him, and keep your distance.*

Vanderveen had no patience for these little games, but he had no choice but to play along. He needed what the controllers had to offer; namely, the specifics regarding Thomas Rühmann and his office in Berlin. The Austrian's business relationship with the insurgency had started long before Vanderveen arrived on the scene. He had met Rühmann only once, and briefly at that. The purpose of the meeting was to describe the kind of weapon he needed for the attack in New York, and Rühmann had come through in spectacular form. Of course, circumstances had changed since then, and now, through little or no fault of his own, he had become a liability to the whole operation. The word had been sent up the line, sealing his fate.

Time was the other factor here. For the moment, Vanderveen had no idea what Kealey was up to. He had to wait for the wheels to turn in Washington, which meant that he had to move faster than he might otherwise have liked. He had every intention of placing a second call to the States by the end of the day, but for now, there were other things to consider.

Raseen lowered her cup to the table and leaned forward conspiratorially. "Russell, can we talk here?"

Vanderveen cast a subtle glance around. Due to the weather, the tables on the terrace were nearly deserted. The closest patrons were four tables over, but judging by their advanced age, elevated voices, and blunt Estuary accents, they would not be able to understand—or even hear—a murmured conversation in French from the next table, let alone at a distance of 15 feet.

Vanderveen smiled and said, "If you think it's safe to talk, Nina, you don't need to call me Russell."

She smiled back demurely but without hesitation, and Vanderveen shook his head in amusement. Her unflinching ability to blend into her surroundings was something that continued to amaze him. Despite the privileged upbringing that al-Tikriti had described, Yasmin Raseen had spent her youth in a country that hindered women at almost every turn. He had not seen her wear a headscarf, yet she appeared at ease without it. He had not seen her pray once—let alone five times a day—yet she appeared unrepentant. The holy month of Ramadan was scheduled to start in less than two weeks, and it was clear she had no intention of fasting. At every turn she had defied his ideas of how she should act. Her indulgence in Western behavior only made her presence more confusing. Her controllers, if they had their way, would severely limit the future liberation of Iraqi women. He could not understand her motivation in helping them.

"Will, how much do you know about the man we're going to meet?"

"Next to nothing. Why do you ask?"

She seemed to hesitate. "Doesn't it worry you? Not knowing, I mean? This man could have switched sides. He could be working against us."

"Perhaps," Vanderveen conceded. "But it's not likely. Take my word when I say that your people have a great deal of money and time invested in this. They're not going to risk the entire venture on a man they can't trust."

"But how do they know?" she persisted. "What if—"

"They can't know." Vanderveen leaned forward and lowered his voice, even though no one was close enough to hear. "The whole thing is a risk, but we don't have a choice. We *need* what this man is bringing us. Rühmann knows too much; not the target, perhaps, but he acquired the weapon. He knows what it can do, and he knows how it's disguised. He can't be allowed to live."

"I suppose you're right," she murmured. A few minutes passed. She finished her tea and ordered another pot as Vanderveen picked at his meal. The waitress hovered nearby, a pretty girl whose gaze had been locked on their table ever since they'd arrived. She had just stepped up to clear their plates when a flicker of movement caught Vanderveen's attention. A man in a gray suit and green tie was taking a seat on the other side of an enormous concrete planter, which, at this time of year, was filled with nothing more than sandy soil and cigarette butts. The newcomer placed his briefcase down by his feet, unfolded his paper, and signaled the waitress. Seeing this, Vanderveen leaned back in his seat and looked at Raseen.

"You might as well make yourself comfortable," he said. "I think we're going to be here a while."

An hour slipped past. Raseen ordered a basket of scones as the surrounding tables started to fill, despite the overcast skies. Vanderveen both welcomed and despised the lunch-hour crowd, which was made up of weary tourists, well-groomed clerks from the Strand, and government workers from Somerset House. The other patrons helped them to blend in, but also made it much harder to detect surveillance.

He had been watching closely since they boarded the ferry in France, and felt reasonably sure they had not been followed. Unfortunately, he could not say the same for the courier. To make matters worse, he was struck by the same tingling sensation he'd felt the previous night in Calais. His instincts were telling him something was wrong, and yet, he had no choice but to go forward with the meet. If they pulled out now, they would lose valuable hours—even days— setting up a second attempt. That was time they just didn't have. More to the point, al-Douri might begin to question his commitment, and he would undoubtedly forfeit the second half of his fee. Vanderveen had no intention of letting that happen.

Finally, the man in the gray suit called for the check. Vanderveen didn't need to follow suit; he had already paid for their meal. From the corner of his eye, he watched as the courier stood, collected his briefcase, and left the terrace. He was clearly visible for some time as he moved northwest through the little park, heading toward the Strand. Once he was nearly out of sight, Vanderveen rose to his feet and slipped a few pounds under an empty glass. Raseen took his arm, and they left the terrace in turn, following at a discreet distance.

The Strand, running from the west end of Fleet Street to Trafalgar Square, the site of the National Gallery, is one of the busiest streets in London. In a city with nearly 8 million inhabitants, "busy" can be a very misleading term. Although the Strand was home to a wide variety of shops, theatres, and restaurants, the congestive vehicular traffic should have done much to dissuade tourists, Vanderveen thought. Nevertheless, the street was completely packed. If there was any surveillance in place, it would be almost impossible to spot. It was this fact that was troubling him as he walked northeast with the flow, Raseen's arm tucked loosely beneath his own. The man in the gray suit was 30 feet ahead of them, his dark head weaving in and out of sight. There was a constant din: the sound of rushing feet as pedestrians swept past, jabbering into their cell phones; the noise spilling from the open doors of the restaurants and pubs; and the steady rumble of traffic a few feet to their left. Exhaust poured over the sidewalk in a thick, constant cloud, but nobody seemed to notice. When a sound emanated from the folds of Raseen's new coat, it took her a few seconds to realize her phone was ringing. She pulled it out with a puzzled expression. "Hello?"

She handed it over, and Vanderveen lifted the phone to his ear. "Do you know the Savoy?"

The voice bore the crisp, upper-class diction of Eton or Sandhurst, which was fitting; the Savoy was one of London's oldest and finest hotels, located only a few blocks away, close to the river. "Yes."

"I need to collect a package at the concierge. Wait in the bar for twenty minutes, then head upstairs. Room 508. The desk will call up for you."

Vanderveen hesitated before realizing he could use any name he wished. The clerk would not ask for identification, just the number of the room he wanted to call. "Agreed. Twenty minutes."

The phone went dead, and he handed it back to Raseen. "You should have told me you gave him the number," she whispered reprovingly. "I was going to get rid of that phone yesterday."

"We'll dump it before we leave the city."

"What did he say?"

He relayed the instructions, hesitated, then spoke his mind. "What do you think?"

"I don't know." Her voice dropped a notch, and she leaned in close, switching to French. "Something doesn't seem right. It's nothing I can see, but still . . ."

Vanderveen nodded uneasily. He slowed and stepped to the right, pretending to examine a shop window as people brushed past on the sidewalk. The overcast skies caused the window to act like a mirror, reflecting everything behind them. They stayed that way for about twenty seconds, looking for anything too familiar, ignoring the bright display of fall fashions. Raseen, looking deeply, deeply into the makeshift mirror, suddenly spoke up. "Green Opel. Right behind you."

Vanderveen tracked the car in the glass, straining to see through the slight gaps in the passing crowd. The small, two-door sedan was moving in the same direction they were, but apart from that, there was nothing unusual about it. There was one occupant—an older male, from what he could see. The vehicle was moving at a steady clip, and it passed from view a few seconds later, followed by a battered white van and a Renault hatchback.

He turned to find Raseen had worked her way to the edge of the street and was staring after the Opel. As he moved next to her, she said, "I saw the license the first time . . . R313 CVG."

"The *first* time?"

"The same car passed us about a minute ago. It was going in the same direction."

He had not seen her look for it, and she had been on his right arm, farthest from the street. "You're sure?"

"Yes, of course." Her voice was insistent, but it caught at the end. "I'm almost certain. One older man in the driver's seat, no passengers. He's wearing a blue shirt, I think, but that doesn't matter. It's the same car."

Vanderveen kept walking, wondering how she could have seen all that, given the speed of the passing traffic. She followed reluctantly. "Maybe he's lost," he said.

"He must have been driving very fast to make it around the block that quickly," she replied doubtfully, her mouth very close to his ear. "I know what I saw. We're being followed."

The whispered words sent a chill down his spine. He cast off the doubt and tried to think it through. What had she really seen? There was just one car. If they were using more than one vehicle, they wouldn't have stood out so easily. On the other hand, there might be watchers on foot, rotating in and out of the lead position. If that was the case, they wouldn't know until the trap was sprung.

Still, something didn't make sense. The only place they could have been picked out was at customs in Dover, and if that had happened, they would have been arrested on the spot. The Security Service wouldn't wait and risk losing its quarry. Neither would the Special Branch, and they certainly wouldn't attempt to apprehend their targets on a busy London street, where hostages were plentiful.

So if there was surveillance, Vanderveen realized, it was focused on the man they were planning to meet in less than thirty minutes. The realization filled him with a strange combination of apprehension, anger, and relief.

They passed a group of noisy teenage boys lounging in the doorway of a Pizza Hut. The young men stopped joking around to leer at Raseen as she walked past, but she was oblivious, her face troubled. Vanderveen waited patiently, giving her time to reach her own conclusion. As they continued walking, the restaurants started to fade away, to be replaced by the historic, weathered stone façades of the West End's theatre district. Finally, she leaned in and said, "It's not us. They would have moved in already, Will. They would have arrested us in Dover."

"I agree."

"Then we can't make the meet," she said, stating the obvious.

Vanderveen felt something cold and wet hit his hand, then his face, the drops coming down in rapid succession. The people passing by seemed to take it in stride. Umbrellas appeared out of nowhere, springing up into view like the bulbs in a flowering field. Raseen huddled close and pulled her hood over her dark head. "What are we going to do?" she asked, her voice muffled by the waterproof fabric in front of her face.

He thought for a moment, weighing the risks. One car meant they were watching the man in the gray suit, but they weren't ready to move. Pulling out was not an option; he couldn't afford to wait. It was worth the stretch.

"We're going ahead with it. Just stay on your toes, and be ready to do what I say."

Five minutes after Vanderveen and Raseen entered the lobby of the Savoy, the green Opel sedan shuddered to a halt on Southampton, a narrow road feeding into the Strand from the north. Ian Haines, the man in the driver's seat, picked a Starbucks container out of the holder between the seats, shook the empty cup, and scowled. Cracking a window, he unbuttoned his blue flannel shirt, pulled it off, and tossed it into the backseat. Underneath, he was wearing a plain gray T-shirt. The rain was starting to come harder now, rattling against the windshield as he thumbed the TRANSMIT button on his two-way radio. "Mike, what do you have?"

A hiss of static, then, "Nothing at the moment. I've got eyes on the front of the building."

"Good. You get anything useful?"

Mike Scott was easily the best photographer in the unit. He ran his own successful business on the side, shooting family portraits out of a small studio on the east end of Fleet Street. "I got him from both sides of the road. Kind of hard to pick out his face in the crowd, but I think we'll end up with some usable shots." A pause, then the other man said, "I'm bloody soaking out here."

Haines chuckled mildly. "Our relief shows up in an hour. You can hang on 'til then, right?"

"Whatever you say, mate. You're the boss."

Haines laughed again at the inside joke. He and Scott had worked together for six years, yet strangely enough, neither man knew where the other fell on the government pay scale. Both had served in the British Army, Scott with the Blues and Royals, Haines with the 2nd Battalion of the famed Parachute Regiment. Scott was by far the younger of the two, having left his unit as a corporal in '98. Haines, on the other hand, finished two tours in Northern Ireland during the late seventies, then went to the Falklands to play his part in the brief war with Argentina. He nearly applied to the Special Air Service—God knows his commanding officer had suggested it often enough—but more than a decade of sustained, bloody combat was enough for the young sergeant.

Instead, Haines decided to get out altogether, leaving the regiment in '84. After years of mediocre, unsatisfying jobs, he decided to apply for a position with the Security Service, otherwise known as MI5. The Service was primarily tasked with countering terrorist activity, both at home and abroad. He wasn't expecting much, considering he'd never attended university. Much to his surprise, he was vetted after an intensive screening process and assigned to a mobile surveillance unit.

Haines took to the work immediately; his only regret was that he hadn't applied sooner. The work was interesting, the scenery changed, and the job was not as physically challenging as he'd been led to believe. After his time with 2 PARA, everything else was easy by comparison, including the seventy-five-day training course the Service had put him through. Even now, at fifty-two years of age, Haines was by no means the oldest member of the unit. Watchers came in all shapes and sizes, and for good reason. Variety made a good surveillance team almost impossible to spot.

Looking over to the passenger seat, Haines lifted his copy of the *Times* and stared at the full-color photograph underneath. Generally speaking, members of the mobile surveillance unit were given very little information about the people they were assigned to track. Such was the case here; with respect to the man they were trailing now, Haines knew only the basics. Samir al-Askari was twenty-seven years old, a graduate of Eton College and the London School of Business. Currently, he was an account manager for the Export & Finance Bank in Amman; for this reason, he had been assigned the code name

"Banker." He had flown into Heathrow that morning on a Jordanian passport, and was immediately picked up by one of the watchers who staffed MI5's airport office. Interestingly enough, the watch list that named al-Askari had been generated by MI6, but it fell to the Security Service to keep tabs on him on British soil. Haines wasn't sure how al-Askari had earned himself a following, but to be honest, he didn't really care. All they had to do was keep track of him until the relief showed up, and then they could get an early jump on the weekend.

Haines glanced at his watch, then ran a hand through his iron gray hair. Fifty minutes to go.

They had used their time in the lobby efficiently. The shop on the ground floor offered a small selection of exorbitantly priced clothing, most of it bearing the Savoy logo. After a few minutes of searching, Vanderveen managed to find a plain navy ball cap and a black windbreaker, which he brought to the counter. Raseen picked out a bright red anorak with a detachable hood. Vanderveen frowned at the color, but there wasn't much else to choose from. Once he had paid, they made their way up to the fifth floor. Raseen tapped lightly on the door. It swung open, and they stepped inside.

Vanderveen moved into the room and looked around quickly, vaguely taking note of the cream-colored walls, dark wood, and opulent furnishings. The door from the hall opened into a small sitting room. Passing through, he poked his head into the bedroom, finding it empty. Closing the door, he turned and walked to the rain-streaked windows, where he pulled the drapes shut, blocking out an impressive view of the Thames and the South Bank. Then he opened the credenza, turned on the television, and upped the volume to a dull roar. Finally, he flicked on the lights and turned back to their host.

The courier had been watching all of this with a slight smile on his dark, narrow face, as if amused by the American's paranoia. Vanderveen was instantly annoyed; everything he had just done was based on common sense, and it should have already been taken care of. His mind was still locked on the car Raseen had pointed out, and the courier's seemingly lax attitude was doing nothing to improve his disposition.

"What do I call you?"

The courier shrugged. He had removed his suit jacket and loosened his tie. "It doesn't really matter, does it? I suppose you can call me Khalil."

"You have what I asked for?"

"Of course." He pointed toward the desk facing the windows. The black briefcase was on top, along with a large brown envelope and the torn remains of a FedEx overnight box.

Walking over, Vanderveen picked up the envelope and withdrew the contents. The first ten pages were typed. These would be notes thoroughly detailing the Austrian's security measures. Setting them aside for the moment, he picked out a stack of 8 x 10s. Each full-color photograph was taken from a different angle, though they all depicted the same building. Finally, he got to the last two shots. One bore the image of Rühmann's assistant. The other was a picture of Thomas Rühmann himself, obviously taken from a distance, but with a high-quality telescopic lens. The image resolution was remarkably clear.

"What's in the case?"

"Nothing. Just a few earnings reports to satisfy customs at Heathrow."

"Have you examined this file?"

"Of course," Khalil repeated. The knowing smirk returned to his face. "Who do you think took the pictures? I was ordered to compile an extensive dossier when we first entered into our relationship with Mr. Rühmann. You see, a group such as ours has to be prepared for all eventualities. As I'm sure you know, Mr. Vanderveen, information is the greatest commodity of all."

Vanderveen's head shot up, his eyes boring into those of the man standing 4 feet away. He could not disguise his astonishment, and as the seconds ticked past, it was a struggle to keep his control from slipping away . . . This man, this courier, who in all probability was being watched by the Security Service, knew his real name and his next target. Looking over to Raseen, he could see that she was equally stunned.

Khalil, misreading their shared expression, raised his hands in a placating gesture. "Please, don't be alarmed. I'm only here to help. I'm flying back to Amman tomorrow morning, and once I board that plane, you will never see me again. But as I'm here, I have something else for you. Look in the newspaper. It's on that chair over there."

Raseen was closest. Picking it up, she flipped through the large pages awkwardly until a single, smaller sheet slipped to the floor. She picked it up, turned it over, and froze.

"What is it?" Vanderveen asked, struggling to keep his voice even.

Raseen looked up, her face stricken. "It's you."

He motioned silently, and she walked over, handing him the sheet. Vanderveen didn't need to read the fine print to know what it was; the header said everything, as did the photograph.

He studied it carefully, though he recognized the picture instantly. It had been taken ten years earlier during his army service. He scanned the text, looking for the distribution date. When he found it, his chest tightened, and a jolt of anxiety passed through his body; the Red Notice—an international arrest warrant—had been issued by Interpol a full two weeks earlier.

"Every airport in Western Europe has one of those," Khalil said quietly. The airy attitude was gone, and his face had settled into a grim expression. "Both commercial and private, along with most of the major hubs in South America, Africa, and the Middle East. The information was being tightly held until a few days ago, but somebody made the decision to give it wider distribution, which is how we learned about it. England is no longer safe for you. MI5 has watchers at train stations and ferry crossings. It's a miracle you weren't picked up this morning . . . As it stands, you look exactly like the picture. You have to change passports as soon as possible."

Vanderveen barely heard a word, still trying to wrap his mind around this newest development. His most recent information indicated that the U.S. government believed he was dead. Dead for the past year, drowned in the Atlantic, off the coast of Maine. Something had happened in the past couple of weeks to change that, something that even his contact in Washington didn't know about.

Then something else occurred to him. Lifting the sheet, he said, "You had the newspaper at the café. Have you been carrying this around all day?"

"Yes. I didn't want to leave it lying around for a maid to find."

Khalil paused uncomfortably, then said, "There's more, I'm afraid. You've been placed on the 1267 Committee List. I have the documentation, if you want to see it."

Raseen had taken a seat next to the windows, looking distinctly unhappy. Turning toward them, she said, "Committee List? What is that?"

Khalil was the one to explain as he handed Vanderveen the relevant paperwork. "The 1267 Committee," he began, "was created under a UN resolution in 1999. Its sole purpose is to enforce sanctions that have already been imposed by the Security Council. The sanctions are limited to people and companies controlled by the Taliban, al-Qaeda, and Osama bin Laden, and the Committee List is simply a list of everyone who falls under that designation. Individually speaking, the sanctions are used to restrict travel and seize assets. . . ."

The courier was clearly enjoying his little recital. In the meantime, Vanderveen had found his name on the last page of the 1267. He was flanked by a senior lieutenant to bin Laden and a Moroccan financier being detained in Italy. He read through the entry quickly.

204. *Name: 1: WILLIAM 2: PAULIN 3: VANDERVEEN 4: na

*Title: na Designation: na DOB: 6 July 1966 POB: Piet Retief, South Africa *Good quality aka: a) Jason March b) Nathan Camden c) Joseph O'Donnell, born 1 Dec. 1968 Low quality aka: "the American" *Nationality: South African *Passport no.: a) Counterfeit Danish driving license no. 20378893, made out to Michael Jørgensen b) Swiss birth certificate, issued for Ernst Baumann, born on 24 Sept. 1968 in Lausanne c) German travel document ("Reiseausweise") A 0064881 National identification no.: SSN: 438-91-5391 (U.S.A.) Address: na *Listed on: 08 Sep. 2008 *Other information: Reportedly killed in November 2007 in the United States (amended on 07 Sep. 2008)*

When he reached the end, he set down the document and ran a hand over his face, thinking it through. He was slightly relieved. Almost all of the information Interpol and the Security Council had compiled was worthless. He had discarded the German papers in

2004 after using them once. The same was true of the Swiss and Danish documents, and he had ceased to be Jason March eight years earlier in Syria. Somehow, they had managed to verify his involvement with Al-Qaeda, but that was old news. The aliases, while accurate, were severely outdated. Still, seeing his name on a document of this nature was hardly reassuring, and the tables had undoubtedly turned. The opposition knew he was alive, and that took away his greatest advantage. Khalil was right; he had to change passports—and his appearance—at the earliest opportunity.

"I don't understand," Raseen was saying. "Why would they issue a Red Notice *and* put you on the 1267? Isn't that sort of . . . redundant?"

"No," Vanderveen replied. "In fact, it makes perfect sense. Wider distribution means more attention. In a way, they're simply covering their bets."

Raseen suddenly went rigid in her seat. "Can I see the list?"

He handed it over and watched as she sped through the pages. It was interesting that she wanted to check for her name, Vanderveen thought. At the very least, it meant that she had worked directly with Al-Qaeda at some point in the past.

Finally, she seemed to heave a sigh of relief and slumped back into the chair. Apart from their strange encounter the previous night, it was the most emotion he had seen her exhibit since their first meeting in Paris.

"Good," Vanderveen said. His satisfaction was genuine. "At least one of us can move freely. You may need to take on a larger role when we get to New York."

Khalil nodded slowly. "Everything is working as expected. The Iranian—that is, the informant in New York—has performed admirably. He has convinced even the senior members of the FBI, and they are undoubtedly working to sway the president. Moreover, the meeting at the UN has been finalized. It will take place on the expected date and time. The specifics will be sent to you once you arrive in the city, which will be . . . ."

"In three days' time," Vanderveen said. "Barring any unforeseen complications. Are you sure that Rühmann is still in Berlin? He hasn't been warned?"

"He's still there, but he knows you're coming."

Vanderveen looked up sharply. "What?"

"I informed him that you wished to discuss the arrangements in person," Khalil clarified. "Anywhere in Western Europe. He was reluctant, but agreed after I threatened to terminate our business arrangement. As you know, he's earned a great deal of money through our organization."

Vanderveen nodded slowly. Using cutouts such as Anthony Mason, Thomas Rühmann had provided more than fifty tons of small arms to the Sunni insurgency over the past six months. Nearly all of the weapons were currently being stored across the border in Syria. The day before the Iraqi delegation was to be taken out in New York, the weapons would be distributed to Sunni insurgents and Syrian-based members of Hamas and Hezbollah. Appropriate targets in the western provinces of Iraq had already been selected by Izzat al-Douri and members of his senior staff. With the Iraqi Parliament in complete disarray, the wave of attacks would have a profound effect, further devastating the integrity of the government and creating a vacuum of power. At least, this was what al-Douri and his advisors anticipated. Vanderveen had his doubts, but he had his own reasons for going forward with the plan; namely, money and the chance to launch a devastating attack on U.S. soil.

"Rühmann will meet you tomorrow in Potsdam," Khalil continued. "Three PM at the Brandenburg Gate. The details are in the envelope, and you've already seen the pictures. Needless to say, he can't be allowed to live. We have more than enough weapons for the upcoming offensive, and Hamas will supply a good deal of their own. At this point, the Austrian is more of a liability than an asset."

"I understand that," Vanderveen replied coldly. It had been his suggestion to kill the man in the first place. "What about the other materials I requested?"

"Yes, an interesting list," Khalil murmured. He could barely be heard over the roar of the television. "A *very* interesting list. I can understand the handguns, but why do you need a long-range weapon? Why do you need explosives?"

"That is not your concern." Vanderveen had asked for a quick description of Rühmann's residence in Berlin the previous night. The list of items he'd requested was based on what he'd been told. "Can you supply them or not?"

"Yes. There is a man waiting to meet you now. Do you know the city well?"

"Well enough."

"Take a taxi to the British Museum, then another to Charing Cross. Hold on to the phone, and I'll call you in ten minutes to give you further instructions. A car is waiting to meet us, but it's best if we leave here separately. It's also better to take different routes. Once we reach the final destination, he will supply what you asked for."

"That doesn't help at all," Raseen said. Her unsettling gaze was locked on the courier. "How are we supposed to get the explosives from here to Germany? We can't exactly take them through customs, you know."

"I understand that," Khalil replied. "And so does the supplier." His voice was tight; clearly, he was sorely tempted to put Raseen in her place. That he could not bring himself to do it said much about the woman's place in the organization, Vanderveen thought. It was yet another indication of how important she actually was.

"This man has a way to bring the explosives and the weapons into Germany by boat. He'll explain it to you once you've examined the goods. Is that satisfactory?"

There was an edge of sarcasm there, but Vanderveen ignored it, nodding his agreement. "When are we supposed to meet him?"

Khalil looked at his watch. It was a flashy Breitling chronograph, perfect for drawing unwanted attention. "In less than an hour, so we'd better be going. Are you ready to leave?"

"Yes."

"Good. I'll just be a minute."

Khalil walked into the bathroom and shut the door. A few seconds later, they could hear him urinating noisily.

Raseen was out of her chair in an instant. Moving close, she rested a light hand on his chest and whispered urgently into his ear. "The Security Service may have your picture, Will, but they have this man in their sights *right now*. He knows your name, and he knows about Rühmann. He knows too much. You have to kill him. It means forfeiting the explosives, I know, but there's no other choice."

Vanderveen turned his face into her fragrant hair, lowering his voice to a murmur. "I agree, but losing the gear means changing the plan, and it's a little bit late in the game for that."

Her eyes drifted away for a moment, and then she snapped back to reality. "I might be able to get what we need, but I'll have to place a few calls."

"You have a supplier in Germany?"

"Yes. I worked with a man in Dresden three years ago. If he's still active, he should be able to meet our needs."

He looked at her, questioning. This was the first time she had mentioned another possibility, a contact of her own. The information would have been useful earlier, but there was no point in getting into that now. "Okay. We'll follow him out, but then I want you to walk away. Don't go too far, and keep the phone . . . I'll call you once it's done."

"Very well." She was about to say something else, but the courier was back in the room, reaching for his suit jacket. He pulled it on, grabbed the black case, and moved to the door. Vanderveen replaced the documents, sealed the envelope, and slipped it under his coat before following them out.

They left the hotel separately, as instructed. Khalil was the first to depart, nodding politely to the doorman as he stepped out into the rain. Raseen followed two minutes later, wearing the bright red anorak. As she approached the doors, she pulled the hood over her head and shot the doorman a little smile, which he eagerly returned. Vanderveen was wearing the black windbreaker, the ball cap pulled low over his blond hair. Raseen took a right after leaving the building, heading back down toward the Embankment, but Vanderveen crossed Savoy Street, poked around a newsstand for half a minute, then walked quickly back down the Strand.

He already knew why the courier had asked them to take a taxi. The British Museum was well out of the way, and the unnecessarily long trip could only mean that he intended to reach Charing Cross on foot. The station was located on the other end of the Strand, and if they had followed his instructions, they would have arrived at roughly the same time. Vanderveen's suspicions were confirmed after a short while, when he again spotted the dark head of the man named Khalil weaving in and out of the crowd.

At least, it *looked* like the same man. Vanderveen knew he would have to get closer to make a positive identification, but he had done this kind of thing before, and he trusted his instincts. He was getting ready to close the gap when the courier solved the problem for him, pausing to examine a window display of expensive watches. A little break in the crowd gave Vanderveen a clear view of the other man's profile. It wasn't much, but enough to make a solid ID, and there was the last piece of evidence: the black case, dangling loosely from his right hand. The gap suddenly closed, obscuring the view. The street was no less busy now that the lunch hour was over, a great rush of humanity sweeping by on the sidewalk. The rain had started to clear a little as well, a few errant drops angling down from the low gray clouds.

He kept moving, letting the crowd carry him forward. Having spotted the courier, Vanderveen was now looking hard for signs of surveillance. The green Opel appeared on schedule, and this time, he got a good look at the license plate. He was slightly chilled to see that Raseen had been right; it *was* the same car. The sedan passed him once more in the space of five minutes, but it was the only visible sign. Vanderveen couldn't pick out any familiar faces on foot, but that didn't mean a thing; he could be surrounded by watchers and never know it. Unfortunately, he couldn't drop back in the hopes of picking them out; Charing Cross was less than five minutes away. If he was going to act, it had to be now.

The courier was 30 feet ahead of him. He picked up the pace, closing the distance rapidly.

In the driver's seat of the Opel, Ian Haines leaned on the horn, angrily scanning the traffic that was currently snarled along Maiden Lane. The rain had started to slow, so he flicked off the wipers and leaned back in the seat, where he took a deep breath and tried to resign himself to a long wait. He still couldn't believe the Arab had decided to leave the hotel before the shift change. The fucking *nerve* of these people . . . If the inconsiderate bastard had stayed in his room for another five minutes, they would have had time to move the next team into position. Unfortunately, it hadn't worked out that way. Now they could easily end up spending the next several hours trailing him around the city, just waiting for an opportunity to switch out the surveillance teams. Judging by the terse, humorless transmissions coming over the radio, Scott was just as unhappy with the situation as he was.

"Ian, he's still moving southwest on the Strand. Where the hell are you?"

"Maiden Lane. Some kind of accident . . . Christ, I don't know. Any idea where he's going?"

A crackle of static, then, "Your guess is as good as mine, mate. But I'll tell you one thing. If he gets on the tube, we're fucked."

"Got that right," Haines muttered to himself. In spite of the situation, he could console himself with one fact: if they ended up losing Banker, it probably wouldn't mean much to the people in charge of "A" Branch, Section 4 at Thames House. After all, he reasoned, the man couldn't be that important; if he was, a full team would have been tasked with trailing him. Then again, that might have been wishful thinking on his part. Haines knew the Service was spread too thin on the ground, despite the constant threat of terrorist activity and a marked upsurge in public interest following the London bombings of July 7, 2005. Manpower wasn't the only problem, either. The Service was also badly in need of additional funding; the annual budget, which was shared with MI6 and the Government Communications Headquarters (GCHQ), had risen a scant 250 million pounds over the past year. At the same time, expectations had risen tenfold.

Yet another impediment was the public's ignorance when it came to matters of national security. Many people tended to forget that MI5 had no arrest powers, which meant that it was entirely dependent on actual government entities, such as Special Branch, to act on domestic intelligence. Haines had learned firsthand how hard it was to let others take the credit after months of thankless surveillance, but generally speaking, he didn't mind operating in the shadows, and he didn't mind the hard work . . . at least not most of the time. Right now, however, he wanted nothing more than to get on with the weekend; the Temple Bar was calling his name. He shifted in his seat wearily. If the little shit would just sit down for a meal somewhere, they could bring in the next shift and get this over with. . . .

Haines was jolted out of his daydream by a horn blared from behind. The traffic had cleared up ahead. Easing his foot off the clutch, he rolled forward and turned onto Southampton. Twenty seconds later, he stopped at another light, ready to make the right turn onto the Strand. He had just finished relaying his position to Scott when the light turned green, and he swung onto the busy street for the fifth time that day.

Vanderveen had closed to within 5 feet. Everything else had fallen away: the jostling crowd, the cacophony of voices, and the constant roar of the cars sweeping by. All he could see was the man named Khalil: the elegant cut of his Savile Row suit, the attaché dangling from his right hand, the hair curling over the back of his collar. He had stopped somewhere to purchase an umbrella, a lime green monstrosity, which was now bobbing over his head. If he had put it up earlier, it would have made Vanderveen's task much easier, but the rain was only now starting to increase in tempo and force.

He paused to sweep some water out of his eyes. The courier, clearly accustomed to large cities, was an expert at navigating the packed sidewalk, sliding from left to right, avoiding the crowd with surprising grace and agility. Vanderveen realized he was falling behind. Adjusting his pace, he looked to the left, waiting for the right moment. The vehicular traffic was moving far too fast for these narrow roads. The city officials seemed to have considered this inevitable, as their preventative measures were mostly passive. Police constables were positioned at the major crosswalks, and white letters on the cement warned tourists to "look right." Khalil was passing one of the crossings now, and with a start, Vanderveen realized that they were drawing close to Villiers Street. The entrance to the station at Charing Cross was less than two blocks away.

As if reading his mind, the courier dipped a hand into his suit jacket and came up with a cell phone. He held it in front of his body as he dialed, obscuring Vanderveen's view. Then he lifted it to his ear. Vanderveen looked past his target, checking the road. Traffic was hurtling past him at full speed. Coming up were a white Rover sedan, a Renault wagon, a black cab, and beyond that, a double-decker bus. Khalil stepped to his left to avoid an elderly woman with an armful of bags, and Vanderveen seized the chance. Coming up on the courier's right side, he let the Rover go racing past, along with the Renault and then the cab. Khalil, with the phone raised to his ear, was giving Raseen instructions when his head turned to the right and his eyes went wide. At the moment of recognition, Vanderveen used both arms to shove him as hard as he could, directly into the path of the bus. Then he turned and disappeared into the crowd as the brakes squealed and the screams rose behind him.

"Fucking hell!"

Haines swore viciously and slammed on the brakes as the cars fishtailed in front of him. Craning his neck, he could see people running toward a double-decker bus. The vehicle was three cars ahead of his own, and every instinct he had told him that this was relevant. Pulling out his earpiece, he turned off the ignition and got out of the car, jogging toward the commotion. As he approached, he could see a few people stumbling away from the scene, their faces white, eyes wide in shock. To his right, a young woman was bent over at the waist, vomiting noisily onto the pavement. Her friend, looking nearly as sick, was standing by her side, rubbing her back and murmuring calming words.

Pulling his eyes away from this strange scene, Haines skirted another car and pushed to the front of the building crowd. An older man in uniform was standing front and center, hands wrapped in his ginger hair. He was screaming something that didn't make sense. Listening closely, Haines heard a few words cutting through the hysterical rant: ". . . wasn't my fault. I swear to God, it wasn't my fault. They just fell right into the road. You all saw it. . . ."

And then he saw the front of the bus.

It looked as if somebody had splashed red paint all over the grill. Despite the obvious signs, it took him a few seconds to realize what had happened. His eyes involuntarily moved down to the wheels, and he saw the twisted remains of a human body, part of it wrapped up in the axle, the rest scattered along the street. Moving forward, Haines caught sight of another body, that of a teenage boy. He was lying behind and to the right of the bus, his limbs broken and resting at strange angles. A middle-aged woman—presumably the mother— was draped over the lifeless form, sobbing uncontrollably. As he watched, a pair of police constables moved out of the crowd. One went to the woman, gently lifting her up and away from her son, while the other started ordering people back from the scene of the accident. Haines felt somebody tap his arm, and he turned. It was Scott. His animated expression was difficult to read; there were equal measures of horror and excitement on his young, unlined face.

"Did you see it?"

"No," Haines replied slowly. "Did you?"

Scott grabbed his arm and pulled him away from the crowd. People were milling about, talking in low, horrified tones, and it was difficult to hear over the babble of voices. When they were far enough away, the younger man said, "I saw it all. Christ, I was right behind the poor bastard when it happened. The driver dragged him halfway down the fuckin' road before he had the sense to stop."

Haines did not respond. All he could think about was the woman hunched over her son's body; he couldn't get her anguished face out of his mind. Finally, the words leaked into his head. "What happened?"

"He was pushed. I—"

"*Pushed?* Are you sure?"

Scott nodded firmly. "Like I said, I saw it clear as day. The kid was just in the way. Wrong bloody place and time, is all, but the Arab was definitely pushed. It was deliberate as hell."

Haines allowed himself to be dragged along, still thinking about the woman. He couldn't understand his reaction, as he had seen much worse in his years with 2 PARA. He had seen men torn apart by machine gun fire on a shingle beach in the Falklands, the aftermath of a mortar attack during the Battle of Goose Green, and the destruction caused by a pair of massive bombs in Warrenpoint, Northern Ireland. In that incident, both the primary and secondary devices had been strategically placed on a dual carriageway near the border.

The bombing claimed the lives of 18 men in Haines's regiment. He had been among the first to arrive on the scene—indeed, he had nearly been killed by the secondary blast—but it all seemed like a distant memory. More to the point, it had been war, and the people who'd died were trained soldiers, brave men who knew the risks. None of it seemed as bad as the stunned look of shock and despair he had just witnessed, and even now, just minutes after turning his back on the scene, he knew he'd be seeing the woman's face in his dreams for years to come.

"Who pushed him? Why didn't you follow?"

"The crowd closed up right away, and I lost him in the confusion," Scott replied. "I didn't see much, anyway. He was wearing a baseball cap and a black jacket, and I think he was blond, but I couldn't swear to it. . . ."

Scott continued to relay what he'd seen as they turned off the Strand. Soon they were moving northeast on Chandos Place, heading toward Bedford Street. "What about the car?" Haines asked.

"Fuck the car. No one's getting off that street for at least an hour, mate. We have to get back and make a report. Robeson won't be happy, but if you ask me, there wasn't a damn thing we could've done to—"

"The pictures."

Scott turned. "What?"

"The pictures," Haines repeated. "You've got shots of our man, right? Whoever shoved him in front of that bus will be in the background."

"Jesus, you're right." The young watcher thought for a minute, then shook his head. "No, I don't think it'll work. You saw how busy the street was . . . There's no way we'll be able to pick him out. I didn't even get that good a look."

"Maybe not, but that falls to the techs, not us. If there's anything there, they'll find it."

A Vauxhall sedan pulled up to the curb, and Scott said, "That's us. I called before you arrived on the scene."

Haines moved toward the back of the car, pulled open the door, and got in. Scott found a seat in the front and tapped the driver's arm. "Let's go."

CHAPTER 34

LANGLEY, VIRGINIA

It was just after 2:00 in the afternoon as Jonathan Harper reluctantly entered the room on the seventh floor of the OHB at Langley, pulling the door shut behind him. The sound of the secretary's typing was blocked out instantly, replaced by an uneasy silence. He had expected the summons, but as he crossed the deep pile carpet, there was something about the resigned look on the director's face that threw him off-guard. He had expected anger, bluster, and shouted accusations from the start. Anything but this quiet, restrained anger.

Rachel Ford's demeanor was much easier to read. She was staring at him intently from the seat opposite his. Her mouth was set in a straight, thin line, her eyes glittering dangerously behind a pair of elegant reading glasses. Her presence could only mean one thing: she had been brought up to date on the contents of Anthony Mason's hard drive, and she had learned about the previous day's meeting at the White House.

It had been Harper's decision to keep her out of the briefing, based on Kealey's request. He had called in every favor he could to keep Science and Technology out of the loop, as Roger Davidson, the head of the directorate, was one of Ford's staunchest supporters. Harper had then persuaded Andrews to go along with the idea, based on the fact that somebody had slipped the Bureau information about the laptop's whereabouts. Harper had pointed out Ford's relationship to Samantha Crane, the FBI agent tasked with the raid in

Alexandria, and the subsequent accusations she had leveled at Kealey. This evidence, while extremely circumstantial, was enough to convince the director to keep Ford out of the way, at least temporarily. It now appeared Andrews had changed his mind; otherwise, the deputy DCI would not be present.

Harper took the proffered chair and ignored Rachel Ford's unwavering stare. Instead, he looked past the large mahogany desk as the DCI arranged a few loose papers. It was midday; through the large, soundproof windows, pale sunlight flitted over the tops of the trees. It was a pleasant scene, but hardly fitting. An autumn gale would have been more appropriate to the dark, strained mood that enveloped the room.

Finally, Andrews looked up and appraised his guest. "So, have you seen him yet?"

The opening question was not what Harper expected, but he recovered quickly. "Yes, I saw him this morning."

"And how bad is the wound?"

"Not bad, but painful . . . You can tell just from looking at it. The bullet scraped a rib and left a nasty gouge. He's lucky as hell. A few inches to the right and he never would have made it out of the building."

"And this situation would be much worse," Andrews added, running a tired hand over his face. He leaned back in his chair. "Of course, it's already a complete disaster. Worse would be . . . well, *unthinkable*. What happened out there?"

Harper cleared his throat, bracing himself for the coming storm. "I can't say for sure. What I *do* know is that we have a location for Thomas Rühmann. He's living in Berlin under the name Walter Schäuble. If we move quickly—"

"Let me stop you right there." Andrews jerked forward in his chair and planted his feet beneath the desk, his face tightening. Ford was shaking her head in disgust. "We're not going to talk about the one good thing that came out of this fucking mess," the DCI continued, "because we can't act on that piece of information. So let's talk about *reality*, okay? At 4:45 this morning, a security guard from the German Embassy was admitted to University Hospital in Georgetown with a gunshot wound to the upper arm. Ten minutes later, a D.C.

Metro police officer was brought in with a Grade V concussion and severe lacerations to the face and neck. In case you didn't know," he continued in a strained tone, "a Grade I concussion is the least severe. Grade V is the worst, with a period of unconsciousness lasting more than ten minutes. In this case, the officer did not regain consciousness for nearly five hours."

Andrews stopped to arrange his thoughts. When he spoke again, his voice was taut and barely controlled. "Thirty minutes after the police officer was brought in, a blue Ford Taurus—a car from *our* motor pool, I might add—arrived at the gate off Dolley Madison Boulevard. The driver was none other than Ryan Kealey. He had no credentials, nothing to identify himself. He was made to wait while they called through and verified his status. Then they called in a doctor, but not before Kealey managed to bleed all over the floor of the gatehouse." The DCI smiled tightly. "It's a tile floor . . . lots of cracks, you know? I hear they're still trying to clean it up."

Andrews rested his arms on the desk and interlaced his fingers. "I have to tell you, John, it pisses me off that you knew about this before I did. Of course, we both know it's more than that, don't we?" The director's gaze was probing. "After all, you supported the embassy raid from the start."

"Bob, if you're suggesting that I signed off on what happened last night—"

"I'm not 'suggesting' anything. I'm *telling* you that I know what you did. How else would Kealey get access to a car from the motor pool? I know he's done a lot for us, but he's only been here four years. He doesn't know the procedure, and he doesn't have the authority. You covered your tracks well, John, but I don't have the time or the patience to beat around the bush. What were you trying to accomplish? Rühmann's ties to the attacks in Baghdad and Paris are sketchy at best. Do you really think his location is worth the kind of fallout that we're about to endure?"

"Sir, we managed to link Rühmann to Kassem, Vanderveen, *and* al-Umari—"

"Maybe so, but it wasn't enough to convince the president, was it? And when the break-in comes back to us, what happens then?"

Before Harper could answer, the telephone chirped softly. Andrews snatched it up and spoke a few harsh, dismissive words. He replaced the receiver, but Ford stepped in before he could pick up the thread. "Well?"

Harper ignored her. "Bob, the Germans can search every database they have, and so can the FBI. They're never going to find a record of Kealey's fingerprints. They might have his blood, but they have nothing to match it to. I talked to him. I know he disabled the cameras before he went in. There is no feasible way this can be traced back to us. People were hurt . . . okay. So what? That happens occasionally in this business. No one was killed. This will all be forgotten in a matter of weeks, and because of Ryan's efforts, we are now in a position to move forward."

Ford scowled. "Jonathan, I don't think you fully appreciate the severity of this situation. If anyone even *hints* at our involvement, our diplomatic relations with Germany will be damaged beyond repair."

"This is not the State Department," Harper shot back. "And you're not on the oversight committee anymore. We are not charged with maintaining diplomatic relations. Will Vanderveen has murdered U.S. soldiers and citizens. He has attacked this country on several occasions. In my opinion, the chance to track him down is worth a few hurt feelings on the international front and a damn sight more."

It was the unvarnished truth, or at least the way he saw it. Harper fully expected his little speech to make things worse, but while Ford's face turned a deep shade of scarlet, the DCI merely nodded plaintively.

"What about a career, John? Would you say that finding him is worth the career of, say, a talented young CTC analyst? One of our best and brightest?"

Harper tensed involuntarily. "Kharmai?"

"Exactly."

"What are you talking about? She wasn't even there."

"That's bullshit," Ford announced. Turning to her right, she said, "You can't possibly believe that. He knew damn well where she was last night, because he sent them both."

Andrews frowned. Harper could see him wavering, but finally, he seemed to accept the denial at face value. "I don't know where

Kealey left her—she didn't come back to Langley with him—but she was definitely at the embassy," the director said. "The Metro police cruisers all have dash-mounted cameras."

"You saw the tape?"

"No. I didn't need to. The officer woke up this morning and gave his statement, which we got hold of shortly thereafter. The name the woman gave him was Sara Brown. Not real, of course, and not particularly original, but that's beside the point. His description matched Kharmai to a T, right down to the accent.

"The dots connect themselves," Andrews continued, his voice dropping to a more reasonable level. "People are going to figure this out, John. It might come out of this building, or it might come out of the White House, but the point is, it *will* come out. She's got to go. Kealey too. Their days at the Agency are numbered. It's that simple."

Harper nodded stiffly, vaguely aware of Ford's triumphant smile. "When?"

"They're suspended without pay, effective immediately. We'll ease them out by the end of the month. I'll let you deal with Kealey; frankly, I'd be happy to never see him again. You've known him for a long time, and he's done a lot for us. That's the only reason he's not facing charges. The same for Kharmai, and she has my word on that: she's free and clear if she goes quietly. I want to talk to her face-to-face. We can bring her up now, if you like. Or you can break the news to her first. It's up to you."

"There's no point in drawing it out," Harper decided at length. "She'll be expecting it anyway."

"Fine." Andrews lifted the receiver and punched a button. "Diane, ask Naomi Kharmai to report to my office, please. You should find her in Science and Technology. If she's not there, try McLean."

He replaced the receiver, leaned back in his chair, and appraised his guest. After a time, he turned to Ford and said, "Rachel, would you mind excusing us for a moment?"

She didn't look happy, but she'd gotten her way, and for the moment, that seemed to be enough. She nodded curtly, stood, and walked out.

Andrews looked at his desk for a long time, a number of emotions passing over his ruddy features. Clearly, the whole situation was not sitting well with him, and it wasn't just anger at the way things had turned out.

"John, what happened here?" he finally asked. "How many times have I looked to you for advice since I was nominated? How many times have you pulled my ass out of the fire? You're probably the smartest man in the building. It doesn't make sense."

Harper shook his head wearily. "I looked at the facts, and I made a decision. What else can I say?"

"You didn't 'make a decision.' You violated a direct order from the *president*, for Christ's sake. What the hell were you thinking?"

"The president is wrong," Harper replied flatly. "I don't know what kind of bullshit the Bureau is feeding him, but the Iranians were not involved in Baghdad or Paris. This all comes down to somebody in the insurgency. Vanderveen can tell us who that is, and the only way to find *him* is through Rühmann. It was the right call, and I'd do it again."

Andrews shook his head in disbelief. He had worked in bureaucracies all his life. He believed in the rules, and on the rare occasion he decided to break one, the decision did not come easily. Harper's unapologetic attitude was beyond his experience. "Well, Kealey and Kharmai are your people, and you know how it works. Unfortunately, their sacrifice is not enough."

The DDO nodded once. His chest tightened, even though he had expected as much. "So, how do we handle it? Is it a minor health issue, or do I suddenly feel the need to spend more time with my wife?"

"Neither," was the surprising response. "I spoke to Brenneman this morning, John. He's not happy, to say the least, but he can't afford to lose you right now." Catching the look on the other man's face, he hastened to add, "He's not doing this out of personal loyalty, so don't get comfortable. It's politics, like everything else. With the election coming up, he can't afford to lose any more public support, especially over something he can actually control. So for now, we keep the status quo."

Harper was too surprised to react right away. He couldn't suppress the wave of relief that swept over him, although it was quickly followed by guilt. Two of his best people, after all, were about to lose their jobs. He could have done more to dissuade Kealey, and he definitely could have done more to stop Kharmai from getting involved. Before he could speak, the director's intercom came to life. "Sir, Ms. Kharmai has arrived."

"Okay, Diane. Send her in."

Andrews stood, adopted a sober expression, and straightened his tie as the door swung open. Getting to his feet, Harper took a deep breath and tried to prepare himself. This was going to be painful, to say the least.

It was perhaps ten minutes later that Naomi found herself in the cafeteria on the ground floor. She looked around in a daze, only dimly aware of the tacky plum-colored walls and industrial seating. A few employees breaking for an early lunch were scattered around the room, spaced well apart in the way people do when they have a choice in the matter.

With little else to do, she walked up to the counter and purchased a large cup of coffee, momentarily forgetting that she hated the stuff. A liberal amount of sugar and cream made it bearable, and she carried the lukewarm beverage back to a seat. She took a small sip and squeezed her eyes shut, resisting the urge to lay her head on the table and let it all out.

She had known this could happen, of course, but nothing compared to the reality. Worst of all was the speed with which she had been dispatched. It had been so *quick*; the director had cut her loose in a matter of minutes, barely giving her time to wrap her mind around the idea that her career with the CIA was essentially over. His words had been rattling around in her head since the moment she'd stepped out of his office. *I'm sorry, Naomi, but you've given me no choice . . . blatant disregard for authority . . . clear violation of standing orders . . . administrative leave pending further inquiries.*

The words, as well as what they meant for her future, had left her numb, at least for the first few minutes. Now that the shock was starting to pass, reality was settling in. She would still be able to get a job—her academic credentials would see to that—but that wasn't the point. She loved her work; it was that simple, and after everything she had done at the Agency, she knew that nothing else would ever be able to hold her interest. It was awful to know that she had reached the peak of her career at thirty-one years of age, and with that thought, it became too much. She put her head on her arms and did her best to hold back the tears.

A shadow crossed the table, and she looked up, startled. Jonathan Harper was standing there, holding a cup of coffee. There was a subdued expression on his face. "Mind if I join you?"

"No," she said miserably, quickly wiping a hand across her eyes. It was beyond embarrassing to be seen this way, but she hadn't expected him. She waved at the opposite seat. "Be my guest."

He took the proffered chair and waited as she composed herself hurriedly. "How are you doing?" he asked.

"I'll be fine, sir. It's just that . . ." She shrugged helplessly. "I've been here five years, and now it's over. It's just a little hard to believe."

Harper nodded sympathetically. Even though she was doing her best to hide it, she was clearly devastated by her dismissal. He was tempted to remind her that she wasn't supposed to have played the role she did, that she couldn't blame anyone but herself for the mess she was in, but the last thing she needed at this point was a lecture. She'd be telling herself the same thing anyway.

"The funny thing," she continued slowly, "is that I would probably do it again." There was a strange wonderment in her voice, as though she could scarcely believe her own words. "Ryan couldn't have done it by himself, after all, and I happen to think he's right."

"About Vanderveen?"

She nodded. "Sir, when it comes to that man, we can't afford to wait for ironclad proof. By going forward with the meeting at the UN, the president is virtually daring him on. I'd be shocked if he *didn't* make a play in New York, and the only way to stop it is to find him first."

"I happen to agree," Harper said quietly. "But you're out of it, so I don't suppose there's much you can do, is there?"

It was a blunt, brutal thing to say, but she absorbed the words silently. "I suppose you're right."

"What will you do now?"

She tried to hide her sudden curiosity; it was almost as if he was measuring her up for something. "To be honest, I don't really know. Maybe I'll take some time off, see what turns up. It's just not fair, though . . . We managed to track Rühmann down, and the Agency isn't going to do a damn thing about it."

"What's your point?"

She straightened and shot him a hard look. "My point is that I'm involved as well, sir. I was involved from the start. I want to finish this."

"With Ryan."

"Yes," she confirmed. "If anyone has earned—" She stopped herself. "That's not the right word. If anyone *deserves* the chance to go after Vanderveen, it's him."

"So if he wanted your help, you would be willing to offer it."

"Yes, but I'd want to know what I'm dealing with." She hesitated again; she knew the two men were good friends, and there was a limit to what she could ask. "I'd need to know if he's . . ."

"Stable enough? Is that what you're trying to say?"

"Sir, I don't—"

"Relax, Naomi. It's a reasonable question, considering what you've given up for him."

Harper fell silent. She stayed quiet, letting him think it through. Finally, he got to his feet abruptly.

"Come on, let's take a walk."

They made their way up to the ground floor and passed through the turnstiles, stepping out into a small courtyard. The open area was positioned between the OHB and the New Headquarters Building, the cement littered with black plastic picnic tables. The sun was out, and the air was agreeably warm. A few people had taken advantage of the weather to eat lunch outside, but most of the tables were free. Harper picked one apart from the others, which gave them a little privacy. Once they were seated, he leaned back and stared morosely into his coffee. His brow was furrowed, as if he was deciding where to begin, or whether to talk at all. Naomi remained silent, trying not to appear too anxious. She desperately wanted to hear what he had to say, but she knew he would only talk if he wanted to.

Finally, he said, "How much do you know? About what happened in Maine, I mean?"

"Only what you told me over the phone, sir."

Harper nodded. "Well, I'll try to fill in the blanks, but don't get the wrong idea. I know this is the first time you've seen him in nearly a year, and I'm guessing you've made the natural assumption: that it all comes down to what happened that night. But that's not the case. Ryan was on the edge of things a long time before he lost Katie Donovan. You have to remember, he's served in some of the worst places on earth, and he's seen a lot of terrible things."

Naomi nodded slowly, remembering a story she'd heard the previous year. There had been a Muslim girl in Bosnia who'd fallen hard for the young Special Forces lieutenant. Kealey had gone out of his way to be kind to her, talking to her every day on patrol, accepting her little tokens of chocolate and flowers, much to the amusement of his fellow soldiers. Then tragedy struck. The Serbian militia found out she was talking to the Americans. The girl disappeared, and two days later, her badly beaten body was discovered on the bank of the Miljacka River by a passing army patrol.

There had been little chance of justice; in a city where dozens of innocent people died each day, a thirteen-year-old girl did not count for much in the larger scheme of things. Kealey had taken matters into his own hands, and three days after her death, her killer—a militia leader by the name of Stojanovic—was found dead in a safe house in Sarajevo, his throat cut from ear to ear. Kealey had nearly been court-martialed, but while rumors abounded, no proof could be found linking him to Stojanovic's death. Naomi, for one, didn't need proof; she had seen him in action, and she knew what he was capable of.

"The point I'm trying to make," Harper was saying, "is that after all of that, Katie meant everything to him, and I do mean everything. She was completely innocent, untouched by all the shit he'd seen in his life. She was a way to start over, a chance at, well, *redemption*, for lack of a better word, and when she died, all of that died as well."

Harper looked away, slightly embarrassed. "At least, that's the best way I can explain it."

Naomi nodded again. The deputy director was clearly uneasy discussing this. Maybe he thought he'd revealed too much, or maybe he thought it wasn't his place to tell her the truth. For a moment, she didn't think he'd continue, but then he surprised her.

"Anyway, I flew down as soon as I got the news, but the doctors didn't let me see him until the following morning. I wasn't sure what I was going to find, but what struck me most was his demeanor. He was strangely unaffected. Dangerously calm, as if it hadn't sunk in. But it did, and it's been there the whole time."

She felt for him, of course, but she was also interested, leaning forward in her seat. "What has?"

"The anger, the grief . . . all of it. Mostly it's guilt. He put the hunt for Vanderveen ahead of her, and he thinks that's what got her killed. He might even be right, but that's not the point. He can't let it go."

Harper set down his coffee and stared absently over the court-yard, remembering. "He came to me a month later, once his wounds were healed and the doctors gave him a relatively clean bill of health. He wanted to come back inside, and I made it happen. Four months in Afghanistan hunting the Taliban with Delta, then a short break, and the next six months in Iraq. I thought it would help him, that staying busy might keep his mind straight."

"And now?" she asked quietly. "Would you have done it the same way?"

She had definitely crossed the line, but he didn't seem to notice. Instead, he shrugged and shook his head. "I'm not sure. It doesn't matter now, but I'll tell you what I do know. He's been taking risks ever since that night, and it's only getting worse. After Ryan came back from Afghanistan, Special Operations Command made it clear to me that they didn't want him back on their turf. Strangely enough, his time over there was hugely productive. Delta nabbed a number of key figures, guys who'd bribed their way into what they thought was a safe haven in Pakistan, but it was the way Kealey carried it off that had them worried. They said he was too reckless, not taking the proper precautions. Coming from those guys, that's saying a lot."

Her next question came naturally, and while she was afraid of the answer, Naomi knew she would never find Harper this forthcoming again. She had to ask it.

"Sir, is he . . . trying to get himself killed?"

He seemed to take the question seriously. "Maybe. Maybe not . . . It's difficult to tell. I think Vanderveen's reappearance has given him something to latch on to, at least for the time being. The point is, if you follow him into this, you'll be completely outside the Agency's authority."

"Are you saying I have a choice?"

He smiled but didn't respond. Draining his cup, he stood and placed a hand on the table in front of her. "Whatever you decide, Naomi, I'll do what I can for you. You've done some amazing work here, and for whatever it's worth, I won't forget that. I'll be staying on for a while, so if you need a reference, be sure to come and see me. Don't wait too long, though. I'll be following you out the door soon enough."

"Thanks for the offer, sir. It means a lot to me."

He nodded and smiled again, then walked away. He was out of sight by the time Naomi saw what he had placed on the table: a business card of some kind.

She turned it over and read the hastily scrawled note on the back. She recognized Ryan's handwriting immediately.

Runway at Upperville, 6:00 AM sharp. Bring your passport.

CHAPTER 35

WASHINGTON, D.C.

Night was descending over the city as Samantha Crane hurried along D Street, having just left her government car in a parking garage off Massachusetts Avenue. She checked her watch as she came up on 1st, swearing under her breath. She was flushed by the time she reached her destination, despite the slight chill in the air. It had taken her twenty infuriating minutes to find an open garage, which made her wish she'd taken a taxi or even walked. Crane was staying at the Hyatt Regency on Capitol Hill, not more than five blocks to the west. She had almost set out on foot from the start, but in the end, she decided against it. She wasn't foolish enough to think that her FBI credentials would make a difference if the worst was to happen, and being unarmed, she thought it best to avoid tempting fate. She rarely carried a gun off duty, and tonight was no exception.

She smiled at the doorman and entered the restaurant, shivering involuntarily at the sudden temperature change. She didn't have a coat to check, so she squeezed through the crowd to the bar. The dining area to the left was packed, but that was to be expected. Established in 1960, the Monocle had quickly become the place to be seen in the District, despite the rather indifferent food. A number of local celebrities could be seen on any given night, and since it was Saturday, more than a few were in attendance. Crane didn't recognize most of them—she didn't have much interest in politics—but a few familiar faces stood out. Senator Edward Kennedy was seated in the middle of the room, surrounded by a starry-eyed group of admirers, and someone who looked a lot like Dennis Hastert was sipping a drink at the bar, talking intently to a pair of older men in dark suits.

As she approached, Crane caught sight of her aunt, Rachel Ford, who was sitting two stools down from the House Speaker, a glass of white wine at her right hand. As always, the young FBI agent felt a sudden surge of inadequacy. She'd always thought that Rachel—with her pale, flawless skin and fine-boned features—could have been the queen of some minor country. Her regal posture somehow made that ridiculous bar stool look like a throne, and her clothes—a brown cashmere cardigan over a silk blouse and tan gabardine slacks—fit her slender form to perfection. Just the sight of her made Crane feel like an overfed second-string cheerleader, despite the extra effort she'd put into her appearance. She reluctantly stepped up to the bar, where Ford caught her eye. The older woman got to her feet and gave her niece an affectionate hug. Stepping back, she offered a small, disapproving frown.

"It's lovely to see you, Samantha. I see you're stunningly underdressed, as usual."

Crane looked down at her outfit, then shot a quick, appraising glance around the room. Her chinos were fine, as far as she could tell, but she'd worn a woolen sweater against the brisk night air, and suddenly, the choice didn't seem that inspired. "Thanks, Aunt Rachel," she said dryly. "It's nice to see you, too."

"Yes, well, I'm sorry we couldn't get together when you first got into town. I've been incredibly busy, of course, but so have you, and that's no excuse. I still don't understand why you didn't stay at my place. You know I have plenty of room."

Crane shrugged uncomfortably. The truth was that her career had benefited from her aunt's position, but she didn't like to advertise the fact. A handful of other agents had also been brought into town to act in supporting roles in the Alexandria raid. Some had stayed on to supplement the forensic teams going through the warehouse, including a few techs from the New York office, where Crane was normally based. They were all staying at the Hyatt Regency, and her absence would have been noticed.

Crane was trying to figure out how to explain this without causing offense, but the other woman saved her the trouble, turning instead to summon the bartender. She returned a moment later with a second glass of Chardonnay, which she handed to Crane.

"Is it always like this?" the younger woman asked. "I mean, it's still pretty early for a Saturday night."

Ford pointed up at the ceiling. "Somebody's hosting an event for Hillary upstairs," she whispered conspiratorially.

"Hillary who? Not Clinton."

"Of course, darling." Ford was mystified. "Who else?"

"Hillary Clinton? *Here*? You can't be serious."

"Of course I'm serious. She can't exactly skip out on her own fund-raiser, can she?" Ford raised an eyebrow, taking in her niece's amazed expression. "Try not to look so impressed, Sam. People are watching, and half the Senate will have stopped in before the night is out. You're bound to see somebody more important than her."

Crane nodded and tried some of the wine. Something about the other woman seemed off, and then it became clear; she was getting tipsy. It should have been obvious from the start, but it was so out of character that Crane didn't catch it right off the bat.

Samantha Crane smiled to herself, feeling a weight lift; this was going to be easier than she'd thought. After days of gentle prodding over the phone, she was finally going to get the answers she needed.

Rachel Ford was on a first-name basis with the maître d', which made all the difference. He found them a table in short order, and although it was far from the best in the house, it was a vast improvement over the cramped, standing-room-only space at the bar. Better yet, the small table was set apart from the others, so they could talk freely. They ordered crab cakes and grilled zucchini, and the wine continued to flow. It wasn't long before the conversation turned to work, and Ford brought up the laptop. "You got it back today, didn't you?"

"We did. Our techs are working on rotating shifts for the next twenty-four hours, but I have the feeling you could save them a lot of trouble."

The other woman seemed to hesitate. "I only got the whole story today. The people in Operations were doing their best to keep me out of the loop, and they nearly succeeded." Her voice turned hard. "I swear those people are all the same. You can take them out of the field and stick them in headquarters, but it doesn't make a bit of difference—"

"I agree," Crane said quickly, not wanting to hear another lengthy exposition on the politics of Langley. "But you said you found out what was on the laptop?"

"I did, but I can't tell you a thing, sweetie. You'll have to wait for the Bureau results. I'm already on thin ice with the director. He knows I told you we had it in the first place."

"What? How did he find out?"

"It had to be Harper," Ford said without thinking, her face tightening in anger. "That bastard has been doing his best to—"

"Harper?" Crane pounced on it immediately. "That's the same guy who showed up with Kealey in Alexandria. I called and told you about that after the raid, and you changed the subject, remember?" There was a brief, uncomfortable silence. "Aunt Rachel, who *is* he?"

The other woman seemed to waver, but not for long. "He's the DDO, Sam. He's the man in charge of the operations directorate, and you can forget I told you that. It's highly classified."

Crane nodded slowly, a satisfied smile spreading over her face. "I knew there was something about him. It didn't make sense from the start. For one thing, Agency lawyers don't show up at Bureau raids."

Ford nodded, her face twisting into a scowl. "He's been trying to undermine my position for months. After a while it became too much, so I did a little digging of my own, just to see if I could get some leverage."

"And what did you find?"

"Nothing." Ford drained her glass and shook her head, barely suppressing an incredulous laugh. "The man is an asshole, but he's amazingly clean."

"You just said he's the head of the DO," Crane protested. "That means years and years of fieldwork, right? Those guys are used to working outside the lines. He can't be totally clean. There has to be something there. A marital infidelity, for example, or a questionable bank deposit . . ."

"*Nothing*," Ford repeated. "I looked at the money angle, of course. He owns a brownstone on General's Row, and when I found out, I thought that must be it. I mean, a government employee can hardly afford a place like that, right? But as it turns out, the answer is simple: he did well in the stock market back in the eighties, then bought at the right time. He's actually quite wealthy, though most of his money is tied up in the house."

"Interesting," Crane murmured. "If he's that rich, I wonder why he still shows up for the daily grind."

Her aunt was pouring the last of the wine. Setting the bottle back on the table, she said, "I don't know, but he may need the equity sooner than he thought." A little smile crossed her face. "As it stands, he's on borrowed time at the Agency."

Crane perked up, sensing important information. "What do you mean?"

In a self-satisfied tone, the other woman started to go over the day's events, including the suspensions of Ryan Kealey and Naomi Kharmai, the latter of whom she described as a mid-level analyst in the CTC. She also explained Harper's tenuous position as the head of the DO, but the story was missing one thing: the cause for the shake-up. Crane was listening absently, trying to figure it out. Then it hit her.

"All of this wouldn't have anything to do with the break-in at the German Embassy, would it?"

Ford suddenly looked uncomfortable. She toyed with the stem of her wineglass for a moment, then looked up and said, "I heard you were trying to get assigned to the case. Is that true?"

"It's important, and there's a lot of pressure to solve it quickly. Whoever gets it will—"

"You don't want it," Ford said, cutting her off. The alcohol seemed to have temporarily lost its effect, as her tone was completely serious, and she looked worried. "Trust me, darling, it's career suicide. That one will never be solved, and once you get your name on the paperwork, I won't be able to get you out of it. When the case is still open a few months from now, the Bureau is going to start looking for a sacrificial lamb. Someone's neck will be on the chopping block, and I don't want it to be yours."

"You know something, don't you?" Crane's eyes opened wide, and she leaned forward in her seat, her voice taking on a demanding edge. "Come on, tell me the truth. Did the Agency have something to do with the break-in?"

"Don't ask me that, Sam." Ford shot her a pleading look, then glanced around hurriedly, as if realizing for the first time that they weren't alone. "Just stay out of it, okay? And you can keep that hurt look to yourself. It won't get you anywhere."

"Aunt Rachel, I just—"

"Samantha, *stay out of it.*"

"Okay! God, I was only asking. . . ."

"Promise me."

"Fine." Crane slumped back in her seat and looked away, folding her arms in frustration. "I promise."

Ford's expression softened immediately. Reaching over, she placed a hand on the younger woman's arm. "Darling, you have to trust me." She hesitated, then went on. "I know I never told you this, but before your mother died, she made me promise that I would look out for you if anything happened to her. Believe me, that's all I'm trying to do."

Crane lowered her eyes, and when she spoke, her voice was brittle and barely audible. "She didn't *die*, Aunt Rachel. Nothing *happened* to her. She killed herself. There's a difference."

Ford cringed, instantly wishing she could take back the words. "I know, and I'm sorry. I shouldn't have brought it up. Still, the point is the same. I gave her my word."

"If you want to look out for me, you can tell me what your people found on Mason's computer."

Ford sighed in exasperation. "You're not going to let this go, are you? Why does it matter, anyway?"

"It matters because I don't think the trail ended with Anthony Mason. He was working for somebody else, and I want to know who it was. His laptop is my best chance to figure it out." Her eyes shined. "Don't you see? Mason was dealing in some heavy stuff, so whoever he was working for must be huge. Getting *that* guy could make my career."

"Sam, you have no idea what you're talking about," Ford said, shaking her head sadly. "This goes way beyond Anthony Mason."

"What do you mean?"

"Well, you know about the ties between Mason and Arshad Kassem, right?"

The younger woman looked puzzled. "Of course, Harper told me about the Iraqi connection the morning of the raid in Alexandria. That guy Kealey mentioned it, too. It didn't seem too solid to me, but what does that have to do with the laptop?"

"I can't really get into it. Suffice to say, you'd be amazed."

"Aunt Rachel, I'm on *your* side, remember?" Thinking quickly, Crane shifted forward and lowered her voice. "Think about what happened here. If the CIA had pushed its way into a Bureau operation and stolen evidence from a crime scene while you were on the oversight committee, would you have let it pass?"

Ford shook her head slowly, obviously torn. "No."

"Well, in this case, it was *my* crime scene and *your* people doing the stealing. If Harrington hadn't been there, I would have been in charge, and it would have been my career in the toilet. Frankly, I think I deserve the truth."

Ford considered these words for a long time, but she couldn't fault her niece's logic. Finally, she nodded her agreement. "Okay, I'll tell you everything."

Crane brightened immediately. "Thanks. I knew I could count on you—"

"On one condition," Ford clarified. "You keep it to yourself until your own people get a break on the laptop. Wait until they give you a name . . . It won't take long."

"And what's the name?"

Ford hesitated one last time, but she had said too much to back out now. "Mason was being run by a man named Thomas Rühmann. He's an Austrian arms broker living in Berlin, where he's using the name Walter Schäuble. If your technicians are any good, they'll get the Rühmann identity off the hard drive, but not the location. And there's something else: I have it on good authority that Kealey is going after him."

The dam broke. Ford talked for twenty minutes, reiterating the initial link between Arshad Kassem and Anthony Mason. To this, she added everything the director had told her earlier—the same information Harper had done his best to keep from her. She went over the links between Rashid al-Umari and Will Vanderveen. She described their involvement in the bombing of the Babylon Hotel, and she mentioned the possibility of an Iranian connection. She went into al-Umari's background, and she brought up the possibility that the most recent attack in Paris was somehow related. The only thing she left out was the Agency's involuntary role in the embassy break-in. Crane appeared stunned by the scope of the conspiracy.

"When did you find out that Vanderveen was still alive?" she asked when Ford was done. She didn't need to ask who he was; a year earlier, the former U.S. soldier had been near the top of the FBI's most wanted list.

"Nearly two weeks ago."

"*What!* Why hasn't it been circulated?"

"It *has* been circulated, but only at the highest levels. The Bureau wasn't told until a few days ago. Don't you see? The president wanted to keep this quiet, and that meant limiting the number of people in the know."

"Well, you could have told *me*."

"You didn't need to know, darling," Ford replied, somewhat disingenuously. "However, the decision has now been made to release the information on a wider scale. He should be back on your top ten in a matter of days, so I didn't see the harm in giving you a little heads-up."

Crane was thinking hard, her brow furrowed in concentration. "There's one thing I still don't get. How is Kealey going after Rühmann if he's out of the Agency?"

"Apparently, he's taken it upon himself to finish the job. Ryan Kealey is a man of some means himself. He booked a private plane this afternoon. It leaves Upperville for Berlin at seven a.m. tomorrow."

"How do you know that?"

Ford smiled. "I have my sources, too, Samantha. The Agency has long cultivated relationships with patriotic, wealthy landowners in

Virginia, Maryland, and the District, all of whom have airfields on their property. All it took was a few innocent calls."

"Hmm." Crane swirled the contents of her glass thoughtfully, then came back to reality. "It's an interesting story, I'll give you that. I have to tell you, though, that the Agency is definitely wrong about one thing."

"What's that?"

"The Iranian connection. I don't know why al-Umari was chosen to play a role in Baghdad, given his background, but the hard-liners in Tehran are definitely behind it. All of it. The Iraqi insurgency is not capable of carrying something like this off."

Ford frowned. "You sound pretty certain."

"Well, I should be." Crane lifted her glass and smiled knowingly. "You see, I've been working directly with the informant in New York for the past month."

CHAPTER 36

POTSDAM, GERMANY

The following afternoon, Will Vanderveen and Yasmin Raseen crossed the Luisenplatz in the shadow of the Brandenburg Gate, angling toward an outdoor café on the far side. The temperature was hovering at 60 degrees, the air heavy and still beneath towering storm clouds. Having arrived earlier than intended, they had passed the time by seeing the sights. They'd strolled through the gardens of the Orangery in Sanssouci Park, admired the Marble Palace on the Holy Lake, and stopped for coffee in a redbrick café in the Dutch Quarter. The lengthy trek gave them the chance to look for signs of surveillance. Nothing seemed out of place, which meant they had guessed right in London: the surveillance had been placed on Khalil and not on them.

Still, since the courier's revelations at the Savoy, they had taken nothing for granted. For Vanderveen, in particular, every move from this point forward was fraught with danger. Knowing his face was posted at Passport Control was especially daunting; boarding the plane at Heathrow had been an exercise in extreme self-control, and he had been secretly surprised when they managed to pass through the airport in Berlin without incident.

Shortly after arriving, they acquired the necessary tools through Raseen's contact in Dresden, a former Stasi officer who'd since turned his hand to more profitable ventures. The man had come through in spectacular form, supplying all that was needed. As it turned out, he was still very much in the game, which made him slightly more trustworthy than he might otherwise have been. They were banking on the fact that he would not risk his reputation—or something worse—by cheating them. Vanderveen had taken a chance and wired the funds from London in advance, not wanting to have that much cash on his person when boarding the plane. The chance had paid off, and for an extra ten thousand Euros, the ex-Stasi officer had supplied them with a late-model Mercedes and a Globalstar SAT-550 mobile phone. The car was now parked on the Charlottenstrasse, and the bulky phone was in his jacket pocket. Everything else they had acquired that morning was packed away in the trunk of the Mercedes, which was not ideal, but it couldn't be helped, and it wouldn't be for long.

When they reached the café, Raseen left his side, took a seat, and waved for the waiter. Vanderveen retrieved the satellite phone from his coat and continued around the square. Since the courier's death in London, everything had gone according to plan, with one major exception. The previous night, he had placed a call to his contact in Washington, D.C., and there had been no answer. Now he dialed the number again and waited.

"Hello?"

"It's Taylor. Where have you been? I called yesterday."

"I know, but I couldn't get away. Have you reached your destination?"

"Yes. Anything new?"

"Quite a bit, actually . . ."

Vanderveen returned to the table ten minutes later. The food had arrived: sandwiches for him, yogurt and freshly baked bread for her, coffee for two. He took a seat but left the food untouched, and she noticed immediately. "What is it? What's happened?"

He leaned forward, dropping his voice to a murmur. "Kealey is already on the way."

She stopped buttering a slice of bread and studied him carefully. "So he knows about Rühmann."

"So it would seem. He left a private airfield in Virginia at 6:00 AM eastern time, which means he should arrive sometime this evening.

He has someone with him, a woman named Kharmai. Undoubtedly, they'll want to talk with our friend."

"And you think they'll move tonight?"

Vanderveen thought for a moment. "I think there's a good chance they will. But that's not a problem . . . In fact, it means we'll be able to leave the country sooner than we thought."

She nodded her agreement.

"Try and eat something," Vanderveen said. "We may not get the chance later tonight."

On the return trip around the square, he had stopped at a news-stand to pick up a few papers. As Raseen dutifully tucked into her food, he unfolded a copy of *Die Welt* and read the cover story. The news from Iraq was predictably dire; the day before, a suicide bomb-ing at the shrine to Imam Musa al-Khadam—one of the holiest sites in Baghdad—had resulted in 45 deaths. According to the Interior Ministry, a secondary device placed in a truck outside the Khadamiya hospital claimed the lives of 32 more as the injured were rushed from the shrine to the hospital in makeshift ambulances. Soon there-after, angry crowds gathered at checkpoints leading into the Green Zone, and several U.S. military vehicles were fired upon as they tried to leave the American enclave. Sixty-three American casualties had been reported by the Pentagon over the past three days.

In the European edition of the *London Times*, however, Vanderveen found a much more interesting article. An investigative journalist in Karbala had uncovered the circumspect sale of an oil refinery east of Samawah. The refinery, originally owned by Rashid al-Umari and the Southern Iraqi Oil Company, had been sold to a conglomerate of Sunni investors, several of whom had direct ties to Iranian president Mah-moud Ahmadinejad. The *New York Times* had picked up the story on the AP, as had every other major newspaper in North America and Western Europe.

In response, Ahmadinejad aired a speech in which he denied Iran-ian involvement, but praised Moqtadr al-Sadr and the Mahdi Army for what he described as "God's work in ridding Iraq of the Zionist in-vaders." That Nuri al-Maliki—the Shiite prime minister—had also been targeted in the recent wave of attacks seemed to have escaped the Iranian leader's attention, but his remarks had had the expected effect. The U.S. ambassador to the United Nations called for a full inquiry into the circumstances surrounding the death of Nasir al-Din Tabrizi in Paris, and a former secretary of state appeared on *Meet the Press*, where he stated his belief that Iran was actively working to undermine U.S. policy in Iraq. He also remarked that such activities would not go unchecked by "this or any other administration."

Vanderveen folded the newspapers and absently sipped his coffee, which tasted as if it had been made several hours earlier. Everything was working according to plan. The Iranians were under escalating suspicion, and the various factions in Iraq were at each other's throats. The American troops were caught in the middle and sustaining huge losses with each passing day. Once the delegation in New York was taken out, Iraq would almost certainly slide into civil war. Izzat al-Douri was about to get his wish.

Thunder overhead pulled him out of his reverie. He glanced at his watch. Raseen, catching the gesture, looked over her shoulder. Tourists were clustered on the other side of the square, standing around the Brandenburg Gate, apparently unaware that there was a much grander specimen—with the same name, no less—on the Pariser Platz in Berlin, just a few kilometers to the east. Most of the tourists were toting cameras and daypacks, and a few carried umbrellas in anticipation of the building storm. As Vanderveen watched, one man walked to the center of the square, turned, and fired off a series of shots with a digital camera.

"That isn't him," Raseen remarked softly, her eyes trained on the figure in the near distance. "He's wearing the right clothes, but that isn't Rühmann. Why didn't he come?"

Vanderveen slowly shook his head. He hadn't really expected the Austrian to show up in person. The man standing in the center of the square, looking around impatiently, without a hint of subtlety, was Karl Lang, Rühmann's bodyguard and personal assistant. His picture and background information were in the file they'd been given the previous day. Before leaving London, Vanderveen had memorized the contents and dropped the file down a grate on the King's Road.

"I'm not sure," he said, raising a hand to wave Lang over. "But this man is here for us, so let's say hello."

* * *

Lang was in his late thirties, short and heavily built. An expensive Nikon was draped around his neck, the strap tucked under the grimy collar of a light cotton jacket. His features were strangely androgynous, not in keeping with the rest of his body. As he walked to the table, he removed a blue daypack from his shoulders. Once he was seated, he tossed it casually under the table, where it landed next to a nearly identical pack.

"How did you get here?" he asked in English. His tone was distinctly confrontational.

"We have a car," Raseen told him. "No one followed us."

Lang snorted but did not reply.

"Where is Rühmann?" Vanderveen asked. "I was told he would be here."

The words earned him a disdainful look. "My employer is a very important man. He can't afford to waste time dealing with trivialities. Besides, meetings are dangerous. This could have been handled over the phone."

"What about the key to the storage facility?"

"That could have been sent by mail." The man leaned forward, his face pinched in anger. "Let's get something straight. I don't want to be here, and you don't impress me. For a professional, you take a lot of foolish risks. I know who you are, Vanderveen, and so does Herr Rühmann. Did you honestly believe that he wouldn't learn your identity? How do you think he lasted this long?"

"Certainly not by employing arrogant little shits like you," Vanderveen replied in a calm, measured voice. The German bridled instantly, reaching over the table, but Raseen quickly batted his hand away.

"Stop it," she hissed, glaring at each of them in turn. "We're in the middle of a public square." She focused her cold gaze on the courier, and there was something in her face that made him sit back instantly. "Since you're here, I assume you've received the final payment."

"Yes. The wire transfer came in yesterday," Lang confirmed. "The key is in the pack. It will open a ground-level unit at the Lake Forest storage facility in Montreal. Unit 124, to be precise. Directions from Montreal-Trudeau are in there as well, along with an invoice for the boiler. All that leaves is the equipment. You know what you need, correct?"

"A truck and a forklift," Vanderveen replied.

"That's right." Lang had a pedantic way of speaking, as though he were addressing a child. "But not just any truck and forklift. It's important that you get it right, or you won't be able to move the device, at least not safely. The truck needs to have a gross vehicle weight rating of at least thirty thousand pounds, with multi—"

"Multi-leaf spring shocks, I know. And a pneumatic forklift rated at twenty thousand pounds. I'm well aware of the specifications."

Lang's face tightened into a sneer. "Well, you seem to be very well informed, which only proves my point. This meeting was entirely unnecessary." He nodded toward the clear glass table, beneath which both packs were clearly visible. "You have what you need. We've received the money. Is there anything else?"

Vanderveen smiled pleasantly. "No, that should do it. Thanks for your time."

"Right," Lang said curtly. He retrieved the pack that Vanderveen had brought, stood, and walked away.

"What a nice man," Raseen remarked, her voice heavy with sarcasm. "You know, I don't think Mr. Rühmann is too pleased with us."

"Well, he doesn't really know us, does he? Let's see how he feels in a few hours. Maybe we can improve his disposition."

After paying the check, they started back toward the car, which was parked on the other side of the Brandenburg Gate. As they walked, Vanderveen retrieved the satellite phone from his pocket and punched in a number.

"Who are you calling?"

"A friend in Manhattan." He looked over. "We need to find a copying place. Any ideas?"

"There's one on the Charlottenstrasse. I saw it when we left the car."

"Good. I need to send him something."

CHAPTER 37

NEW YORK CITY

It was just after 10:00 AM in a warm, cluttered office in the garment district of Manhattan. The room was enclosed by low cement walls and glass panes, the interior blinds pulled down. There was almost no natural light in the room, owing to the height of the surrounding buildings. On the other side of the glass, Amir Nazeri could hear his employees at work: the low rumble of voices, the whine of a small forklift, the thump of heavy pallets hitting the smooth cement floor. Behind him was the steady rumble of morning traffic on West Thirty-seventh Street. Caught in the middle, Nazeri was lost to the sounds, immune to the racket that constituted his daily work environment. As he flipped through the accumulated mail, his telephone rang. He looked up, startled. The sound caused a ripple of apprehension to run through his body, just as it had done for the past several weeks. He hesitated for a long moment before reaching for the receiver.

"Amir, it's Erich."

Nazeri's mouth went dry instantly, but he forced himself to speak, his spare hand tightening around the arm of his chair. "Kohl." He caught himself and said, "I've been expecting your call."

"Good. I'm glad to hear it." The voice on the other end was calm and confident. "It's time, my friend. Have you made the arrangements?"

"Yes. The transportation is waiting, along with the forklift. The second vehicle is already in Ithaca."

"What about the other materials?"

"Here at the warehouse, locked in a spare room."

"Good." There was a rustle of paper, then, "The manifest needs to list a 150-horsepower commercial steam boiler. The width of the cabinet is fifty-six inches, the length is one hundred and fifty-six, and the height is one hundred and forty-five. That includes the barometric dampener. I'm going to fax you the commercial invoice. What else do you need?"

"The manifest, of course, but I can fill that out myself. My people in Montreal will fax it to the U.S. broker."

"Fine. Amir, I want to be sure you can handle this. We don't have time to waste. Today is Sunday. We need to be ready by Tuesday morning."

Nazeri had written down the dimensions. He looked at the numbers and ran through them quickly. "It's longer than I expected, but that's not a problem. How heavy is it?"

"The actual shipping weight is 15,340 pounds."

"Fine. I have a vehicle prepared." Nazeri hesitated. "Will this stand up if I'm stopped on the bridge? I can't risk—"

"It won't have to stand up if you fill out the manifest correctly. You're a naturalized citizen, and you're known to customs. You come in and out of Canada all the time. You have nothing to worry about."

"Yes, I . . . I suppose you're right."

There was a lengthy pause. "Amir, you're not having second thoughts, are you? I thought you wanted this. I thought you wanted to set things right."

Nazeri felt sweat running over his ribs. It had all been talk to this point, but now the time for talk was over. In theory, he could still go back. In reality, he had sealed his fate with the promise he'd made six months earlier. He steeled himself and said, "I'm willing to do whatever it takes. I haven't forgotten, Erich." He paused, and a face flashed into his mind. It was a face he had not seen in many years. A face he would never see again, at least not in this lifetime. Suddenly, all doubt was gone. "I could never forget."

"Then I'll see you in Montreal, my friend. The Lake Forest storage facility, unit 124. Ten a.m. tomorrow."

Nazeri looked at the clock on his desk. "If I'm going to make it by morning, I need to make some calls."

"Then I'll leave you to it. And Amir?"

"Yes?"

"Be ready to work all night. It all comes down to Tuesday."

The phone went dead. Nazeri held it for a minute longer, staring absently at the far wall. His chest felt hollow, his mind buzzing with fear and adrenaline. It was hard to believe it had all come down to this.

When Nazeri looked back on his life, he could not help but feel a certain amount of pride; by any standard, he had accomplished a great deal in his forty-four years. He had been born in Tehran, the fifth of seven children. His mother was French, his father a professor of physics at the Iran University of Science and Technology. From an early age, it was clear that he had not inherited his father's aptitude for science, though his intelligence was never in doubt. At the same time, he had little interest in school, and even less interest in the impoverished state in which his family existed. When Amir was a child, his uncle had spoken of Europe in glowing terms, and it was this thought that had consumed his teenage years. He wanted nothing more than to leave Iran and never return, and following the fall of the shah in 1979, the opportunity finally presented itself. He immigrated less than a year after Khomeini assumed power, but he did not travel to Europe, as he'd originally intended. Instead, he went to America.

The United States was everything he could have hoped for, though at first, he'd been unsure of how to approach his newfound freedom. Owing to his lack of formal education, he was forced to work a series of mediocre jobs. Eventually, he went to work for a transport service based out of Ithaca. The company was owned by an Iranian American, a man who'd built his wealth in real estate before branching out to freight. The owner took a liking to the hardworking Nazeri and brought him into the front office in the summer of 1985. Over the next two years, the owner taught his young apprentice everything he'd ever need to know, and then he sold Nazeri the company, Bridgeline Transport, Inc.

At the time, the company consisted of two associates, three tractors, and five trailers. Now, more than twenty years later, Bridgeline had a fleet of twenty trucks and fifty trailers. The company employed more than 30 staff and drivers. Opportunities had come along in recent years, the chance to expand at a faster rate, but Nazeri had preferred to keep things on a manageable level. He had no desire to take on a partner, and by keeping things small, he'd never been forced to do so. The company specialized in cross-border transportation; for this reason, Nazeri owned a small terminal just outside Montreal, on the St. Lawrence River, in addition to the original facility north of Ithaca. The hub on West Thirty-seventh was used primarily for administrative purposes, though he also used it to run a vending service for businesses in Manhattan.

To the casual observer, Amir Nazeri appeared to epitomize the American dream. He had come from humble roots, survived an oppressive regime, and risen to considerable wealth and success in a new land. But the things Nazeri thought and felt in his private world would have shocked the people closest to him—if there had been people close to him. The truth was that he had never felt a connection to his parents, and his siblings meant nothing to him. He had never had any real friends or romantic attachments to speak of. The only person he'd ever truly cared for—ever really loved—was his cousin Fatima.

She was his first cousin, the daughter of his father's youngest brother. As children, they had lived two houses apart in Tehran. From the very start, he had been confused by his devotion to her. She was a plain girl at best, not particularly pretty, not especially charming. But she had returned his affection, and there had been something between them that he could never hope to duplicate. In short, she was his whole world. He had watched with bursting pride when she was admitted to Azad University, with burning jealousy when her marriage to a fellow student was arranged, and with overwhelming, guilty satisfaction when her suitor was killed in a car accident two days before the wedding was to take place. Once Nazeri gained financial security in the United States, he had begged her to join him, but she had refused, citing her work. They remained extremely close, however, and he traveled to Tehran as often as possible to visit her. He had repeated the offer on dozens of occasions, but she always declined. At least until the previous year, when her correspondence had stopped without warning. No telephone calls, no letters . . . nothing at all.

The silence was unbearable. He was desperate for answers, but there was nowhere to turn. Her parents were dead, as were his, and he had not been in touch with his siblings for years. Fatima's only brother was also deceased, an indirect casualty of the Iran-Iraq war. Nazeri had no idea where she worked: she had always avoided the topic, and when confronted, she addressed it in vague generalities. He'd always had the impression that her position was with the government. He couldn't be sure, though, and even if he was right, it didn't help; he had no contacts within the regime. In short, no one could tell him what had become of her. He labored for months, distracted at work, unable to let it go.

And then came the fateful day. Five months after her disappearance, a man telephoned Nazeri at his Manhattan office, claiming to have information about Fatima's disappearance. Nazeri agreed to meet at once, already aware of a crushing weight in his chest. He met Erich Kohl for the first time the following day, and the news the German brought only confirmed his worst fear: his beloved cousin was dead.

Kohl never explained how he knew of Fatima's fate. Nor did he explain how he'd acquired the proof, and Nazeri, consumed by grief, never thought to ask. As far as he was concerned, it didn't matter. The German had showed him government documents detailing an FBI raid in Washington, D.C., an incident that claimed the lives of two Iranian nationals, including that of his cousin. It had taken place exactly five months earlier, around the time she had stopped returning his calls. For Nazeri, it suddenly became clear: her work with the Iranian government was far from ordinary. According to the FBI account, however, her death had nothing to do with politics. Instead, it was the result of a high-risk arrest warrant gone bad. The file contained a detailed account of the raid, concluding with a description of Fatima Darabi's final moments. The dry, economical prose had left Nazeri trembling with rage.

The file was accompanied by pictures. He had not been able to look at them for long, but what he had seen remained in his mind and swelled in his chest, turning his love for his adopted country into something else entirely. Kohl had given him a week to ponder what he had learned, and then he'd returned with a simple offer. At some point in the future, he said, he would return with an opportunity. A way to show the Americans that their actions were not without consequence. For Amir Nazeri, the decision was easy to make, and now, nearly half a year later, he was bound by his word. Despite his fears, he did not regret making the promise.

Turning to a metal filing cabinet, he found the appropriate documents and placed them on his desk. He heard the fax machine start up as he began filling out the manifest. When he was done, he went to the fax and retrieved the invoice that Kohl had sent. He scanned it quickly. Everything seemed to be in order.

He looked at the phone. All he had to do was place the call to his U.S. broker. Once he did that, there was no turning back.

He picked up the phone and started to dial.

CHAPTER 38

BERLIN

When Thomas Rühmann's business brought him to Western Europe, he worked from the top floor of a five-story building in central Berlin, on the south bank of the River Spree. The front of the squat, gray stone structure faced a narrow road lined with parked cars, and the back dropped straight into the river, flush with the retaining walls that guided the waterway through the heart of the city. The apartment building was flanked by a crumbling antique shop and a store that sold secondhand musical instruments, the façade of which was covered in graffiti and leaflets advertising upcoming shows throughout the city.

Thick black clouds were still moving in as Karl Lang walked up the sidewalk quickly, avoiding the withered trees sprouting out of the cracked cement and the cluster of youths arguing loudly outside the music shop. The trip from Potsdam had taken him twice as long as it should have, owing to a lengthy stop at a roadside café, where he'd consumed a simple meal of veal schnitzel, roast potatoes, and sauerkraut, all washed down with a strong wheat beer. After the first *Hefeweizen*, he'd consumed another two with surprising speed, still trying to clear his mind of the meeting he'd just attended.

He knew he'd hidden it well, but the truth was that the woman had terrified him. Her presence alone was deeply unsettling, and although it was difficult to pick out the precise reason, he thought it might well stem from the way she moved. Every gesture was graceful and slow, but to an unnatural extent. It was almost as if she'd written down everything she was going to do for the day, and was taking great pleasure in prolonging each and every performance, immersing herself in the smallest details. Even more frightening was her voice. It was low, throaty, and strangely erotic, but it also held an odd quality that he couldn't quite define. To Lang, it sounded as if she were trying to earn the trust of a small animal, only to strangle it once she had it in her arms.

He shivered involuntarily, just thinking about it. Fortunately, he'd never have to see them again. He'd make a point of suggesting that Herr Rühmann deal with more savory people in the future, but he set the thought aside as he approached the door and punched a button with his thick forefinger.

Rühmann employed a bookish young woman on the ground floor as the building's caretaker. She answered immediately and buzzed him in. Lang crossed the cracked linoleum of the foyer and made his way to the elevator, unaware that the door behind him had hung open longer than usual. The brass doors to the elevator slid open, and he paused, hesitating. Rühmann had asked him to fax some paperwork to the storage facility in Montreal, effectively terminating the lease, and he'd left the originals in the car. He was about to turn back, but before he could, he felt something cold and hard pressing into the base of his neck. He stepped forward instinctively, moving into the elevator. A familiar voice said, "Stop right there. Hands out by your sides."

Slowly, Lang complied, his mind racing, stomach churning. Once his hands were up and cocked at the elbows, the muzzle moved away.

"Turn, slowly."

Lang turned. Will Vanderveen was standing inside the doors, holding a suppressed HK Mark 23 in his right hand. The gun was now at waist level and close to his body; he was holding it more like a useful accessory than a murderous tool. Lang instantly thought of the Glock .40 concealed beneath his thin cotton jacket, but he knew he would never get it out in time. Behind Vanderveen, the woman stepped into the elevator. She examined the controls for a moment, then turned to face him.

"You need a key, correct? To get to the top floor?"

Lang nodded, trying to stop from trembling; even now, he couldn't meet her eyes. "It's in my pocket."

"Take it out, but do it slowly."

He did as she asked, holding it out in his right hand, but she shook her head. "Throw it to me."

Lang could barely understand her heavily accented English, but Vanderveen, seeing the confusion on his face, quickly repeated the instructions in German. Lang tossed Raseen the key. She picked it out of the air, then turned to the controls. Seconds later, the elevator jolted upward.

For no apparent reason, Lang looked up at the sudden motion and didn't see what happened next. Vanderveen raised the Mk23 and fired twice. The first shot pierced Lang's heart. The second tore through his chest, coming to an abrupt halt against his spine. The German dropped to the floor of the elevator, groaned once, then went still.

The elevator shuddered to a stop, and the doors slid open.

The entrance hall in the fifth-floor apartment rivaled the foyer on the ground floor in size, but easily surpassed it in style. Recessed lighting played over neoclassical wall murals, and the antique parquet floor glistened beneath their feet. After pulling Lang's body out of the elevator, Vanderveen checked the empty compartment quickly. There was no blood on the metal floor, and neither of the low-velocity rounds had exited Lang's body. The doors closed, and Vanderveen paused to listen. He could hear music playing softly through a pair of double doors—Mendelssohn's Piano Concerto No. 1. He adjusted the pack he was wearing and started to move toward the music. Raseen trailed softly behind him, a suppressed Beretta .22 in her right hand.

The entrance hall led into a small drawing room. They skirted the cluttered furnishings and stepped into a large office. The pale yellow Regency draperies were pulled back from the massive casement windows, which overlooked the slow-moving, gray-black waters of the Spree. The office was elegantly appointed, the walls upholstered with moss green velvet, a nineteenth-century chandelier hanging from the plasterwork ceiling. Couches covered with silk cushions were scattered over the Brussels weave carpet, and at one end of the room, a series of leather-bound bookcases held a vast quantity of expensive tomes. To the left, there was a second doorway, leading to an expansive dining room. Just inside the door, an eighteenth-century desk was positioned at an angle to the windows, affording its owner a fine view of the river.

Behind the desk sat Thomas Rühmann, his neat silver head hunched over a series of documents. He glanced at his watch as they entered and started to speak without looking up. "Karl, where have you been? I need you to . . ."

He looked up and trailed off, his eyes narrowing slightly. There was nothing in his face that hinted at fear; if anything, his expression was one of mild irritation. Vanderveen had expected as much; Rühmann had not reached his current station in life by being easily intimidated.

"Who are you people? What are you doing here?"

Vanderveen was not surprised that the Austrian arms dealer didn't recognize him. He'd changed his appearance yet again the previous day. His close-cropped hair was now black and streaked with gray; his eyes were a pale, watery blue. They had only met once before. He had appeared in his natural state on that occasion, though he had used the name Erich Kohl.

"It's me, Thomas." Vanderveen moved farther into the room, but Raseen hung back, tapping the Beretta against her denim-clad thigh. "Don't you recognize my voice?"

Rühmann's face turned white, but it was his only concession. When he spoke, his voice was surprisingly strong. "What do you want? We've finished our business. I fulfilled my end of the bargain."

"Stop right there," Vanderveen said. Rühmann had started to move his right hand down to a drawer. "Stand up, please, and have a seat over here. I'm not sure what's in the desk, but I think it's best to remove any temptation."

The Austrian complied, selecting the armchair next to the one Vanderveen had indicated in a pointless display of disobedience. Meanwhile, Vanderveen checked the desk quickly. The second drawer held a nickel-plated Walther PPK. He tucked the handgun into his pocket and started going through the rest of the drawers.

Rühmann had turned slightly in his seat. His back was arched in indignation, his face a picture of aristocratic outrage. "Kohl, what do you think you're doing? You're making a terrible mistake, my friend, if you think you can barge in here and threaten me like this. . . ."

While he was speaking, Raseen had crossed the room to take the chair opposite his. The Beretta was still in her hand, but she held it down by her side, out of view. Rühmann could not help but look at her, and when she opened her mouth, her melodious voice poured forth. From that point on, Vanderveen became part of the furniture.

"Herr Rühmann, we are only here to ensure our security." She leaned back in her seat and crossed her legs, tilting her head to the side. Everything about her posture suggested a calm, relaxed disposition. "We need all of the documents pertaining to the storage facility in Canada. We need anything that might link you or us to the device, including financial transactions, and we need it immediately. You see, we have reason to believe a man from the U.S. government is on his way to interrogate you, and we wish to stop that from happening."

"You mean you intend to kill me," Rühmann said stiffly.

"I didn't say that," Raseen pointed out softly. "All we want are the documents. You'll have to come with us, of course, but we have no intention of killing you. You and your contacts are much too important to our organization."

"And where is Karl?"

"I have no idea. We left him in Potsdam."

Rühmann seemed to draw into himself for a moment. His face was expressionless, but Raseen could see that his mind was moving quickly behind those dark blue eyes.

"You say the U.S. government is behind this?"

"Yes."

"How did they track me to Berlin?"

"We're not sure. They got your name from Mason, but that doesn't explain how they tracked you here." Raseen paused thoughtfully. "Of course, it might have something to do with the break-in at the German Embassy. I assume you heard about it."

"Bastards," Rühmann hissed, his face contorting. "I told them they had to take me out of the database. I told them that a thousand times. . . ."

Raseen waved it off. "It's not important. All that matters is getting you somewhere safe, along with any relevant documents."

"*Relevant* documents? If the Americans are coming here, I'll have to destroy everything."

"How?"

"Burn bags," Rühmann answered absently. "They're used by the military and the CIA. The ones I have are designed for instant use in the field. They burn the contents while the bag stays intact. I managed to get hold of them through my friends in the *Bundeskabinett*."

"What about a computer? I assume you have one."

"Yes, I have a laptop. I'll have to pull out the hard drive."

He fell silent for a long moment, studying his hands, thinking it through. Finally, he said, "Where are you planning to use the device?"

Vanderveen looked up to address the question. "You don't need to know that."

"Bullshit!" Rühmann turned to glare at the younger man. "I'm the one the Americans are after. I think I deserve to know."

"It doesn't concern you."

The Austrian didn't seem to hear, and appeared to wither before their eyes, his face crumpling. "I knew this was a mistake from the start," he said in a low voice. "It's too big . . . It was always too big. Don't you see? If you use the device in the States, I'm finished. The Americans know I was at Al Qaqaa. They managed to keep the story quiet, but a select few still know what was stolen out of that facility."

He looked at each of them in turn, finding nothing in their neutral expressions. "This has something to do with Paris, doesn't it? That Iraqi minister who was killed." His voice started to rise. "What about the prime minister in Baghdad? Was that part of it, too? Answer me!"

"You supplied the weapons," Vanderveen remarked quietly. "You had some idea where they were going. What do *you* think?"

Rühmann didn't seem to hear. "I should have stayed out of this," he muttered. "It's too big. I'll never be able to move again."

"It doesn't matter," Raseen said. "You took the money. You can't back out now."

"They'll trace the device to me." The Austrian arms broker looked sick. "Thousands will die. They'll never stop looking."

"They can't prove a thing," Vanderveen lied. He knew that Rühmann was the primary suspect with respect to the theft at Al Qaqaa in 2003. It was never intended that the Americans should learn of the Austrian's involvement in the upcoming attack, but since he had been tied to Mason, the connection would eventually be made; it was all but inevitable. Still, the situation could be fixed easily enough. All Vanderveen had to do was pass additional instructions to the informant in New York. The informant, in turn, would suggest to his FBI handlers that Rühmann was working for the Iranians, which would further muddy the waters.

"We've taken many precautions, Mr. Rühmann." Raseen's voice was low and strangely seductive. "Your continued well-being is very important to us."

"I see," Rühmann replied. He was clearly skeptical. "You have an interesting way of showing your gratitude. You come here to warn me of danger, yet the first thing you do is show me your guns."

Raseen smiled gently, shooting a quick look at Vanderveen. He had already discovered a number of pertinent documents, which he'd stacked neatly on top of the desk. "Well, we didn't know if you'd see it our way, Mr. Rühmann. You did have a gun of your own, after all."

"Right." He looked over at Vanderveen, an annoyed expression crossing his face. "If you want my help, you can start by getting away from my desk." He motioned to the Beretta in Raseen's hand. "Do you mind?"

She shook her head. "Go right ahead."

The Austrian stood warily and moved to the desk. Vanderveen stepped aside as the older man started pulling paperwork out of the drawers. The frustration was clearly taking hold, and he finally let it out in a bitter tirade. "This is ridiculous," he spat, accidentally knocking a sheath of paperwork to the floor. "I don't know how you found me, and I don't care why you're here. This kind of intrusion is completely unprofessional. I'll never work with you people again, no matter how this—"

"Don't be stupid," Raseen said, interrupting him calmly. "Our business relationship is very profitable for you. If you have any sense at all, you won't throw it away over some hurt feelings."

Rühmann did not reply, his anger fading as he shot a curious glance to the door. Vanderveen was examining the frame, running his fingers over the lacquered wood. He walked the length of the wall, bouncing his knuckles against the velvet-covered surface. After a moment, he looked back to the Austrian.

"What's behind this wallpaper? Plaster?"

Rühmann frowned. He seemed annoyed at the suggestion that his exquisite surroundings could be constructed of something so crude. "It was exposed brick when I bought the place. I had it covered with plaster to hold the wallpaper. Why?"

Vanderveen frowned in turn. Ignoring the question, he walked back to the windows, his gaze fixed on the flat roofs of the buildings across the river. Realizing he wasn't going to get an answer, the Austrian turned to a painting behind the desk, a large Turner landscape. He lifted it gently from the wall, revealing a safe.

"Stop," Raseen commanded. Vanderveen turned instantly, alarmed by the sharp note in her voice, but she waved him away.

Walking over, she gestured for Rühmann to step aside. "What's the combination?"

He gave it to her, and she opened the safe. Inside, there were a number of burn bags and a small pile of numbered folders. No weapon. She gestured for him to continue. He pulled out the folders and started to push them into the bags, along with the documents stacked on the desk.

It took less than five minutes to fill all the bags. Raseen used the time to unscrew a small panel on the bottom of Rühmann's Hewlett-Packard laptop. Once she had the hard drive out, she slipped it into her pocket. Rühmann pulled the tabs on the burn bags, destroying the contents. All that emerged was a thin whisper of smoke. Vanderveen watched everything from his spot by the windows. His face was neutral, the gun resting on the ledge by his hand. He had dropped the backpack by his feet, and on several occasions he'd caught Rühmann staring at it with interest.

The Austrian fell into the seat behind his desk and sighed wearily. "So, that's it. When is this American supposed to arrive?"

"Sometime tonight," Vanderveen said. Kneeling, he unzipped the pack and started removing items. Some of the equipment had been supplied by the man in Dresden; the rest he had picked up himself at an electrical supply store. He pulled out the Semtex first, two half-pound blocks of grayish white material wrapped in green polyurethane.

Rühmann, leaning over his desk, recognized what he was looking at immediately. His eyes went wide. "What the hell are you doing with that?"

Vanderveen did not reply. Setting the plastic explosive aside, he reached into the pack and produced a bundle of electrical blasting caps, a bulky roll of insulated copper wire, wire strippers, a handful of clothespins, and a pair of 6-volt batteries. Finally, he removed a soldering iron and a plastic bag filled with hundreds of steel ball bearings.

"What the hell are you doing?" Rühmann repeated.

Vanderveen looked up, but he didn't offer an explanation. "Tell me something, Herr Rühmann. The door in the entrance hall . . . Does that lead to the stairwell?"

This was information that had not been contained in the file. "Yes," Rühmann said, obviously struggling to see the relevance. "It opens to a brief flight of stairs; then there's another secure door on the fourth-floor landing. You need a code to get through."

"Is there an alarm?"

"Yes, but it only activates my security monitors."

"Give me the code."

The Austrian recited four digits from memory.

"Good." Turning to Raseen, Vanderveen switched to Arabic. "I'm going to need some type of metal containers. Can you find me something like that? Coffee cans, for example? Look in the kitchen."

She went out as the Austrian looked on in utter confusion. Vanderveen was busy stripping the ends of a 20-foot length of wire when Raseen returned a minute later, bearing two large silver cans.

"What are you doing with those?" Rühmann asked, still standing behind his desk. His gaze swung between them rapidly. Receiving no reply, he elevated his tone. "I asked you a question, Kohl. *What the fuck do you think you're doing?*"

Without looking up, Vanderveen murmured a few words in Arabic.

Rühmann looked to Raseen. "What does that mean? What's he saying?"

She didn't reply. Her arm swung up, and she fired into the Austrian's face from a distance of 2 feet. The three shots came in rapid succession, so close together they sounded like one. Rühmann was already slumping when she fired the last round, his ruined face slack, his eyes and mouth open in a final expression of pure astonishment. He fell into his seat at an angle, flipping it over, coming to rest on the floor with one leg strewn over the upended chair.

Raseen lowered the gun and took a seat on a nearby couch. Then she leaned back and closed her eyes.

Twenty minutes later, she was in the kitchen making coffee when Vanderveen walked in. "I'm finished. Are you ready to go?"

She nodded. "I walked down to the door on the fourth floor. The code works fine. If someone really wants to get in that way, they'll be able to do it."

"Good."

After an extensive search for any paperwork they might have missed, they walked back to the entrance hall and entered the elevator. Vanderveen had dragged Lang's body out of sight, but Rühmann was still in the office, lying exactly where he'd fallen. The doors closed, and Vanderveen punched the appropriate button. As the doors slid open on the ground floor, he snapped off the key in the lock. Anyone trying to reach the penthouse suite would be forced to take the stairs.

They stepped into the dingy, empty foyer. There was just one apartment on the ground floor, that of the caretaker. Her number was posted on the buzzer outside the building. Raseen rapped on the door lightly as Vanderveen stood off to the side, out of view of the peephole. After a few seconds, they heard a muffled "*Ja? Was benötigst sie?*"

"Frau Hesser?" Raseen called lightly. "I'm Sara, Herr Rühmann's new assistant. He sent me down to ask you a favor. Do you have a minute?"

There was a long pause. Finally, the door cracked open. Raseen offered a friendly, appealing smile, and the door opened all the way, light spilling into the foyer. Vanderveen, standing off to the side, only saw part of what happened next. Raseen pushed her way into the caretaker's apartment, slamming the door shut behind her. Stepping forward, Vanderveen heard a brief scream, followed by two dull thuds. Then the door swung open, and Raseen reappeared. She didn't need to speak; a brief nod said it all.

They left the building and turned west. It was just after 6:00 p.m. Night had drifted over the city, and it started to rain as they walked, thunder booming in the near distance. They reached the Mercedes five minutes later. Vanderveen started the engine as Raseen climbed into the passenger seat. Soon they joined the light traffic moving north on the Friedrichstrasse. As they crossed the river, Raseen lifted the pack out of the backseat, where Vanderveen had tossed it before starting the car. Opening the main compartment, she extracted a pair of two-way radios. Like the rest of their equipment, the Motorola radios had been supplied by the man in Dresden. She turned each unit to the appropriate channel, then plugged in the headsets.

Vanderveen turned onto a narrow street running along the river, trying to gauge his position. As he looked to his left, a gap appeared between the buildings, and he saw a flash of Rühmann's building on the other side of the Spree. Vanderveen eased his foot off the accelerator. The curb was choked with cars, so he stopped in the road and flicked on the hazard lights. Fortunately, there was no traffic behind them.

"Here," Raseen said, handing over the pack. One of the radios was still inside, along with several bottles of water, a shooting mat, and a large poncho. Getting out of the car, Vanderveen slung the pack over his shoulder. There was one other pack in the backseat, but he ignored it and walked to the back of the car. He retrieved a black plastic case from the trunk as Raseen slid into the driver's seat.

She lowered the window as he approached. "Do you think it will work?" she asked, looking up at the surrounding buildings.

"I think so." Vanderveen was wearing an anorak over a thick sweater, and he pulled the hood over his head as he turned to follow her gaze. "I just need to find a good vantage point. It shouldn't take long. We can expect our friends in a few hours."

"Fine. I'll let you know when they arrive. I'll be in front of the building."

"Make sure you keep some distance. They won't be expecting us, but it's best to be safe."

"Right. See you later." She dropped the car into gear and accelerated quickly, the tires kicking up a spray of rainwater. Vanderveen crossed the road, black case in hand, and melted into the side streets bordering the river.

CHAPTER 39

BERLIN

By the time Ryan Kealey and Naomi Kharmai stepped out of the terminal building of Berlin International Airport at Tegel, 8 kilometers from the city center, the rain was coming down in great wind-blown sheets. White and beige Mercedes taxis were lined up at the curb, waiting for passengers, as were a few limousines and a number of dark SUVs. Lights on the façade of the terminal shone down like miniature moons, indistinct in the deluge, and although they were surrounded by groups of people engaged in conversation, their voices could barely be heard over the sound of the rain pounding onto the overhead canopy.

From her brief discussion with Ryan on the plane, Naomi knew they were going to be met by a man named Bennett. According to Jonathan Harper, Bennett was a CIA operations officer based out of the U.S. Embassy in Berlin, an Air Force veteran who'd seen combat in Panama and the Gulf. More importantly, he had worked directly under Harper in the past. The DDO had gone out of his way to help them one last time. He had placed a call before they left Upperville that morning, securing Bennett's assistance for their impromptu visit. Despite Harper's assurances, Naomi wasn't sure what to expect; Bennett might not enjoy the idea of operating without the approval of his immediate superiors. She would have discussed this possibility with Ryan, but he didn't seem to be in a talkative mood, so she hadn't pushed it.

At first, it had been difficult to keep quiet on the plane. She had so many questions. What did he hope to get out of Rühmann? Did he really think the Austrian would lead them to Vanderveen? Mainly, she wanted to know why he had asked her to come along. She suspected it was mostly guilt, but she hoped that wasn't the case. After all, it had been her decision to join him in raiding the German Embassy. He had tried to talk her out of it, but she had insisted, and it wasn't his fault it turned out badly. She much preferred to think she was there because she had earned the right, because she had proved her value. Because she had a stake in how it all played out. Either way, she was glad for the chance. This was an immediate task, a way to take her mind off the fact that she'd just lost the only job she'd ever really loved. With little else to do, she had spent hours on the plane trying to figure out a way to redeem herself. Unfortunately, she wasn't sure how she could make up for violating a direct order from the president. If anything constituted a firing offense, that was it.

Lost in thought, she didn't notice that a Range Rover had braked to a halt in front of them, the black paint glistening beneath a sheen of rainwater. The man who jumped out of the driver's seat was short and built like a bull. His blue eyes were small and bright in his square face, his upper lip completely obscured by a thick brown mustache. He came around the vehicle a little too quickly, almost as if he were about to pick a fight. Naomi resisted the temptation to take a step back as he marched up and extended a hand.

"Shane Bennett," he said in a low rumble. "You're Kharmai, right?"

Naomi nodded, hoping she didn't look as intimidated as she felt. "Yes, that's me. It's nice to meet you."

"Same here." He offered a warm smile, and she felt herself relax a little.

Bennett turned to Kealey and shook his hand. "And you're Kealey. Good to meet you."

Kealey returned the sentiment, but Bennett frowned as though he were trying to place the other man's face. Suddenly, recognition sparked in his eyes, and his mouth dropped open. "Holy shit, I know you. You were in the Shahikot, weren't you?"

Kealey looked uncomfortable. "That's right. I remember you, too. Mako 31. You were the combat controller."

"That's it." Bennett grinned broadly. "Never thought I'd see you again. Anyway, I don't mean to hold you up. You have everything you need?"

Kealey looked down at Naomi's bag. "Yeah, looks like it."

Naomi scowled, catching the sarcasm. Ryan's only luggage was a tiny black grip, which was slung over his right shoulder. She didn't know how he could travel so light, and she felt a certain satisfaction when Bennett lifted her large suitcase with one arm and tossed it easily into the back of the Range Rover.

Ryan moved to the front, so she climbed into the backseat. As soon as the doors were closed, a shrill noise penetrated the warm, still air inside the vehicle. Bennett lifted a satellite phone from between the seats and answered. Listening quietly for a few seconds, he handed it over to Kealey. "It's Harper."

Kealey accepted the phone and got out of the truck, closing the door behind him. He moved off immediately, getting some distance between himself and the people standing outside the glass doors of the terminal. Kharmai and Bennett were left to sit in uncomfortable silence.

"So," he finally said, turning slightly in his seat. "How long you been with the Agency?"

"About five years," she replied, thinking it best not to mention the fact that she'd just been fired. "What about you?"

"Less than a year," Bennett said, running a hand over his close-cropped hair. "Director Harper brought me in personally. I did some work with his people when I was still with the Air Force."

"Don't take this the wrong way, but when I think of people moving from the military into the CIA, the Air Force doesn't exactly spring to mind. Except for pilots, that is, and you don't seem to fit the profile."

He emitted a short, barking laugh. "Can't argue with that. You've got a sharp eye, missy."

Missy? She looked out the rain-streaked window, shrugging it off. She didn't think he was being intentionally condescending, and she didn't want to get off to a bad start. She decided to change the subject. "So what were you saying about the Shahikot? Where is that, anyway?"

"Afghanistan," Bennett replied. He lifted a cup of coffee from between the seats and showed it to her, raising his eyebrows. She shook her head. He shrugged and peeled off the lid, taking a long sip.

"When were you there?" Naomi pressed.

"In 2002. You remember Operation Anaconda?"

"Vaguely. That was a while ago." She hesitated. "You said Ryan was there?"

Bennett nodded and laughed without turning around. "Yeah, and it's a good thing he was, too. The man saved our asses."

She leaned forward in her seat, suddenly interested. "What happened?"

He turned to face her. "Well, you have to know a little about what was happening at the time. It was less than a year after 9/11, four months after the fall of the Taliban. Six weeks after we missed bin Laden in Tora Bora, the decision was made to sweep into the Shahikot Valley in eastern Afghanistan. Our intelligence indicated a large number of al-Qaeda fighters were holed up in the area, including a number of HVTs."

Catching her confused expression, Bennett explained. "High-value targets. Senior al-Qaeda leaders. Anyway, Anaconda was a huge endeavor, involving more than two thousand soldiers from 10th Mountain and the 101st Airborne. The Rangers were in on it, too, along with a bunch of SF. The big push was to come on March second. Two days beforehand, reconnaissance units were sent in to the valley to set up observation posts, what we called OPs."

"And you were in one of those units?"

He nodded. "Mako 31. Our goal was to reach what we called the Finger—a ridgeline extending into the southern half of the valley, eleven thousand feet of razor-sharp rock. It was a two-day, seven-mile climb through knee-deep snow just to get to the top, but when we did, we got the surprise of a lifetime. Two men on a DShK machine gun, Soviet-made, with more than two thousand rounds. They had everything: a heated tent, fuel, food, plenty of small arms. They were in perfect position to ambush the Chinooks coming through the next day. So we called it in to AFO—that's Advanced Force Operations—and the decision was made to take them out."

"But something went wrong?"

"It was a complete disaster," Bennett said cheerfully. "There were six men in Mako 31: three guys from SEAL Team 6, one of whom was the commander, a Navy explosives expert, Kealey, and me. Everyone knew Kealey was with the Agency, but he'd been in-country from the start, so when he asked to come along, no one really complained. One guy threw up a few objections, but Kealey was in tight with the head of AFO, a guy he knew from Delta, so he got the okay. His presence in the Shahikot was never recorded."

Bennett paused to take another sip of coffee. "Anyway, the commander sent the other two SEALs over the ridge to take a closer look. Everything went fine. Then, just after four a.m., one of the fighters went looking for a place to piss, and he stumbled onto our position. He ran back to the tent, screaming his head off. The two SEALs on watch got over the ridge and fired on the enemy encampment, but their weapons jammed after the first couple of rounds. It was just one of those things. They cleared them as fast as they could, but the bad guys were already alerted. They pulled the tarp off the DShK and started to turn it around, but Kealey shot the guy loading the gun, then the gunner himself. He caught a bullet himself for his trouble."

"Unbelievable," Naomi breathed. She looked out the window. Ryan was still on the phone, his back to the Range Rover. "What happened then?"

"The SEALs managed to clear their weapons and started to engage. The commander grabbed Kealey and pulled him to cover while I called in our air support. The gunners on board laced the mountain with 105mm rounds. There wasn't much left of the enemy when it was over, I can tell you that."

"And Ryan?"

"He let one of the SEALs patch him up, but he refused an evac. He hung on for the duration." Bennett fell silent for a moment, then let out a laugh. "You know the funny thing?"

"What's that?" Naomi asked.

"The only guy who objected to Kealey joining Mako 31 was an army colonel, the commander of Task Force Rakkasan. He was scheduled to be on board the lead Chinook coming through the pass the very next day. If we hadn't taken out that machine gun, he probably would have been shot to pieces, along with most of his men."

Naomi fell back in her seat, taking it in. It was an amazing story, but before she could consider it further, Ryan was back at the vehicle, pulling open the front door. He handed the phone to Bennett as he climbed in. Looking between them, he seemed to sense that something had transpired while he was out of the vehicle, but he let it pass. "Let's go."

The drive into the city took forty minutes; the traffic slowed to a near halt on the A111. Kealey used the time to question Bennett thoroughly, and what he learned was not encouraging. The former Air Force sergeant didn't have the rank to allocate resources, and his other responsibilities had kept him occupied for most of the day, which meant that Rühmann's residence in Berlin had gone unwatched for hours on end. The lack of surveillance prompted Kealey to ask the obvious question.

"How do you even know he's there?"

"I checked three times this afternoon," Bennett replied. "The name he's been using in Berlin—Walter Schäuble—is listed on the buzzer at the front door. Rühmann has the penthouse, and the lights have been on all day. I also ran a discreet check through the TÜV . . . That's the agency that carries out safety inspections for vehicles registered in Germany. Under the Schäuble identity, Rühmann owns a Mercedes CLK coupe. The car wasn't parked in the street the first time I looked, but it was there when I passed the apartment later."

"That doesn't mean a thing," Kealey said. "Maybe he has an assistant. Rühmann might not even be in the country."

"If that's the case, wouldn't the assistant be traveling with him?" Naomi put in.

"Maybe . . ." Kealey fell silent, thinking it through. "We'll just have to look and see."

Bennett swung the Range Rover onto the Friedrichstrasse and followed it down to the river. Even seen through the curtains of rain, the black water shone with multicolored lights, most of which spilled from the immense blocks of flats on the south bank. A few houseboats were moored near the Reichstag, where the Luisenstrasse crossed the Spree. To their left, a towering pinnacle of light marked the TV Tower in the Alexanderplatz. Naomi gazed through her window, admiring the view for as long as possible. Then Bennett turned onto a narrow street just south of the river, and the squat buildings looming over the sidewalk replaced the luminous skyline. A few seconds later the vehicle started to slow.

"That's it," the ops officer said. They followed his gaze immediately.

"Doesn't look like much," Kealey remarked. "Rühmann knows how to keep a low profile."

"Yeah, he's smarter than most of his peers," Bennett agreed. He started to put his foot on the brake, but Kealey said, "No, keep going to the end of the street. We'll park there."

Bennett nodded. As they approached the intersection, he found a spot near the curb and pulled in.

"What do you have for weapons?" Kealey asked.

Bennett pulled back his jacket to reveal the butt of a Browning Hi-Power. Then he turned and said, "See those cases next to you, Kharmai? Hand one of them up, will you?"

She did as he asked. Following Kealey's lead, she opened the other. It contained a field-stripped Beretta Tomcat. She stared at the pieces for a long moment, trying to remember the weaponry course she'd taken at Camp Peary five years earlier. It took her two minutes longer than necessary, but she finally managed to put the .32 caliber pistol together. Dry firing it once, she heard a satisfying click. Then she slipped a 7-round magazine into the butt and chambered a round.

The other case contained a Sig P229, the standard-issue weapon of the U.S. Secret Service. This one happened to be chambered for 9mm rounds. Kharmai paused to watch Kealey put the weapon together. She had handed him a case at random, and she couldn't help but wonder what his reaction would have been if he had ended up with the smaller gun. She didn't think he'd care that much, but she knew that men could be surprisingly superficial about such things.

Bennett looked uneasy. "You know, I'm not supposed to have those weapons in-country. They're not registered with the embassy. If anything happens—"

"I don't think we'll need them," Kealey cut in. "But I'm not going in there unarmed."

"You'll try to keep this clean?"

THE ASSASSIN   333

"If I can. It's up to Rühmann."

"Well, that's the other thing." Bennett shot him a curious look. "How do you plan on handling this?"

"I assume Harper briefed you over the phone."

"He did."

"Then you know why I'm here. All I want is Vanderveen's location."

"And the weapons," Naomi reminded him. "We need to know who was ultimately taking possession at those ports in the Middle East."

"Right," Bennett said. "But then what? You can't leave him alive. He'll be on the phone before we leave the building."

Kealey's face turned hard. "I realize that. Let's just get up there and see what he has to say. I'll figure out what to do after that."

Bennett shook his head, but he pushed open the door and stepped into the rain. Kealey and Kharmai concealed their weapons and followed his lead. They moved at a quick pace down the flooded sidewalk, reaching the entrance to Reichstagufer 19 a moment later. Bennett punched a button at random, and a voice came over the intercom. "Yes?"

Bennett looked at a loss. Kharmai pushed him aside, scanned the list, and hit the same button. In rapid, exasperated German, she said, "Delivery for 4B. I'm not getting an answer, and I have other stops to make. Do you mind?"

A few seconds later, the door sprung open, and they stepped inside.

On the other side of the road, 20 meters west of the doorway, Yasmin Raseen watched them enter the building. She was sitting in the driver's seat of the Mercedes, the engine on, the heater running at full capacity. She was clearly visible to cars passing by in the road, but that was intentional; she wanted to appear like she was waiting for someone. A magazine was sitting on the passenger seat, the German edition of *Vogue*. She pushed it aside to reveal the Motorola radio, then pressed the TRANSMIT button. The earpiece was already in position, the wire concealed beneath her hair. "They're here. Two men and a woman. They just entered the building."

* * *

At that moment, Vanderveen was on the north side of the river, lying prone on the gravel roof of a four-story apartment building. The shooting mat was tucked beneath his body, the olive drab poncho draped over his back. The rain was beating against his back so hard it nearly hurt, and the cold had numbed his exposed skin hours earlier. The weapon that lay before him, the barrel propped up by an integral folding bipod, was a Steyr Scout Tactical with a 5-round box magazine. Through the preinstalled Kahles ZF95 mil-dot scope, he had an excellent view of Rühmann's brightly lit office, which was not more than 100 meters away, on the far bank of the Spree. As soon as Raseen's transmission came over the radio, he lowered the stock and returned the call.

"Give it a minute; then get inside." Raseen had taken the caretaker's key; she wouldn't need to be buzzed in. "Stay in the foyer until I give you the word."

There was a brief crackle of static, and then she acknowledged his words. Vanderveen lifted the rifle back to his shoulder and looked over the river with his naked eye. Under normal conditions, the Steyr Scout was a highly accurate weapon. In this case, however, it was practically useless, and it wasn't because of the rain. He had picked up the weapon that same afternoon, which meant that he didn't have time to acquire a zero. The dealer in Dresden had assured him the weapon was sighted in, but that didn't mean a thing; zeros were different for each shooter.

Even with time to sight in, though, he would have needed to break the Steyr back down to get it up on the roof, as he couldn't exactly be seen walking around with a fully assembled rifle. Either way, the weapon was less accurate than it was supposed to be, which explained why he wasn't going to try to take Kealey on the street. He had considered the option, but 5 rounds didn't leave much room for error, and Kealey was a world-class marksman in his own right. And there was another, more important factor at play: he had brought at least one other person along, the woman named Kharmai.

Vanderveen smiled to himself beneath the poncho. He had anticipated this possibility; in fact, he had anticipated everything. He was satisfied with his preparations, but there was something else, an undercurrent of pure adrenaline, that he couldn't ignore. It seemed as though everything since Maine had led up to this moment, his chance to finish the work he'd started eight years earlier.

What was waiting for Kealey in Rühmann's office was simple in concept and design, but extremely lethal in practice. The improvised device he had created was modeled after the M18A1 Claymore anti-personnel mine. Both cans were filled with hundreds of steel ball bearings, the open ends sealed with duct tape. Beneath the ball bearings were thick layers of cardboard, which would act as a buffer, and then the half-pound blocks of Semtex. Vanderveen had punched a hole in the bottom of each can, through which he'd routed the electrical blasting caps. The caps, in turn, were wired to separate 6-volt batteries, and from there to the clothespins.

The clothespins served as improvised detonators. Preparing them had been the trickiest part. He'd glued metal contact plates to each prong, then soldered the free ends of the wire to the plates. The prongs were now separated by nothing more than the glass panes of the windows in Rühmann's office. All it would take was one round from the Steyr. The window would shatter, causing the prongs to close. This, in turn, would complete the circuit, firing the Semtex. The pressure wave would shatter every window in the room, setting off the second device and filling the office with nearly two thousand quarter-inch ball bearings, each moving at a speed in excess of 500 feet per second.

The design was less than perfect, owing in part to the time crunch. The angle left much to be desired—the shape of the cans would limit the dispersion of the projectiles—and the trap was largely dependent on the ricochet effect the brick walls would provide. Still, he felt sure it would work. Raseen would see that the ground floor was impassable; if Kealey and Kharmai weren't shredded in Rühmann's office, they'd burn on the stairs. As far as Vanderveen was concerned, both were acceptable outcomes.

There was nothing to do now but wait. Vanderveen adjusted the stock of the Steyr, pulling it into his shoulder. His right eye was an inch behind the glass, his finger tapping the trigger guard lightly.

Nothing to do but wait.

CHAPTER 40

BERLIN

Kealey was the first through the door. He took in the scene quickly: a cramped, dirty foyer; a bare bulb hanging overhead; the elevator on the far wall. Turning left, he spotted the staircase. He went up the stairs quickly, Kharmai behind him, Bennett taking up the rear. It took less than thirty seconds to make it up to the fourth-floor landing, where they were confronted with the first real obstacle.

The door was simple enough; what caught Kealey's attention was the self-contained keyless entry system housed on the wall to the right. He examined it closely, then turned and looked up to the opposite wall, near the ceiling. A small Sony camera was mounted in the corner, aimed toward the door.

He turned to Bennett. "What do you think?"

The other man shrugged. "This isn't my forte. I have no idea how you're going to get in without the code."

Kealey swore and looked back at the door, thinking it through. His lock picks were buried in Kharmai's suitcase, but he didn't see how they'd help much in this situation. Then something came to him. "There's an elevator on the ground floor. Check it out, will you? See if we can get up that way."

Bennett nodded and went down the stairs. Kharmai moved to examine the keypad. After a moment she looked up and smiled. "No problem."

He looked at her incredulously. "What are you talking about?"

"Come here." He leaned close as she pointed to some of the keys. "These aren't strictly 'keys,' Ryan, because they're not independent of each other. The whole thing is a single pad, with circuitry underneath. The problem with this kind of system is that the same buttons are heavily used, and that makes them distinctive. You see? The numbers on these three are starting to wear."

Kealey followed her finger. On closer inspection, he saw what she was talking about. The 3, 7, and 9 keys were all worn down, the numbers starting to fade.

"They're also darker than the others. That's because of the oil on the user's fingers. It takes a long time, but eventually, it leaves a kind of signature."

"I won't ask how you know that," he said, shaking his head. "Where does this leave us?"

"Simple. I recognize this keypad . . . We had ones just like it on the interior doors at Grosvenor Square. It's a four-digit code, but only three of the buttons are worn. In other words, one number is used twice."

"Which number?"

She looked closely, her face barely an inch from the keypad. After a minute had passed, she said, "Nine. The 9 key looks a little darker then the other two."

"Are you sure?"

"No," she said, shaking her head in frustration. "I'm not sure at all. But it's my best guess, and that's all I can give you."

"So if you're right, that leaves us with ten possible combinations."

"Sounds right. No, wait . . . Make that twelve combinations."

Kealey looked up at the camera. "That helps, but I think we've lost our biggest advantage. Rühmann already knows we're here."

"Maybe not. I don't see any wires or conduit. Everything is behind the walls. That camera could be activated by the keypad, and we haven't touched it yet." She frowned. "Which could be a problem, actually."

"What do you mean?"

She looked worried. "This keypad is designed to deny access after three incorrect entries. If we get it wrong, we'll never get in."

Kealey paused to consider that. Bennett turned on the staircase a few seconds later, looking grim. "I checked the elevator," he said. "Somebody broke the key off in the lock for the fifth floor."

Kealey glanced at Naomi. He didn't speak, but he knew they were thinking the same thing: somebody else had gotten to Rühmann first.

"I went outside to check the list again. The caretaker lives on the first floor, so I banged on her door. I was going to feed her some bullshit story, thinking maybe she'd give us the code, but no one answered."

"She wouldn't have known it, anyway," Naomi muttered. "She's just there for the residents."

They all fell silent. Finally, Kealey said, "Fuck it. Let's give it a shot."

"Ryan, I don't think—"

"Come on, Naomi. The odds are one in four. The numbers are three, seven, and nine. Give me your best guess."

She took a deep breath. "Three, seven, nine, nine."

He punched it in, but nothing happened. The light on the unit stayed red. She shot him a pleading look, begging him to spare her the responsibility, but he wasn't about to let her off the hook. "Try again," he said.

"Three, nine, seven, nine."

Nothing.

"Last try," Kealey said. His voice was completely neutral. "Make it count."

"Umm . . . nine, seven, nine, three." He moved to punch it in, but she grabbed his arm. "No, wait." She closed her eyes and pressed her palm to her forehead, as though she could somehow draw the code out with her mind. "Nine, seven, three, nine."

He entered the numbers. There was an aching pause, and then the light flashed green. Kealey flashed a rare smile at Naomi, who had slumped against the wooden railing, looking as if she'd just run a marathon. "We're in."

They came to the second door. Naomi released an audible groan, but Kealey stepped forward and turned the knob. The door opened instantly. He pushed it forward carefully, listening for anything amiss. When the gap was large enough, he slipped into the entrance hall, followed by Bennett and Kharmai.

Kealey drew his Sig, and the others followed suit. He waved Bennett down a narrow hall, then gestured for Kharmai to stay close. She looked ready to argue, but he held a finger to his lips and moved before she had the chance. They turned left and started to clear the apartment.

The long, dimly lit hall led into a kitchen. The whole place seemed eerily quiet. They passed through to a dining room: wood-paneled walls, gilt-framed landscapes, elaborate chairs clustered around a mahogany table. The polished surface shone beneath a sterling silver chandelier. Kealey pointed to the kitchen, gesturing for Kharmai to hold back, but she ignored him and moved to the doorway of the office. The room was open and brightly lit, light playing over the moss-colored walls. There was a desk to the left. As she leaned in and examined the scene, her eyes went wide. She tugged on Kealey's sleeve and pointed. Leaning his head round the corner, he saw an overturned chair. A single leg was hiked over the upended piece of furniture.

"Is it him?" Naomi whispered. "I can't see his face."

"It's him." Kealey leaned against the wall and closed his eyes. It was over. He felt a sinking weight in his chest; he had come this far for nothing at all.

Kharmai was shaking his arm, but he pushed her away. She tried again. Reluctantly, he opened his eyes and straightened, turning to follow her gaze. Bennett was at the other door, moving into the office. Kharmai was still caught up in the moment, so she followed his lead. Kealey trailed reluctantly. He knew it was pointless; whoever had killed the Austrian would have thoroughly sanitized the apartment. There was nowhere to go; in losing Rühmann, they had lost their only lead.

Kharmai joined Bennett, who was standing over the Austrian's body. Kealey stepped into the room and started rifling through the desk. There wasn't a single scrap of paper to be found. Opening the computer, he punched the POWER button, but all that came up was an error message. He caught sight of the burn bags scattered over the floor. Picking one up, he looked inside and was greeted by the faint odor of smoke. It was just as he'd feared; they were far too late.

Bennett had walked over to the windows. Now he stretched his arms and stared over the river. "I can't believe it," he finally said. His voice was filled with regret and embarrassment. "I'm sorry about this, guys. I should have had people watching the building."

"It's not your fault," Kharmai said, staring down at the bloodied, distorted face of Thomas Rühmann. It was strange, but the sight didn't seem to affect her at all. It didn't make sense; losing her job had brought her to tears, but this terrible image meant nothing to her. It made her wonder if she had seen too much in her few years with the Agency, if she had lost something fundamental. "We were just too late. We should have been here a week ago."

"Maybe you're right, but still . . ." Something caught Bennett's attention, and he shifted the draperies aside. "Hey, what the hell is this?"

Kealey, looking at the other man, caught sight of something wrong, something flashing silver in the bright light of the room. He reached for Naomi's arm and screamed, "GET OUT! GET THE FUCK OUT NOW!"

Bennett turned instantly, his eyes opening wide, but Kealey didn't see the other man's final expression. All he could think about was getting back to the dining room. He dove to the floor, pulling Naomi down with him. She was shouting a question, probably demanding an explanation, but Kealey couldn't hear a thing. The roar came behind him, the whistle of hundreds of projectiles, the sound of instant death.

Then everything turned black.

Vanderveen swore as he watched the scene unravel. His vantage point was less than ideal, he'd known that from the start, but the options were few. All he could see was the big man, the one who'd come in from the hall. He knew Kealey and the woman had entered from the dining room, because the big man had turned to his left, and his mouth was moving in conversation. But then he'd reached for the draperies, and Vanderveen was left with no choice but to fire.

At 100 meters, there was no need to compensate. He lined up the crosshairs and squeezed the trigger gently.

The explosion was drowned out by a sudden boom of thunder, which somehow minimized the effect. Lightning flashed overhead as the fifth-floor windows exploded outward, glass raining down to the river. The lights blinked out in the office, even as the lights came up on the floors underneath. Vanderveen didn't wait to see if his plan had worked. Instead, he grabbed for the radio lying next to his side, under the poncho.

"They're up on the fifth," he shouted over the storm. "Get in there. *Now!*"

Yasmin Raseen flung open the door of the Mercedes and ran through the torrential rain to the door of the building. In her left hand she carried a pack filled with half a dozen 2-liter containers of liquid propane. She'd collected the fuel from a service station on the Müllerstrasse two hours earlier. She slipped the caretaker's key into the lock, then entered the foyer.

There was one person present, a teenaged girl with braided blond hair. She paused on the stairs, a confused frown on her face as Raseen rushed in. She opened her mouth to speak, but she never got the words out. Raseen raised her suppressed Beretta and fired twice. The only sound was that of the slide moving back and forth. The first round left a neat hole over the girl's right eye. The second missed entirely, tearing into the wood-paneled wall. The girl dropped without a sound, her lifeless body bumping over the remaining wooden stairs, coming to rest in the foyer.

Raseen crossed the linoleum floor quickly. There was a trash container next the elevator. She punched the button for the fourth floor. When the doors opened, she grabbed the container, placed it between the doors, then punched all the buttons at once. Racing back to the entrance, she tossed the backpack onto the stairs. Retreating as far as possible, she lifted the Beretta once more, covered her face, and squeezed the trigger. The backpack exploded, showering the stairs and the walls with burning propane.

Lowering the gun, she removed the Gemtech suppressor quickly, stuffing it into her pocket. She slipped the gun into the top of her jeans, under her shirt at the small of her back. She pushed out the door, aware of the screams on the first floor, aware of the shrill thump of the fire alarm. Seconds later she was back in the car, pulling onto the road, grabbing for the radio.

"It's done. I'm on my way to your location."

There was no reply. She pressed the TRANSMIT button and repeated the message. Still nothing. Dropping the radio, she shifted into second gear and punched the pedal, squealing onto the Friedrich-strasse.

Kealey came back to consciousness slowly, the plasterwork ceiling swimming into view, everything shifting crazily. He tried to sit up, but his limbs didn't seem to be working. He forced himself to think, to gain a sense of his surroundings. First, he was aware of the dark. It hadn't been dark a few seconds ago, but now the room was pitch black. He was completely blind. Worse was the ringing in his ears, which was more like a constant, high-pitched whine than anything else. He put down his hands for support, then pulled them back sharply; the wood floor was covered with shards of glass. He could feel warm, wet pain in his palms as he rolled unsteadily to his feet, trying to clear the haze in his mind.

Naomi. When it cut through the gloom, the thought hit him hard. Where was she? Was she even alive? He fell to his knees, ignoring the stabbing pain of the glass, and felt around on the floor. A sound caused him to turn to his right. Crawling forward, he reached out and felt something warm beneath his hand. He felt his way up to her hair, brushing it back from her face.

"Naomi?" His voice sounded far away, like it belonged to somebody else. "Can you hear me? How bad is it? Where does it hurt?"

She let out a low moan and tried to sit up. He moved behind her and helped her into a sitting position. "Can you hear? Come on, talk to me. Say something."

"My . . . my arm. My left arm. Something's wrong with it."

Kealey's eyes were starting to adjust to the dark. Turning her carefully, he could see several tears in her light blue pullover, wet stains spreading around the holes. A sick feeling washed over him instantly.

"It's nothing," he said, trying to sound more confident than he felt. "You're going to be fine. But we have to get out of here. Come on, I'll help you up."

"What about Bennett?" she asked, stifling a cry as he hefted her to her feet. "Where is he?"

Kealey moved carefully to the door and looked into the office. The light was weak, but he could see that Shane Bennett was clearly dead. He was lying on his back in the middle of the room, arms outstretched, his face and chest reduced to a mass of bloody pulp.

Kealey moved back to Kharmai, who was leaning against the dining-room table. "He's gone. Come on, we have to get out of here."

He guided her back through the kitchen. The lights were still on in the entrance hall, and it was there that he got his first good look at her wounds. Her left sleeve was virtually shredded, but there didn't seem to be as much blood as he'd initially thought. Her eyes were glazed over, though, and she could barely stand on her own; she was clearly in shock.

There wasn't time to be gentle; he had to check something out, but he couldn't leave her standing, not in the shape she was in. He pushed her down to the floor, propping her against the wall. Then he pulled open the service door. He was instantly greeted by a gust of hot air and the stench of acrid smoke. Down the stairs, he could hear people screaming on the other side of the second door, the one with the keypad. The stairs were clearly impassable. On the fifth-floor landing, there was an aluminum ladder leading up to the roof. He had noticed it before, but now it was more than a visual distraction— it was their only means of escape.

He went to the base of the ladder and looked up. There was a cheap combination lock on the hatch that led up to the roof. He hesitated; he could shoot the lock off, but the bullet would probably ricochet. Still, there was no other choice. He raised his Sig, took aim, and fired. He flinched involuntarily as the round bounced off the steel and slammed into the floor by his right foot, but looking up, he could see that the shackle had popped open.

He climbed the ladder quickly but awkwardly, the gun still in his hand. Bracing himself inside the concrete shaft, he pulled off the broken padlock and pushed open the hatch. Rain instantly started to pound his upper body as he threw back the metal cover, planted his hands on the roof, and lifted himself up, examining his surroundings. There was a large air-conditioning unit right in front of him, partially obscuring the buildings on the other side of the river. He could hear rapidly approaching sirens, but not much else over the thunderous rain.

Kealey dropped back into the shaft and descended the ladder, heading back for Naomi. When he turned the corner, he saw she was standing, leaning against the wall for support. She had obviously shaken off some of the shock, but her eyes were still glazed over, and he couldn't help but wonder if she had suffered a concussion. He grabbed her good arm and pulled her back to the ladder. The screams on the lower floors were starting to intensify. Kealey knew there was no fire escape, but there wasn't a thing he could do for the building's residents. All he could think about was getting Kharmai out safely.

He guided her to the ladder and turned her to face him. "Naomi, you have to climb. Do you hear what I'm saying? Nod if you understand."

She nodded, her eyes momentarily clearing. She reached out for the ladder and started to climb. She'd only gotten up a few rungs before she stopped. Kealey, following right behind, wedged himself up against her body to see what was wrong. Her face was pained and covered in sweat, and her eyes were squeezed shut.

"I'm sorry," she gasped. "My arm is killing me."

"I know, but we have to move." The smoke was starting to fill the shaft, choking them and stinging their eyes, even though the hatch was still open and rain was drilling in through the gap. "We have to get out. Come on, climb. *Climb!*"

A few seconds later, she reached for the next rung, then the next. After what seemed like an hour, they were on the roof. Naomi collapsed on the wet gravel, her chest heaving, her face contorted in pain. Kealey grabbed her shirt, dragged her over to the air conditioner, and drew his weapon.

The relentless rain seemed to have revived her. She sat up and leaned against the unit, then noticed the gun in his hand. "What are you doing?"

Kealey didn't answer; his mind was whirring. Something about the explosion seemed very familiar. He tried to block out the sound of the storm, the scream of the sirens, and the hoarse shouts of the people in the street to his rear. He tried to project himself back to the stunned silence that had followed the explosion. When he'd gone back to check on Bennett, the floor had been littered with steel ball bearings. Kealey knew of only one device that utilized that kind of projectile: the M18. But when Bennett had pulled back the draperies, he had seen the device for a split second, and it didn't look like a Claymore.

But if it wasn't that, it was something similar, and he knew he'd seen it before. . . .

And then it hit him. Will Vanderveen had demonstrated the exact same thing at a demo range nine years earlier. Suddenly, everything became clear; not only had Vanderveen killed Rühmann, he had signed his work. The improvised explosive device bore all of his trademarks, and with this realization, Kealey knew exactly how he'd detonated the device. Vanderveen was one of the finest marksmen he'd ever known, a graduate of the U.S. Army Sniper School. He would have set the trap with a sniper's mentality, which could only mean one thing: he'd used an electrical gate to complete the circuit. A rifle would have afforded him the protection of distance, and the roofs on the other side of the river offered a perfect vantage point.

There wasn't any solid evidence to support this theory, but Kealey had survived for years on the edge by trusting his instincts, and right now, they were telling him he'd gotten it right. There was no doubt in his mind that Vanderveen was responsible, but there was something else: somehow, he knew the other man was still out there, waiting to finish the job.

Pressing his back to the air conditioner, he moved sideways to the edge of the unit. He was completely involved in the moment, but he also felt a little sick, realizing how naïve he had been. The only reason they hadn't died in the office was luck. The same was true of their venture onto the roof; Vanderveen would have fired if he'd had a bead on the hatch. At the same time, Kealey knew that they'd used up whatever luck they had started with. Now the slightest mistake would result in death. If his head showed around the side of the air conditioner, the other man would take instant advantage. All it would take was a split second; the bullet would travel faster than he could possibly react.

He crouched, leaned his head against the unit, and tried to think it through, aware of Naomi's pained, questioning gaze. Turning toward her, he said, "Did you see this building when we crossed the bridge?"

She looked at him blankly. "From the north, you mean?"

"Yes. When we approached from the north, did you see this building?"

"I guess so." He could barely hear her over the sound of the storm. "I wasn't sure which building it was, but I must have seen it."

"Did it drop straight to the river? Or was there a—"

"They all dropped straight to the river."

He moved back to her, trying to stay low, the gravel scraping beneath his legs. "Are you sure?"

She looked confused. "Yes. Why?"

"Because we have to jump for it." Her eyes opened wide, and he quickly explained his theory.

"So you think he's still out there? On the other side of the water?"

"It's the way I would do it," Kealey confirmed. "We can't sit around. He's probably looking for a better shot right now. We have to move."

She looked uncertain. "I don't think I can swim. I mean, my arm . . ."

He looked at her torn, bloody sleeve. "Can you move it?"

She started to lift it out by her side. Her face was contorted with concentration at first, and then agony as the movement stretched the wounded area. Despite the rainwater running over her face, he saw tears spring to her eyes with the effort. He gently grabbed her elbow to stop her.

"That's enough," Kealey said. He instantly regretted the question; he shouldn't have asked her to show him. "I know it hurts, but we have to take the chance, Naomi. You climbed the ladder . . . You can do this. I'll be in the water right after you. There's light on the river. Try to stay out of it, and look for me."

She looked terrified. "Ryan, I—"

He grabbed her hand and pulled her to her feet. "Come on, let's go." He guided her to the edge of the air conditioner. The rain was following the wind, which was howling along the course of the river. Lightning rippled over their heads, the jagged forks of electricity obscured by side-blown clouds of water. The thunder was so close it seemed to shake the very foundation of the building.

"On the count of three, turn the corner and jump," Kealey shouted. "I'll fire to cover you." She shook her head instinctively, but he knew she would do as he asked. "I'll be right after you. Ready? One . . . two . . . three. *Go!*"

She turned the corner instantly, exposing her body to the roofs on the other side of the river. Kealey was aware of distant flashes as he blindly squeezed off 2 rounds of his own, then instantly adjusted his aim, shooting toward Vanderveen's muzzle signature. He heard the supersonic crack as a round passed by his ear, no more than a few inches away, but Naomi was already over the edge. He fired twice more as he dived after her, falling into the darkness, something plucking at the sleeve of his shirt. Then he hit the water, and everything went black.

On top of the opposite building, Vanderveen threw off the poncho as he got to his feet, running to the edge of the roof. He looked down at the river. The view was almost completely obscured by a curtain of rain, but he lifted the rifle anyway, having already loaded a second 5-round magazine. Peering through the scope, he thought he caught sight of a dark shape in the water. He fired quickly, emptying the magazine in a matter of seconds. He was beside himself with rage; the dealer in Dresden had obviously lied about the weapon being sighted in. He was almost certain he'd missed Kealey on top of the roof. The other man's covering rounds had passed several feet over his head, which was shockingly close for a handgun, given the range. The covering fire had thrown off his aim at the crucial moment, giving Kealey the chance to dive after the woman. He suddenly realized that Raseen had been right all along: they should have simply waited and taken them on the street. With the advantage of surprise, the ambush would have worked perfectly.

There was nothing to be done about it now, though, and he could see emergency service vehicles racing over the bridge to his left. He dismantled the rifle, removed the scope, and placed everything back in the case. Then he retrieved the poncho and the mat, stuffing them into the pack. Ninety seconds later he was back on the street, jogging through the rain to the idling Mercedes. He opened the back and tossed in the pack. Moving around to the passenger-side door, he got in and propped the case between his legs.

Raseen dropped the car into gear. "Did you get them? Did it work?"

"I don't think so. I might have clipped the woman, but I can't be sure." He swore viciously and slammed his hand into the dashboard, causing Raseen to jump in her seat. "That fucker in Dresden. . . ."

"What are you talking about?"

"Your supplier lied to us, Yasmin. That rifle was never sighted in. I had Kealey on the roof at one hundred meters, and I missed. I fuck-ing *missed*."

"It must have been the rain," she protested. "You can barely see your hand in front of your face. I've worked with that man before, Will. I don't think he would—"

"It was the rifle," Vanderveen insisted. "But it doesn't matter. I'll come back and settle up when I get the chance." He leaned back and took in a deep breath, trying to calm himself. "We need to get out of here. Stop near the Oberbaumbrücke. I'll toss the case in the river, and then it's the airport."

She looked at him. "Canada?"

He nodded and glanced at the dashboard clock. "Our plane leaves in two hours. We're due in the morning. With any luck, we'll be in the States by tomorrow evening. Driving time from Montreal to New York City is about seven hours, but it'll take nearly twice as long since we're using Nazeri's normal route." During the drive from Potsdam to Berlin, he had told her about Amir Nazeri and his part in the up-coming attack. "I don't want to deviate from the norm."

"And then?"

"And then we finish it. We may have left them alive, but we left them with nothing." He smiled at her. "They can't do a thing to stop us."

Kealey hit the water hard, his stomach imploding, the air rushing out of his lungs. He went down fast, then started to kick for the surface. Just as it seemed he was about to lose consciousness, he broke the surface and took a huge breath. The rain was bouncing off the surface, finding its way into his mouth and nose. He fought to keep his head above the water, looking around blindly.

He was tempted to call her name, but something deep inside, some lingering thread of rational thought, told him it would be a waste of time. Then he spotted her. She was trying to swim with the current, but even through the rain he could see she was having a hard time of it, her right arm doing all of the work. He started toward her. When he reached her side, she grabbed for him instantly.

"I can't do it," she sputtered. "I tried, but . . ."

"Just hold on to me," he said. "Don't panic, and try to keep your head out of the water."

She nodded weakly, and he started to swim, aiming for the house-boats beneath the Luisenbrücke. Her wounded arm was wrapped loosely around his torso. She was definitely slowing him down, but he knew she was trying to do her part, because she wasn't struggling, and he could hear her splashing the water with her free arm. Finally, they reached the wooden ladder of the pier. Pulling her forward, he guided her arms to the ladder.

"One more time, Naomi." He tried to sound reassuring. "Come on, it's just a few rungs."

She was obviously exhausted, but she reached up with her right arm and grabbed hold. Her left arm came up slowly, and she struggled to make it up the ladder. Kealey followed right behind her, supporting her body, helping her whenever he could. They reached the pier, and she rolled onto the wooden planks.

He helped her up and paused, looking around, trying to figure out his next move. He looked to his right. There were five house-boats tied up in a row. The first two had lights in the windows, and he could hear the low hum of portable generators. The next three were dark.

He looked over and saw she was shivering violently in the cold rain. A brief flash of lightning lit her pale face; her lips were tinged with blue. The temperature had plummeted since nightfall, and he knew it couldn't be more than 40 degrees Fahrenheit, maybe closer to 30. She needed to get inside immediately.

He grabbed her good arm and pulled her down to the last houseboat. It was a large craft—nearly 60 feet in length—with a fiberglass arch over the flying bridge. Kealey climbed over the rail and helped her over. There was an aluminum table bolted to the deck, surrounded by chairs, potted plants by the rail. He went to the sliding glass door and tried to open it, but it was locked. There was a mat under his feet. He lifted it but didn't find a key. Looking around, his gaze was drawn back to the plants. Ignoring Naomi's bewildered expression, he crossed the deck and kneeled by the clay containers. He started dumping the soil out of them, one after the other, running his fingers through the dirt. Finally, he saw something glinting silver. He grabbed the key and went back to the door.

"How did you know that was there?" Naomi managed to ask. She was leaning against the exterior wall, shaking impossibly hard, her arms wrapped tightly around her body.

He didn't reply, unlocking the door and sliding it open. He stepped inside, and she followed him in.

The salon was filled with comfortable, overstuffed couches, worn rugs on the floor, the galley beyond. There was a little light from the riverside lamps, enough to make out the general layout. Naomi went to one of the couches immediately. She collapsed onto the cushions and curled into a tight ball, her whole body trembling. Kealey went straight through to a side hall, finding the master stateroom a few seconds later. He searched the room, but it quickly became apparent that no one had been on the boat for a while. Unable to find any clothes, he stripped the blanket off the bed, then went through to the head. He rinsed the dirt from his hands in the sink. There was one towel on the rack. He grabbed it and went back to the salon. Kharmai was still in the same position.

"Naomi, you have to get out of those clothes." She didn't respond, her face pressed into the back of the couch. He sat on the edge and shook her gently. "Come on, sit up."

She slowly did as he asked, and didn't protest when he lifted the fleece pullover over her head, only wincing slightly when her left arm came up. Kealey thought the cold must have numbed the pain. The T-shirt came next. Then he pulled off her shoes, socks, and finally her jeans. Kealey quickly grabbed the towel and pressed it into her hands. She absently started to rub it over her damp skin. He looked away, resisting the urge to appreciate her seminude form. When she was mostly dry, he wrapped the blanket tightly around her and used the towel to finish drying her hair. Then he sat next to her and pulled the blanket down from her left shoulder.

"How bad is it?" she asked, turning to look for herself. Her voice was stronger now; she was starting to warm up a little. Her lips had returned to their normal color, and there was a pink glow to her cheeks which he found encouraging.

"Not as bad as I thought," he said honestly. He could only find three puncture wounds. Two of the bearings were just beneath the skin, but the other was much deeper. He was guessing the first two were ricochets, the third a direct hit. She had been behind and to the left of Bennett when the explosion occurred; it was possible that the bearings just beneath her skin had passed through Bennett's body before hitting her, which would explain why the wounds weren't deeper. He felt a sudden, insane urge to laugh out loud. "You have no idea how lucky you are."

"What about you?" she asked, looking suddenly alarmed. "Were you hit?"

Kealey hadn't had time to think about it. He'd pulled off his pullover in the river, so he checked his exposed arms, then looked for holes in his T-shirt. The cuts on his hands had been rinsed clean, and he could see they weren't too bad. He tried to focus, letting the adrenaline ebb, feeling for anything wrong. Nothing seemed to be out of place.

"I don't think so," he said. "Listen, you have to get to a hospital. Your arm isn't bad, but you can't leave it. Not even until the morning."

She shook her head immediately, the anxious expression falling away, replaced by a look of intense concentration. "The police will be checking the emergency rooms. We can't risk it."

"What about the embassy?"

She closed her eyes and leaned back on the couch, desperately trying to think of a way out. Bennett had been working with them as a favor to Jonathan Harper. Nobody else at the embassy even knew they were in the country, let alone what they were doing, but once they went to the CIA's chief of station, they'd have to explain what had happened. His reaction would not be pretty, but that would be nothing compared to the fallout at Langley.

Naomi shook her head, realizing that there was no way she could fix the situation. The truth would come out sooner or later, and when it did, her career would be beyond saving. She suddenly felt a hot wave of guilt; she was thinking about her career while Shane Bennett—a fellow officer, a decent man—was lying dead in Rühmann's apartment. She remembered what had popped into her head as she'd stared down at Rühmann's ruined face, and she suddenly realized it was true: she *had* lost something fundamental, some inner sense of compassion. Somehow, without even noticing the change, she'd become a harder person than she'd ever thought possible.

"I guess we have no choice," she finally said. Her voice was heavy with resignation and something else that Kealey couldn't quite place. "The truth will come out sooner or later. Let's just get it over with."

"I have to find a phone. It won't take long. I looked around . . . I don't think anyone's been here for a long time. You'll be fine until I get back."

He started toward the door. Naomi hesitated, then called his name. He turned to face her.

"Ryan, I . . ." She looked away and pulled the blanket tighter around her shoulders, hoping the dark obscured her features. Her face felt hot. Once again he had saved her life at the risk of his own. If there was ever a time to express her feelings, this was it. But even though the words were on the tip of her tongue, she just couldn't get them out.

"Don't take too long, okay?"

CHAPTER 41

BERLIN

The U.S. Embassy in Berlin is a boxy, charmless building of gray stone located in the embassy district south of Tiergarten, shielded behind a vast array of red and white barriers, concrete planters, and rows of razor-sharp concertina wire. The guardhouse is manned by unsmiling German police officers bearing automatic weapons; to stumble upon the sight, a tourist might start to wonder if the tangible divide between East and West was still in place.

Just after 7:00 the next morning, Ryan Kealey lay on a bunk in a spare room on the second floor. A television tuned to CNN was mounted against the far wall. The volume was barely audible, as Naomi was sleeping soundly in the next bed, but he could hear enough to get the general drift. The situation in Iraq was escalating day by day. Twelve hours earlier, a series of coordinated attacks had taken place in Basra, propagated by Syrian insurgents. Three police stations were bombed in the space of forty minutes, along with a local office of the International Red Cross. Since the attacks occurred in the evening, the number of reported casualties was surprisingly low. As a result, the story took a backseat to the more dramatic events in Baghdad. Six hours before the bombings in Basra, a truck laden with seventy pounds of HMX had crashed into a Green Zone checkpoint. Seventeen were reported dead, including 5 U.S. soldiers, among them a captain in the 1st Marine Expeditionary Force.

The images on the screen changed, and the newscaster moved on to a different story. Kealey let his mind drift, thinking about the events of the past few weeks. It was hard to see any kind of pattern in the recent escalation of violence, but the truth was that everything seemed to stem from the attempted assassination of the Iraqi prime minister and the murder of Nasir Tabrizi in Paris. Both men were powerful, influential politicians, and that made them natural targets, but there was something else to consider. Nuri al-Maliki and Nasir Tabrizi were also on either side of the most prominent divide in Iraq, that between the Shia and Sunni faith. After the bombing of the Babylon Hotel, the Shiite-controlled Mahdi Army had publicly accused the Sunni insurgency of masterminding the attack. As a result, the violence over the next week seemed to primarily target Sunni businesses and places of worship. But then Tabrizi had died, causing the violence to swing the other way. Shiite places of worship had suffered the brunt of what appeared to be retaliatory strikes, despite the discovery that Tabrizi's assassins were Iranian nationals.

Given the current situation, Kealey couldn't see a solution on the horizon, and apparently, he wasn't the only one. A number of prominent Democrats had already revived an old debate on the floor of the Senate, arguing that U.S. troops were not trained to intervene if the situation dissolved into civil war. A number of retired generals had also weighed in on the issue. Most seemed to believe that the military would not be able to control the situation if the Iraqi government fell into disarray. Privately, Kealey agreed, but it threw the whole situation into a new light, and he couldn't help but reconsider his earlier thoughts. What if someone wanted to destroy the Iraqi National Assembly? What if someone had retained Vanderveen's services to that specific end? The former U.S. soldier had definitely participated in the bombing of the Babylon Hotel—that much was fact—but had Vanderveen somehow played a part in the assassination of Tabrizi in Paris? If so, he had covered his tracks remarkably well.

Naomi stirred on the other bunk, and Kealey looked over, his thoughts switching to the previous night. The car from the embassy had arrived less than ten minutes after he made the call. The driver had brought clothes for Kharmai, and once she had changed, they'd driven straight back to the embassy. The chief of station, a florid, portly Texan by the name of Fichtner, had met them at the gates. He had screamed at Kealey for twenty minutes while a doctor removed the shrapnel from Naomi's arm. Fichtner then made the call to Harper in Washington. Kealey had no idea how Harper had reacted—he had only heard one side of the conversation—but he knew that the DDO would not be pleased with what had transpired. A man he had personally recruited was dead, Rühmann was gone, and they were no closer to finding William Vanderveen. The whole thing was a complete disaster. For the first time since his dismissal from the Agency, Kealey was starting to feel that he'd earned his walking papers.

Naomi stirred again and sat up, rubbing the sleep from her eyes. She pulled back the covers and swung her feet to the floor, revealing a white T-shirt that hung like a dress on her slender frame. Kealey could see the bandage beneath the fabric near her left shoulder, but his attention was quickly drawn elsewhere, as the bottom edge of the shirt barely reached the top of her bare thighs. He looked away, embarrassed, but then he felt her eyes on him, and he turned back. She was wearing a slight smile, obviously amused.

"You didn't seem so shy when you were pulling my clothes off last night," she said, pulling her hair back from her face.

The comment caught him off-guard. "You were soaking wet, Naomi, and it was freezing out there. I was just trying to—"

"I know, I know. Relax. I was only joking." She stood and looked around for her jeans. Once she had pulled them on, she sat back down on the edge of the bed. Kealey saw that her smile had disappeared. As if reading his mind, she studied him with a serious expression. "This isn't good, is it?"

He shook his head, then seemed to hesitate. "I'm sorry I brought you into this. If I'd known it would turn out this way—"

"Don't, Ryan." She fixed him with a steady gaze, hoping to convey her sincerity. "Don't apologize. You didn't make me get on that plane, just like you didn't make me help you in Washington. I wanted to do those things. I wanted to be part of it, and I don't regret it."

"What about your career? And don't tell me it doesn't matter, because I know it does."

She shrugged. "Yeah, it matters. I didn't want to lose my job . . . I mean, who does, right? But it's done, and that's that. Besides, some things are more important."

"Like what?"

"Like helping the people you care about."

They looked at each other for a long moment, each trying to figure out what to say next. The moment was shattered by a knock at the door. A woman with feline features and short auburn hair poked her head in, her gaze instantly moving to Kealey's bare chest. Naomi recognized her as Fichtner's aide. She spoke between loud smacks of the gum she was chewing. "Ryan, Mr. Fichtner would like to see you in his office."

"Okay," Kealey said. He reached for his shirt, which was still slightly damp. "Thanks, Becky."

"No problem." The woman beamed at him for a few seconds, then turned to Naomi, the smile fading. "You're Kharmai, right? You have a telephone call. You can take it in the next room."

Naomi was bewildered. "Did they say who they were?"

"Her last name is Peterson," the aide said, sliding her gaze back to Kealey. "Apparently, she called Langley looking for you, and Mr. Harper had it routed through to our switchboard."

"Okay," Naomi said. "I'll be out in a minute." The woman didn't move, and Naomi repeated herself loudly. Finally, the aide left reluctantly, the door closing behind her.

"You have a fan there," she said wryly.

"What are you talking about?"

"Yeah, right." Naomi shook her head as she stood and walked to the door. "Like you didn't notice."

She followed the aide down a narrow hall. They came to the secure phone, which was housed in a small, windowless office. The aide gestured in a bored, dismissive kind of way, then went back the way she had come. Naomi glared at the retreating woman as she reached for the phone and punched the HOLD button. "Kharmai."

"Naomi, it's Liz. How are you?"

At the sound of the other woman's voice, she couldn't help but smile, her spirits lifting. At the same time, she felt a tinge of self-pity.

She didn't miss much about London, but Peterson definitely qualified.

"Could be better," she replied honestly. They exchanged pleasantries for a minute; then Naomi related the events of the previous night, leaving out the fact that she was no longer officially with the Agency. Peterson was slightly stunned when she finished, and Naomi had to prompt her to get back to why she'd called in the first place.

"Well, it has to do with the name we pulled off the tape. Jason March, aka William Vanderveen."

Naomi instantly perked up. "What do you have?"

Peterson explained quickly about Samir al-Askari, the Jordanian banker, and his untimely end on the Strand. "Two of our best watchers were tracking this guy, Naomi. One was taking photographs from across the street. When we went back and digitally enhanced the shots, two faces kept popping up in the background, a man and a woman. We ran a check through our facial recognition software, looking for nodes. Vanderveen came up; the match was ninety-five percent."

Kharmai interpreted quickly. Nodal points were visual markers on the human face. The markers could be nearly anything distinctive: the width of the mouth, the distance between the eyes, the spacing of the cheekbones. The human face contained eighty nodal points, but for the software to make a match, only fourteen to twenty-two points were needed, with twenty-two rated at 100 percent. Ninety-five percent was encouraging; it meant that twenty-one nodal points had linked the file photograph of Will Vanderveen to the shots taken in London. "And this was when? Two days ago?"

"Al-Askari died two days ago, but we didn't get the match until yesterday."

"Huh." Naomi thought about it, unsure of how this information could help. They didn't have any hard evidence, but Ryan was certain that Vanderveen had set the trap for them in Rühmann's apartment, and Naomi agreed. London was old news.

Then something hit her. "Wait, you said there were *two* faces?"

"That's right," Peterson replied. "The second is a woman, but she didn't come up on the database. We have no idea who she is, but she was definitely moving with Vanderveen. They're close together in all the shots, and in one, you can see that she's holding his arm. According to the report, al-Askari entered the Savoy and stayed inside for approximately thirty minutes. We don't have shots of Vanderveen entering the hotel, but we managed to get hold of some footage from the Savoy's CCTV cameras. He was there, and the woman was with him inside the hotel as well."

Naomi instantly thought back to the night before. She'd been dazed shortly after the explosion, but she could remember the thick smoke rising up from the ground floor. If Vanderveen was shooting from across the river, who had started the fire? It seemed strange that she hadn't considered it earlier.

"Liz, do me a favor and send me those shots through Langley. We'll run them through our own database and see if we can't come up with something more."

"Already done," the other woman said. "When I called looking for you, I was put through to a man named Harper. He has the photographs, and you'll have the security tape from the hotel tomorrow. I just wanted to tell you in person."

"Thanks. I owe you one."

"Don't mention it. When are you coming back?"

Naomi sighed, thinking about her recent dismissal. The States didn't feel much like home at the moment, and London definitely had its perks. She *was* a British citizen, after all, and MI5 was always looking for experienced people. Maybe Peterson could pull some strings.

"I don't know," she finally replied. "But I'll be in touch. Don't forget about me, okay?"

"Not a chance."

Naomi was ushered into the chief of station's office a few minutes later. Ryan was already there, seated in front of the other man's desk and looking decidedly unhappy. Ken Fichtner was shouting into the phone, his face blotchy, his tie loose and stained with some unknown substance. He looked like he was on the verge of a heart attack. He scowled at Naomi as she walked in, then turned back to the single window behind his desk. Naomi took a seat next to Ryan and pulled her chair close to his. In a low voice, she relayed what Liz Peterson had just told her.

Kealey nodded thoughtfully when she was done. "You're right . . . There must have been somebody else to start that fire on the ground floor."

"He couldn't have done it himself?"

"I don't think so. I've been thinking about this, Naomi. That IED in Rühmann's office was very sloppy. We were barely out of the office when it went off. It should have killed us both. Then there's the fact that he missed us on the roof. That probably means he didn't have a night scope, or maybe it means he didn't have time to sight in. Either way, we shouldn't be here right now."

"What's your point?"

"The point is, I don't think he was well prepared. I think we caught him off-guard. He picked an electrical gate because it was the only thing he had time for. Because he could set it off with a rifle. In other words, he didn't have time to rig something more sophisticated for the stairs. Certainly not something he could trigger remotely."

"Maybe you're right." She paused. "Of course, there's always the question of how he knew we were coming in the first place."

"I've been thinking about that, too," Kealey said, remembering Samantha Crane's unexpected visit to his room at the Hotel Washington.

"Any ideas?"

"I'll tell you later."

"What do you think about the woman? Do you think we'll have a record on her?"

"I doubt it," Kealey murmured, aware of Fichtner's building irritation. "MI5 has a huge database. If they don't know who she is, I doubt we can do better."

Fichtner suddenly slammed down the phone and turned to them without warning. "Okay, you two. You don't deserve to know this, but since you're here, I'll fill you in. According to the preliminary coroner's report, Thomas Rühmann died of multiple gunshot wounds to the head. The gun used was a .22. The body of his assistant, a man named Karl Lang, was discovered in the master bath. He also sustained gunshot wounds, two to the chest, but the gun that killed him was different than the one used on Rühmann."

"Well, sir, that fits into what I just—"

"Don't interrupt me!" Fichtner shouted, slamming a hand onto his desk. Naomi shrank back into her chair, and he continued, his voice turning dangerously low. "You two cost me one of my best officers. I don't give a shit what you have to say." He shifted his gaze. "And I don't care about your theories, Kealey. You can't prove that Will Vanderveen killed Rühmann, just as you can't prove that he set the trap in the office. As far as I'm concerned, you've done nothing but cause problems since you landed on German soil. You're lucky it isn't up to me. Frankly, I'd like nothing more than to call the local police and let them know about your little part in last night's disaster."

He paused to catch his breath, then said, "You know what was found in the apartment? You know what you got for your trouble? Nothing. Not a damn thing. No incriminating papers, no hard drive . . . nothing. In a matter of hours, the Germans are going to figure out who Shane Bennett really was. When that happens, the shit is going to hit the fan, and it won't help to have you two hanging around. Jonathan Harper wants you back in the States. You're already booked on a flight to D.C. The plane leaves in two hours."

Kealey and Kharmai nodded in unison; they hadn't expected anything less.

Fichtner shuffled some papers on his desk. "A car will pick you up downstairs in ten minutes. They already have your baggage and passports." He reached for the phone, ready to tackle the next problem. "Now get the fuck out of here. I'm done with both of you."

It was raining when they stepped outside a few minutes later, though the weather had calmed substantially since the previous night. The vehicle was already waiting for them, a black Chevy Suburban. Kealey went up and knocked on the passenger-side window. When it came down with a light whir, he leaned in and said, "You're here for us?"

The driver nodded. The frown on his face seemed to indicate that he knew they were no longer welcome in Germany. "Your stuff's in the back. Got everything you need?"

"Yeah. Let's go."

They climbed in, and the vehicle started to move. They passed through a number of checkpoints on the Neustädtische Kirchstrasse before leaving the embassy district. Before long they were racing north on the A111. The driver flicked through the channels on the radio incessantly, finally settling on the latest teenage pop sensation. He hummed along tunelessly as the wipers flicked light rain from the windshield. In the back, Naomi stared out the opaque window, her mind going in a thousand different directions at once. It was hard to believe that they had come this far for nothing, but she felt as though she was missing something, something Bennett had said the day before. She tried to clear her thoughts, knowing it wouldn't come if she tried too hard, but it didn't hit her until they reached the airport.

The driver pulled up behind a fleet of vehicles outside the main terminal. He didn't get out and offer to help with their bags. Instead, all he said was, "Your tickets are at the counter. Have a good flight."

Kealey went to the back and pulled out his light grip, then reached in for Kharmai's larger bag. When he had the bags on the wet cement, he saw that Naomi's gaze was fixed on something in the near distance. "What are you looking at?" he asked.

"That car," she said slowly. "It's pretty nice."

He followed her gaze and found himself looking at a late-model Mercedes coupe, shining silver in the lights on the building's façade. A middle-aged man in a suit was leaning against the rear fender, smoking a cigarette. "A CLK. What about it?"

She turned to meet his eyes. "What did Bennett say last night when you asked him about surveillance? He said that Rühmann had a CLK registered under the name Schäuble."

"So?"

"So we never checked the car, Ryan. It's probably sitting right outside his apartment."

Kealey shut the rear cargo doors of the Suburban, then banged on the window twice. The vehicle had disappeared into traffic before he addressed her words. "Why would we check the car, Naomi? It doesn't seem like a good place to store documents, especially documents relating to illegal arms sales."

She caught the sarcasm and was instantly annoyed. "I realize that," she said as she snatched up her suitcase and extended the handle with more force than necessary. She winced as the movement jarred her injured shoulder. "But it's worth checking, isn't it? I mean, what do we have to lose?"

"Yeah, I guess you're right," he replied at length. The glass doors slid open as they approached the terminal. "I need to talk to Harper anyway. I'll ask him to call the embassy directly . . . That's the only way Fichtner will make the effort."

She shivered slightly as they entered the warm building. "Do you think Harper will even do it? I mean, he can't be too happy with us right now."

"Maybe not, but that won't stop him from making the call. He'll save the rest for when we're on the ground in Washington."

She didn't reply as they stepped up to the counter. They displayed their passports and picked up their tickets. Kharmai checked her bag, and then they walked through to security. Once they had passed through, they followed signs up to the third floor. Naomi headed off to a place called Miller's Bar while Kealey found a telephone. He dialed the appropriate number and asked for Harper. The DDO came on the line almost immediately.

"Ryan, where the hell are you?"

Kealey immediately took note of the other man's tone. He didn't sound angry, which was surprising enough, but there was an undercurrent of urgency there that Kealey recognized immediately. He knew it meant they had a break in the case. "We're at the airport. Fichtner couldn't get rid of us fast enough. We're about to catch a plane to Washington."

"What the hell happened? Why did—"

"I'll explain everything once we get back. Right now I need you to do something for me." He explained quickly about Rühmann's car, using as few words as possible. "I know it's a long shot, but we have to check everything."

"It's way beyond a long shot, but I'll make the call."

"Thanks." Kealey paused, then said what was on his mind. "John, Vanderveen was there. Don't ask me how I know—I didn't see him—but he was definitely there. He set the trap in Rühmann's office. He knew we were coming. Someone tipped him off."

"Well, I might be able to shed some light on that, but we'll wait and see. I want you to look at the evidence. In any case, a lot has been happening here. You need to get back as soon as possible."

Kealey was tempted to ask, but he knew that Harper wouldn't say anything more on an open line. He glanced at his watch, which strangely enough had survived the events of the previous night. "We'll be there in eight hours."

Two hours after Kealey and Kharmai boarded a United flight bound for Dulles International, a number of dazed tenants were clustered around the entrance of the apartment building on the Reichstagufer, watching from a distance as police officers and firefighters went about their business, salvaging what they could of the ruined apartments. The bodies—those of three men and two women, including the caretaker—had been removed hours earlier. The injuries sustained in the fire were minor: a few cases of smoke inhalation, a couple of first-degree burns. The onlookers now gathered on the cold, rainy street were primarily concerned with the state of their homes. No one seemed to notice when an unmarked sedan slowed to a gentle halt on the road behind them.

The passenger door swung open, and a man stepped into the road. He was in his mid-thirties, lean, with brown hair, a thin mustache, and plain features. In short, his appearance was completely unremarkable, a trait befitting a four-year veteran of the Central Intelligence Agency. He quickly scanned the line of cars parked in front of the building. Spotting the one he was looking for, he crossed the road at a brisk pace, his head swiveling slowly. No one was watching him. When he reached Thomas Rühmann's black Mercedes, he stood close to the passenger-side door and let a thin strip of metal slide from his sleeve. In less than twenty seconds, he'd popped the lock.

The alarm went off immediately, but he ignored it and scoured the vehicle. He found a small pile of paperwork on the passenger seat immediately, then checked the rest of the car: the glove compartment, under the seats, the trunk. Finding nothing else, he walked back to the sedan, the paperwork tucked under his arm. The alarm on Rühmann's CLK had been blaring for less than thirty seconds. A few of the onlookers had turned in curiosity; finally, someone brought the matter to the attention of a harried police officer. The officer disentangled himself and started forward to investigate, but the sedan was already gone, almost as if it had never been there.

CHAPTER 42

WASHINGTON, D.C.

As it turned out, their plane didn't arrive until 7:00 PM eastern time, owing to a delayed connection at Heathrow and bad weather on the ground at Dulles. By the time Kealey and Kharmai had collected the checked bag, they were both exhausted and ready to drop in their tracks. As they left baggage claim, a man in a neat blue suit approached them, looking uncertain. Kealey didn't recognize him but took a chance and assumed he was with Harper. It turned out he was right. They followed the driver out the glass doors, stepping into the cool air. There was a black Suburban waiting at the curb. Kealey threw their bags in the back, then joined Naomi in the backseat. As the vehicle pulled into traffic, Jonathan Harper shut off his cell phone and turned to appraise them both. His first words were hardly surprising.

"You two look like hell."

"Fichtner practically pushed us out of the building," Kealey said. The truck was a little overheated, so he cracked the window. A light rain was coming down, but it wasn't enough to slow the traffic. "I haven't showered in two days."

"Neither have I," Naomi chimed in. She suddenly looked embarrassed, as though it had been a personal choice instead of a situation beyond her control. After removing the shrapnel from her shoulder the night before, the doctor had given her a powerful sedative to help her sleep. It was a miracle she'd woken up in time for their flight.

"Well, you'll get the chance soon enough," Harper said. "In fact, we—"

"John, I don't mean to interrupt, but you said this morning that you had something new."

"And I do. Unfortunately, my regular driver is out sick, and Talbot here isn't cleared for it, so it'll just have to wait." He glanced over and said, "Sorry, Jake."

"No problem, sir," the driver said as he merged onto the airport access road.

"I *can* tell you this," Harper continued. "I placed a call to Fichtner right after we talked this morning. He sent some of his people out to the Austrian's residence, and believe it or not, they got something out of his Mercedes. Papers terminating a lease in Canada."

Kealey sat up in his seat. "What kind of lease?"

"A lease to a storage facility. A ground-level unit in Montreal." Harper hesitated. "A large one."

Kealey frowned, his mind racing. "Why would he leave that in the car?"

"Well, if you were right about Vanderveen being there, he was the last person to see Rühmann alive. Maybe they had a legitimate meeting before Vanderveen shot him. Whatever the reason, I think we have to consider the possibility that he's collecting something in Canada."

"Well, we can stop that from happening, right?" Naomi asked. "All we have to do is get word to the Canadian government."

"It's not that simple," Harper said. "I'm prepared to take you at your word, Ryan, but you can't expect others to do the same. We have no real proof that Vanderveen was in Berlin, so we can't prove he killed Rühmann. Remember, it's a well-known fact in intelligence circles that he was being protected by the German government. The Canadians won't get involved unless they absolutely have to. The request is going through State as we speak, but I'm not hopeful."

"What about our own people? We can have them talk to whoever owns the facility. Give the owner whatever he wants. Money for information. Then we set up surveillance and wait for Vanderveen to show."

"Already done. Unfortunately, the owner is out of the country, and the security cameras only cover the entrance. We already got hold of them."

"And?"

Harper shrugged as the Suburban swung onto MacArthur Boulevard. "The tape isn't very clear. Our people showed the guards a photo of Vanderveen, and they didn't recognize the face. Of course, he wouldn't look the same anyway, so that doesn't mean much."

"Why are they wasting time with photographs?" Kealey demanded. "We need to get inside that unit and see what's there."

"Not possible. Besides, it wouldn't help. If Vanderveen already picked up the cargo, going in now won't make a difference, and if he's on the way, our people will pick him up when he arrives. Believe me, it's covered to the best of our ability."

The younger man leaned back in his seat. He was frustrated, but he couldn't find fault with what Harper had said. He looked over to see that Naomi was just as troubled as he was.

The Suburban slowed to a halt. Kealey looked out the window and frowned; it took him several seconds to figure out where they were. The vehicle was parked outside Jonathan Harper's brownstone on General's Row.

Harper turned in his seat, anticipating the younger man's objections. "Julie's been cooking all day, so don't even think about saying no." He looked at Naomi. "Kharmai, you're more than welcome to stay. In fact, I'd prefer it if you did . . . We have plenty of spare bedrooms. I need to bring you both up to speed, but if you like, Jake can run you into the city, and I'll fill you in tomorrow."

She was surprised at this turn of events, but she shook it off quickly. "I'd like to hear it tonight, sir, if it's all the same to you."

"Good. Let's go."

CHAPTER 43

WASHINGTON, D.C.

The sky was pitch black, the rain drifting down as they stepped out of the vehicle. The driver retrieved their bags from the back, and Kealey hung back to help as Naomi hurried up the steps. Julie Harper, a short, slightly overweight woman with a warm smile and a pleasant nature, met them at the door. She kissed her husband perfunctorily and pulled Kealey into the warm, brightly lit foyer, brushing the cold drops from his sleeves. She looked up at him and placed a hand on his cheek.

"How are you, Ryan?" Her voice was soft and tinged with sympathy. "It's been so long."

"I'm fine, Julie. It's good to see you again."

Watching this scene unfold, Naomi realized that they hadn't seen each other in a while, maybe not since Ryan's full-time return to the Agency. Clearly, they knew each other well, and she couldn't help but wonder if Katie Donovan had ever visited the Harper home. The thought gave her a jealous ache, although the feeling was quickly replaced by a wave of guilt.

She stood by awkwardly until Harper introduced her. She tried for a pleasant smile, even though she was completely exhausted and not feeling very sociable. The other woman shook hands with her warmly.

"It's nice to meet you, Naomi. Here, let me take your coat." Julie Harper glanced at her husband as she hung it on a rack near the door. "I assume you all have things to discuss."

"We do, but it can wait until after dinner."

Julie brightened. "Good. It'll be ready in half an hour. You'll have to excuse me."

She hustled back to the kitchen, and Harper nodded toward the stairs, reaching for Naomi's large case. "I'll show you upstairs. If you like, you can get cleaned up before we eat."

Kealey could not disguise his impatience. "John, I appreciate this, but we have a lot to go over. Now is not the time for—"

"Hold that thought." Harper looked to Naomi and said, "Could you give us a minute? We'll follow you up."

"Of course, sir." She walked up the stairs, and Harper turned back to Kealey, his face set in a firm expression.

"Ryan, you've been pushing yourself hard for days on end. As it stands, all the bases are covered."

"I realize that, but—"

"Are you personally going to drive up to Canada? Are you personally going to check every vehicle coming through every border crossing?" Harper let the rhetorical question sink in, then said, "Stressing yourself now is counterproductive. We have all night to figure out our next move, so right now, go upstairs and clean yourself up. We'll get down to business after we eat. Okay?"

Kealey couldn't do much but nod tightly. Everything the other man had just said made perfect sense, and he wasn't in a position to argue. "Fine."

They presented themselves at the table twenty minutes later. Both had taken the time to shower and change, Kealey into a gray University of Chicago sweatshirt, Kharmai into a white woolen turtleneck. They were both in jeans. Despite the similarity of their outfits, Naomi felt distinctly underdressed. She knew it was probably just psychosomatic—the effect of being in her employer's home for the first time—but knowing didn't alleviate her sense of unease. The feeling didn't subside until Harper came down in similar attire, having exchanged his suit for khakis and a black crewneck sweater. He poured the wine as Julie emerged from the kitchen. Once everything was laid out on the table, she started to fill their plates.

The meal was simple but excellent: vegetable soup to start, followed by linguine with red sauce, sautéed shrimp, Italian bread, and salad on the side. Julie made an obvious effort to promote conversation, but watching her, Naomi realized that the talk was only a cover for the concerned, motherly glances she kept shooting in Ryan's direction. When the meal was done, she pushed back from her seat and offered to help clear the dishes, hoping to get Julie alone for a private discussion, but Harper waved it away.

"We have some things to talk about upstairs. Sorry to eat and run."

"It was wonderful, though," Naomi said quickly. She wanted to leave a good impression. "Thank you, Mrs. Harper."

The other woman beamed as she cleared the plates. "I'm glad you enjoyed it, dear. And please, call me Julie."

Naomi had to smile. Even though Julie Harper was clearly shy of her forty-fifth birthday, her personality seemed to be that of a woman years older. It wasn't a bad thing, but Naomi couldn't help feeling slightly awkward; it was strange being called "dear" by a woman barely ten years her senior.

She turned and followed the two men up the stairs. Jonathan Harper led them into a wood-paneled study. It was a distinctly masculine room, with leather club chairs, an enormous desk in the corner, and Persian carpets scattered across the floor. Harper gestured for them to sit and went to his desk, retrieving the suitcase he had taken from the Suburban earlier. As he opened it and pulled out a number of documents, Julie entered with coffee on a tray. She deposited it on the center table, pausing to rest a light hand on Kealey's shoulder. Then she left, closing the door softly behind her.

"Okay," Harper said, settling into a free chair. "Where to begin, that's the question."

Naomi jumped on the opening. "Sir, what about the woman? Liz Peterson said she was going to send you the surveillance photographs from London."

Harper nodded and slid a number of 8 x 10s across the table. Naomi picked them up and began perusing them instantly, handing some of them off to Ryan. "Do we know who she is?"

"Unfortunately, we don't," Harper replied. He started to pour black coffee into one of the mugs. "We ran her through our facial recognition software, which, as you know, is similar to that used by MI5. We had one hit, but it only came back with nine markers. That's a forty percent match . . . not exactly definitive."

"Not definitive, maybe, but it's a start," Naomi said, trying to remain optimistic. "Who came up?"

Harper handed her another photograph. "Samara Majid al-Khuzaai, thirty-eight years old, a Sunni born in Baghdad. Her father was part of the Special Republican Guard, Saddam's innermost circle. The 1st Brigade, responsible for security. He was arrested in Najaf shortly after the invasion, and he didn't go quietly. As they pulled him out of the house he was hiding in, he started screaming that it wasn't over, that his daughter would carry on the fight. Even though it was made in the heat of the moment, the remark prompted a brief investigation. As it turned out, he only had one child, and that was Samara."

Naomi looked at the two photographs. She studied al-Khuzaai's face, then the surveillance photos of Vanderveen's traveling companion. The two women did not look that similar.

She handed the shots to Kealey and said, "What does that mean, 'carry on the fight'? Was that a legitimate threat?"

"It's hard to say," Harper replied. "But she isn't in custody, and she hasn't shown up in Jordan or Syria looking for political asylum. The Middle East desk at the CTC seems to think she's still in Iraq, working with the insurgency."

Kealey looked up from the photographs. "I don't think it's the same person, John. Is this our best guess?"

Harper sipped some of his coffee and hesitated. "Well, some of the analysts brought up Nouri Hussein, but they tend to do that whenever a photograph like this pops up."

"Nouri Hussein?" Naomi asked. "You don't mean . . ."

"Nouri Saddam Hussein. His fourth daughter."

Naomi was amazed, and let it show. "I thought she was a myth."

"She is," Kealey put in, his voice laced with disgust. "Her very existence is based on a single document."

"What document?"

"A letter," Kealey specified. "It was found in a house in Tikrit in 2003, typed and addressed to 'Nouri, my dearest and eldest.' It was signed at the end, supposedly by Saddam. Handwriting experts were brought in to verify its authenticity, but they couldn't reach any firm conclusions."

"What about photographs? Has anyone—"

"No photos have ever turned up," Harper said, cutting her off. "The letter is the only evidence of her existence."

"And that isn't evidence," Kealey snapped. "I'm telling you, John, you need to put those analysts in their place. They're letting their imaginations get the best of them. Nouri Hussein does not exist, and the name does nothing but distract them from workable leads."

"Maybe you're right," Harper said, "but it doesn't really matter at this point. We have no idea where the woman is, anyway. When we find Vanderveen, we'll find her. Until that time, learning her identity is not a priority."

He paused, then said, "I do, however, have another piece of information you might find interesting."

This was what Kealey had been waiting for. He felt himself shift forward on the warm leather chair. "The Iranian informant?"

"That's right. His name is Hakim Ghasem Rudaki, a native of Tehran. He's forty-two years old, a Harvard grad, and a visiting professor at Columbia. He's also heavily involved with the National Iranian American Council in New York." Harper paused. "Rudaki approached the Bureau several months ago, and the decision was made to hear him out. He passed on some low-grade intelligence at first, but it all checked out, so he was given more attention."

"How did you get this information?" Kealey asked.

"One of the agents at the New York office wasn't buying into what Rudaki was saying, so he started complaining to anyone who would listen. Last night he relayed his concerns to his former supervisor at the Los Angeles field office." Harper smiled. "My old college roommate."

"So who's running Rudaki in New York?" Naomi asked.

Harper's face turned grim. "Since the end of August, he's been dealing with just one person. Special Agent Samantha Crane."

Kealey sprung to his feet and swore loudly, causing Naomi to jump in her seat. "That *bitch*. I knew it. I knew there was something about her . . . She's working with Vanderveen, John. She has to be."

The other man nodded slowly. "I know it looks that way, but we can't jump to conclusions. Let's think it through, and then we'll decide how to handle it." He gestured to the empty seat. "Come on, sit down."

Kealey took his seat and fell silent, but the furious expression was fixed on his face. It was Naomi who said, "Sir, Rudaki is the same man who predicted the bombing of the Babylon Hotel, right?"

"No," Harper said. "He predicted the attempt on the life of Nuri al-Maliki, but he was wrong about the place and time. Just like he was wrong about the place and time with Nasir Tabrizi."

"Quite a coincidence," Kealey said sarcastically. "He knew the targets, but nothing else. I don't buy it. I never did."

"Neither do I," Naomi put in.

"That makes three of us," Harper said. "Rudaki was very quick to blame the Iranian government for the Babylon Hotel and the shooting in Paris. A little too quick, if you ask me."

"Where is Rudaki getting his information?" Kealey asked.

"His cousin is Reza Bagheri, the Syrian defense minister. According to Rudaki, his cousin is displeased with the actions of the government. Bagheri believes Ahmadinejad is making a mistake by trying to subvert U.S. policy in Iraq, and he's worried that U.S. troops will invade Iran if the regime's true role in Tabrizi's assassination is discovered. Obviously, that would mean a much larger U.S. military presence in the region, which is the last thing Bagheri wants. Of course, he can't exactly talk to us directly, so Rudaki is his mouthpiece."

"That's a lie," Kealey said automatically. "I don't buy a word of it."

Harper nodded slowly, looking over the rim of his cup. "Because of Crane."

"That's right." Kealey paused and looked at his hands. He saw they were balled into fists, and he forced himself to take several deep, calming breaths. "John, Ford told Crane I took the laptop in Alexandria. We know that for a fact, but it begs the obvious question: What other information has she passed on?"

Harper leaned back in his chair, staring thoughtfully into his cup. "Rachel knew about the embassy break-in, and that means she knew about Rühmann. She could have told Crane where he was hiding, what name he was using . . . everything."

"Everything," Kealey repeated. "And what did Crane do once she had that information? She gave it to Vanderveen." He paused, letting them reach the natural conclusion. "How else would he know we were coming, John?"

The room fell silent. They were each lost in thought when the telephone rang. The DDO stood, went to his desk, and lifted the receiver of his secure phone. "Harper."

He listened for a long moment, asked a few questions, then hung up. Kealey and Kharmai had heard enough to know it was relevant, and they waited for an explanation.

"Our people in Montreal managed to track down the owner of the Lake Forest storage facility, a guy by the name of Liman. He remembers the delivery of an item to Rühmann's unit. That occurred about six months ago. Before that, he says the unit was empty."

"Does he know what was delivered?" Naomi asked.

"No, but he remembers what it looked like, and he remembers the approximate dimensions. He sketched it out for our people. It's on the way by fax."

Kealey said, "Are they still watching the building?"

"Yes. No movement so far."

"Okay." Kealey leaned back in his seat and tried to set aside his anger. He had no idea why Samantha Crane would betray her agency and her country, especially given her background, but he couldn't think about it now. Instead, he focused on Thomas Rühmann. Above all else, he was wondering what the Austrian arms broker had placed in the Lake Forest storage facility.

"John, how did we know about Rühmann in the first place? I mean, how did he come to Langley's attention?"

"Because of Al Qaqaa," Naomi said, beating Harper to the punch. "Remember? He was suspected of arranging the theft of explosives back in 2003."

"That's right," Kealey mumbled. "What was taken again?"

"Three hundred eighty tons of HMX and RDX." Naomi shrugged. "Conventional explosives. Nothing special, really, except for the quantity. There was a lot of speculation in the press, of course. People thought that something else might have been stored in the buildings, but if there was, it never came out."

Kealey pondered her words as the fax machine started up on Harper's desk. The DDO collected two sheets of paper and examined them quickly.

"It doesn't mean much to me," he said, handing over the second sheet. "Do you recognize this?"

Kealey looked at the drawing, aware that Naomi had gotten out of her chair and was leaning over his shoulder. The picture was relatively crude, but it looked like a large cylinder with a conical protrusion on one end. It seemed vaguely familiar, but he couldn't quite place it.

Harper was reading through the cover sheet. "According to the owner of the storage facility, this thing was about"—he paused to convert from metric to standard—"eleven feet long and four feet high."

Kealey suddenly felt sick to his stomach. "What color was it?"

Harper scanned the text quickly. "Dark green."

"Shit." Kealey shook his head in disbelief. "That's military ordnance. I think I know what it is, John."

Harper froze and looked up from the cover sheet. "Well?"

CHAPTER 44

WASHINGTON, D.C.

"It's called a BLU-82," Kealey said ten minutes later. He had used the office computer to download several high-resolution images of the bomb, and Kharmai and Harper were both examining printouts. They had also faxed some of the images back to Montreal and were waiting for confirmation from Liman, the owner of the storage facility.

"It stands for Bomb Live Unit," Kealey continued, "but it's more commonly known as a 'daisy cutter,' owing to the distinctive pattern it leaves after detonation. Until recently, it was the largest conventional explosive in the U.S. arsenal, and as you can see, it's *very* large, with a total weight of about fifteen thousand pounds. It's also extremely simple . . . nothing more than GSX slurry in a big metal container. The container itself doesn't weigh much; nearly all the weight comes from the explosives. Twelve thousand six hundred pounds of ammonium nitrate and aluminum powder."

Harper looked up. "It says here it was used primarily for clearing helicopter landing zones in Vietnam. That makes it a pretty old design."

"But still very effective," Kealey assured him. "We used them in Afghanistan and Iraq, mostly for psychological purposes. Let me give you an idea of what I'm talking about. Back in the first gulf war, a C-130 dropped a daisy cutter on an Iraqi position just outside Kuwait City. Five minutes later, a Special Air Service recon patrol called in and asked if someone had dropped a tactical nuke in the area. At the time, the patrol was a hundred and ten miles away from the site of the bombing. What they saw was the signature mushroom cloud . . . They mistook the daisy cutter for a nuke. That's how powerful it is."

Naomi looked up from the paper in her hands, an expression of mixed confusion and concern on her face. "What does that mean for an urban area? What will this thing do?"

He looked at his hands, trying to think of the best way to explain it. "Think about Oklahoma City," he finally said. "The bomb that took out the Alfred P. Murrah Building was about a third the size of this one. If Vanderveen actually has one of these and sets it off in New York City, it will destroy every structure within one thousand feet, and the pressure wave will shatter windows for miles. Depending on where he detonates it, casualties will probably be in the thousands."

"Jesus," Harper breathed. His face had turned white.

The room was completely silent for half a minute. Then Naomi said, "It was our weapon originally, right? Rühmann must have gotten it from Al Qaqaa. If we can find someone who will say it was there, we can put everything together and bring it to the president. He'll have to cancel the meeting at the UN. I mean, it's not just the United Iraqi Alliance that's scheduled to attend. The secretary of state will be there as well, not to mention the entire General Assembly. If we give him something tangible, he'll have to call it off."

"We don't have time for that," Harper pointed out. "The meeting is set for tomorrow afternoon. The Iraqi delegates arrived in New York this morning. Even if I *could* get an audience with Brenneman in time, he'd want a lot more proof than what we have. Remember, I'm persona non grata with him at the moment, and you two are out of the loop completely."

"Well, we have to try," Kealey argued. "I assume we investigated the incident at Al Qaqaa. Let's see if we can get a list of all the agencies involved in the investigation, the individual people if possible. Maybe we'll find a friendly face, someone willing to give us a full account of what was being stored at the facility."

"I can get that by morning," Harper said. "There'll be a lid in place, of course, but I'll work around it."

"The main thing," Naomi said, "is getting access to Hakim Rudaki. If anyone knows what's coming next, it's him."

"Or Samantha Crane," Kealey muttered.

"Ryan, I agree it looks bad," Harper said, "but the evidence against Crane is purely circumstantial. We have to keep that on the back burner for as long as possible. Let's see if we can get to Rudaki first."

Before anyone could say anything more, the phone rang again. Harper answered it, said a few words, and replaced the receiver. Turning toward them, he said, "Liman just verified it. The item stored in Rühmann's unit was definitely a BLU-82. He gave our people permission to go in and check it out. The unit was empty."

"Damn it," Naomi said bitterly. "We must have missed him by hours."

"Any chance we'll get it at the border?" Kealey asked.

"I don't think so," Harper said slowly. "It sounds like Vanderveen timed this well. I don't think he'll show up without the necessary paperwork, and if it's all in order, he'll be waved right through."

"Can we at least get the word to customs?"

"I can't do it myself. That has to go through Homeland Security. The wheels are already in motion, but now I need a statement from Liman in Montreal. Once it arrives, I can get it out to the right people. Chances are, he's already crossed the border, anyway."

"So what does that leave us with?" Naomi wondered.

"Rudaki," Kealey said, repeating her earlier words. "We have to get to him, John. Immediately."

Harper hesitated. "The last few days haven't exactly done wonders for my credibility. I'm all out of favors. I don't think the director will pull any strings for me based on what we've managed to dig up so far."

"He has to. There's too much resting on this. I don't care how you make it happen, but I need to talk to him. Face-to-face, first thing in the morning."

"I can still get you an Agency plane," Harper said. "I'll call the director first and see if I can get him to work it out with the assistant director in charge in New York." The DDO felt the need to point something out. "If it happens, Ryan, and it probably won't, you'll be surrounded by FBI agents. I hope you realize that. And if Rudaki is hiding something, a friendly discussion isn't going to get it out of him."

"I'll worry about that when I'm on the ground," Kealey said. "Just get me the meeting, John."

"I'll do my best." He reached for the phone, checking his watch in the process. "This will take a while. Why don't you two get some rest?"

"Actually, I—"

"Get some sleep," Harper ordered, his voice taking on an authoritative tone. "You should take a look in the mirror . . . You're dead on your feet. If I manage to get you in there, it'll be first thing in the morning. You need to be ready."

Reluctantly, Kealey nodded and stood, followed by Kharmai. They left the room as Harper started to dial.

CHAPTER 45

WASHINGTON, D.C. • FORT ERIE, CANADA

Much later, Ryan Kealey lay still on a bed in one of the second-floor guest rooms. He had stripped off his sweatshirt but was still in his jeans. The room was draped in shadow, the far wall rippling with light from the streetlamps beyond the double-hung windows. He had tried to sleep, knowing he needed to get some rest, but his mind was far too active. After leaving Harper's office, he had gone downstairs with Naomi. They had talked with Julie Harper for a while, the two women sharing half a bottle of wine. Kealey had settled on beer, but he limited himself to two, as he wanted to be sharp for the morning.

After an hour of this, Harper had called them up to the office. The news was not what they had hoped for, though it wasn't entirely bad, either. Director Andrews had bought into the theory, mainly because Harper had done his best to leave Kealey's name out of it. The DCI had then called the FBI director at home and explained the situation. Twenty minutes after the initial call, Harper had the ADIC of the New York field office on the phone. Arrangements were made for Naomi Kharmai to sit in on an interview with Hakim Rudaki at 11:00 AM the following morning. The meeting was to take place at 26 Federal Plaza in Manhattan. It was the best Harper could do; Andrews wasn't about to allow Kealey anywhere near the Iranian informant, especially in a federal building. He had made an exception for Kharmai, whose sins—at least in his eyes—were less egregious than Kealey's.

Kealey was glad that one of them had the chance to confront Rudaki, but he knew that it was a long shot. Naomi didn't have much of a chance at penetrating the Iranian's defenses. After all, the man had managed to convince the senior FBI leadership that his information was genuine, probably with Samantha Crane's help. And that was the other thing: Crane would never allow Kharmai to see Rudaki unless she was present.

Despite Harper's restraining words, Kealey was certain that Crane was working with Vanderveen. The idea that the former U.S. soldier was now heading for New York City with a device capable of killing thousands made Kealey feel sick. He didn't know how it had gotten this far, but there was no doubt in his mind that Vanderveen intended to use the bomb the following day, and if he succeeded, the death toll would rival that of 9/11. It simply could not be allowed to happen.

He thought it through for as long as possible, but eventually exhaustion set in, and everything started to blur. Kealey closed his eyes, listening to the whisper of rain against the windows, the occasional rumble of a passing car in the damp street. The house was almost completely quiet. For some reason, he wanted noise and sound, anything to distract him from the memories that encroached in the dark. He held them at bay for as long as he could, but he couldn't stop the inevitable.

He wasn't surprised that the past should get to him here. He hadn't visited the Harper home in nearly a year, and the last time he had stepped foot through the door, Katie had been at his side. He could remember that night with startling clarity, and for good reason: it was the night he had asked her to marry him. After they left for the hotel, he'd surprised her with a moonlight visit to Rock Creek Park. They had walked in the snow, and on a bridge over a frozen stream, he had shown her the ring. Against all odds, she had said yes, and in doing so, she had made his life complete.

Kealey pushed the memory away, but it was no good. For a moment he wished he was back in Iraq, where he could go on pretending that nothing had ever happened, that she was still alive and well. He would give anything, everything he had to go back to the house on Cape Elizabeth and find her waiting, arms open, eyes shining, a pretty, precocious smile on her face. The thought caused a stinging pain to build on the bridge of his nose, but just as the image threatened to overwhelm him, he heard a slight tap at the door, and a shaft of light slipped into the room.

Kealey sat up to see Naomi at the door, her figure bathed in the warm light of the hall. She was wearing a loose-fitting T-shirt and cotton drawstring pants, her feet bare. She took a few hesitant steps in, as though second-guessing her decision, but then she came to the edge of the bed and sat down. Ryan eased back and waited, but she clearly didn't know what to say. After a minute, he broke the silence.

"How's your arm?"

He saw her smile in the half-light of the room. "You know, that's the first time you've asked me about it."

He realized she was right. "I'm sorry, Naomi. I've just been caught up in everything."

"Me, too," she said. "Anyway, it's fine. Julie changed the bandages for me after you came up. She used to be a nurse, you know."

"I could have done that for you."

She nodded once, but didn't respond. He realized she was distracted, lost in thought. "Ryan, what's going to happen tomorrow? What am I supposed to say to Rudaki?"

"I don't know," he replied truthfully. "This is not how I pictured things working out."

"Why would he talk to me? What could I possibly say to make him give up the truth?"

"I have no idea. I've been thinking about it for hours, but we'll just have to see how it plays out. Honestly, I'm too tired to think anymore."

"I feel the same way."

She moved up next to him and leaned against the headboard. They stayed that way for a few minutes, neither finding anything to say. Eventually, he heard her voice in the dark. "I stayed downstairs when you came up." She hesitated. "You know, talking to Julie."

Kealey instantly went on guard, but he didn't speak.

"She told me about the last time you were here. With Katie, I mean."

She waited for a reaction, but it didn't come. "Did you ever—"

"Naomi, what do you want from me?"

She froze at the bitter, angry tone of his voice. His mood had changed without warning, like the flip of a switch. As the shock wore off, she realized she had made a huge mistake. She swung her feet to the floor, intent on getting out of the room, hoping she could make it to the door without embarrassing herself further. Before she could take the first step, though, she felt his hand reach out to lightly grip her arm.

"Wait . . . I'm sorry." He was instantly repentant. "I didn't mean that. Don't go."

She paused, unsure of her next move. Finally, she retook her place at his side, her mind racing, body trembling. Something told her it would be better to stay quiet, so she sat back and struggled to restrain her many questions.

"I've never talked about it," he said. "Not with anyone. I didn't mean to . . ."

"It's okay," she assured him softly. "It's my fault. I shouldn't have brought it up."

"No, I want to tell you." He hesitated, then said, "I need to tell you."

She waited for what seemed like an eternity, staring at her hands, too nervous to look at his face. Finally, she heard his voice in the dark. From his distant tone, she could tell he was no longer there by her side, but instead reliving that terrible night on the coast of Maine.

"It was late when I got back. There was a hell of a storm, and the roads were . . ."

He trailed off inexplicably. "After everything that happened, all I could think about was seeing her. I mean, it was finally over. I knew Vanderveen wasn't dead. We all knew that, but we stopped him in Washington, and that seemed to be good enough at the time. I thought we'd get a second chance, you know? That he'd show up in Africa or Europe and we'd go after him and finish it. But then I walked in that very same night and saw him standing there, with the knife to her throat, and I just . . . I just couldn't believe it."

He fell silent, and after another lengthy pause, he said, "I've never seen her grave, Naomi. I killed her, and I've never even seen her grave."

She finally looked up, aware of the bottomless pain in his voice. She knew he couldn't say anything more. His eyes were squeezed tightly shut, his face damp. Seeing this, she felt a sudden ache in her chest, and she couldn't stop herself. She gently wiped away his tears with the back of her hand and wrapped her arms around him. He didn't try to stop her, but he didn't respond, either.

They stayed that way for a very long time. Naomi couldn't be sure of what she was seeing; she didn't know how much was grief and how much was guilt. As far as she was concerned, it didn't really matter. The important thing was that he was finally letting it go. His shoulders were shaking, the tears running free. She felt a strange sense of pride that he had chosen her, that he was willing to show her the things he had buried inside for nearly a year. Eventually, though, he lifted his head and looked away, as though embarrassed by his show of emotion. She desperately tried to think of something to say, anything to fill the silence. She didn't want him to feel ashamed of the tears he had shed. They were a long time in coming.

"It's not your fault, Ryan. You didn't kill her, and you can't keep doing this to yourself."

"I couldn't protect her," he mumbled. "I failed her when she needed me most. The look in her eyes at the end was just . . ."

Naomi was shaken by his words, but she tried not to show it. She released him and pulled away, resting a light hand on his arm. "Ryan, look at me." He kept his head down for a long time, obviously struggling with some inner turmoil. Finally, he looked up, and their eyes met.

"I know how much she meant to you, but you've suffered enough. You've made mistakes in the past . . . I understand that, but everyone makes mistakes, and you've made up for yours a thousand times over. How many lives did you save last year? How many times have you saved *my* life?" She reached up and touched his face, her expression softening. "You've never let me down, and I know you never will. I trust you completely."

She looked away and let her hand fall to her side. Suddenly, she felt very self-conscious. "I don't know if that means anything to you, but—"

"Of course it means something, Naomi." She lifted her gaze and saw that something had changed in his face. "It means more than you probably know."

They looked at each other for a long moment, the tension building steadily. Then she found herself shifting forward. Her body seemed to be moving of its own accord as she rested a hand on his bare chest, her heart thumping wildly. He put his hand over hers as their lips met, his left arm sliding around her waist. She moved forward and straddled his hips, kissing him harder, digging her fingers into his chest. Naomi knew she was being too aggressive, but she couldn't seem to stop herself. She had wanted this for so long, and now it was finally happening.

She forced herself to slow down, to prolong the moment. She brushed her fingertips over his bare skin, careful to avoid the closed wound on the left side of his abdomen. Ryan sat up, and she wrapped her legs around his waist, pressing her lips to his, aware of him rising beneath her. He lifted the T-shirt over her head, easing the fabric over the bandages on her left shoulder. She closed her eyes as his hands drifted down to her lean waist, moving around to the curves of her back. She sucked in her breath as his head dipped to her small, firm breasts, his left hand touching her inner thigh, his right sliding under her hair, stroking the base of her neck.

They finished undressing each other. Naomi lay back and closed her eyes, lost in the moment. She let out a long, low moan when he entered her, lifting her hips to his body. It was the first time in a long time for both of them, and it couldn't last; they came quickly and in unison, their limbs intertwined, fingers wrapped in each other's hair. When it was over, she rested her head on his shoulder and let out a slow, shaky sigh. She was pleasantly out of breath. She had never felt happier, more content, but as the minutes passed, her brain kicked back into gear. She couldn't help but wonder what was coming next. Like it or not, everything had just gotten a lot more complicated.

As if reading her thoughts, Ryan said, "This could be tricky."

"Mmm." She was still trying to catch her breath. "I always . . ."

"What?"

"Wondered if you had an interest," she finished lamely.

By way of response, he lifted her chin and kissed her softly. She responded immediately, and they made love for the second time, their bodies moving in slow, simple harmony. The act carried less urgency than it had the first time, but no less desire. Twenty minutes after they started, Naomi couldn't hold on any longer. She cried out, then caught herself and tried to restrain her passion, aware of the thin walls that surrounded them. When they were done, they were both too tired to consider things further. They fell asleep in each other's arms, and for the moment, the trials that awaited them the following day were forgotten entirely.

At that same moment, a light rain was drifting over the Peace Bridge between Buffalo, New York, and Fort Erie, Canada, so named to commemorate one hundred years of peace between the two neighboring countries. Despite the temperature, which was hovering near 45 degrees, Tom Logan was relatively warm in his booth on the Canadian side of the Niagara River, a small electric space heater resting on the floor behind his stool. Logan, a twenty-six-year-old Buffalo native, had just started his third year with U.S. Customs & Border Protection, otherwise known as CBP. He didn't think much of the work, but it seemed to pay the bills, and he'd never really aspired to more than that. As he reached for the second half of the turkey sandwich he'd brought in for dinner, a truck rolled up to his window, having approached unseen on the Queen Elizabeth Way while Logan was digging for his food.

Logan sighed and dropped the sandwich back in the bag, then slid open the window. He hoped the driver's paperwork was in order; otherwise, the man would be stuck in Canada for at least another four hours. The Commercial Vehicle Processing Centre had closed at midnight; if the computer indicated the need to contact the carrier's U.S. broker or conduct a physical inspection of the cargo, it would just have to wait, and Logan would probably be in for an argument, the same argument he endured dozens of times each day. Most drivers did not appreciate the delay that secondary inspection entailed, even though it was usually their fault to begin with.

The driver's window came down. "Hey, how's it going?"

"Good enough," Logan replied languidly, looking the man over. He was near forty, he guessed, with shaggy brown hair, brown eyes, and an unshaven face. The collar of his checked flannel shirt was turned up. He looked weary, but nearly every driver coming through Primary looked like that. Driving for a living obviously took a toll on the human body. Knowing this made Logan appreciate his job a little bit more, but not much.

"Got your paperwork?"

The driver handed over two documents. Logan accepted them, checked them quickly, and nodded his approval. The carrier—like every other company seeking to import commercial goods into the United States—subscribed to the Pre-Arrival Processing System, otherwise known as PAPS. The advantage to the relatively new system was a quick turnaround on paperwork, which resulted in fewer delays on the bridge. Before the CVPC was finished in '99, more than seven hundred vehicles a day were referred to Secondary in order to complete missing paperwork. Since nearly four thousand vehicles made the crossing daily, the delays had made the Peace Bridge nearly impassable. The introduction of PAPS and the CVPC in recent years had smoothed things out considerably.

The first document was Customs Form 7533, the cargo manifest. The PAPS bar code was affixed in column one. The second document was the commercial invoice, which wasn't strictly necessary, though most drivers handed it over as a matter of course. Logan scanned the CF7533 quickly, looking at his monitor. The label itself meant nothing; any carrier registered with customs could get the labels; in fact, the carrier could print them off themselves. Once the label was affixed to the manifest, the carrier was required to send the manifest to a U.S. broker, who would then forward the document on to customs for prerelease. If none of that had transpired, the monitor would instruct Logan to direct the truck to Secondary, which would result in a long wait for the driver.

In this case, however, it looked like the man was well prepared. The words "No Exam" came up on the monitor, indicating that the truck was allowed to pass. Like 82 percent of the commercial vehicles that came through daily, this one would proceed unhindered into the United States.

"Looks like you're good to go," Logan said, handing the driver his paperwork. He glanced at the manifest one last time before releasing the document. "That's a heavy load."

The driver grinned. "We got a deal on the boiler from one of our clients in Montreal. It's actually for us . . . . The old one gave out in our terminal in Ithaca a week ago."

Logan laughed. "I feel sorry for the poor bastards working in that building. Ain't it hard to believe it's only September? The guys on the night shift must be freezing their asses off."

"Well, if I wasn't here, I'd be one of them. This is one of the few times I'm glad to be on the road."

Logan grunted his amusement. "Well, drive safe, and welcome to the United States."

Will Vanderveen dropped the truck into gear and smiled out the window. "Thanks. It's good to be back."

CHAPTER 46

WASHINGTON, D.C.

In the second-floor bedroom on Q Street, Kealey woke with a start and sat up, his eyes moving to the bedside clock. It was just after 5:30 in the morning. He looked to his left, expecting to see Naomi's sleeping form, but he was surprised to find the other side of the bed empty. His gaze moved to the adjacent bathroom. There was no light under the door, so he assumed she must have gone back to her room while he had been sleeping. He couldn't help but wonder what that meant. Did she regret what had happened? Or was she just uneasy sharing his bed in this particular setting?

Kealey stood and moved to the window. It was still dark, the street shining beneath the sidewalk lamps, sodden leaves piled up at the curbs. As he stared out at the calm, silent scene, he found that he couldn't stop thinking about her. It was strange, but he felt more at peace than he had in months, and he thought he knew why: after months and months of black despair, the shadow caused by Katie's death was finally starting to lift. He knew that no one would ever replace her, but for the first time since that terrible night in Maine, he thought there might be room in his life for somebody else.

He knew that the guilt would never entirely fade, just as he knew that his memories would haunt him forever. Still, now he thought he saw a way to build some new memories. Some good ones. He shook his head, realizing his thoughts might be a little presumptuous, or at least premature. He and Naomi obviously still had a lot to talk about, but that conversation would just have to wait. Hopefully, she wanted the same thing he did, to build on what they had started.

He turned away from the window and went into the bathroom, flipping on the light. He shaved and brushed his teeth, then turned on the shower. Twenty minutes later he was dressed for the day in jeans, a black, long-sleeve layering T-shirt, and Columbia hiking boots.

He left the room and started down to the other end of the hall. Before he hit the stairs, he heard Harper talking on the other side of the office door, as well as the sound of a television set at low volume. He tapped lightly and heard the other man call him in.

When Kealey stepped in the room, he was slightly shocked at the DDO's appearance. His eyes were bloodshot, his hair unkempt, and he was still dressed in the same clothes. Obviously, he had stayed up all night, giving orders and chasing down additional information. From the look on his face, it was clear that he had news to impart.

"All hell has broken loose in Iraq," he said, gesturing to the television.

"What happened?"

"Mortar attack on the Green Zone from across the river," Harper replied wearily. "Just after midnight. Six people were killed outright, another dozen injured, most of them critically. Two hours later, a Huey carrying the 25th Infantry Division's deputy commander was shot down near Kirkuk. The crew was killed in the crash, along with the ADC's aide, a full colonel. The general is still missing, presumed dead."

"Jesus." Kealey knew that this was big. To date, the highest ranking officer killed in Iraq since 2003 was a colonel in the National Guard. "How did they—"

"Looks like a portable missile launcher. Stinger, maybe. We're looking into it." Harper shook it off and held up a handful of paper. "This just came in. You might want to read it."

Kealey accepted the paperwork and sank into one of the leather club chairs. "What is it?"

"A list of people involved with the investigation at Al Qaqaa, following the theft of the explosives in March of 2003. The investigation involved the multinational force and the Iraq Survey Group. I assume you know what I'm talking about."

Kealey did. From the start of the war until January 2005, the ISG had been tasked with finding Saddam Hussein's phantom WMDs. The group consisted of more than 1,000 nuclear, chemical, and biological experts, as well as private security contractors and military officers. Although the ISG never completed its main objective, it was one of the war's most cohesive, efficient units, losing only a handful of people to accidents and enemy fire over a two-year period. At the same time, it managed to dispose of hundreds of tons of conventional munitions.

"The ISG was divided into three Sector Control Points: North, Baghdad, and South," Harper continued. "The Baghdad SCP was responsible for Al Qaqaa, so I narrowed the search to that group of people. What you have there is the name of everybody who, at some point or another, was involved with the investigation."

Kealey scanned the list quickly, but nothing jumped out. He forced himself to reread it carefully. There were nearly three hundred names on five sheets of paper. He was halfway through the fourth page when he stopped and said, "Jesus, I don't believe it."

Harper had been watching the television, which was tuned to CNN. "What do you have?"

"I know this guy, John. Owen . . . Paul Owen. He's a lieutenant colonel with Delta. He used to be my CO at Bragg."

"Hold on, wasn't he—"

"Yeah," Kealey cut in, anticipating the question. "He and his boys were with me in Fallujah when I went after Arshad Kassem."

"So he can either prove or disprove that BLU-82s were being stored at Al Qaqaa," Harper said. A shadow crossed his face. "As I recall, he wasn't too happy with you after what happened with Kassem."

"That's true, but the brotherhood is a strange thing, John. You never served, so you don't really know, but what happened in Fallujah is over and done with. I'll explain the situation, and he'll tell us what we need to know. I guarantee it."

Harper didn't reply for a long moment, sizing up the younger man's statement. Finally, he seemed to take it at face value. "You can call him on the way to the airport."

"It might not be easy to track him down," Kealey pointed out. "Last I heard, he was at Camp Fallujah, but that might have changed by now. Guys like Owen never stay in one place for long."

"I'll get you a telephone number before we leave. In the meantime, there's something else you need to know about. I called my guy in Los Angeles and asked him to lean on that agent in New York. You know, the one who wasn't buying into Rudaki's story."

"This is how we got Rudaki's name in the first place, right?"

"Exactly. Anyway, as it turns out, he's been meeting with Samantha Crane at a Bureau safe house. Apparently he didn't want to show his face at the field office, which isn't really surprising, considering the sensitive nature of what he was passing on. Lies or no lies, he wouldn't want to be seen schmoozing with agents in a federal building. Supposedly, the safe house is in the Bronx. The agent thinks it might be on Vyse Avenue—the street popped up once in conversation—but he doesn't know the address, and he's not in a position to ask for it."

The younger man thought it through. "That's interesting," he finally said. "If something is going down today, Rudaki will want to be sure he's free and clear of any involvement. A Bureau safe house would be a good place to be, especially if he's surrounded by agents and nowhere near the UN. You couldn't ask for a better alibi."

"That's makes sense, but without the address, the information isn't much good."

"Maybe. I'll have to think about it, but this meeting at the field office isn't much good, either. Even Naomi knows there's no way Rudaki will tell her the truth. She doesn't have any leverage. We have to get Rudaki alone, and I have to do it myself."

Harper hesitated. "What if he's telling the truth, Ryan? What if the Iranians really are behind the Babylon Hotel and Tabrizi's death in Paris?"

"We both know that's not the case, John. The Iranians have more to lose by interfering in Iraq than they have to gain. Ahmadinejad is a crazy bastard, but not that crazy. He won't risk sharing Saddam's fate by killing that many people on U.S. soil. Vanderveen may be the man on the ground, but ultimately, someone else is behind this, and it's not the regime in Tehran. Hakim Rudaki is feeding the Bureau lies, and so is Samantha Crane."

"So what will you do?"

Kealey thought for a moment. "I'm going to see if I can find out where this safe house is. Naomi can go to the FO and sit in on the interview as planned. If Rudaki doesn't want to be seen in a federal building, he won't want to dawdle. Maybe I'll catch him coming in or out."

The DDO shook his head. "Do you have any idea how that sounds? You're basically hoping for a miracle."

"Well, that's what we're left with, isn't it?"

Kealey made his way downstairs a few minutes later. Despite the early hour, he found Naomi in the kitchen. She was sitting at the table, still in her bedclothes, eating a bowl of cereal. Her jet-black hair was mussed, her green eyes shining with some inner light. She smiled when she saw him, but there was some hesitation behind it. Kealey didn't understand why at first, but then it hit him. She was probably having the same thoughts he was, namely, wondering if he wanted more than what they had shared the previous night.

Julie Harper was busying herself with coffee at the counter. She turned when he entered and smiled. "Good morning, Ryan. Did you sleep well?"

Out of the corner of his eye, he saw Naomi's face turn red. She suddenly became much more interested in her cereal, pausing to shovel a huge spoonful of Cheerios into her mouth.

"Great, thanks," he said, responding to Julie's question. "It definitely beats a cot in Kabul. Or a tent in the Bekaa, for that matter."

She laughed and turned back to the coffee. Kealey waited until Naomi had swallowed her cereal, then took the opportunity to lean down and kiss her. When he pulled away, her smile was so radiant that he couldn't help but grin himself. He immediately realized that his fears were completely unfounded: judging by the happy look on her face, she didn't regret what had happened at all. He took a seat at the table as Julie walked over with a mug of coffee, which he accepted gratefully.

"Well, you look better, anyway. Much better, in fact." She shot a suspicious but not unfriendly look at Naomi, who managed to look reasonably innocent. "What time are you heading out?"

"Less than an hour. Our plane leaves at nine."

"Well, we had you for one night, at least. You won't leave it so long next time, will you? I don't want to wait a year to hear from you again."

"Not a chance. You'll be sick of me before you know it."

"Not a chance," she said, smiling to show she'd intentionally borrowed his words.

Harper walked in from the living room a few minutes later. He accepted a cup from his wife and glanced at his watch, taking in Naomi's disheveled appearance. "Kharmai, you'd better get moving, or that plane will be leaving without you."

She nodded and pushed back from her chair, shooting Kealey one last look before she left the room. Harper pushed a scrap of paper across the table.

"According to Special Forces Command, Colonel Owen is currently based at Camp Diamondback at Mosul Airport. He's been running search-and-destroy missions out of the garrison with a select group of men from 'B' Squadron. They've been tracking a mortar team that's attacked the airport on four separate occasions since June. They think it's the same team that hit the Green Zone this morning. That number will put you in touch with him."

"Good."

"If you get hold of him before you hit the airport, give him my name and tell him to expect my call," Harper continued. "If he can affirm that Rühmann got the BLU-82 from Al Qaqaa, it'll go a long way in convincing the president to bulk up security around the UN. It's already tight, of course, but I won't be happy until all the surrounding roads are blocked off."

"What time does the meeting begin?"

"The General Assembly convenes at five PM. They're holding it off as some of the Iraqi delegates won't arrive until later this afternoon."

"So if Vanderveen wants to get them all in the same place, we have until five."

"That seems to be a reasonable assumption."

Julie Harper had gone upstairs while they were talking. Kealey stood and went to the counter, where he poured himself a second cup of coffee. As he returned to the table, he said, "I've been thinking about something you said last night, John. If Vanderveen already has the daisy cutter here in the States—and I think we have to assume he does—how did he get it over the border?"

"A truck."

"Right, but that's risky. What if he got stopped? He couldn't risk a customs inspection."

"If the weapon was disguised he could."

"It's kind of hard to disguise a fifteen-thousand-pound bomb."

"But not impossible," Harper pointed out. "Besides, there are other ways to circumvent customs. Like I said before, just having the right paperwork makes a huge difference."

"Exactly," Kealey agreed. "But how do you get the right paperwork?"

The older man frowned. "I don't know as much about this as I probably should. I know there are systems in place to facilitate companies that do a lot of cross-border trade."

"I think that's where we need to look. A company based in the New York area that spends a lot of time going in and out of Canada."

"That's a lot of companies."

"Yeah, but who files the paperwork with U.S. Customs? The owner, right?" Kealey fell silent for a moment, thinking it through. "The question is, who would risk everything to help Vanderveen with this, and why? What's the motivation?"

"Money."

"Money is one possibility," Kealey said absently. "Let's get this to the New York FO, John. Ask them to start looking at businesses in the five boroughs listed with the CBP. Have them focus on companies owned by people of Middle Eastern descent."

"That's the worst kind of racial profiling, Ryan."

"I'm aware of that," the younger man said, unable to hide his irritation, "but we're not asking them to break down any doors, are we? If they check discreetly, no one will be the wiser. We have to look at all the angles, and I don't care if we hurt a few feelings along the way. We don't have time to fuck around anymore."

By 6:45 they were ready to leave. They had opted to leave their luggage behind, so they were traveling light. Naomi had changed into a snug cashmere sweater, along with a pair of stretch chinos and suede flats. She was unarmed, owing to the fact that she would be spending most of the trip at the Bureau's FO, but Kealey had his Beretta, which he'd left with Harper before departing for Berlin. He planned to check the weapon at the airport, knowing that whatever happened in New York, he would almost certainly need it. If, by some miracle, he did manage to get his hands on Hakim Rudaki, the man would not be quick to volunteer the truth.

Julie Harper walked them to the door. She hugged Ryan briefly and urged him to come back soon. As Jonathan pulled him aside to deliver some last-minute instructions, Kharmai found herself alone with the other woman. To her surprise, she found herself being drawn in for a warm embrace.

"Take care of him, Naomi," Julie murmured. "He deserves to be happy again."

Naomi nodded when the other woman released her, touched by the gesture. She was also a little embarrassed; she wasn't aware they had made it so obvious. "I'll do my best. It was great meeting you."

"You too, dear. Take care."

The Suburban was already waiting at the curb. Naomi walked down the stairs, followed by Kealey and Harper. She got in first. Kealey moved to follow, but Harper pulled him back for a second. There were equal amounts of hesitation and steadfast determination on the older man's face.

"Ryan, I asked my driver to bring along a couple of cell phones. I have the numbers, and you have mine. If there's anything I can do from here, don't hesitate to let me know."

Kealey nodded. "Thanks, John. I'll remember that."

"And good luck," the older man said. He looked up at the overcast sky and frowned, as if the weather could foretell the day's events. "I think you're going to need it."

CHAPTER 47

NEW YORK CITY

In the parking area outside the warehouse on West Thirty-seventh Street in Midtown Manhattan, Will Vanderveen lifted the rolling door of an Isuzu truck, placed his hands on the cold metal floor at the back, and stared in at the contents. Thomas Rühmann's men had done their work well; to look inside, one would never guess that, concealed beneath the thin metal walls of a Parker commercial boiler, was an elaborate, delicate wooden framework, and beneath that, a device capable of unleashing incredible destruction, a device capable of destroying the heart of the Iraqi Parliament, the United Iraqi Alliance. As he gazed upon the sight, he was aware of Raseen at his side. He looked at her and saw she was equally rapt, her dark eyes shining. Behind her, standing off to the side, was Amir Nazeri. He looked calm and assured, his glasses reflecting the pale morning sun, but there was an undercurrent of tension there that had not escaped the other two. Vanderveen, in particular, was still trying to figure out how steadfast Nazeri was. It was the last—but most important—thing he had to consider. Nearly everything else was done.

The previous day, they had used a forklift from the Montreal terminal to load the device at the Lake Forest storage facility, after which they returned the forklift and started west to the border crossing at Buffalo. After passing through customs on the Peace Bridge, Vanderveen had followed I-95 to Syracuse. From there, it was a short drive to Ithaca. The Bridgeline warehouse was located just north of the city, in a commercial sector that had seen better days. Yasmin Raseen and Amir Nazeri had entered the United States hours earlier in a passenger vehicle owned by Nazeri's company. Vanderveen met them in Ithaca just after 5:00 a.m., where they transferred the bomb to an Isuzu H-Series box truck with a GVWR of 33,000 pounds. The rear axle was capable of withstanding loads up to 19,000 pounds, which was more than adequate for their purposes.

According to Nazeri, the vehicle was completely untraceable, meaning that no link would ever be found between the shattered remains of the Isuzu and Bridgeline Transport, Inc. Vanderveen didn't know if this was true or if it was just wishful thinking on Nazeri's part, but it didn't really matter. Nazeri had no idea what was about to happen. He didn't know that he was about to embark on a suicide mission, and when it was over, Bridgeline would be implicated almost immediately. An anonymous call to the FBI would point the investigators in the right direction. The death of thousands of American citizens would, in due course, be attributed to the Iranian who had come to America in search of a better life, only to find that the U.S. government had stripped him of the only thing he had ever cared about.

The death of Dr. Nasir Tabrizi in Paris at the hands of Iranian fundamentalists—combined with the revelation of Iranian funding for the purchase of Rashid al-Umari's refinery in Iraq—had already generated enormous suspicion in the Western media. Many people already believed that the regime in Tehran was behind the escalating situation in Iraq, and Nazeri's actions would only clinch their suspicions. The American public would never believe that the Iranians did not have a hand in it, and with thousands dead in the worst attack on U.S. soil since 9/11, President David Brenneman would be under immense pressure to exact swift, harsh revenge on the Iranian capital.

The idea that Mahmoud Ahmadinejad was ultimately responsible would also be reinforced by Hakim Rudaki, the FBI's coveted informant. Vanderveen had already called Rudaki directly to provide additional instructions; at the moment, Rudaki was busy establishing ties between Thomas Rühmann and the Iranian president, some of which were imagined, others real. Vanderveen had called his source in the Bureau hours earlier to confirm that everything was on schedule. He had not been surprised to learn that Kealey had survived the trap in

Berlin, along with the woman, Kharmai, but he had been disturbed to learn that Kharmai had been granted an audience with Rudaki shortly before noon. Somehow, the CIA was aware of what had been stored at Lake Forest. But that couldn't be helped now, and it didn't really matter. They didn't know about Nazeri, and they didn't know about the warehouse on West Thirty-seventh. The intense security surrounding the UN would prove to be worthless. Kealey may have cheated death yet again, but he would never be able to stop what was about to happen.

Vanderveen stood up and stretched, gazing around at the open cement. Using Nazeri made things more complicated than they should have been, but the same was true of the men they had used in Paris. Implicating the Iranians wasn't strictly necessary, but it did have the effect of diverting attention from the Iraqi insurgency. Vanderveen had listened to the news on the drive east from Ithaca. Iraq was already on the brink of civil war, and in a matter of hours, the Shiite alliance would be wiped from the face of the earth, along with several thousand U.S. citizens. The U.S. military would no longer be able to control the mass chaos that would ensue in Iraq. In other words, Izzat al-Douri was about to reclaim the country he had lost just a few years earlier.

Vanderveen turned to Nazeri. "Where's the box?"

"In my office."

"Show me."

They followed the Iranian through a set of double-glass doors and into the warehouse. The smooth cement floor was littered with wooden pallets, all of which were weighed down with thousands of bottles of water and soda. Behind the pallets were redbrick walls leading up to a low ceiling. Vanderveen recalled that the warehouse was used to distribute soft drinks to area businesses. Fortunately, Nazeri had had the foresight to dismiss his employees for the day, a point that Vanderveen had overlooked.

They came to the glass-enclosed office. There was another door on the far side of the room. Nazeri pulled a key from his pocket with trembling hands, unlocked the door, and pulled out a large box sealed with masking tape. He used the key to slice the tape along the fold, then pulled open the cardboard flaps.

Vanderveen looked inside. The package had come courtesy of Anthony Mason several months earlier. It contained five half-pound blocks of Semtex, two 50-foot coils of what appeared to be time fuse, a pair of wire crimpers, and a cloth-wrapped package. Vanderveen pulled out the package, placed it on the nearby desk, and unfurled the cloth. Inside were several nonelectric blasting caps and three nylon tubes with pull rings on one end. Nazeri walked over, and Vanderveen lifted one of the tubes.

"I'm going to show you how this works," he said, adopting the instructive tone he'd used as an E-7 in the 3rd Special Forces Group at Fort Bragg, North Carolina. Nazeri's distracted mien was instantly replaced by an expression of sober, undivided attention.

"This is an M60 fuse igniter," Vanderveen began. He pointed to the bottom part of the tube, opposite the metal pull ring. "This is the fuse holder cap. You unscrew it"—he demonstrated—"and remove the shipping plug, like this. Now you're ready to install the time fuse, but first we'll prepare the blasting cap. Do you have a knife?"

The other man nodded. Raseen was standing off to the side, watching with interest. Vanderveen went to the box and pulled out one of the coils of the time fuse. Nothing changed in his face, and the hesitation was barely noticeable, but he checked both coils quickly, then selected the one on the bottom. He brought it back over and accepted the Iranian's pocketknife.

Vanderveen cut off the first 6 inches of the time fuse and tossed it aside. The box was dry, but he knew it was still possible for moisture to contaminate either end of the fuse. Then he cut off approximately 3 feet from the remaining length. Selecting one of the blasting caps, he checked the open end for debris and, finding none, gently pushed it onto one end of the fuse. Then, with exquisite care, he used the crimpers to secure the cap to the time fuse.

"You see what I did?" he asked Nazeri. The other man gave a jerky nod. "Now, do you have a blanket around here? Some kind of soft material?"

"I have a sweater. Will that work?" Vanderveen nodded, and Nazeri retrieved the sweater from a cabinet near the office door. Vanderveen wrapped it around the blasting cap and placed the sweater on the far side of the office, well away from the cardboard box. Then he took the free end of the fuse and slipped it into the well of the M60 igniter. Finally, he tightened the fuse holder cap and held up the tube.

"Watch what I'm doing." He waited until he was sure he had Nazeri's attention. Then he pulled out the safety clip, pushed the pull ring into the M60, turned it to the right, and pulled it all the way out.

Nazeri looked confused. "Why is nothing happening?"

"That's three feet of fuse," Vanderveen explained. "It burns at roughly forty seconds a foot, so it'll take about two minutes. Then the cap will detonate. You'll hear a little pop . . . Just wait."

They waited, and in due course, the cap went off. Nazeri jumped at the noise, even though he'd been told to expect it. Vanderveen walked over and unfolded the sweater, showing Nazeri the scorched, torn material. "If the cap had been surrounded by explosives, it would have set them off. But do you understand what I'm talking about? You'll have plenty of time once you pull the ring to get out of the truck and into the subway. We'll be using about twelve feet of the time fuse, so you'll have nearly five minutes to get clear."

"But won't the police be able to get inside the truck by then?"

"No," Raseen put in. "But even if they do, they won't know how to stop it in time. Policemen in America are not trained in such matters."

Nazeri seemed to take this at face value, though he didn't look in Raseen's direction as she spoke. Vanderveen had already noticed that the Iranian businessman was uneasy in her presence. He didn't know if this was due to a cultural phenomenon or the fact that Yasmin Raseen had a way of making people uncomfortable. He assumed it was a little of both.

"Okay," he said. "We're going to do it again, only this time, you are going to set it up, and I'll watch. It's vital that you know how to use the igniter. It's not a difficult procedure, but it has to be done correctly."

Nazeri nodded. He appeared calm, but when he reached out to accept the next green nylon tube, his hand was shaking ever so slightly. Vanderveen studied him for a few seconds, face impassive, then gestured with his head for Raseen to join him outside. They left the office, Raseen closing the door behind them. A moment later they stepped outside. Their breath steamed in the cool morning air.

The Isuzu shined white in the pale sun, which had just topped the surrounding buildings.

Vanderveen turned toward her. "What do you think?"

"He's nervous."

"I agree. Is the cousin enough to push him forward?"

Raseen had ridden with Nazeri from Montreal to Manhattan, and she'd used the time to peel back the layers with infinite care. She started with questions about him, probing his fears, dreams, and desires. Then she ventured into the life of Fatima Darabi. Finally, she incorporated the two, asking about their childhood together, the pivotal moments they had shared in their youth. Nazeri had been reluctant to talk at first, Raseen explained, but that was only because she was a woman, and it hadn't stopped him for long. Amir Nazeri had been in the States for many years, and the cultural strictures imposed on him as a child had faded with time. As the miles and hours passed, she had managed to break through his defenses.

"I think he loved her a great deal," Raseen concluded. Her voice was neutral; in Iran, romantic love between cousins was viewed differently than it was in the United States, as marriage within the family helped ensure the preservation of land and other material assets. "He believes she felt the same way. Her death changed everything for him."

"Has it changed him enough, though?" Vanderveen mused. "That's the question."

Raseen shrugged. "Have you shown him the document?"

"Not yet."

"When you do, his doubts will disappear, along with his fears. I would wait until the last possible minute; that way, it will have more of an effect. You shouldn't worry, though. He's prepared to see this through."

Vanderveen nodded. "You have your phone?"

Nazeri had purchased several pay-and-go phones before driving up to Montreal. They each had one. "Yes, I have it."

"And money?"

"I have that as well. I'll call you once I'm in position."

"Good." Vanderveen paused. "We'll meet again this evening, and then we'll discuss how we're going to get out of the country."

"Fine." She hesitated. "Will, do you remember what you told me in Germany? About Jonathan Harper?"

He nodded. During the brief trip from Potsdam to Berlin, he had relayed everything he had been told by his Bureau contact over the phone in the Luisenplatz, right down to the identity of the CIA's deputy director of operations.

"Do you think we'll get the chance to take care of that?"

"Possibly." It was a tremendous opportunity, Vanderveen knew. The identity of the DDO was highly classified. Now, thanks to his Bureau contact, they had not only the man's name, but an approximate address, a brownstone on General's Row in Washington, D.C. "If the opportunity presents itself, we'll pay him a visit. For now, we have enough to worry about."

"I suppose you're right." She crossed the open cement, walking to the gate leading out to the street. Vanderveen followed. He unlocked the gate, then pulled it open. She stepped onto the street and turned to face him. There was an awkward pause while they each considered some kind of affectionate gesture, but then the moment was gone.

"I'll be in touch." Before he could reply, she turned and walked off, heading east toward Eighth Avenue. Vanderveen watched her go for nearly a minute, wondering if he would ever see her again. Then he shut the gate, locked it, and headed back to the warehouse.

CHAPTER 48

NEW YORK CITY

As the taxi she'd taken from LaGuardia Airport left Brooklyn and sped over the Williamsburg Bridge, Naomi Kharmai gazed out at the East River. The bridge offered an incredible view of FDR Drive and the Lower East Side, the Manhattan skyline beyond, but she was too distracted to appreciate the view. Her mind was wrapped up in the meeting she was about to attend, as well as the events of the previous night.

Naomi could still scarcely believe what had happened with Ryan, but she didn't regret it at all. It had been everything she'd hoped for and more. The only reason she'd gone back to her room was to avoid a potentially embarrassing scene in the morning. After collapsing onto her bed, she had stared at the ceiling for hours, worried that if she fell asleep, she'd wake to find it had never happened, or—worse yet—that he regretted the encounter. It was a strange dichotomy; it had been one of the best and worst nights of her life, a bewildering mixture of lingering happiness and dread for what the morning would bring. She needn't have worried; all of her fears had melted away with the kiss he'd given her over the breakfast table. She felt sure that, everything else aside, it was the start of something incredible. Part of her just wanted to get the day over with so they could talk about it properly. At the same time, she knew she couldn't afford to let what had happened distract her. She did her best to push it aside as the taxi turned onto Kenmare Street, then swung a left onto Lafayette Street.

Naomi still didn't know how she was going to handle the interview with Hakim Rudaki. She felt sure that Ryan was right—that he was stringing the Bureau along with false information. Judging by the information that Harper had managed to dig up on the Iranian informant, Naomi knew he wouldn't break easily. He was an intelligent man: a Harvard graduate, a respected member of the academic community. She wasn't intimidated by this—she had reached comparable heights at Stanford, after all—but she knew she couldn't discount his academic achievements. At the very least, it meant that he would not succumb to crude psychological manipulation. This realization left her deeply concerned. She had faith in her abilities, but she wasn't a trained interrogator, and she just couldn't conceive of a way to get him to confess his true role in the recent events. All she could do was play it by ear and hope that Ryan had more luck in the South Bronx.

They had separated after their plane landed at LaGuardia. His destination was Vyse Avenue, where he was going to try and track down the Bureau safe house. Privately, Naomi didn't think he would have much luck. The ADIC had assured the DDO that Rudaki would be present when Naomi arrived at 26 Federal Plaza, which meant that Ryan would find himself with no one to question, even if—by some miracle—he did manage to find the safe house. It would all come down to her.

It was strange; the full implication of this thought took a long time to sink in, but when it did, it hit her like a ton of bricks. If Vanderveen *was* planning to use a daisy cutter in the city that same afternoon, the only way they could stop him was by breaking Rudaki.

And that fell to her. No one else.

Her mouth went instantly dry. The thought made her feel dizzy and sick to her stomach . . . How could she not have seen this before? If they were right about Vanderveen's intentions—and she felt sure that they were—the lives of thousands of people rested in her hands. The thought was so overwhelming that she didn't notice they had reached their destination until the driver turned in his seat to scream at her in Spanish, trying to get her attention.

She handed over the money with shaking hands, then stumbled out onto Lafayette Street. The Civic Center was a block to the south, and for a minute, she wondered why the driver hadn't continued. Then she realized that the roads surrounding the Bureau's building were probably blocked off to vehicular traffic. She walked on weak legs down the sidewalk, following the crowds. The people around her were engaged in their daily routines, oblivious to the looming disaster. She couldn't look at them. Her realization of a moment ago had left her numb . . . It was so unfair. How could the deputy director have put this on her shoulders? Maybe even *he* didn't realize what he'd pushed her into, but she didn't think that was the case. She felt a bitter anger join the piercing ache in her chest . . . Jonathan Harper was a lot of things, but he wasn't naïve. He'd known exactly what he was doing.

She reached Duane Street and turned right, passing a series of concrete barriers and a small guard shack. The U.S. Customs House was on her right, and past that, the east entrance of the Jacob K. Javits Federal Building. She went up the brief flight of stairs, pulled open the glass door, and stepped inside. There were a number of turnstiles off to the right, but they were reserved for building employees with government-issued smart cards. Since she was technically no longer with the Agency, Naomi had only her British passport and her driver's license. She was forced to wait in line with a group of sullen immigrants and their screaming children, all of whom were destined for the INS offices on the fourth floor. When it was her turn, she passed through the metal detector and endured a brief search of her purse. Then she explained to the security guard her reason for visiting. He placed a call and gestured for her to take a seat on a nearby bench.

Five minutes later she was approached by a man with dark, wavy hair; broad shoulders; and square, chiseled features. He was handsome enough, with one exception: his nose had been badly broken at some point in the past. It was pinched at the bridge and shaped like an hourglass. Naomi made an effort not to stare at it as she stood up and accepted the proffered hand.

"Ms. Kharmai? Or is it Agent Kharmai?" The man grinned. "Sorry, but I still haven't figured that out. As you can probably imagine, I don't have a lot of interaction with you people."

She tried to return the smile, but it wasn't easy, given her recent epiphany. It felt like the weight of the world was resting on her shoulders. "You can call me Naomi."

"I'm Special Agent Foster, but call me Matt. Sorry you had to wait."

"That's fine," she said. "I got here only a minute ago."

They started toward the elevator. *Matt Foster.* Something about the name seemed familiar, but she couldn't place it. Where had she heard it before? She was still thinking about it as the elevator stopped on the twenty-third floor and the doors slid open. They stepped into a reception area. There was a desk near the far wall, the FBI seal displayed prominently behind the secretary's blond head. Trailing behind, Naomi couldn't see Foster's face as they passed the desk, but he must have done something, because the secretary blushed and looked away. For some reason, the harmless flirting annoyed her deeply. She no longer felt like wasting a second; all she wanted was to find and stop Will Vanderveen, and that meant getting the truth out of Hakim Rudaki.

The bullpen was incredibly noisy, the open space filled with agents talking on phones and working on computers. Crossing the room, they came to a glass-enclosed office. The door was open, so Foster tapped on the frame and was told to enter. Aware that she was probably about to have a very unpleasant conversation, Naomi tried to adopt her most stoic expression. She wanted to appear unflappable, which was a lot to aspire to, given the situation. She took a deep breath and felt some of the fear and apprehension slip away. Then she stepped through the door.

CHAPTER 49

NEW YORK CITY

Vyse Avenue, between East 173rd and East 176th Street, was symptomatic of the cheap, surface-deep changes that greedy developers had forced upon the South Bronx community in recent years. During the seventies, the city, in a disastrous policy move, opted to relocate a large number of welfare households to the area between 152nd and the Cross-Bronx Expressway. The results were predictable: crime shot up, working-class families moved out, and the neighborhood was left worse off than it had been to start with. In truth, not much had changed since then, despite successive mayoral claims of extensive urban renewal. According to statistics compiled in the 2000 census, the South Bronx belonged to one of the poorest congressional districts in the nation.

In short, it was just about the last place one would expect to find an FBI safe house. As Ryan Kealey moved down the irregular sidewalk on foot, his attention was not focused on the redbrick housing units wedged tightly against the road, but on the few cars lined up at the curb. He'd rented a Honda Accord at the airport, and he'd used it to check the length of Vyse Avenue before proceeding on foot. While he was slightly impressed with the Bureau's decision to keep this safe house in such an unlikely area, he didn't think the New York ADIC would go so far as to purchase vehicles that blended into the neighborhood. That kind of thing just wasn't in the budget. Government vehicles were typically easy to spot, and he'd already come up with a likely candidate. Now he wanted to see it close up, which explained why he was moving on foot.

The car was a dark blue Crown Victoria, a typical Bureau vehicle. He checked the license plate first. They weren't government tags, but that wasn't surprising; even the FBI—one of the government's more arrogant agencies—knew how to keep a low profile when circumstances dictated. Next, he looked in through the window. The interior was abnormally clean, at least, abnormally clean for this neighborhood. He checked the front. He didn't see any type of radio, but again, that wasn't really surprising. The Bureau didn't use vehicle-mounted radios to the same extent that local law enforcement did. There wasn't a light bar in the back window, either. He still couldn't be sure—it could be an NYPD detective's unmarked car—but if Harper's contact at the Bureau was right about the location of the safe house, this was probably his best bet.

Kealey turned away from the car and checked his surroundings. The street was strangely empty. He'd parked the Accord a few blocks away, and during the brief walk, he'd only passed a few kids playing baseball in the middle of the road. The housing units on either side of Vyse Avenue were three-story duplexes: redbrick façades on the first floor, cheap vinyl siding above that. The buildings looked innocuous enough, but a closer inspection revealed bars on the first-story windows, and the short driveways were blocked off by black-iron fences that rose to chest height. There was very little vegetation, a scrap of grass here and there, a few scraggly trees rising out of the sidewalk. A few empty lots were filled with nothing but bare soil, rubble, litter, and milkweed.

He turned and walked back the way he had come, thinking about it. Even if he was right about the car, the problem was obvious: he had no way of knowing which unit was being used by the Bureau. More to the point, he had no way of getting inside. If Samantha Crane was in one of these buildings with Rudaki, she would probably have at least one other agent with her. If Kealey tried to force his way inside, he would quickly find himself at a disadvantage.

He was still thinking about it when he reached the Accord a minute later. A few Latino teenagers in baggy clothes were standing nearby. One was drinking from a bottle wrapped in a paper sack; another was sitting on the hood of the rental car. Kealey thought he knew why; aside from the Crown Vic, the Accord was easily the nicest vehicle in a four-block radius. They were probably just looking for someone to fuck with. As Kealey approached, one of the youths standing said something to the one sitting on the car. The teenager grinned and waited; he seemed to be relishing the upcoming confrontation.

Kealey stopped and studied them each in turn. Finally, the kid perched on the hood said, "This yours, man?"

Kealey nodded. "Yeah."

"It's nice. Wouldn't mind a ride like this myself. Could use some twenties, though." The kid bounced up and down once, testing the shocks. Then he kicked his heels against the front fender, leaving a mark. "Maybe some new paint. White people always go for the same old shit."

The others snickered; clearly, they were waiting for him to react. Instead of protesting, Kealey walked a few steps closer, stopping about 5 feet away from the nearest youth. He looked them over quickly. He didn't think they had anything larger than a knife between them, but he had to be sure.

The guy on the car looked to be the oldest and, therefore, the de facto leader, but the teenagers standing nearby were the greater threat. Turning to the one who had both hands free, Kealey said, "I'm going to show you something, and I don't want you to panic, okay?"

They laughed again, but it was slightly forced, and he knew he had their attention. Dropping his gaze to their hands, he lifted the right side of his long-sleeve T-shirt, revealing the Beretta 92FS holstered on his right hip. He didn't look up, but he could tell that seeing the gun had sobered them up. The youth on the car slid off and backed up immediately, muttering something in Spanish. Kealey assumed they thought he was a cop or something similar, since he wasn't brandishing the weapon like a maniac.

Still watching their hands, he said, "I want you all to do something for me. Lift your shirts slowly. Come on, you too."

They did as he asked. Just as he'd expected, they didn't appear to be carrying. "Turn around," he ordered. "Keep your shirts up."

Still nothing. Relaxing slightly, Kealey said, "Okay, drop 'em and face me." When they turned back around, he finally looked at their faces. He could see that the two younger men were nervous, but the leader appeared unfazed. Kealey knew he had guessed right from the start. These young men were far from hardened criminals, but they weren't exactly Boy Scouts, either. In short, they were exactly what he was looking for.

He lowered his shirt back over the butt of the Beretta. Then he smiled and showed them his open hands.

"You guys feel like making some money?"

Terry Best, the assistant director in charge of the New York field office, was fifty-three years old, a large man with ruddy features, heavy jowls, and a fringe of coppery hair. When Naomi followed Matt Foster into the room, Best half-stood and shook her hand perfunctorily, then waved her into a seat. She looked around the office quickly, unimpressed with what she saw. For a man in charge of the largest FO in the country, Best didn't seem to have a great deal of space to himself. Then again, she reflected, that might be intentional. It was rare, but sometimes men in Best's position actually preferred to play down their authority. Normally, Naomi would have considered Jonathan Harper such a man and meant it as a compliment, but she still wasn't feeling very charitable toward him, given the current situation.

The ADIC looked to Foster and said, "Thanks, Matt. That'll be all for now. How are we doing on those carriers?"

"We just got the list back from customs, sir. Apparently, use of the Pre-Arrival Processing System became mandatory for land-based carriers back in 2002. In order to qualify, a U.S. carrier needs a Standard Carrier Alpha Code."

Best gestured for the younger man to explain.

"It's a two-to-four letter code that customs uses to identify individual carriers. We're cross-checking all the carriers in the state against the information Langley sent us this morning."

"Good. Keep me up to date," Best said. Foster shot Naomi a little grin and left the room, closing the door behind him.

"As you can see," Best continued, "we're taking the information you people sent us very seriously. Even though you don't seem to have any hard evidence that this . . . What do you call it?"

"A BLU-82, sir." She was annoyed by his show of ignorance; she knew he'd spent half the morning on the phone with Harper, who would have sent pictures and specifications. "Also known as a daisy cutter."

"Yes. Despite the fact that you can't prove this 'daisy cutter' is even in the country."

Naomi straightened in her seat. "Sir, the evidence may be sketchy, but it's there."

"By which you mean this storage facility in Canada, right?"

"That's right, sir. The unit was leased by Thomas Rühmann. He was in Al Qaqaa when the explosives went missing in 2003. He was killed two nights ago in Berlin, almost certainly by William Vanderveen. I'm sure you're familiar with the name."

Best nodded to show that he was. He picked up a ballpoint pen and began to twirl it clumsily in his fingers. "Is there any proof that BLU-82s were being stored at Al Qaqaa? That Rühmann would even have access to one?"

"Actually, there is. This morning we managed to get in touch with a man named Paul Owen, a lieutenant colonel in the U.S. Army. He was involved with the unit responsible for investigating the theft. Colonel Owen told us that in addition to three hundred and eighty tons of convention explosives, four BLU-82s were taken from the facility at Al Qaqaa. That fact was never admitted by the U.S. government."

"Four? I thought we were looking for one."

"Two of the bombs were located at a warehouse outside Karbala a month after they were taken, and the third was picked up a month after that. It was discovered in the back of a dump truck at the Iranian border. The fourth was never recovered."

Best leaned back in his seat, dropped the pen, and studied her plaintively. "So again the Iranians come into it. The information you've given us so far is shot full of holes, Ms. Kharmai, but Vanderveen's part in this seems to be the biggest leap of all. I don't appreciate your trying to confuse the issue by bringing his name into it."

"Sir, we know that he was involved with Rühmann, and we know he took part in the bombing of the Babylon Hotel in Baghdad."

"But you can't prove he was in Berlin, and you can't prove he's here in New York."

Naomi lifted her hands in exasperation, then instantly regretted the gesture. This man was just a couple steps below the FBI director himself, and he wouldn't appreciate a show of insubordination. "Sir . . . okay, I'll give you that. But even if we assume that he doesn't have a part in this, it doesn't change the fact that this bomb is almost certainly here in the U.S., as evidenced by the documentation found in Rühmann's car and the statement given by the owner of the storage facility in Montreal. Given everything that's happened in Iraq over the past few weeks, and the fact that half the Iraqi Parliament is scheduled to be at the UN this afternoon, I think we have ample cause for concern."

"'Half the Iraqi Parliament' is quite an exaggeration," Best pointed out. "But security couldn't be tighter, and frankly, I don't know what else we can do. Fifty of my agents are there, along with the entire Manhattan Traffic Task Force and a good part of the Manhattan South Patrol Borough. Everything east of Second Avenue is completely closed off to traffic, along with the through streets between Forty-first and Fifty-first. It's easy to stop vehicles, though. The pedestrians are where it gets tricky."

Naomi nodded. She'd caught part of the news that morning, and she knew that a massive antiwar demonstration was scheduled to take place at the corner of Fifty-first and First. The protesters had requested a permit to march past the UN complex. Predictably, the request was denied by city officials, but that hadn't deterred the organizers of the event. By the time she and Kealey had left for Dulles, 20,000 people had already arrived at the police barricades on Fifty-first Street, the crowd stretching up to Fifty-fourth. Unfortunately, that was just the beginning. More than 100,000 people were expected to show up by the time the General Assembly convened, and Naomi knew that the NYPD would have its hands full with crowd control. Nearly every street surrounding the UN enclave would be completely packed by day's end.

She hadn't considered it before, but now she realized that the huge crowds would be just as good a target as the UN itself. The thought brought on a fresh wave of nausea, but she managed to push it down before Best noticed anything wrong.

"So," he said, jolting her out of her reverie. "How exactly do you think Hakim Rudaki fits into this, ah, rather cryptic scenario?"

"Sir, we haven't been able to link Rudaki to any of this, but the fact remains that there is a huge discrepancy between what he's been telling you and what we've dug up on our own. Most of what we have is pointing toward an Iraqi mastermind, probably someone associated with the insurgency. Rudaki, however, has insisted all along that the Iranians were behind the bombing of the Babylon Hotel and the assassination of Nasir Tabrizi."

Best nodded slowly, but instead of addressing her point, he made one of his own. "As far as I'm concerned, Ms. Kharmai, the question is not the veracity of what Rudaki's been telling us, but how you even know who he is. His identity was tightly held within this office."

Naomi knew that this was not a time to step back. "Sir, this is a big place, and people talk. To be honest, I'm not privy to that information, but either way, it doesn't really matter how we know. What matters is whether or not he's telling the truth."

"Why would he lie?"

"That's exactly what I plan to ask him." They looked at each steadily, neither giving an inch.

Finally, Best leaned forward in his seat and rested his arms on top of his desk. "Ms. Kharmai, do you know why you're here?"

The question caught her off-guard. "What do you mean?"

"You're here because the director of Central Intelligence called my boss in Washington and asked for a favor. To be honest, we don't want anything to do with you people after what happened with Anthony Mason in Alexandria, but the director does not want to bring the president into another interagency spat. We're taking this information seriously—we can't afford not to—but we don't appreciate your interference, particularly when it comes to our confidential informants."

Naomi couldn't believe what she was hearing. "Sir, this isn't about credit or some stupid rivalry. This is about stopping a major terrorist attack on U.S. soil."

Best clenched his jaw, his face turning purple. "I'm aware of that,

Ms. Kharmai, and I don't appreciate being lectured in my own office. I don't know how they do things at the Agency, but—"

His tirade was cut short by a firm knock at the door. Easing back into his chair, Best shot her a menacing glare and spoke in a loud voice aimed at the door. "What is it?"

Matt Foster poked his head in. "Sir, Crane just called in. She's held up at the minute, but she said she'll be back by two."

Best looked annoyed. "What's the holdup? She's with Rudaki, right?"

Foster shot a curious look at Naomi, obviously wondering why Best would use the informant's name in her presence. "That's right, sir. By the way, I'm out of here."

"Why, what's happening?"

"We got a lead on one of those carriers. The company is run by an Iranian right here in Manhattan. According to our records, he was naturalized back in '86. He has an SCAC, he's listed with customs, and one of his trucks came in from Canada carrying a heavy load last night. It looks like a solid lead. I'm gonna run over and check it out."

Best looked at his watch and said, "Take somebody with you. O'Farrell."

"O'Farrell isn't here, sir, but I'll find someone on the way out."

"Fine."

Naomi had listened to the conversation with interest, each sentence sparking a different emotion. She was annoyed that Rudaki wasn't going to arrive until 2:00 p.m., which was nearly three hours away, but she was thrilled that he was with Crane, which probably meant they were at the safe house on Vyse Avenue. Ryan might still have a shot at getting to them. Above all, she wanted to know more about this possible lead. *Iranian owner, SCAC, heavy load . . .* It sounded promising. But again, with the Iranians . . . Despite herself, she couldn't help but feel a twinge of doubt. Maybe they'd gotten it wrong all along.

Before the young agent had closed the door, she called out for him to stop. He poked his head back in and shot her a curious glance. Best looked equally perplexed.

Naomi addressed the older man. "Sir, I was told I'd be able to see Rudaki immediately."

"I'm sorry, but it can't be helped. I'm sure there's a good reason for the delay."

"Good reason or not, I don't want to sit around for three hours waiting on him. With your permission, I'd like to tag along with Agent Foster."

Best laughed. "Absolutely not."

The smug look on his face pushed her over the edge. She shot him the hardest look she had and said, "Sir, you said you wanted to avoid an interagency spat, right? Well, my superiors are behind me a hundred percent on this, so if you jerk me around here, I'll be forced to call them and say we're not getting the cooperation we were promised. I don't know about you, but I could see word getting to the president pretty fast after that, and I don't think he'd be too happy . . . especially if it turns out that we were right and you were wrong."

Best stared at her incredulously. From the corner of her eye, Naomi could see that Foster was also completely stunned.

"Kharmai, I don't know who the hell you think you are, but you have some fucking nerve, coming in here and—"

"Sir, there's no harm in it," Foster said, recovering quickly. The two men shared a meaningful look, and Best sat back in his chair, breathing heavily. Naomi suddenly got the impression that the ADIC was a man with a quick temper who relied on his subordinates to help him keep it in check. "As long as she's not armed."

Best looked at her. "Are you?"

"No." She decided it was time to back down a little. "Sir, I don't want to cause any problems. Just let me tag along with your agent here until Rudaki gets back." She looked at Foster. "It won't take too long, will it?"

He shook his head. "We only need to make a few stops. I want to talk with the Iranian and two others. I don't have to cross the bridge. Shouldn't take more than a couple of hours."

Naomi turned back to Best expectantly. Finally, he nodded slowly. "If it gets you out of here, I guess I don't see the harm."

"Good. And thank you." She grabbed her purse and avoided his angry gaze as she followed Foster out the door. The confrontation had left her drained, and suddenly, she couldn't wait to be out of the building. When the door closed behind them, Foster gave her a look that fell somewhere between disbelief and admiration.

"You have some guts. I don't think anyone's ever talked like that to him in his life."

She shrugged like it was nothing, but in truth, she was feeling quite proud of herself. "Well, I think he was asking for it."

He looked at her for a moment longer, shaking his head in amusement. Then he nodded toward the exit. "You ready?"

"Yep. Let's go."

CHAPTER 50

NEW YORK CITY

O n Vyse Avenue in the South Bronx, Kealey sat behind the wheel of his rented Accord, his whole body taut, his eyes alert and watchful. The vehicle was parked just north of 173rd Street, directly behind a rusting, paint-stripped Camry covered in peeling bumper stickers. In front of the Camry was the blue Crown Victoria. The street was completely empty, but after a few minutes, he looked up at his rearview mirror and saw what he'd been waiting for. The three Latino teenagers that had confronted him earlier were approaching from the south, walking side by side like something out of a bad gangster movie.

The proposition Kealey had put to them was simple: for fifty dollars each, all they had to do was carry out a minor act of vandalism. He couldn't trust them, of course, so he'd gotten the leader—the only one of them old enough to drive—to hand over his license. Kealey checked it quickly and decided it was authentic. Then he handed it back with a promise: if they backed out of the agreement, he'd pay Miguel Morales a very painful visit. Morales, he assured them, would be more than happy to point out where the other two lived, and they could expect the same. Kealey didn't enjoy making threats of this nature—they were just kids, after all—but he needed their help, and he needed to get his point across. They had agreed without hesitation, so he'd given them the location of the vehicle, then the money. Now it looked like they were about to come through.

Kealey unconsciously felt for his Beretta as the three youths passed his passenger-side window. A few seconds later they stopped beside the Crown Vic. Morales was holding an aluminum baseball bat. As Kealey watched, he used it to knock off the Ford's passenger-side mirror. Then, as the others cheered him on, he let loose with a wild swing, which caved in part of the front windshield.

Kealey heard the dull crunch and the ringing sound of the bat, but he wasn't watching the action. His attention was focused on the housing units beyond the iron fence, and after a few seconds, his patience was rewarded. One of the doors flew open, and a tall, lanky man in a dark suit came running down the sidewalk, swearing at the top of his lungs. The three youths instantly scattered in what was clearly a prearranged fashion; by moving in different directions, they were virtually assured of escape. The man in the suit started to chase one of them, then stopped, realizing the futility of his actions. He walked at a fast pace back to the mangled car. Kealey could see him swearing and shaking his head as he assessed the damage.

This was his guy. With his neat hair, striped red tie, and bulge beneath the jacket, the man had agent written all over him. Kealey made sure his weapon was covered by his T-shirt, then got out of the Accord and walked around to the sidewalk, doing his best to avoid his target's peripheral vision. The agent was already making his way back down the short path to the safe house. During his sprint from the building, he'd left the front door wide open. He was still swearing viciously, and Kealey silently urged him to keep going, as the noise helped cover the sound of his approach.

He silently closed the last few feet. As the agent put one hand on the door and prepared to step inside, Kealey lifted his shirt with his left hand and drew the Beretta with his right. Raising his arm, he brought the butt crashing down on the back of the agent's neck. It was a bad angle; the man was much taller than he was, and he didn't have good leverage, but the blow had the intended effect. The man let out a strange croak and dropped to the ground. He instantly tried to get up, but Kealey hit him again. This time he connected solidly, the blow sending a shiver along his forearm. He immediately raised the gun, ready for someone to come through the door.

Nothing. Kealey grabbed the back of the man's shirt collar and pulled him inside, then closed the door. He took in the scene instinctively: a few worn couches, a beat-up recliner, a Samsung TV on a cheap wooden stand. Only the necessities. There were no prints on the walls, no rugs on the floor. He listened carefully. There was no noise coming from the kitchen, but he heard voices drifting down from the stairwell. Moving back to the unconscious agent, he checked the man's coat pockets with practiced speed and skill. He found the gun first, then a leather billfold. He flipped it open. Inside were credentials identifying the fallen man as Special Agent Nicholas Mackie of the FBI.

"Nick?"

Kealey's head shot up. He raised his Beretta instinctively, but then he realized the voice was coming from upstairs. "Nick, what's going on down there?"

Kealey was thinking as fast as he could. He couldn't risk moving the agent; if Samantha Crane caught him in the act, she'd have the drop on him. At the same time, he didn't relish the idea of climbing the stairs. It was too exposed; besides, she had the elevated position, and it would be too easy for her to duck out of view and get to her gun.

Still, there wasn't much choice. The recliner was in the middle of the room, positioned next to an overstuffed couch. As he passed it, he shoved Mackie's 9mm down between the cushions. Then, holding his Beretta in a modified Weaver stance, he approached the stairs in a crouch and looked up to the second floor, ready to fire.

The landing was empty. He moved up the stairs two at a time, painfully aware of the wood creaking beneath his feet. When he reached the last few steps, he paused. There was bare drywall to his right, the second-floor rooms beyond. Moving slightly to the left, he could see part of the room in front of him, but not the people inside.

There wasn't much of a choice; he'd just have to risk it. Before he could move, though, he heard the sound of approaching feet. The sound sent a jolt of electricity running through his body, but he didn't have time to react. Without warning, Crane appeared in the doorway in front of him. Her eyes opened wide, and there was a moment when everything froze. Then he advanced quickly, grabbed her by the shirt, and put the gun to her head.

"Don't move. Who else is up here?"

She didn't respond. He slammed her against the opposite wall and repeated the question. Her mouth was working silently. Finally, she managed to find her voice. "What are you doing here? What—"

"Who else is up here?"

"No one! Where's Nick? What did you do to him?"

"He's sleeping." Kealey stepped back, but he kept the gun at arm's length, aimed at her forehead. "Where's your weapon?"

"My right hip."

"Show it to me."

She was wearing a black merino sweater over a white cotton blouse. Slowly, she lowered her right hand and lifted both layers. A Glock 10mm was tucked into her DeSantis holster.

"Take it out very slowly, and drop it."

She did as he asked, her lips slightly parted, her eyes fixed on the muzzle in front of her face. When she dropped her weapon, it clattered away. Suddenly, Kealey sensed movement to his right and turned to look. Hakim Rudaki was standing in the doorway. The Iranian was of average height, with narrow, intelligent features. He was dressed in jeans and a Columbia University T-shirt, and appeared stunned by the scene unfolding before him.

"I thought you said no one was up here," Kealey snapped. He grabbed her and turned her around roughly, jamming the muzzle of the Beretta into her lower back. Leaning down quickly, he picked up her gun and, using only his left hand, ejected the magazine. He positioned the upper receiver against his thigh and pushed forward, shucking out the remaining round. Then he dropped the useless weapon and pushed her into the room at the back of the house. Over her shoulder, he spoke to Rudaki. "You, get back in there. Hands where I can see them."

A few seconds later, he had them sitting side by side on the bed. He could see that Rudaki's mind was already working, trying to figure a way out of the situation. Crane, on the other hand, looked furious. Her face was flushed, her blond hair sticking out at crazy angles. "Kealey, I don't know how the hell you found this place, but you're going to—"

"Stop talking, Crane. There's nothing you can say . . . I know what you did. Your only option now is to cooperate. If you do exactly what I tell you, I might even let you live. Until then, keep your mouth shut." He turned the gun on Rudaki. "You're the reason I'm here."

The Iranian managed to look confused. "I don't understand. What do you mean?"

"I know who you are, Hakim. I know what you've been telling the Bureau, and I know you're full of shit. The Iranians were never part of this. Individual people, maybe, but not the regime in Tehran."

Rudaki shook his head slowly. "Everything I've said is the truth."

"No, it isn't," Kealey snarled. "The Bureau may have bought it, but I don't." He looked at Crane. "What's he been telling you now? That Ahmadinejad is targeting the UN?"

Crane looked startled. "As a matter of fact, yes. But security is so tight that—"

"Save it, Samantha. Don't try to play dumb. I know you have a part in this."

She stood up, her fists balled by her side. "What are you talking about?" she shouted.

"*Sit down!*"

"No!" She planted her feet and glared at him. "You'd better explain yourself right now, Ryan, or—"

"The raid in Alexandria," Kealey said, cutting her off. He stared at her intently. "You were so fucking quick to go in, weren't you? Why? Was it just to shut Mason up?"

"What the hell are you talking about?"

"What happened after that? Hold on," he said sarcastically. "Let me guess. You found out that we had Mason's laptop, and you knew you had to get it back, because it had Thomas Rühmann's name on it. But that didn't happen in time, did it? We got the name before you could act, so instead, you told Vanderveen where to find us."

She didn't rise to the bait, so Kealey raised his voice, trying to get through to her. "He nearly killed me and Naomi Kharmai in Berlin,

Crane. It had to be you . . . Aside from you and Ford, no one else knew we were going to Germany."

"I don't know what you're—"

"Stop." She fell silent, and he shook his head in disgust. "The only question is, what are you getting out of it?" He looked at her hard, trying to see what was behind those angry brown eyes. "It's money, isn't it? How much did it take to buy you off, Sam?"

Rudaki was starting to look nervous, Kealey noticed, which wouldn't mean much by itself, but combined with Crane's expression, it was cause for concern. She looked furious, but also genuinely confused, and while he knew it could be an act, he had seen people try to act their way out of bad situations before. This looked real, and for the first time since he'd learned that Crane was running Rudaki, he felt a tremor of doubt.

"Vanderveen? *Will* Vanderveen?" She gave an incredulous laugh. "You think I've been passing him information?"

"I know you have," he said through gritted teeth. His finger was tightening on the trigger, the muzzle level with Crane's heart. "You can't lie your way out of this. It had to be you. Don't you get it? Even if you discount the other shit as coincidence, *no one else knew about Berlin.*"

Crane scoffed. "What, I'm supposed to take your word on that? If anyone's been feeding Vanderveen information, it's probably someone at Langley."

That's not possible," Kealey said, but he hesitated. Even through the blustering and the sarcasm, her innocence shone through like a beacon he couldn't ignore. "Crane, I'm only going to ask you this one time. Did you tell anyone what Ford told you? Anyone at all?"

She shrugged, as if the question was meaningless. "I told my partner, of course, but I tell him—"

"Who's your partner?"

"Matt Foster," she reminded him. "From the warehouse in Alexandria, remember? He's the one who shot Mason."

"And what did you tell him?"

"Everything," Crane replied, finishing her earlier sentence. She was starting to sound annoyed, and Kealey realized that, gun or no gun, her cooperation was coming to an end.

"He was on administrative leave while they investigated the shooting," Crane continued. "But after they cleared him, he decided to stay in Washington instead of coming back here." Her mouth twitched, a light coming on in her eyes, and Kealey had a sudden insight. It was subtle, but the look on her face suggested that her relationship with Foster went beyond a mere partnership. "I had drinks with my aunt a few nights ago, and when I got back to the hotel, I told him everything."

"What night did you see your aunt?"

"Tuesday. Tuesday night at the Monocle."

The night before he and Naomi had flown to Berlin. Kealey shook his head, trying to think it through. "So what happened in Alexandria? You said you got an anonymous tip that Mason was there . . . ?"

"That came through Matt," Crane confirmed. "He took the call in New York, and I asked the ADIC to call Washington and get us in on the raid. After all, we had been looking for Mason for months, and the tip came through our FO. It was only fair that we should have a part in bringing him down."

"Could Foster be sure of being there?"

"Of course," Crane shot back. "He's my partner, for one thing, and I have . . . advantages." Kealey knew she was referring to her relationship with Rachel Ford. "Besides, Matt has connections as well. His father spent twenty years as an agent. He finished as the SAC in Houston, and he still has plenty of friends in the Bureau."

He looked at Rudaki. "So you've been working with Foster."

"No! I have no idea what you're—"

"Matt had nothing to do with this!" Crane shouted, cutting off Rudaki's denial. "And you can't prove otherwise, so stop accusing him!"

"Save it," Kealey snarled. He gestured to Rudaki. "What else has this guy been telling you? What's supposed to happen today?"

She looked at her informant and took a deep breath, as if deciding how much to say. "He said the Iranian government was working with Rühmann. They're supposed to hit the UN this afternoon."

"How?" Kealey addressed the question to Crane, even though Rudaki was right there. He still wasn't sure of Crane's role in all of this, but he definitely didn't trust the Iranian to give up the truth, even at gunpoint.

"He didn't say," Crane said. "But it doesn't matter. We've already locked down the whole area. It would have to be a bomb, but even if the Iranians have one, they won't be able to get it within two blocks of the target. It would never work."

"The Iranians are not behind this, Sam. It's Will Vanderveen, and he *does* have a bomb. A very large one." Kealey turned back to Rudaki and pointed the gun at his face. "And you know something about it, so start talking."

"I have no idea what you're—"

"I'll ask you once more," Kealey said, struggling to keep his voice calm. "And then I'm going to shoot you. Do you understand?"

Rudaki looked to Crane, who looked in turn to Kealey. She scowled and said, "You'd better be bluffing, Ryan. If you do this, I will personally make sure you spend the rest of your life in prison."

"I have the gun, Samantha, and I'm still not convinced of your innocence. You might want to keep that in mind. The only reason I'm not putting these questions to you is because of your position."

"What are you talking about?"

"I can't hurt you to get the truth," he explained. "And I don't want to, even though you probably deserve it. But I *can* hurt him, and that's just what I plan to do unless he starts talking."

"Bullshit," she said simply. "You're bluffing."

"You can't let this happen," Rudaki said, looking at Crane. Some of his bluster was starting to fade. "You're with the FBI, and this man is threatening me. *Do something.*"

"Where's the fucking bomb?" Kealey shouted.

Rudaki looked at the gun, then at Kealey's face. "I don't—"

The shot sounded like an explosion in the small room. Hakim Rudaki screamed in agony, his eyes wide in horror. He clutched at his ruined knee and slid from the bed to the floor, blood pumping between his fingers.

"Jesus Christ!" Crane screamed, dropping her arms. "What the hell are you . . . ?"

Kealey never heard the rest of her question. He was on the ground, his left hand wrapped in Rudaki's hair, his gun jammed under the other man's chin. He was screaming the same question over and over, his face an inch from Rudaki's. "Where's the bomb? Where is it? Tell me, you piece of shit! *Tell me!*"

Kealey was aware of Crane's hands on his shoulders. She was trying to pull him back, and it briefly occurred to him that if she was in on it, she wouldn't even be in the room; she would have gone for her gun in the hall. The fact that she hadn't only reinforced her innocence.

He shrugged her off and kept screaming the question. Finally, through gritted teeth, Rudaki howled a name.

"What? What was that?"

"*Nazeri! I don't know anything about a bomb! I only know the name, I swear to God. . . .*"

"Nazeri? Who is he? *Where* is he?"

"*I don't know!*"

"The Iranian government was never behind this, was it?" Rudaki seemed to hesitate, and Kealey shouted the question again.

"No," Rudaki gasped. His face was covered in sweat, and Kealey could tell he was about to pass out. "Tehran never had a hand in it. The whole thing started in Iraq."

"With who?" Kealey demanded. "Who in Iraq?"

Rudaki shook his head, his face contorted with pain. "I never dealt with the top people. Just intermediaries."

"Like Vanderveen, right? You dealt with Vanderveen?"

"Yes. I dealt with Vanderveen and . . ." He nodded at Crane, who had been watching the exchange with a mixed expression of shock and disbelief. "Her partner."

It was irrefutable proof; at this point, Rudaki would gain nothing by lying. Kealey shot a glance at Samantha Crane. She was staring at the Iranian informant, her face frozen. "This whole time?" she finally managed to choke out. "I don't believe it. You're lying."

Rudaki shook his head weakly. "It's the truth. I swear it."

"You're lying," Crane repeated, but the words had lost their conviction. "It can't be true. It's not possible. It's just not . . ."

Her voice faltered, but instead of collapsing into herself, she suddenly sprinted forward. "*You fuck!*" she screamed. "*You fucking—*"

Kealey was caught off-guard by the sudden outburst, but he managed to restrain her in time, wrapping her up from behind. "We don't have time for this," he said in a low, urgent voice. "He'll get what's coming to him, and so will Foster."

He could feel her trembling in his arms; her whole body was shaking with rage. "Come on, calm down, okay? I'm going to let you go. Don't do anything crazy. Stay calm."

He released her cautiously. Then he asked for her phone, having left his in the car. As she pulled it out of her pocket and handed it over, he pushed her into the hall, then followed her out. He was careful to keep his body between her and Rudaki, who was still lying on the floor in the bedroom, moaning in agony.

"We have to call the FO," Crane said. She was still flushed and breathing hard. "They can get a location on Nazeri in less than a minute."

"In a second," Kealey said. He was already punching in Naomi's number. He wanted to give her a heads-up first, and then they would bring the whole world crashing down on this Nazeri character. He let out a long breath, letting some of the tension ebb. It seemed like everything was in hand; the meeting at the UN was still hours away. Soon he would have Nazeri's location, and when he got there, Kealey had no doubt that he would find Will Vanderveen and the BLU-82. At this point, the only thing he had to worry about was killing Vanderveen before he could set off the bomb.

But then he lifted the phone to his ear, and everything changed.

CHAPTER 51

NEW YORK CITY

"Hello?"

He pulled the phone away from his ear and looked at it, wondering if somehow he'd dialed the wrong number. Bringing it back to his ear, he said, "I'm looking for Naomi Kharmai, but I think I have the wrong—"

"Is this Ryan? Ryan Kealey?"

"Yeah." A little shock there, with the name recognition. "And you are . . . ?"

"Matt Foster. We've met before."

Kealey froze, a quiver of fear running through his chest. What was Foster doing with Naomi's phone? He glanced at Crane. She looked back at him inquiringly, but he didn't have time to bring her into this. "Uh . . . yeah, I remember you."

"I thought you might. We met in Alexandria."

"That's right," Kealey said. His mind was racing. "Where are you?"

"Just out and about." There was a smile in the other man's voice, but there was nothing pleasant about it. "Checking leads, following up, you know. The usual."

"Right, well . . . Is Naomi there?"

There was a long silence. "I'm afraid she's indisposed at the moment."

Kealey closed his eyes. *Indisposed?* What did that mean? Surely not what it sounded like. Surely not that.

He couldn't have killed her; there was no reason to do so. Unless Naomi had somehow figured it out first and confronted him, and Kealey didn't see how that would be possible. But this wasn't getting him anywhere. He had to get off the phone and think it through. "Will you tell her I need to talk to her?"

"Sure." Foster's tone was a little too pleasant. "Can I have a quick word with Samantha?"

For a second, Kealey thought the other man was trying to trick him into giving something away. Then he remembered that he was using Crane's phone, and the number would have come up on Foster's screen.

He looked at Crane. Her face had lost all of its color, and her eyes were wide and glazed over. The rage was gone, at least for the moment, but she looked utterly drained. He knew he couldn't put her on the line; she was still reeling from Foster's betrayal on two fronts. Judging from the show of emotion he'd just witnessed, she would give it away in a second.

"She's also indisposed," Kealey said, "but if you want, I can—"

"Tell me something, Ryan. Since you're using her phone, I assume you've had a talk with her. Did you happen to talk to Hakim Rudaki as well?"

Kealey was gripping the phone so hard he thought it would break, but he forced himself to stay calm. "Agent Foster, I don't know what—"

"Sure you do," the other man said amiably. "You know exactly what I'm talking about, but I'm afraid that leaves us with a little problem. Have you called the Bureau yet?"

Kealey struggled to keep his voice even. It was clear they were done with the false pleasantries. "No."

"Good. If you want your friend to live, you won't try to track us down, and you won't call the FO. Because if you do, and my fellow agents show up to gun me down, the last act of my life will be to cut her pretty little throat. Do I make myself clear?"

"You fuck," Kealey rasped. "If you touch her, I swear to God, I'll—"

"You'll do nothing," Foster said, his voice turning hard. "That isn't too much to ask, is it? Just do nothing for the next hour. Unless you want Naomi back in pieces, that is."

"Foster, you—" Kealey stopped and looked at the phone. The other man had already cut the connection. "Fuck!"

"What?" Crane asked. She'd already collected and reloaded her weapon, and was slipping it back into her holster. "What happened?"

"It's your partner. He's got Naomi."

Crane shook her head slowly; she was still trying to get her mind around what she had just learned. This was just too much to handle. "How is that even possible?"

"I don't know, but he said if we call the FO, he'll kill her." Kealey leaned against the wall and closed his eyes, trying to block out the sound of Rudaki's low moans in the next room. He felt numb. Finally, he opened his eyes and started for the stairs. Crane followed, and as they bounded to the ground floor, he spoke to her over his shoulder. "I have to get in touch with Langley. They'll give us an address for this Nazeri guy, and I'll just . . ." He shook his head, unsure of how it had come to this. "I'll just have to go in alone."

"Not a chance," Crane said. Her voice was imbued with sudden determination. They hit the bottom of the stairs and moved for the door. Special Agent Mackie was still lying where Kealey had dragged him earlier. Behind him, he heard Crane ask, "Is he going to be okay?"

"He'll be fine," Kealey said. They reached the Accord. Kealey thought it said a lot about the neighborhood that no one had come to investigate the shot he'd fired into Rudaki's leg, but there were sirens on the horizon as he unlocked the door and looked over the roof at Samantha Crane.

"I don't think you should be part of this," he said. "I have a habit of wrecking people's careers, including my own."

"At this point, that's the last thing I'm worried about." She hesitated. "He may have your friend, Ryan, but he betrayed my trust, and he betrayed the Bureau. I can't let that go. I'm coming with you, and that's final."

He nodded; he couldn't argue with anything she'd said. "Fine. Let's go."

On the corner of Thirty-fourth and Eighth, Special Agent Matt Foster disconnected the call, aware that he'd cut Kealey off in mid-sentence. He stared out the windshield for a few seconds, wondering how it had come to this. All he'd wanted to do was keep Kharmai busy until the bomb reached its target, but somehow, Kealey had managed to find Crane and Rudaki. His arrangement with Will Vanderveen had made him an extraordinarily wealthy man, but even in his wildest dreams, he'd never thought he would need the money so soon. With this development, he had no choice; he'd have to leave the country immediately.

He cursed under his breath. He was completely unprepared. At the very least, he would need a false passport, but getting one would take time, time he didn't have. In a matter of hours, he would become one of the most wanted men in the world. Given the situation, there was only one option left to him.

Foster lifted the phone and punched in a number.

"Yes?"

"It's me," Foster said, struggling to keep his voice level and calm. He didn't know the other man well—they had only met in person a few times—but he suspected that Vanderveen would not react favorably to panic. "I have a passenger, and we have a small problem." He put emphasis on the "I" and the "we." "Open the door. I'm heading your way."

"Not possible," Vanderveen said instantly. "This wasn't part of the plan, Foster."

"I realize that, but it can't be helped. Listen, it's the Kharmai woman, the one you missed in Berlin. She might prove useful."

There was a long pause. "What happened? Why do you need to bring her here?"

Foster swore under his breath. He didn't want to relay the bad news over the phone, but he didn't have a choice. He explained quickly.

"Did you talk to him?"

"Kealey? Yes. I told him to keep the field office out of it, or I'd kill the woman."

"He'll come anyway. How far is the safe house from West Thirty-seventh?"

"Twenty minutes or so, but it's the middle of the day, and the roads are busy as hell. Besides, he'll need to call Langley to pin Nazeri down. We probably have about half an hour."

"And where are you?"

"A few streets down. I can be there in a couple of minutes."

"Where's the woman now?"

Foster looked out the passenger-side window. Naomi Kharmai was just walking out of the Starbucks on the corner, holding a cup in each hand, nodding at the man who'd held the door for her. "She's walking back to the car."

Another long pause. "Okay, bring her in. The door will be up, and I'll be waiting. We'll figure it out when you get here."

The phone went dead. Foster slipped it into his pocket as Kharmai placed the cups on the roof and opened the door. He thanked her as she handed one in, then took her seat with the other. Once the door was closed, he pulled back into traffic.

Naomi took a sip of her tea and flinched as the hot liquid touched her lips. "Ouch . . . too soon." She looked around for a cup holder. Not finding one, she held the container gingerly on her knee and turned to face him. "Matt, I was thinking we should head back to your office. Rudaki's probably already there, or at least on the way."

"Actually, I just called. It'll be another half hour or so. In the meantime, we have one more stop to make."

She looked at her watch and frowned. "Will it take long?"

"No, I don't think so." He smiled reassuringly. "Not long at all."

CHAPTER 52

NEW YORK CITY

As the Bureau Crown Vic turned left onto West Thirty-seventh Street, Naomi looked at her watch again, then scowled out the window. She no longer cared if her impatience was obvious. This was taking much longer than she'd expected, and she really wanted to talk to Rudaki. They were running out of time, but then again, she thought the delay might be a good thing. If Ryan had gotten to Rudaki already, that would explain why the informant had yet to show up at the New York FO. On the other hand, it seemed like if that had transpired, Ryan would have called to let her know. With this thought, she realized that she hadn't checked her phone in a while. Her purse was down by her feet. Leaning down, she rooted around for a minute but didn't find it.

"Agent Foster, did you see what I did with my phone?"

"Oh, shit," he said, digging into his pocket. He pulled it out and handed it over. "Sorry . . . Some guy named Kealey called while you were getting the coffee. He asked me to tell you that he struck out."

"Damn it," she muttered. "Is that all he said?"

"That's it."

She looked at her phone, thought about calling him, then decided against it. If he'd struck out with the safe house, he wouldn't want to hear that the New York FO had been wasting her time for the better part of an hour. The first person they'd visited had been a naturalized Iranian just west of the Brooklyn Bridge, the owner of a small freight company. He had been adamant in his denials of wrong-doing, and there had been something about his manner that convinced her immediately. Then they'd moved on to a Saudi immigrant in the financial district. That interview proved equally fruitless, ending with the man screaming obscenities at them in Arabic as they'd hurried back to the car. In short, the whole trip had been pointless, making her wish she had just stayed in the Javits Building. Unfortunately, it was a little late for that now.

Without warning, Foster swung the car to the right. They bumped over a little concrete lip, passing beneath a worn wooden sign. The car slowed to a halt in the middle of a large parking area, a brick warehouse off to the right.

Naomi turned to her left, confusion spreading over her face. She was about to ask what they were doing there when she saw the gun in his hand. She froze, unsure of what was happening. For a split second, she thought it was some kind of sick joke. Then she was aware of the metal door sliding down behind the car, blocking the view of the street. Before Foster could say anything—before she could even ask what was happening—her door was pulled open. She turned instinctively and looked up into a face she had only ever seen on her computer screen and in distant surveillance shots: the face of William Vanderveen.

She tried to speak, but no words came out. Vanderveen seemed to realize the effect he was having on her. He smiled, revealing two rows of very even, very white teeth. "You must be Naomi. It's nice to meet you. Would you mind dropping that phone and stepping out of the car?"

She took note of his voice: flat, calm, devoid of emotion. There was no hint of his native South African dialect, but that wasn't surprising; according to the files she had read on countless occasions, he had not returned to his homeland in many years. She felt like this must be a dream; in the year since she had learned of his existence, she had almost convinced herself that he wasn't real, that he was nothing more than a figment of their collective imaginations. But now, sitting before him, she could see he was definitely real. Just like the gun in his right hand.

Seeing no other option, she dropped the phone on the floor, got out of the car, and shut the door. She looked around quickly as Foster got out of the driver's seat and moved around the car. Aside from the roll-down vehicular door, there was also a pedestrian gate set in the 10-foot metal wall that separated the parking area from the street. A short, heavyset man with glasses and dark features was standing next to the door he had just pulled down. To her right was the warehouse; she could see an incongruous set of glass doors directly behind the back of a large Isuzu box truck. The doors were propped open with red clay pots, but it was the truck that held her attention. She knew instinctively that it contained the BLU-82, even though she could not see the contents from where she was standing.

Vanderveen looked to Foster and said, "Bring her inside and secure her."

"We should just—"

"We will," Vanderveen said. "But not yet. Just do as I say."

Foster grabbed her arm and pushed her toward the glass doors of the warehouse. Naomi was still too stunned at this turn of events to think it through properly, but she forced herself to concentrate. It was now clear that Foster had been feeding Vanderveen information all along, but the question remained, how did he get it in the first place? Did Samantha Crane still have a part in it? Ryan had been so sure about that, and it still seemed like the only possible explanation.

Only now did she remember what he had told her in the bar at the Hotel Washington, that Foster had taken part in the raid in Alexandria. That was why the name had seemed so familiar, but Ryan had mentioned him only in passing, which explained why it had slipped her mind.

She cursed herself silently, bitterly, realizing she had probably made the last mistake of her life. Even though Vanderveen had cut off Foster's last sentence, it had been all too clear what he was about to say: *We should just kill her.* She knew what was coming, but she couldn't dwell on it. If she hesitated, or if she froze completely, she would lose any chance of survival. She forced herself to keep putting one foot in front of the other, not wanting to give them the satisfaction of seeing her fear.

They entered the warehouse. Foster grabbed her arm and seemed to hesitate, then pushed her toward a large piece of machinery, a freestanding commercial lathe. Vanderveen walked in behind them, the gun held loosely in his right hand. Seeing that the other man had Naomi covered, Foster set down his service weapon on a nearby stack of broken wooden pallets. Then he produced a pair of handcuffs and pulled her over toward the lathe. She resisted slightly, so he grabbed her hair and pulled her head back sharply. Tears sprang to her eyes with the pain, but she refused to cry out.

"Put your hands around that bar," Foster hissed. "Do it."

The stinging sensation at the back of her head was unbearable, and she knew it wouldn't help to struggle. She put her hands on either side of a horizontal bar that ran the length of the lathe, and he snapped the cuffs tightly around her wrists, securing her in place.

"Step away," Vanderveen said. Foster hesitated, then did as he was told. The former U.S. soldier walked over and stood very close, eyeing her steadily. There was a smile on his handsome face, but the look in his eyes revealed his true intentions and etched away at whatever self-control she had left. She could tell he was deciding how best to hurt her before taking her life.

"Naomi . . . You don't mind if I call you that, do you?" She didn't reply, knowing it wouldn't matter what she said. "As you can see, you're in a very bad situation here. I'm afraid you used up all your luck in Berlin."

Naomi closed her eyes. "So you were there."

"Of course." He paused and looked at her carefully, then reached out and touched her cheek. She recoiled instantly, but he merely smiled.

"Tell me, how long have you worked for the CIA?"

"I don't work for them at all." She did her best to sound defiant. "They fired me."

"Really?" He looked amused. "I'm impressed. And how long have you known Ryan?"

She set her jaw and looked away. He stared at her for about twenty seconds, as if gauging her conviction. Then he nodded once and walked off toward the office, disappearing from sight. Naomi heard a door bang, the rattle of blinds against glass panes, and then he returned, carrying a green metal toolbox. Setting it down on the smooth cement floor, he opened it and started perusing the contents. As he rummaged, he spoke to her without raising his eyes.

"You know, Naomi, this is the last time we're going to talk. Make no mistake, you're going to die very soon, but before you do, I thought we might have a civilized discussion." He straightened, holding a pair of needle-nose pliers. "Of course, it doesn't *have* to be civilized. That's up to you."

Foster, standing nearby, shifted uneasily. "We don't have time for this. Kealey will be here any—"

"We have plenty of time," Vanderveen said quietly. Foster shifted again, but didn't push the issue. "Go outside and watch the gate."

Foster muttered something under his breath, then retrieved his weapon and made his way to the glass doors. At the same time, Nazeri hurried forward and seized Vanderveen's arm. He was sweating profusely, and his brown eyes were wide, amplified by his thick glasses. In Farsi, he said, "What is this woman doing here, Erich? You have to get rid of her."

"Relax, Amir. Times Square isn't going anywhere."

Naomi spoke four languages, including Farsi. She struggled to keep her face blank, not wanting to reveal what she'd heard, but Vanderveen's words were hitting her hard. *Times Square?* Why would they choose that particular spot? Maybe it was just an alternate target, she decided. Maybe they had decided the UN was too well protected.

"She'll be gone soon enough," Vanderveen added gently, pulling himself free. He placed a hand on the other man's shoulder. "Just focus on what you have to do. I'll take care of the rest, okay? Go outside and wait for me. This will all be over soon."

The Iranian looked distraught, but he did as he was told. Vanderveen turned back to Naomi. He was still holding the pliers. He couldn't help but notice the hopeful expression on her face.

"Oh, that's right. What did Agent Foster say?" Vanderveen made a show of trying to remember. "Kealey will be here any . . . what? Any second? Any minute?" He smiled broadly, clearly enjoying the moment. "Either way, it won't be in time to do you any good. I only wish I could stick around to see his face when he finds what's left of you."

He paused thoughtfully, examining the steel prongs of the pliers.

"Tell me . . . Is your relationship with Ryan purely professional? Or is it something more? Because if you have any insights, I'd very much like to hear them. Has it been difficult for him, coming to terms with what happened in Maine? Have you helped fill the void, so to speak?"

He studied her dispassionately, then said, "You're quite beautiful . . . I can't imagine he would be able to resist you for long. I know I wouldn't be able to." He leaned close, touching the tip of the pliers to her cheek. As the cold metal brushed against her skin, Naomi nearly lost it, but she pushed down her terror with one last tremendous effort.

"Naomi, Naomi . . ." He repeated her name in a singsong kind of way, then shook his head in amusement. "I can see that there's something between you two. It couldn't be more obvious. Do you think you can replace his dead fiancée? Answer me."

"I don't know," she mumbled.

"Do you want to?"

She didn't reply, and he let it go. He leaned down to the toolbox and replaced the pliers, then came up with a retractable utility knife. Extending the blade with his thumb, he examined the edge, then tossed it back in the box. "That won't work. Plastic surgeons can work miracles with clean cuts these days. Let's see if we can't find something a little more . . . interesting."

She didn't want to ask it, but she couldn't stop herself. "What are you doing?"

"Well, it's simple," he said, still digging around in the toolbox. "Killing you outright would be too easy and, frankly, a little boring. I think I'll make you suffer first."

He looked up to catch her reaction, and when he spoke, his voice was matter-of-fact. "You really shouldn't have interfered in what I'm trying to do here. In your case, I could almost put it down to ignorance, but Ryan should have known better. Unfortunately, he's not around to take his share of the blame, which leaves only you." He dug around for a minute more, then produced a fixed-blade scoring knife. He held it up so she could see the hooked edge. "This is better." He smiled gently. "Now, let's see what we can do with that pretty face, shall we?"

As he advanced, Naomi pulled away as far as she could, aware of a low moan building deep in her throat. The steel cuffs were digging into her wrists, tearing the skin, but the pain didn't register; all she could think about was getting away from the knife.

It was no good; there was nowhere to go. She felt flailing panic in her chest, felt her legs giving way as he pinned her painfully against the lathe. She could hear herself saying no and repeating the single word over and over as the jagged parts of the lathe dug into the lean muscles of her back. She was intensely aware of what this man had done to Katie Donovan a year earlier, and knew that she was about to suffer much, much worse. Her arms were pulled to the right, her left pinned between his body and hers. Naomi was wedged in place as he grabbed her throat with his left hand, pushing her head back, bringing the knife to her face with his right. She closed her eyes as tightly as she could and waited for the tearing pain to begin, praying it wouldn't last too long.

But it never came. There was a sudden noise at the entrance, and Vanderveen stopped, looking left. Foster was standing inside the glass doors, about 20 feet away. "We can't wait any longer," he said uneasily. "Nazeri has to get moving. Right now."

"In a minute," Vanderveen replied. "This won't take long."

"Will . . ."

Vanderveen looked from Naomi's terrified face to the door, then back again. He was clearly torn, but finally, he released her. Her strength failed her, and she slumped to the floor, only stopping when the cuffs pulled her arms taut over her head.

"Okay, I'm coming." He looked back at Naomi, who had buried her face in her right shoulder. "Don't go anywhere."

At that same moment, Ryan Kealey's rented Accord was racing south on FDR Drive, having just crossed the Triborough Bridge over the Harlem River. As soon as they'd left the safe house on Vyse Avenue, he had placed a direct call to Jonathan Harper at Langley, requesting a check on the name Nazeri in the New York area. Fortunately, the search yielded only a small number of results, and through the process of elimination, they were able to narrow it down to one probable address.

It was indeed that of Bridgeline Transport Inc., a freight company with terminals in Montreal and Ithaca, was owned by a man named Amir Nazeri, who'd emigrated from Tehran in the early eighties. The company also owned a vending service based on West Thirty-seventh Street, which was their current destination. Harper had demanded to know what was happening, but Kealey had cut him off in mid-sentence, not wanting to tie up the line. Repeated calls to Kharmai's cell phone had gone unanswered, and he knew they were running out of time.

Up ahead, brake lights flashed as vehicles slowed to a halt. So far, they had managed to avoid most of the traffic, but it couldn't last. He swore and slammed his hand against the wheel. Samantha Crane didn't move an inch. She was sitting in the passenger seat. Over the past ten minutes, she had recovered slightly from Hakim Rudaki's revelation. Now, she appeared neither drained nor angry. Her body was unnaturally still, her mouth set in a straight, tight line. Her eyes were unreadable, but Kealey knew exactly what she was feeling. He'd felt the same depth of betrayal when Will Vanderveen had shot him in Syria eight years earlier, right after killing 5 of his fellow soldiers. But that was in the past, and at the moment, all Kealey could think about was Naomi.

He was desperate to get to her, but at the same time, part of him wanted to sit in traffic forever. He was terrified that he'd get to the warehouse to find she was already dead, that he had failed her just like he'd failed Katie. Her words of the previous night were banging around in his head, but now they seemed taunting rather than reassuring. *You've never let me down, and I know you never will. I trust you completely.* He shook his head unconsciously, trying to free himself of the burden, knowing it was pointless to even try. If he proved her wrong—if she died because he couldn't get there in time—he knew he would never be able to forgive himself.

Finally, the traffic broke, and they reached the exit for the Midtown Tunnel. He shot a look over his shoulder, then swerved into the next lane without indicating, punching the accelerator. The Accord shot forward on the service road. A few seconds later, the tires squealed in protest as Kealey swung a hard right onto East Thirty-seventh Street.

As he shifted into third gear, Samantha pulled out her Glock 29. He glanced over and saw her pull back the slide to check for a round in the chamber. She rested the gun on her lap and said, "How many people are we looking at here? I mean, it *is* just the two of us."

It was the first time she had spoken since they'd left Vyse Avenue, and the question caught him off-guard. "Vanderveen, Foster, and this guy Nazeri. No more than that," Kealey replied at length. "But they'll all be there. I don't think they'll have moved the bomb yet. At least, I hope to God they haven't."

"How big a bomb are we talking about?"

"Fifteen thousand pounds."

He didn't look over, but he felt her staring at him. "Are you serious?" she finally asked.

He glared at her, and she was instantly repentant. "Never mind," she mumbled. "Dumb question."

Kealey shot a look at the speedometer: with Third Avenue looming, he was ahead of the traffic and building speed. As he watched, the light ahead turned yellow. People were lined up on either side of the street, waiting to cross, and he was still about 300 feet away from the intersection.

He punched the pedal and hit the horn as the speedometer continued to climb.

Naomi, still slumped against the front of the lathe, didn't look up until she was sure she was alone in the warehouse. As she got to her feet unsteadily, she could hear the three men through the open glass doors. Suddenly, the truck started up and pulled away. She froze, wondering if that was it, if they were too late to stop the bomb, but the noise didn't travel far. She realized that the Isuzu was still in the parking area, probably sitting in front of the roll-down vehicular door. It might not be gone, but it would be leaving soon, and as soon as it did, Vanderveen would be back to finish the job.

The thought filled her with a fresh, crippling wave of terror, but she pushed it down, knowing she had to act immediately. She took a deep, shaky breath and tried to focus, looking down at her cuffed hands. She didn't recognize the machine she was cuffed to, though she noticed it seemed out of place in the building, which was otherwise filled with wooden pallets loaded with bottled water and soft drinks. Her eyes followed the length of the bar that secured her to the main unit. Gripping it with her hands, she shook it as hard as she could, but it didn't give an inch. She went to the left side of the machine and leaned close, examining where the bar joined the larger part of the metal structure. It seemed to be pushed into a well of some kind, but it was machined with precision, and the fit was perfect. There was no room for give.

Breathing deeply again to steady her nerves, she made her way back to the other end of the lathe. When she checked the right side of the structure, she immediately felt her spirits lift; the bar was secured by what looked like simple screws. Instantly, her eyes moved down to the toolbox, which was within reach of her foot. Moving to the middle of the bar, she stretched out her left foot as far as she could, the cuffs tight against her raw wrists, her arms stretched so far it felt like they would pull out of their sockets. Her wounded left shoulder was screaming for her to stop, but she ignored it and kept going. Finally, her foot brushed against the box, then caught the lip. She pulled it back inch by inch until she could move it easier. Then she pulled it directly under her body.

There. A screwdriver right on top. Shifting her body, she examined the screws again. She swore under her breath. She knew there were different types of screwdrivers, but she didn't have a choice; as far as she could see, the box only held one kind of screwdriver, and she couldn't see the tip.

She used her left shin to push off the shoe on her right foot, silently thanking God she had worn flats. When her foot was exposed, she pinched the metal part of the screwdriver between her toes, then lifted it carefully. A sudden noise outside the warehouse made her jump, and she nearly dropped it. She kept going, knowing that what she had heard was the back of the truck being pulled down. The fear started to rise again, and she felt her limbs turn to water; she was out of time. The voices outside were so distinct, they had to be getting closer. She steeled herself immediately, trying to force breath in and out of her constricted lungs. It took everything she had, but finally, the screwdriver was in her hand. From there it was shockingly easy; she had the three screws out in no time at all, and the bar came free.

She looked at her hands, slightly amazed at what she had managed to do. She was still handcuffed, but at least she could move. She immediately started toward the office, intent on getting to a phone. It was the only option left to her, as she didn't have a weapon. But then, just as she put her hand on the door, she heard exactly what she'd feared most: nothing at all. The truck was gone, and that could only mean one thing. Vanderveen was coming back to kill her. She turned back to the building's entrance, seeing nothing at first, but then a shadow loomed on the concrete, drawing closer.

She looked around frantically, but she was boxed in. Her heart hammering, she pushed open the door to the office and stepped inside.

CHAPTER 53

NEW YORK CITY

After pulling the Isuzu up to the gate, which was still lowered, Vanderveen climbed out without shutting off the engine. He walked to the back, where Foster and Nazeri were waiting. Leaning in, he stared at the bomb one last time, aware that he would never again see it intact. The thought was strangely uplifting, but he couldn't ignore the irony: in ceasing to exist, this device would create a whole new world of fear and terror.

For the most part, it still resembled the Parker boiler, with one exception: the panel on the left side had been removed, exposing the curvature of the BLU-82. The bomb itself was strapped to a custom-designed metal pallet and surrounded by an elaborate wooden framework. Wedged inside this framework, tight against the metal shell of the bomb, was 2½ pounds of Semtex high explosive. The Semtex, in turn, was molded around a single nonelectric blasting cap, which fed 12 feet of military det cord through predrilled holes in the box and cab. The M60 fuse igniter was taped to the vinyl side of the driver's seat; to set off the Semtex and the BLU-82, all Nazeri had to do was reach down, rip off the M60, push, turn, and pull. It was an extremely simple, efficient design. As far as Nazeri knew, he would then have approximately five minutes to get to safety before the bomb went off. In this belief, he was fatally mistaken.

Vanderveen had spent the last hour preparing the BLU-82, and in the process, he had replaced the time fuse he'd demonstrated earlier with standard det cord. It had not been difficult to distract Nazeri long enough to make the switch. The time fuse used by the U.S. military was extremely simple: black powder wound in yarn and sealed with bitumen, all of which was wrapped in plastic tubing. The powder was distributed in such a way as to ensure a slow burn. Det cord, on the other hand, was plastic tubing filled with thousands of grains of PETN, which burned at a rate of 8,400 meters per second. From the outside, time fuse and det cord looked remarkably similar, but the difference could hardly be greater. The instant Nazeri pulled the ring on the M60, he would cease to exist, along with the core leadership of the United Iraqi Alliance.

Vanderveen put a foot on the back bumper, reached up, and pulled down the rolling door. Once he'd secured it, he clamped on an ABUS Granit core-hardened padlock, the best that money could buy. Without the key, it would take a very long time to get through this simple piece of security.

And with that, it was done. He turned to Nazeri.

"It's time."

Nazeri nodded, his forehead bathed in a light sheen of sweat. Vanderveen almost reached out to put a hand on the man's shoulder, but decided it wouldn't be welcome. For the moment, it was just the two of them. Foster was standing a few feet away, but he was not a part of what they had started so many months ago, and he seemed to know it. He stayed silent and looked back to the warehouse, clearly uneasy.

In Farsi, Vanderveen said, "I know you've started to question whether you're doing the right thing, Amir. I don't question your love for your cousin, but I do wonder if you're prepared to see this through. Why, when we've come this far, are you hesitating now?"

Nazeri lowered his head. Vanderveen knew exactly what he was thinking: that his hesitation reflected the limits of his grief; that in pausing to think things through, he had somehow marginalized his cousin's death. "When I do this, many people will die. Many people who were not involved in her murder."

"And who *was* responsible? In your eyes, who should pay?"

Nazeri looked up, his eyes burning. "The government. But we're not attacking the government."

"And yet you haven't questioned the target. Why?"

"Because I know why you picked it," Nazeri said slowly. "It's a symbol of the city, known the world over. It's a public—"

"No," Vanderveen said. He shook his head and reached under his coat, withdrawing a single sheet of paper. "This is why."

Nazeri accepted the document. He was confused at first, but he read it quickly, and when he was done, his eyes seemed clearer, sharper, and his body was unnaturally still. "Is this true?"

"Amir, I've never lied to you. I made it clear from the start that I had my own agenda, but I gave you the opportunity to take part because I knew your cousin, and I knew what she was trying to do. She was gunned down in Washington when she could have been taken alive, and her death was covered up so the government could save face."

Vanderveen paused and waited until their eyes met. "The director of the FBI is here, my friend. Here in New York, at the Renaissance Hotel in Times Square. He came to oversee security for the meeting at the UN, and in doing so, he's given you the opportunity of a lifetime. Raseen has already verified his location. He's there as we speak." *Along with thirty-five members of the UIA,* Vanderveen thought.

Nazeri looked at Foster, who was obviously unaware of what they were talking about. "Does he know about this?"

"Yes," Vanderveen replied. It was true; Foster had forged the memorandum himself. "But he can't tell you anything I haven't already, and we don't have time to discuss this further. The man ultimately responsible for your cousin's murder is within arm's reach. Now, are you prepared to take the final step, or have you changed your mind?"

Nazeri looked at the paper in his hand, then tilted his head back and looked up at the sky. It was a strange gesture, and Vanderveen wasn't sure what to make of it. He waited, and in time Nazeri seemed to come back to himself.

"No, I haven't changed my mind."

Vanderveen nodded slowly. Leaving this responsibility in Nazeri's hands was the last thing he wanted to do, but he knew it had to happen this way. In theory, he could have used a regular time fuse and set off the device himself, but Nazeri had wanted the responsibility, and Vanderveen had needed his preferred status with customs to get the daisy cutter inside the country to begin with. If he had denied the Iranian the chance to carry out the act itself, Nazeri might not have assisted him at all. Still, the other man's firm expression—as well as Raseen's earlier words—worked to alleviate most of Vanderveen's lingering concerns.

"Then go. And good luck, my friend. This is the last time we will meet."

Nazeri nodded and moved to the cab. As he climbed up and shut the door, Vanderveen started toward the chain that raised and lowered the roll-down vehicular door. With one hand on the chain, he glanced at his watch and turned to Foster. "Go and take care of the woman. Kealey will be here in a few minutes."

The FBI agent nodded and started back toward the warehouse. As the door cleared the top of the truck, the Isuzu rolled out onto West Thirty-seventh, then turned right, the transmission whining as Nazeri shifted gears, the engine struggling with the weight in the box. Vanderveen lowered the door and looked back as Foster disappeared from view. He hesitated, then turned and walked quickly to the pedestrian gate. As he unlocked it and stepped into the street, he thought he heard Foster shouting something from inside the warehouse, but he ignored it and shut the gate behind him. He thought about locking it, but decided against it.

Directly across the street was a small parking lot. Vehicles in long-term storage were stacked on metal racks, while others were arranged in tight, neat lines on the cement. One of those cars was a red Mercury Sable. Aware of horns blasting to his left, Vanderveen turned to see what was happening. A car was approaching rapidly from the east. He turned to his right and saw that the Isuzu had already vanished into traffic. Nazeri would reach his target in a matter of minutes.

He crossed to the south side of the street, pulling a set of keys from his pocket. When he reached the Sable, he unlocked the door quickly and slipped into the driver's seat. The car was Nazeri's personal vehicle. He was barely inside when a silver Accord squealed to a halt in front of the warehouse, and two people got out. He didn't know the woman, but he would have recognized Ryan Kealey anywhere. As he watched through the windshield, they approached the pedestrian gate with their weapons out, checked it, and found it unlocked. Then they passed through.

As Naomi slipped into the office, her eyes were drawn first to the phone on the desk. She started toward it, aware of someone shouting in the warehouse. She realized it was Foster; she could hear him calling to Vanderveen, screaming that she had escaped. She looked around wildly, forgetting the phone. It wouldn't take him more than a few seconds to figure out where she had gone, and when he did, he would throw open the door and kill her. She had no choice but to act first.

She went to the desk and started pulling open drawers as fast as she could, spilling the drawers and their contents onto the floor. As the third crashed to the ground, she looked down and found what she needed: a Smith & Wesson Model 60 revolver. She didn't believe it at first; it seemed too good to be true, an impossible stroke of luck, but she snatched it up without hesitation. There wasn't time to see if it was loaded. She only had time to do two things: draw back the hammer and level the weapon in outstretched arms. Then the office door flew open, and Foster appeared before her. His eyes went wide at the sight of the gun. He started to bring his own to bear, but Naomi was faster.

The first time, she barely had to touch the trigger. Foster jerked as the .38+P round tore into his chest, but he still managed to get off a shot as Naomi squeezed the trigger again. Foster's single round burned past her ear, slamming into the brick wall behind her head. At the same time, her second round drilled into the right side of his chest. Amazingly, he managed to level the gun again, his face twisted in fury and pain.

Naomi closed her eyes, held her breath, and pulled the trigger until all she heard was the sound of the hammer falling on empty chambers.

Before the car came to a complete halt on West Thirty-seventh, Kealey was already pushing open his door, but Crane beat him to it. She approached the pedestrian gate, gun out, muzzle down, as

Kealey came round the front of the car. He could smell burning rubber from the tires as Crane tried the gate and found it unlocked. She looked at him, nodded once, and pushed through. He followed instantly, less than 2 feet behind her.

The parking area was empty, except for some pallets stacked in the corner and a blue Crown Vic. "That's from the motor pool at the FO," Crane said in a low voice. "He's here."

"But no truck," Kealey pointed out. He felt suddenly numb; they were too late.

As Crane approached the warehouse, he moved to the car, looking through the windows. On the passenger-side floor he saw something that chilled his blood: Naomi's purse. She had to be inside the building.

Involuntarily, his eyes moved to the glass doors of the warehouse, which were still propped open. He knew that as soon as he walked through those doors, there was a good chance he would find her body and nothing more. He found himself frozen, unwilling to take the next step, but then he heard a scream—a woman's scream—followed immediately by shots. Crane, 10 feet from the door of the warehouse, seemed to hesitate for an instant, and then she dashed forward. At the same time, four more shots echoed within the building. Kealey sprinted forward, trying to catch up, shouting for Crane to wait, but she ignored him. She reached the doors and ran through, her 10mm up in a two-handed stance. Kealey heard two more shots as he covered the last 20 feet, heart pounding. He had no idea what he was heading into; all he knew was that he had to get through those doors.

As Foster slumped to the ground, Naomi found herself reaching down to grab his weapon. The revolver was empty, useless, and only one of the three men was down. Her head was buzzing with fear and adrenaline. She couldn't seem to hear anything, and her vision was blurred. Looking down, she could see that the FBI agent wasn't quite dead, but it wouldn't be long. His eyes were still moving, his mouth open, stains spreading wet on his chest. She could hear a strange rattling noise as he tried to breathe through the fluid collecting in his throat. It was the first time she had ever killed another human being, but even as that thought hit her, along with a storm of emotions, a noise cut through the shock. She heard a man shouting, the words indistinct, and knew at once that it had to be Vanderveen.

Her eyes shot up, along with Foster's gun, but Vanderveen didn't come running into the warehouse. Instead, it was a woman—blond hair, black sweater, gun in hand. Her features were instantly recognizable; Naomi had never seen Samantha Crane in person, but she'd seen a number of photographs, and she knew who this was.

Suddenly, everything Ryan had said about Crane came back in a hot, fierce rush: *It had to be her. No one else knew about Berlin. No one else knew. . . .*

Crane's weapon was up and traversing the room. Suddenly, it was swinging right toward the office.

Right toward her.

Naomi squeezed the trigger once, saw she had missed, and squeezed it again. Crane stopped dead in her tracks, her head snapping back. As the gun slipped out of her grasp, she lifted a hand to her face, pressing it hard against the hole in her cheek. Her eyes opened wide, and she let out a choked cry. Then her gaze went blank and she dropped to the floor, almost as if the life had been pulled right out of her body.

At that moment, Ryan Kealey entered the warehouse. Naomi snapped Foster's gun toward him and barely managed to avoid squeezing the trigger again. From that point on, everything happened in slow motion. She saw him stare at her, his gaze drifting down to the gun in her hand. Then he looked from the gun to Samantha Crane. Finally, their eyes met, and from the stunned look on his face, Naomi knew she had just made a terrible mistake.

CHAPTER 54

NEW YORK CITY

In the small parking lot across from the warehouse, Will Vanderveen lifted his phone and dialed a number. Yasmin Raseen picked up on the first ring.

"Yes?"

"Where are you?" Vanderveen asked.

"I just left the hotel," she replied. "The lobby is full of security officers. I think most of the delegates must still be inside."

"Good. Does it look like they're getting ready to leave?"

"No. I don't see any cars outside the building. At least not the right kind of cars."

Vanderveen knew what she meant. The members of the UIA scheduled to attend the General Assembly meeting in less than three hours would be protected not only by their own security teams, but also by sworn agents with the U.S. Diplomatic Security Service. The vehicles that would eventually come to collect the delegates would be Lincoln Town Cars or something similar, undoubtedly bearing diplomatic or government plates. The official vehicles would be easy to spot, especially since they'd be surrounded by NYPD escort cars and motorcycles.

"So we're on track."

"I believe so," she replied. "Is it time for me to leave?"

"Yes." Vanderveen shot a glance at his watch. "In fact, you need to move fast . . . Nazeri left nearly two minutes ago. You don't have time to get to the subway, not from where you are now, so grab a taxi and try to get some buildings between you and the hotel. Otherwise, you're still in the blast radius."

"Understood."

Her voice was unnaturally calm, given the gravity of the moment. Vanderveen smiled and shook his head, quietly impressed. "I'll call you when it's done."

He hung up and leaned back in the driver's seat of the Sable, studying the pedestrian gate on the other side of the street. Kealey and the woman had been inside the warehouse for less than a minute, and he couldn't help but wonder what they had found. He hadn't heard any gunfire, but he knew that didn't mean a thing; the sound wouldn't carry beyond the thick walls of the warehouse. It was a strange feeling, knowing that people were dying a few feet away and not being able to see them meet their end. A rather disappointing feeling.

He waited, wondering who would emerge in the end.

Inside the warehouse, Kealey moved forward instantly, dropping to one knee by Crane's body. Naomi watched him move from a distance, aware of a rising dread, a building fear. After a moment that seemed to stretch on forever, he looked up and stared at her in disbelief. "Jesus, Naomi, what did you do?"

"Wait," she heard herself say. The gun was still in her hands, held down by her waist, but she couldn't feel it; she couldn't feel anything. She was still trying to figure out what was happening here. "I don't understand."

"Why the hell did you shoot her?"

"What are you talking about? She had a gun, Ryan. I—"

"She wasn't part of this." Kealey checked Crane's pulse but looked up a moment later, shaking his head. "She's gone. Jesus Christ, you killed her."

"No, I . . ." Naomi felt a terrible pain swelling up in her chest, rising into her throat. She shook her head in an effort to deny what was happening. "She's with Foster. She was working with Vanderveen. You said it yourself. *She was working against us.*"

She stopped when she saw the grim look on his face. "It wasn't

Crane, Naomi. It was Foster. Just Foster, the whole time. Rudaki confirmed it less than an hour ago."

"That's not possible." She could hear her voice rising, climbing into hysteria. There was no way she had just killed an innocent person. It had to be some kind of nightmare, some kind of horrible illusion. An out-of-body experience, maybe. There was just no other explanation. "That's just not possible."

Kealey got to his feet but didn't look at her. "Naomi, she wasn't involved—"

"Don't say that, Ryan." She backed up a couple feet, shaking her head wildly. *"Don't tell me that!"* Still holding Foster's gun, she clamped her free hand over her mouth, her eyes wide and disbelieving. She didn't move for about twenty seconds. Then, as his words started to sink in, her legs gave way and she half-fell, half-sat on the smooth concrete floor, just outside the open office door.

Lowering her hand from her mouth, she stared into space for what seemed like a very long time, shaking her head slowly. Then it all seemed to hit her at once. Kealey saw the change sweep over her face as the guilt, grief, and regret took hold, squeezing away any lingering hope that this might be a dream. From personal experience, he knew that what he was seeing was only the start. It was painful to watch, but he also knew there was worse to come. Much worse.

He looked away, struggling with several emotions of his own. He was relieved beyond measure to find her alive and unharmed, but he was furious with her for what she had done, for what she had brought on herself. With one impulsive act, she had made a mistake that would haunt her forever. A mistake she could never take back.

He looked down at Samantha Crane. Her soft brown eyes were open, her lips slightly parted. In death, her face was strangely serene. It was hard to believe she was gone; just a moment ago she had been so alive, so vital and real. The small hole in her right cheek was barely noticeable, but as Kealey watched, a thin trickle of blood ran down from the wound to the floor. Gazing into her lifeless face, he was tempted to follow Naomi's example: to sit down, let the exhaustion take over, and wait for the police to show up. But that just wasn't an option; Vanderveen and Nazeri were still out there somewhere, and time was running out.

Snapping out of it, he went over and kneeled by her side, shaking her arm to get her attention. "Naomi, did you talk to Vanderveen? Did he mention anything about the bomb?"

She was still in denial, or maybe shock; it was hard to tell. She opened her mouth, but nothing came out.

"Come on, did he tell you anything? Where are they taking it?"

"He said . . . something about Times Square."

"Times Square? You're sure?"

"Yes."

"When did Vanderveen leave?"

"Five minutes ago. Right before you got here. Nazeri is driving the truck."

"Is Vanderveen with him?"

"I . . . I don't know."

Kealey closed his eyes, shaking his head. It didn't make sense; Times Square was only five minutes away, to begin with. They should have felt the blast already. He flipped open his phone and dialed Harper's number at Langley. "What kind of truck was it?"

"White," she said in a daze. "With a box on the back. An Isuzu, I think."

When Harper answered, Kealey said, "John, I need you to check something for me right now, no questions asked. The delegates with the UIA . . . Where are they staying in the city?"

"Jesus, Ryan, I have no idea—"

"Then find out," he snapped. "And call me back."

"I'm on it."

Kealey snapped the phone shut without responding, thinking furiously. There wasn't much he could do until the DDO came up with an answer, so he moved onto the next problem: what to do about Naomi. He still hadn't heard any sirens, probably because the gunshots weren't audible on the street. Maybe the traffic served to drown out the sound. Either way, it gave him a little time to figure things out.

He looked down and saw that she had started to cry softly. For the first time, he noticed the handcuffs around her wrists. He touched her shoulder, and she looked up through her tears.

"Naomi, did you shoot Foster, or was it Crane?"

"It was me. But I had to. He was trying to—"

"I know, I know. Did you use the same gun on both of them?"

She shook her head, tears rolling down her face. "No, I found a gun in Nazeri's desk, and I used it on . . . Foster. But I fired all six, and then I saw his gun, so I picked it up. I thought Vanderveen was coming back for me. After that, everything just kind of . . . happened."

She broke off, tucked her knees up to her chest, and buried her head in her arms. Kealey was already on the move. First, he went to Foster's body and grabbed the back of his shirt, turning him so he was facing the opposite direction, away from the office. Then he moved back to Naomi, lifting Foster's gun out of her lap. She didn't seem to realize what was happening. He lifted the lower half of his T-shirt and used the material to wipe down the gun as fast as possible, doing his best to erase any sign of her fingerprints. When he was satisfied, he kneeled next to Foster's right hand and let the gun slip from his shirt to the floor.

At that very moment, his phone rang. He flipped it open immediately.

"It's the Renaissance Hotel," Harper said. He sounded amazed and angry. "Forty-eighth and Seventh. Thirty-five members of the Iraqi National Assembly in one fucking place. I don't know who thought that one up, but I'm going to—"

"Okay, thanks." Kealey flipped the phone shut without waiting for a response. It didn't make sense; he didn't know why the bomb was still intact, but it didn't really matter. If he could just get there in time, he might still have a chance to stop it.

He touched Kharmai's shoulder again to get her attention. "Naomi, I have to leave you here. I don't know if what I've done will hold up, but you have to get a grip on yourself and come up with a story, okay? Foster shot Crane; then you shot him. You need to fill in the blanks before the cops get here. Understand?"

"Ryan, I can't do that. I deserve whatever—"

"Don't say that," he said in a hard voice, cutting her off. He softened his tone and kneeled beside her. "It was a mistake, it's done, and spending the next few years of your life in prison won't fix it. You have to get it together, okay?"

She nodded and wiped her eyes with her sleeve. "Okay. I'll try."

"Good."

He glanced at his watch as he ran for the doors. Sanitizing the scene had taken a full minute, a minute he couldn't afford to spare. Before he got outside, he thought of something and went back to Foster's body. He found the keys to the Crown Vic in the man's left jacket pocket, along with FBI credentials in a flip-style billfold. He grabbed both items. Less than a minute later, he had the roll-down vehicular door up and was pulling out onto West Thirty-seventh Street, heading for Eighth Avenue. He accelerated immediately, racing against the one-way traffic, laying his hand on the horn. In his rush to beat Nazeri to the hotel, he didn't notice the man in the Sable across the street, who watched him go with a mixed expression of rage and curiosity.

As Kealey raced north toward the Renaissance Hotel, Vanderveen crossed the street quickly, heading back to the warehouse, wondering what he would find inside.

CHAPTER 55

NEW YORK CITY

Amir Nazeri wiped a film of sweat from his forehead and stared down at his hands, which were wrapped tightly around the steering wheel of the Isuzu box truck. They were steady, but only because they were welded around the wheel; the rest of his body was trembling violently. He willed his limbs to relax but knew that it wouldn't make a difference. Looking up, he stared blankly through the windshield at the traffic passing a few feet in front of him, then turned to his right, absently watching the crowds sweeping past on the sidewalk. He wondered what these people would think if they knew what was going through his mind. Would any of them understand? Somehow, he didn't think so. Only one person had ever really understood him, and she was gone, stripped away by the same government that had given him the chance to prosper in a new and foreign land. The irony of this—that America could give with one hand and take away with the other—had never occurred to him, but he wouldn't have cared to consider it.

The Isuzu had passed through the western half of the theater district and was now idling at the intersection of West Fifty-second and Tenth. He had missed the right turn onto West Forty-eighth several minutes earlier. At first, he told himself it was just because he'd seen a police car make the same turn. But then he'd come up with a similar excuse for the next eastbound street, the street after that, and the street after that. At this rate, he would never reach his destination, but suddenly—inexplicably—he wasn't sure he wanted to.

He wiped his face again as the light turned green. He hesitated, but instead of turning right onto West Fifty-second, he kept going straight. Nazeri shook his head unconsciously, aware of the pressure building inside his chest. He didn't understand what was happening to him. When Kohl had first put forth this proposition, everything had seemed so clear. In killing Fatima Darabi, the U.S. government had stripped away the only thing that had ever mattered to him. When he'd learned what had happened to her, the bitterness had threatened to overwhelm him completely. Nothing had changed since then, so why was he hesitating? Why was he finding it so hard to make the turn?

Suddenly, he was overcome with deep, piercing shame. How could he be so weak? He still didn't know exactly what Fatima had done for the mullahs in Tehran, but he knew that she'd come to the United States to risk her life for her country. She had sacrificed every-thing for what she'd believed in, and while Amir did not share those beliefs, he did respect them. More to the point, he respected her courage. In life, she had possessed a certain strength, an inner vital-ity he could never aspire to, only admire from afar. But now she was gone, and it was his turn to be strong. If he failed her now, he would never again have the chance to avenge her death, at least not to the extent she deserved.

As this realization sunk in, her face appeared, unbidden. When she came, he saw her at ten years of age, splashing in the fountains at the Sheik Lotfallah mosque in Isfahan, a giddy smile on her face, whooping as the water rained down in a silvery cloud.

It was the best memory of his life.

Horns blared behind him, pulling him out of his reverie. As he came back to reality, he wished so much that he could go back to that time, a time when anything seemed possible. A time when they still had the chance to make the right choices. He felt something warm running over his cheeks and realized that he was crying.

When he hit the light at West Fifty-sixth Street, he swung the wheel to the right. The hotel was less than five minutes away, and he knew now what he had to do.

All doubt was gone.

*   *   *

In the warehouse on West Thirty-seventh, Naomi Kharmai was still sitting on the smooth cement floor. For the moment, she was lost to the world, mired in her own private hell. She couldn't seem to settle on any one emotion: the guilt would start to take hold, only to be replaced by a surge of self-pity. These twin tenets of misery were propped up by anger: anger at Harper, for letting her have her way; anger at Ryan, for not walking in first. If Crane had been the second person through the door, Naomi never would have pulled the trigger. But it just hadn't worked out that way, and now an innocent person was gone forever.

She still couldn't believe it. Through the tears in her eyes, she stared at Crane's body in the near distance, silently begging the other woman to stand up and shake it off. It just didn't seem possible. She had taken a life. An *innocent* life. It was the one word she just couldn't shake from her tortured conscience. It was also a word that didn't apply to Matt Foster, and for this reason, Naomi didn't regret shooting him at all. Samantha Crane was the only victim here, but if Crane was innocent, what did that make *her*? The answer was incredibly simple, yet so hard to accept.

She was guilty. Guilty of the worst possible crime. Naomi just couldn't see a way past this mistake. Even if Ryan somehow managed to stop Nazeri, how was she supposed to live with herself? To come to terms with what she had done?

The thought brought on a fresh wave of bitter, scalding tears. They were flowing steadily now that the shock had worn off, but she knew this was only the start; the shock might have faded, but reality had yet to set in. As sorrow welled up in her chest, she heard a noise at the doors and looked up. Suddenly, her grief was replaced by something even worse. As she stared, openmouthed, at the man standing before her, she couldn't help but wonder if this was some kind of divine punishment for what she had just done. If so, the punishment was fully befitting her crime.

Will Vanderveen was standing there, holding a gun in his hand. Her gaze instantly moved to the gun near Foster's hand—the one Ryan had cleaned of her fingerprints—but Vanderveen seemed to sense her thoughts.

"Don't even think about it," he said. Smiling, he gestured for her to stand. "On your feet, Naomi. We're going for a little ride."

The six-minute drive from the warehouse to the intersection of Forty-eighth and Seventh was the longest of Ryan Kealey's life. He was caught up in a surge of emotions: rage that he'd missed Will Vanderveen yet again, sympathy for Naomi and what she had yet to endure, and building despair over the death of Samantha Crane. He hadn't known her, but she had been innocent of this whole mess and, from what he could tell, a good agent, despite the fact that she'd been blindsided by Rudaki and Matt Foster, her own partner. He couldn't really fault her for not seeing the truth earlier; he had been similarly betrayed in the past, and he hadn't seen it coming, either. He only wished he had been able to get to Naomi first; if he'd been able to warn her, Crane would almost certainly still be alive. In truth, he was as much to blame as she was.

He had found the lights shortly after making the turn onto Eighth Avenue, and the siren soon after that. As the Bureau sedan swept toward Times Square, he was scanning the surrounding traffic, as well as the cars lined up at the curb, searching for any sign of a white Isuzu truck. He saw a few possibilities, but he didn't have time to check them. At this point, his only chance at stopping Nazeri would be to get to the target as fast as possible. The only thing he couldn't understand was why he had not heard the blast. It should have happened at least ten minutes ago. He kept waiting for the rising plume of shattered cement and dust, as well as the thunderous explosion, signifying the death of thousands of people, but it never came, not on West Thirty-seventh Street, not on Eighth Avenue, and not as the Crown Vic he had borrowed squealed to a halt at the intersection of West Forty-eighth and Seventh Avenue.

He'd cut the lights and the siren a few blocks earlier, not wanting to warn Nazeri if the other man had already reached his destination. Now he got out of the car and looked around, searching frantically for the truck that Naomi had described. Not seeing it, he took a second to scope out his surroundings. The Renaissance Hotel was on his right, twenty-six stories of black glass and steel. From where he was standing, he could reach out and touch the gleaming façade.

Above his head was a huge sign edged in gold filigree, at least six stories in height, with a large, circular clock on top. He checked the time and saw that the General Assembly was not set to convene for another three hours. In other words, at least thirty members of the United Iraqi Alliance were inside the hotel at that very moment, along with several hundred businessmen, conventioneers, and tourists, all of whom were blissfully unaware of the looming threat.

In the distance was the narrow northern face of the world-famous One Times Square, the Bertelsmann Building off to the left. Times Square Tower rose behind all of it, glistening like a vertical wall of blue-green water in the midday sun. In between, passenger cars flashed back and forth on the through streets, along with dozens of buses and what seemed like hundreds of yellow cabs, though the actual number was far less. The traffic on Seventh Avenue was southbound in four narrow lanes, hurtling toward One Times Square and the intersection with Broadway, the view partially obscured by towering columns of steam, which seemed to gather in ominous clouds in the cool air.

People were everywhere, choking the sidewalks, dressed for the weather in long-sleeve shirts and light sweaters. The temperature was about 65 degrees, much warmer than it had been in Washington the previous night, but still fairly brisk for September. Kealey automatically started looking for police officers and was momentarily shocked when he didn't see any. Then he remembered that half the force—and 90 percent of the Manhattan Patrol Borough South—was conducting crowd control at the UN enclave a few blocks to the east. He wondered why the crowd didn't extend to this area, then recalled that the demonstration stretched north on Second Avenue, from Fifty-first to Fifty-fifth. In other words, this was the perfect place to strike: for the moment, the hotel was completely unprotected. Completely vulnerable.

Kealey swung around and looked north, scanning the approaching traffic. If Nazeri was coming, he guessed it would be from this direction, not from the west. Involuntarily, his right hand drifted down to his hip, where the Beretta was holstered. The butt was covered by the lower edge of his T-shirt. A magazine was loaded, of course, 14 rounds plus one in the chamber, and he had two spare mags as backup. He suspected he might well need them; 15 rounds might not be enough to take out Nazeri, Vanderveen, and the truck. Once he saw the vehicle approach, he'd have to fire through the windshield as fast as possible. It wasn't an ideal scenario, but at this point, he had little other choice. What worried him most were the police officers in the area. He hadn't seen any, but he knew they were there. The minute he pulled the gun, he'd become a target, but there was no way he could explain the situation in time. He had no proof of anything he had to tell them, and the first thing they would do is take his gun and hold him for questioning. Bringing them into the loop simply wasn't an option.

Just as he was trying to figure out his next move, two things happened at once. His cell phone rang, and he spotted the top of a white Isuzu truck approaching from the north, moving at a slower rate than the surrounding traffic. As he watched, it shuddered to a halt at the light at Fifty-first and Seventh, two cars back from the light itself. Never moving his gaze from the vehicle, he reached into his right pocket and withdrew his phone, flipping it open to answer the call. "Kealey."

"Ryan? Is that you?"

He froze, unsure he had heard correctly. Sensing his shock, Vanderveen laughed and said, "How have you been?"

"You fucking bastard. Where are—"

"Easy," Vanderveen said, a warning note creeping into his voice. "That's no way to talk to a man who's holding a gun on your girlfriend."

"You . . ." Kealey was left speechless, his heart pounding against his ribs, every nerve ending seared by anger and fear. He should never have left her alone . . . It just didn't seem real. "Put her on."

"Just for a minute, then." There was a pause, a few mumbled words, and then a sharp, defiant refusal. Kealey heard what could only be a slap, the sound of flesh hitting flesh. He knew that the other man had just hit her, and he was filled with a white-hot rage, his hand gripping the phone so tight the plastic was starting to crack. Up ahead, the light at Fifty-first turned green, and the Isuzu rolled forward. Kealey squinted through the glare of the pale afternoon sun but couldn't see the man behind the wheel.

"Ryan?" Naomi's voice came over the phone, filling him with

dread and despair. She sounded scared as hell, but he could also detect a strange determination. When she spoke, the words came out
in a rush. "Don't worry about me. Just stop the bomb, okay? Just—"

She had spoken as fast as she could, but she was quickly cut off by
another audible slap. Vanderveen came back on the line right away.
"See? I'm a man of my word. Not very good at protecting your
women, are you?" The other man's voice was filled with a kind of
amusement, which bordered on outright glee. "If I hadn't been distracted earlier, I would have left you a little message to that effect. By
which I mean a message carved into her face. Looks like I might still
have the chance."

"You son of a bitch," Kealey managed. His eyes were glued on the
Isuzu. It was approaching fast now, not more than a few hundred feet
away. He quickly searched again for police officers, but if they were
there, they had lost themselves in the crowd. "If you touch her, I
swear to God, I'll—"

"Let it go," Vanderveen said, his voice low and strangely hypnotic.
"Just let it go off. Let it do what it was meant to do. If you stop it, she
dies in the worst way possible. Just like Katie."

Kealey closed his eyes, aware of a crushing despair. The image
came back in an instant: he could see her lying on the kitchen floor,
bleeding out from the wound in her neck, begging him for help with
those frightened blue eyes. The thought of Naomi enduring the
same was just too much, but there was no way to stop it. Vanderveen
would kill her anyway, and besides, he couldn't put her life ahead of
the thousands of innocent people in the surrounding buildings. He
had already risked too much time in the warehouse by trying to
shield her from blame in Crane's death. There was nothing more he
could do for her; he'd just have to prove her wrong.

*You've never let me down, Ryan, and I know you never will. I
trust you completely.*

Vanderveen was clearly waiting for his reply. Kealey took a deep
breath, then made the hardest choice of his life.

He disconnected the call and dropped the phone.

Reaching under his shirt, he drew his Beretta and held it down by
his side for as long as he could. Then he stepped into Seventh Avenue, narrowly avoiding being hit by a passing bus. As soon as it

swept by in a blast of cool air, Kealey took a few more steps, crossing into the second lane. The Isuzu was close now, and judging by the sweaty, agitated look on the driver's face, he had the right vehicle. He was aware of squealing tires, a cacophony of horns, and the shouts of pedestrians rising up from the sidewalk, but he shut it all out. Lifting the gun in two hands, Kealey set his feet, aimed at the man behind the wheel of the approaching truck, and squeezed the trigger.

In the passenger seat of the red Mercury Sable, Naomi Kharmai looked down at her balled fists, trying to ignore the stinging pain on the left side of her face. Her wrists were still cuffed; Vanderveen had thrown a sweater over her hands to hide the evidence as he'd hustled her into the car a few minutes earlier. She could taste blood in her mouth, and she felt dizzy from the three blows he had just delivered. After hitting her twice while on the phone with Kealey, he had administered a third, brutal punch to the side of her head, more out of frustration than anything else. At least, that was her guess. Fortunately, the angle had taken away most of his leverage, so the blow hadn't done nearly as much damage as it should have. Still, she could feel something warm running down past her ear, and looking down, she could see a few spots of blood on her sweater, bright red against the white material.

After Ryan disconnected the call, Vanderveen had thrown the phone onto the floor by her feet. Then he had lapsed into a barrage of biting profanity. She didn't dare to look at him, afraid of drawing his wrath. She was intensely aware of the Glock 19 in his left hand, which was resting in his lap and pointed toward her. She had briefly considered throwing open the door and diving out, but she knew she would never get clear in time. At that angle, the bullet would tear right through her abdomen, leaving her with a wound that would almost certainly prove fatal, but only after an hour or so of excruciating pain.

Far more terrifying than the gun, however, was the knife he'd dropped into his pocket before pushing her out of the warehouse and into the car. It was the same knife he'd threatened her with earlier, and judging by what he'd said to Ryan over the phone, he was anxious to use it. She couldn't stop thinking about that shiny hooked blade, but the gun was right there, clearly visible, and she knew he wouldn't hesitate to fire. By the time they crossed West Forty-second Street, she'd decided the best thing to do was to sit still and wait for an opportunity.

As her mind raced to find one, though, Vanderveen turned the wheel hard to the right. She looked up to see a sign that said WEST 48TH STREET, and she suddenly realized where they were going. The Renaissance Hotel at Forty-Eighth and Seventh.

They were heading right for ground zero.

CHAPTER 56

NEW YORK CITY

Joseph Ruggeri counted himself a fortunate man, despite being in desperate need of a shower and a month's worth of sleep, and for one simple reason: he was one of the very few cops in the five boroughs with the rest of the day off. The twenty-six-year-old Ruggeri had just come off a twelve-hour desk shift at the precinct on the corner of West Fifty-fourth and Eighth, the home of the Patrol Borough Manhattan South, and was looking forward to a good meal and a warm bed, preferably his girlfriend's. The bed would have to wait a little bit longer, but he knew where the meal was coming from, as his uncle co-owned the Stage Deli and Restaurant on Fifty-fourth and Seventh.

He had changed into street clothes before leaving the precinct: a white T-shirt under a brown canvas jacket, worn Levis, and running shoes. His service weapon, a Smith & Wesson Model 5946, was holstered on his right hip, but he hardly noticed it; he carried the gun almost everywhere and was used to its comforting weight.

Ruggeri had been on the force for just over four and a half years. Like many men in his age group, he'd felt the need to serve his country following the events of September 11th, 2001, and as with most of his like-minded peers, that meant one of two things: the military or law enforcement. Ruggeri was Brooklyn born and raised; his parents still lived in the same house he'd grown up in, and his six siblings all lived within the five boroughs, except for one sister who'd strayed to

Trenton, of all places. Leaving them behind to go to Afghanistan or some other godforsaken place was simply not an option. The idea of crossing the Jersey line filled him with a distinct sense of unease; Afghanistan might as well have been on a different planet. So it was the NYPD, and he'd never regretted it. He enjoyed the work, he loved being able to get a home-cooked meal any day of the week, and he especially loved the nice little jump he had just received on his last paycheck.

He crossed Fifty-fourth heading south, the colorful façade of the Stage Deli coming up on his right. Just as he started to open the door, a distant popping noise caused him to turn left instead. After twenty-six years in the city and four and a half on the force, he recognized the sound of gunfire instantly. His hand dropped and slipped under his jacket, finding the butt of his weapon, but his eyes were locked on the scene in the near distance. He had a bad angle—no sign of the shooter—but as he watched in disbelief, a white box truck swung hard to the right on Seventh Avenue, then started to tip.

Drawing his weapon, he instantly ran forward, doing his best to cover the next seven blocks in the least time possible. At the same time, his left hand dipped into his jacket and found his cell phone. The precinct was on his speed dial, so he hit the number and kept running hard.

At the intersection of Forty-eighth and Seventh, Kealey was firing as fast as he could into the windshield of the Isuzu, which was still moving toward him. He saw his first shot crater the glass just left of the driver's head, then adjusted the next three and saw the intended effect. The driver seemed to jerk spasmodically behind the wheel, inadvertently pulling it hard to the right. He fired another three shots as the truck veered sharply toward him. He dived out of the way but wasn't quite fast enough; the grill caught his left ankle, spinning him around in midair, and he hit the pavement hard, ending up in the next lane. A southbound Lincoln Navigator screeched to a halt, tires smoking, the front wheel less than 3 feet from his head. He had no time to consider this further; behind him, he heard a strange, anticipatory silence, then a loud crunch, glass shattering, the scream of metal sliding across the road.

He got to his feet, ignoring the crushing pain in his ankle, and turned to see something that chilled his blood: the truck was on its side, sliding across the pavement, throwing up a shower of sparks. Kealey felt everything stop inside his head. He waited for the bright flash, knowing it would be the last thing he'd see in his life, but it never came. As the truck finally came to a halt, everything started to move again, like a tape coming out of slow motion. People were screaming, running north and south on Seventh, and he was aware of distant sirens. But the cops wouldn't get there in time, and he had to be sure.

Kealey ran forward, his ankle delivering shivers of pain with every step. His attention was completely focused on the roof of the cab, which was facing back toward the Renaissance Hotel. He lifted the Beretta again, silently adding up the shots in his head. He knew he'd fired at least seven, which left him with more than enough to make sure the driver was dead. Just as he was about to fire through the roof, though, he felt someone hit him hard from behind. His lower back arched painfully, his head whipping back as he pitched forward onto the pavement, the gun coming loose. The crushing blow nearly left him unconscious, and his back felt as if it had snapped in half. He did his best to sit up, trying to figure out what had happened.

Looking back, he half expected to see Will Vanderveen, but it was just some guy he'd never seen before, a heavyset man with a thick beard and a look of determination on his face. He wasn't a cop, Kealey knew, or he would have said something to that effect. And then it hit him; his assailant was just a bystander who didn't know any better. Kealey briefly considered explaining it to him, but there wasn't time. Instead, he simply slammed a fist into the man's throat. The bearded man rolled away instantly, his hands shooting up to his throat, a strangled noise coming out of his mouth. Kealey turned painfully back to the truck and reached for his Beretta.

In the driver's seat, Amir Nazeri was hanging on to life by a thread. One of Kealey's bullets had creased the left side of his skull; another had torn into his chest, just beneath his clavicle; and a third had pierced his face, penetrating the right lateral nasal wall before angling up through his left eye, coming to rest in the orbit. Strangely enough, the pain wasn't that bad, and he had the strength, in his final moments, to tear the M60 fuse igniter free from the right side of his seat. He'd been wearing his seat belt when the vehicle tipped over, and his body was now dangling to the right, toward the shattered passenger-side window and the pavement. With tremendous effort, he managed to bring his left arm around—it didn't seem to be working correctly at all—and get one of his fingers inside the pull ring. As he prepared to carry out his final task, he thought of his dead cousin and smiled.

It was the last act of his life.

At that precise moment, Kealey fired six more shots through the roof of the cab. All six found their target, though it was the second that killed Nazeri as it tore through the top of his skull, penetrating his brain and coming to rest in his cervical column. Kealey instantly moved round to the front of the vehicle and crouched, gun up, aiming through the shattered windshield. He could see that the driver was dead, and his thoughts turned instantly to defusing the bomb; until he got inside, he couldn't be sure if it was on a timer or if Vanderveen had rigged up an electrical firing system.

Before he could act, though, he was aware of a voice carrying high over those of the frantic onlookers. He looked up, breathing hard, and saw something that turned his spine to ice. Another vehicle—a red Mercury Sable—was parked directly next to his stolen Crown Vic, about 50 feet north of his current position. A man who looked vaguely familiar was standing next to the open driver's door, his left arm wrapped around Naomi Kharmai's throat. Vanderveen looked different, but Kealey instantly made the connection, looking for the man's right hand. He couldn't see it.

"Let her go!" he screamed, bringing the Beretta to bear. The other man was ducking behind her, giving him nothing to work with. Through the adrenaline, his mind did a quick assessment and gave him the bad news. He had one round left in the chamber, maybe another in the magazine.

Two rounds. Maybe.

"Set it off!" Vanderveen shouted back. Kealey watched with horror as the other man's right hand came up out of nowhere, holding a knife. He flashed on Katie Donovan's death involuntarily, his mind caught up in a whirl of terrible images, past and present. "There's an M60 in the cab, Ryan. Set it off and make it painless for everyone. Otherwise, you watch her die, and I don't have to tell you what that's like."

Vanderveen moved the knife up and touched the hooked, 3½-inch blade to Naomi's right cheek. She was clearly terrified, but Kealey tried not to look at her face, knowing it would only distract him. He was entirely focused on finding a shot, but the other man was crouched behind her, making himself an impossible target. If Kealey pulled the trigger, he would almost certainly hit Naomi instead. He moved forward, his feet crunching over shattered glass, his broken ankle forgotten entirely.

"Stop there!" Vanderveen shouted, using the knife to make his point. Naomi cried out, and a tiny point of red appeared on her cheek. Kealey stopped instantly, his stomach dropping, his heart lurching.

"Okay, okay! Jesus, just . . . let her go. Let her go, you bastard! *Let her fucking go!*"

"You're panicking," Vanderveen shouted back. "That's not a good sign, Ryan. I'll tell you what . . . Forget the bomb. Just kill yourself. Take your own life and save hers. Put the gun to your head and pull the trigger, you fuck. *Do it! Do it or she dies!*"

"You'll kill her anyway." Kealey was desperate, frantic; there was no way to stop what was going to happen. He couldn't believe he was in this position again. He had a gun; he had to take the shot, but Vanderveen was giving him nothing. He could aim for the left arm around her throat, but unless he was incredibly lucky, the bullet would not strike bone but would pass through and into her body. He just couldn't take the risk.

Where were the cops? Why wasn't anyone moving in? It seemed as though someone in a better position should have tried to defuse the situation. But even as he thought it, he could see men edging in from behind, trying to approach unseen. He did his best not to look at them, but Vanderveen seemed to sense their attention anyway.

"Back! Get back or I cut her throat! You want that on your conscience?"

Vanderveen's would-be assailants retreated immediately, raising their hands. Kealey had been ready for them; he was sure the distraction would cause Vanderveen to turn, thereby giving him a shot, but it hadn't happened. The other man seemed to be in perfect control, despite the fact that he was trapped in a busy intersection with police on the way and Kealey waiting for his slightest mistake. He didn't appear to be fazed at all by the hopeless nature of his situation; in a matter of minutes, he would either be dead or in handcuffs. In truth, though, only one of those was a real possibility. Kealey tightened his finger on the trigger, waiting for Vanderveen to make his final mistake.

Vanderveen was doing his best to keep behind the woman, knowing that Kealey wouldn't need much of a target. For a split second, he marveled at his own actions, amazed at the fatalistic nature of the choice he'd made in the car. He had raced into this situation knowing there was almost no possibility of escape, yet he didn't regret it at all. It seemed right that it should come down to this: the two of them face-to-face in Midtown Manhattan. He still had the gun in his pocket and knew he should have used it right from the start. The knife had proved irresistible, though. What better way to remind Ryan of what he had lost? And what better way to set the stage for a loss even more profound, more horrific than the one he had suffered before?

Every fiber of his being was sparked into life by this incredible showdown; he had never felt more alive, more powerful. More *elemental*. But at the same time, he was suffused by a bitter, blinding rage. Kealey had stopped him yet again, ruining what should have been his crowning achievement. His hatred of the other man could not be more intense if it had been instilled from birth, and it was the main reason he'd driven to the hotel instead of just killing the woman and leaving the city. It wasn't enough to take her life. He wanted, *needed* Kealey to see it happen.

Vanderveen pressed his face into the nape of Kharmai's neck and breathed deeply, catching the mingled scents of vanilla, sweat, and fear. An unusual combination, but not unpleasant . . . at least not to him. Carefully, using her hair to conceal as much of his face as possible, he raised his lips to her ear and said, "Naomi, are you ready to die?"

She didn't respond; she didn't even moan. In that strange moment, he was intensely proud of her. He pulled her even tighter, letting his lips touch the lobe of her ear. He was aware of her heart thudding, her body shaking, her breath coming in short, quick spurts. And yet, despite her obvious terror, she didn't scream . . . She didn't even whimper.

What an incredible woman. If he had chosen a different path, a different life, he might well have selected a girl like this to share it with. For a brief moment in time, it seemed as if they had somehow fused, as if their bodies were one.

But she belonged to Ryan, and for that, he couldn't forgive her.

He reversed his grip on the knife, placed the tip at the hinge of her jaw, and pushed it in.

Kealey heard words come out of his mouth when he saw what was happening, but he couldn't be sure of what he was saying, his screams drowned out by those of the onlookers. He fired instantly, knowing that it no longer made a difference; Vanderveen had changed everything by putting the knife in, and Kealey knew instinctively that the other man wouldn't stop until Naomi was dead. His first shot missed completely, but he got lucky with the second, as Naomi wrenched her body to the left, trying to get away from the knife. Vanderveen followed her before regaining control, exposing his right shoulder for less than a second. Kealey's round ripped into his arm just above the elbow, tunneling the length of his bicep before exiting at an angle near his shoulder, catching the edge of his neck.

Vanderveen jerked back, but somehow managed to bring Naomi's body back in front of his own. The knife was still moving up, and there was so much blood . . . impossible amounts of blood. Kealey was still squeezing the trigger, swearing and screaming all at once, but nothing was happening. He dropped the mag and reached for another, slamming it in, racking the slide. The movements were like second nature: mechanical, yet strangely fluid. Despite the speed with which he'd reloaded, precious seconds had been wasted, time which Vanderveen had used to continue his grisly work. Kealey leveled the gun, but the moment was gone. He'd been running forward and was now just 30 feet from the struggling pair. He moved to the right, looking for a shot.

Naomi screamed in agony as the blade crossed under her ear, nicking her jawbone before sliding up to her right cheek. She felt the razor edge cutting deep as it moved over her skin, angling up to her cheekbone. Rationally, she knew what was happening, but her mind was somehow detached, unwilling to accept what was taking place. She couldn't focus on anything but the searing, ripping, mind-bending *pain*; everything she knew was mired in feeling. If she'd been able to hear, her whole world would have been noise: the few people still in the area screaming in horrified disbelief, Ryan's shots and screams carrying over the din, and the sound of fast-approaching sirens covering everything. But since she couldn't hear, she could only feel: the hot blood streaming down the side of her neck, the hooked tip of the knife caught under her cheekbone, Vanderveen's wrenching attempts to pull it free. She felt his body jerk once behind her as Kealey's second round found its target, but Vanderveen was still holding the knife, still trying to get it up to her eye, so she knew he had not suffered a disabling wound.

Her hands, still cuffed, had jerked up the second she felt the knife begin to penetrate. She was grabbing his wrists, trying to pull them down and away, but part of her mind—the small part that hadn't shut down completely—was telling her that if she succeeded, the knife would come down along with his hands, and then he'd be able to cut her again.

She wriggled frantically, trying to pull away, but it just wasn't working. Then she tried to drop down to the pavement, but he seemed to expect it, and his left arm only tightened around her throat, cutting off the last of her breath. Her throat was clogged with blood, her vision blurring. She felt herself start to weaken, to give up the fight. He was just too strong. Way too strong . . . stronger than she would have believed. Finally, he managed to pull the knife out of her face, and she braced herself, waiting for the final, fatal cut.

It had taken Joe Ruggeri a little under 2 minutes to run the full length of six city blocks. Amazingly, he had yet to see any units respond, even though he'd called it in when he was still back on West Fifty-Fourth. There had been two more shots just a few seconds earlier, and the screams were impossibly loud as he crossed Forty-ninth. Suddenly, everything seemed clear; he could spot the back of the overturned truck and two men; one was lying on the ground, his hands wrapped round his throat. The other was 20 feet north of the truck, moving to his right—Ruggeri's left—his hands wrapped round the grip of a semiautomatic pistol. His eyes were wide, and he appeared to be shouting at someone that Ruggeri couldn't see.

Traffic had come to a complete halt on Seventh. Everyone north of Fifty-first was still honking angrily, but the motorists farther south—those to his immediate left—could tell that something was wrong. Some had abandoned their vehicles entirely, while others were standing in the middle of the street, watching from a distance, eyes wide. Ruggeri ran out to the middle of the street, keeping low behind a series of cars. He looked up over the hood of a yellow RAV4, took in the scene, then ducked down again, his gun in two hands between his knees.

The brief glimpse had given him a new piece of the puzzle: a man holding a woman hostage. Ruggeri had seen blood, which meant that he had to act immediately, but he was still too winded from the long sprint to trust his aim. From the angle, it was clear that the other man with the gun—the one near the truck—didn't have a shot, but Ruggeri did. He had a clear line of sight on the hostage taker's head, and he planned to use it.

Taking a deep breath, he stood up, leaned over the hood of the RAV4 for support, and took aim. Then he squeezed the trigger.

Vanderveen didn't know how he'd managed to hold on to the knife after Kealey's second round found its target. Looking down at his right arm, he could see he was badly injured, though the pain had yet to set in. The entire sleeve of his jacket was soaked in blood, and his grip on the knife was rapidly starting to slip. The wound in his neck was not as accommodating. It was becoming increasingly difficult to breathe, though it didn't feel as if the bullet had penetrated his airway. He was surprised to find he no longer cared; all that mattered now was finishing the woman.

She was struggling hard, and the knife was locked in somehow, jammed into her cheekbone or maybe hooked underneath. He couldn't tell, and the second he tried to look, he would expose himself to a fatal barrage. He focused on keeping her upright and in front of his body as he worked the knife loose, ignoring her blood-choked screams. Finally, the knife came free, and he moved it down and around to her throat. Sensing his intentions, she tried to tuck down her chin. He tried to pull her head back and reached around farther, aware of another shot. This one pierced his arm in almost exactly the same place as the first, and this time, the pain was so intense, the knife slipped from his grasp. He screamed in agony just as another round scorched into the left side of his neck. He was thrown against the Mercury, where he bounced off the front fender before dropping to the pavement.

Owing to the angle of the car, he was momentarily blocked from Kealey's view. Realizing this, he took the opportunity to reach into his coat with his left hand, finding the butt of his Glock 19. He pulled it out slowly, painfully, aware of the woman stumbling away, dripping blood all over the pavement. He raised the gun, aiming for her back, then changed his mind. For some reason, he couldn't bring himself to pull the trigger. He would have laughed if he'd still been able to speak; he was willing to cut her to ribbons, but the idea of finishing his work no longer held any appeal. How strange. He tried to breathe but only succeeded in sucking blood into his airway. Incredibly, it was all over. For a fleeting instant, he wondered if he could set off the BLU-82 by firing through the roof of the box but realized it wouldn't work, not at this range. Still, he could try. . . .

Or he could shoot Kealey.

It was a difficult choice to make, and he didn't have long. The other man was probably less than 10 feet away, circling to his position. While he would have much preferred to destroy every building in the vicinity by detonating the bomb, his mind, working through the pain and the absence of air, told him this was all but impossible. And that left him with just one choice.

Unable to use his right arm, he moved his legs round and under his body. He got to his knees, careful to keep his head below the line of the hood. It was difficult to get a feel for the gun in his left hand, and the darkness was already creeping in. If he was going to act, it had to be soon. Normally, it would be occasion enough for a deep, calming breath, but he was past that now.

He was past everything.

Kealey was running forward, crossing the last 30 feet as fast as he could. He was torn between finishing Vanderveen and helping Naomi. He saw her stumble away from the Mercury, hands pressed to her face. Blood was streaming down from between her fingers. As she made it to the first line of cars at the light on Forty-eighth, a few people rushed out from behind their vehicles to pull her to safety. The sight should have relieved some of his anxiety, but he wasn't sure if Vanderveen had managed to get to her throat with the knife. If he had, there was almost no chance she'd survive. He wanted nothing more than to go to her, but he couldn't seem to stop moving toward the car. Vanderveen had taken so much from him, and now it looked as if he'd taken Naomi, too.

The thought of losing her was unbearable, but he tried to push it out of his mind, knowing he had to finish what he had started. He knew he'd managed to hit Vanderveen a second time in the same arm, but it looked like the man to his right had fired the fatal wound. Kealey could see him screaming something about dropping the weapon, but he wasn't about to comply. He was driven forward by a burning desire to inflict on Vanderveen what the other man had inflicted on so many others—namely, a great deal of pain, followed by an appalling death.

He was rounding the car, gun up, ready to finish it. Just as he moved into position for the shot, Vanderveen stood up and leveled his weapon. Thrown off by the sudden, unexpected movement, Kealey's first shot went wide, missing the other man's head by an inch. Vanderveen fired at the same time, and Kealey felt something punch into his left arm, just above the elbow. He fired again, and this time he found his target. A pink cloud exploded like a halo around Vanderveen's head, blossoming into the cool air, just as the man near the RAV4 fired several rounds of his own into the falling body. Vanderveen twisted to the right, bounced off the front of the Mercury, and hit the ground. He didn't move again.

Kealey kept moving forward. Intellectually, he knew that the man was dead, but some part of him didn't register that fact. He fired round after round until his gun was empty, and even then he kept squeezing the trigger, aware that he was shouting at the top of his lungs, but unaware of what he was saying. It didn't seem to matter anymore. Will Vanderveen was gone, but there was nothing to celebrate. Kealey would have given anything to turn back the clock just a few minutes; he would have let the man live forever if it meant keeping Naomi out of harm's way. Unfortunately, it was too late for that now.

It was too late for a lot of things.

A sudden movement to his right caught his attention. Kealey turned to see that the man had moved away from the RAV4 and was now pointing a gun at his chest, saying something and waving his free arm in a downward motion. Kealey couldn't seem to hear the words for some reason, but he understood that he was being told to lose the weapon and get on the ground. He considered this request from a distance, thought about complying, then decided against it. He was starting to feel dizzy, his limbs turning to water. Looking down, he saw that the blood was rapidly spreading around the wound in his left arm; in fact, it was spreading at an alarming rate. He realized that Vanderveen's final round had severed his brachial artery. The wound was starting to throb, but just as the pain settled in, everything else went away.

He felt himself start to fall, tumbling into a black void.

And then there was nothing.

CHAPTER 57

LOUDOUN COUNTY, VIRGINIA

From all outward appearances, the eighteenth-century, three-story manor house at the base of the Blue Ridge Mountains was just another site of modest historical merit, no different from the many similar properties scattered throughout the Virginia countryside. No Monticello, this, but a pleasant environment nonetheless, the kind of place that, in other circumstances, might play host to fourth graders on field trips or families in search of a cheap, educational day in the country. Such visits, however, had never transpired, nor would they, for despite its unspectacular history, Windrush Manor was much more than it seemed.

First constructed in 1770 by William Fitzhugh, an American planter and delegate to the Continental Congress in 1779, the house was willed to Fitzhugh's cousin by letter in 1825, along with 100 acres comprising the grounds. The property was then handed down through a succession of sons and daughters until 1976, when it was quietly purchased by an outside party: Richard Helms, the former director of Central Intelligence. Over the next few years, extensive modifications were made to the building's interior. Then, in 1979, the government signed a fifty-year lease on the property. Although tax records indicated otherwise, Helms never received—nor requested—financial compensation of any kind. When Helms passed away in 2002, the property was willed to a like-minded, closemouthed supporter of the intelligence community, and everything continued as normal.

Since 1979, Windrush Manor had been a place for U.S. intelligence officers injured in the line of duty to convalesce, a place so secret that listing it with the Virginia Historical Society or a similar institution was no longer possible, for the property was no longer known to anyone who might conceive of doing so. Nestled deep within the Virginia Piedmont, Windrush was accessible only by a single service road. Wayward motorists occasionally found their way to the main gate, but when they did, they saw nothing that might give them cause for alarm, just a pair of watchful security guards, the kind of minimal protection often employed by wealthy, reclusive private citizens. The security was designed to be effective, but not obtrusive. The various electronic countermeasures scattered throughout the surrounding forest were just as efficient, and just as invisible. In short, Windrush was the kind of place that the U.S. government would never admit to knowing about, simply because it would never be forced to.

It was just after 1:00 PM when a black GMC Yukon rolled up to the service entrance just off US 421. The window came down with a whisper, and the driver produced his Agency credentials. The guards were not alarmed in the least, as this particular visitor was himself a recently discharged patient. He had left the manor two weeks earlier, but had visited every day since. Used to seeing his face, the guards would have preferred to let him pass without delay, but rules were rules. They called up to the small command post in the house, where another officer turned away from his microwaved lasagna and checked the list. Approval was given, and the driver was waved through.

The Yukon rose and fell over a series of gentle hills, the engine's low rumble breaking the afternoon quiet, tires hissing on the damp, black ribbon road. The oak and hickory trees passing by were skeletal and absent of color, their bark stripped bare by foraging deer. After several miles the trees broke and the house appeared. The Yukon turned off the main road, the tires crunching on gravel as it rolled to a stop, the engine shutting off. Then the door swung open and Ryan Kealey stepped out, dressed in jeans, a black roll-neck sweater, and a corduroy barn jacket.

He took a moment to look around, breathing in the cold air, appraising the low gray clouds that scudded along the wintry sky. It was the first week of November, and a heavy snow had fallen two days earlier, freezing the millpond and blanketing the ground with a layer of clean white powder. The manor house, with its whitewashed field-stone walls, almost looked like an extension of the ground, save for the wood shingle roof. Smoke curled out of the twin stone chimneys, the gray haze drifting east on a cold, steady breeze.

Kealey walked up the path to the banded oak door, aware of a black Suburban sitting off to his right. The engine was running, along with the heater, he guessed. He couldn't see through the tinted windows, but as he moved forward, he shot a quick glance through the windshield. He was surprised to see a man he recognized. It was Harper's longtime driver, apparently recovered from his bout with the flu. There didn't appear to be anyone else in the vehicle, and looking around, he saw no sign of the other man. Kealey decided he was probably inside.

He knocked on the door and was admitted by Jean Everett, the head nurse. Everett was in her early forties, with blond hair going to gray and a kind, careworn face. She smiled at him and held out her arms for the flowers he was carrying. It had become a kind of daily ritual; she would accept the flowers he brought, find a vase and some water, then send him away with a gentle apology and a plea for a little more time. Kealey knew she did not bring the flowers upstairs until he was gone, as she didn't want to give him the chance to explore the house. It was not a subtle gesture, but he couldn't despise her for it; he knew she was just looking out for her patient.

"How is she?" he asked. It was another part of their ritual, and he received the expected response.

"Getting better. Healing." She smiled again, but there was a trace of sadness there. He couldn't be sure, but he thought this woman had lobbied on his behalf. "She's eating a little bit more, which is a good thing. She went outside yesterday after you left, and I think that helped."

"I'm glad," Kealey said. There was the habitual awkward pause. "Will she see me?"

Everett shook her head sadly, just as she'd done every day for the past month. "She can't, Ryan. She's just not ready."

Kealey looked away, struggling to hide his disappointment, but the nurse stepped close and put a comforting hand on his arm.

"It'll happen. Just give her time."

Kealey nodded. When he turned back, his face was set. "As much as she needs."

A noise to his right caught his attention. He looked over, hope springing up, but it was just Jonathan Harper. He'd come out through the kitchen and was holding two steaming Styrofoam cups. He held one out and said, "I heard the gatehouse on the radio, so don't start thinking I'm telepathic. I thought we might go for a walk."

Kealey looked out the window. It was about to snow again, but that was fine; he needed the air. "Sure. Let's go."

They went out and turned right, crossing the grounds toward the pond, moving at a slow, deliberate pace. The gristmill was off to the right, the wooden walls covered in lichen, sagging with time and lack of maintenance. The waterwheel was half frozen in the surface of the pond. They crossed the narrow trestle bridge, heading for the gravel footpath on the other side.

"When did you get here?" Kealey finally asked.

"Just a few minutes before you did," Harper replied. He hesitated, wondering what Kealey was thinking. It was the first time he had come to Windrush since the start of October, and he knew how that must look to the younger man. He hurried to change the subject.

"How's the arm?"

Kealey looked down at his left arm, which was still in a white sling. "Not bad. They fixed it up pretty quick."

"That's bullshit, Ryan. I talked to the paramedics, as well as the doctors. I know you almost bled out on the way to the hospital, so don't try to play it down."

"Yeah, well . . ." Kealey looked away. "What happened to me was nothing, really. Not when you think about it."

The unspoken thought seemed to cloud the air between them, but neither felt up to discussing it. They walked for a time, drinking their coffee, talking around the subject of Naomi. Most of what they went over had already cropped up over the past month, but so much had happened, it was helpful to go back and check the facts.

When the white Isuzu truck outside the Renaissance Hotel in Midtown Manhattan was finally opened by the NYPD's Emergency Service Unit two hours after it tipped over, the contents generated an enormous amount of press coverage. Predictably, the news was followed by public outrage, and Will Vanderveen—even in death—quickly became the focus of an intense media storm. The former U.S. soldier was depicted as a psychopath and a terrorist-for-hire, but those were just two of the less-than-inventive titles bestowed upon him by Western media, none of which were complimentary.

Following the events of September 16th, it seemed as if his face was everywhere. Official U.S. Army photographs acquired through dubious means had appeared on the cover of *Newsweek* and *Time*. Indirectly, the latter image stirred up a storm of controversy, as it depicted Vanderveen standing outside a hangar in Somalia in 1993, deep in discussion with Major General William F. Garrison.

The networks immediately jumped on the opportunity to boost ratings and began speculating that Vanderveen might have deliberately warned the Somali militia of the impending raid in which 18 U.S. soldiers were killed, later known as the Battle of Mogadishu. Before long, the theory evolved into something approaching fact, despite the absence of any supporting evidence beyond the grainy photograph, which wasn't really evidence at all, except in the world of sensationalist journalism.

There was no limit to the coverage, or to America's rabid fascination with the man who had turned against his own. Vanderveen was the subject of an MSNBC investigative report as well as a CNN in-depth special, which aired during prime time. A hastily composed biography had hit the bookstores a week ago and was already topping the best-seller lists. Everyone wanted to know about the Special Forces soldier who'd betrayed his country, lending his skills to some of America's worst enemies, with the goal of destroying thousands of innocent lives. His infamy was only enhanced when it became clear that the bomb he had brought into the country would have wreaked devastation on a scale rivaling 9/11, had Nazeri been allowed to reach his target. Strangely enough, Amir Nazeri was hardly mentioned in the ensuing media storm; Vanderveen alone seemed to have captured the nation's attention.

Harper had done his best to keep Kealey's name out of the whole thing, but it had proved impossible; the two former soldiers had too much shared history, and there was no avoiding it. Even so, the situation would have been tenable were it not for a lengthy article that appeared in the *New York Times* less than a week after the failed attack. The article contained information that could only have been leaked through an Agency source, and while the *Times* reporter had refused to divulge his source—resulting in another Valerie Plame–like incident—it had been clear to everyone who mattered—Kealey included—that the leak could only have come from one person.

It had been clear to the president as well. Rachel Ford had ample motive. It was well known that she'd despised the entire operations directorate to begin with. Beyond that, however, she'd made it clear that she didn't buy the official record of what had transpired in the warehouse on West Thirty-seventh Street. The Bureau's internal investigation had determined that Special Agent Matt Foster had killed his partner, Samantha Crane, before being shot to death himself by Naomi Kharmai. The Bureau would have preferred to avoid the tarnishing link to Vanderveen, but there were just too many fingers pointing toward Foster. Kealey, for one, had demanded that the Bureau come clean, and in the end, he'd gotten his wish.

Ford had instantly started screaming about a cover-up, accusing Kealey of involvement in her niece's death. A few people listened at first, but she lost any support she had when she leaked Kealey's personnel file to the press. Even before that, Hakim Rudaki had been making noises about where Foster was getting his information—namely, from Samantha Crane—and that could only mean one thing: that Ford was involved, at least on the periphery. The president had quietly offered her a choice. She could either endure some painful and very public inquiries, or she could quietly resign her post. In the end, the choice had been easy to make.

Less than a week after the president accepted her resignation, he'd submitted Jonathan Harper's name for the vacant post. The Senate had yet to confirm the nomination, but word had trickled down that Harper was a lock for the job. His skillful handling of the crisis had ensured he would sail through the confirmation process, but there was something infinitely more important at work, and that was the fact that no one else had seen it coming. Had it not been for the work of Harper, Kealey, and Naomi Kharmai, the attack would have easily succeeded, with disastrous consequences. In essence, giving Harper a promotion—with the implied promise of an eventual nomination to the top job—had been the best way for the president to defuse a more thorough investigation into his own personal handling of the entire situation, which was sorely lacking.

Ironically, David Brenneman had gotten the most mileage out of the incident, even though he'd done nothing but stand in their way since the embassy break-in. The plot had failed, and that automatically worked in his favor, but when it became clear that the bomb was meant primarily for the thirty-five members of the United Iraqi Alliance staying at the Renaissance Hotel, Brenneman received some of the credit for preventing—at least indirectly—what might have been a disastrous setback in Iraq. His political advisors milked the story for all it was worth, pointing out that the loss of the UIA's core leadership would likely have led to civil war, resulting in the deaths of hundreds of U.S. soldiers before a suitable plan for withdrawal could be put into effect.

The political spin made Kealey sick; the troops wouldn't even be there without the president's approval, and suddenly he was being portrayed as their guardian, the man watching out for them. But he knew voicing this opinion wouldn't get him anywhere, so he kept his mouth shut. He doubted whether the president would care what he thought, anyway, as Brenneman had won reelection the previous day, with a staggering 58 percent of the popular vote, defeating Democratic governor Richard Fiske in a landslide.

In the meantime, the insurgent activity in Iraq had returned to normal levels, aided in part by public appeals for peace by leading Shiite and Sunni clerics, including Ayatollah Ali al-Sistani, easily the most revered religious leader in the region. The U.S. commanders had done their part to restore the status quo, which was about the best they could hope for.

As they walked, Harper brought Kealey up to speed on the most recent news. First, he mentioned the ongoing hunt for Vanderveen's traveling companion, the woman inadvertently photographed by

MI5 in London. Since that single sighting, she had disappeared without a trace. The Agency still had no idea who she was, and although the surveillance shots had been distributed to a number of friendly security services, no one was holding out much hope for her capture. Kealey didn't speak as Harper relayed this information, but privately, he sided with the majority: the woman would probably never be found. The Agency just didn't have enough background information to conduct an efficient search, and a few distant photographs were not enough to build on. Out of all the collaborators, it looked as if one had walked away clean. While this wasn't really acceptable, Kealey knew there wasn't much they could do to resolve the situation; the woman had simply covered her tracks too well.

Moving on, Harper laid out the specifics of Operation Clean Sweep, a massive endeavor involving 1,400 U.S. soldiers, including units from 10th Mountain, the 75th Ranger Regiment, and the 82nd Airborne. Clean Sweep was primarily geared toward cross-border raids into Syria in search of arms caches, and the operation had proved wildly successful. More than thirty tons of small arms had been seized, then transported back to Iraq, where they were either stored or destroyed. The joint U.S.-Iraqi forces seemed to have regained dominance on the ground, but there was still the question of Hakim Rudaki and his cousin, Reza Bagheri.

"So the Bureau's done with him?" Kealey asked.

Harper nodded. "As far as they're concerned, everything that came out of Rudaki's mouth was a lie. They've washed their hands of it . . . or at least, they've tried to. This has really hurt their reputation, especially since it wasn't that long ago that they had to deal with Hanssen and all the damage he did."

"What do you think?"

"I think Rudaki might have given us some truth, if only by accident."

"Because of his cousin," Kealey said.

"Exactly. The defense minister was supposedly passing us info because he was unhappy with the regime's attempts to disrupt U.S. policy in Iraq by killing Tabrizi and the prime minister. Of course, it wasn't true; Iran was never involved. But if Bagheri had nothing to do with it, why would Rudaki bring him up to begin with?"

"He needed a cover for the lies he was selling us," Kealey pointed out. "Maybe the cousin was just the most convenient excuse."

"Maybe," Harper muttered. "We're still talking to him. I think Bagheri might know a lot more than he's letting on, so we're looking for leverage. If anything comes of it, I'll let you know. The question is, would you want to be involved?"

Kealey looked over. "Is that what you came here to ask me?"

"No, because that would imply a temporary role." The other man paused. "Look, I want you back in the fold. What's it going to take to get you back to Langley?"

Kealey brushed some snow off the wooden railing, watching absently as it drifted down to the frozen surface of the pond. "John, it's a possibility. I want to come back, I think, but for now, my place is here."

"She won't see you, Ryan. She probably won't want to see you for a very long time."

"Then I'll wait," Kealey said simply. "As long as it takes."

Harper thought about saying something but decided against it. He nodded slowly, his gaze drifting over to the manor house and the black government SUVs parked nearby. "Okay. I understand. When you're ready, give me a call."

Kealey nodded. Their eyes met, and they shook hands firmly. "Have a safe trip. Say hi to Julie for me."

"Will do."

Kealey watched him go, but before long, his gaze drifted back to the house. For a brief instant, he thought he saw a face swathed in bandages at one of the third-story windows, but then it was gone.

He stayed that way for a long time, staring out at the frozen pond, just thinking about things. What he had said was the plain truth, but he knew Harper didn't really understand. Kealey would stay in town and drive out here every day forever if that was what it took. He wasn't sure how Naomi had come to mean so much to him in so short a time, but he couldn't deny his feelings. All he wanted was to see her again. There were things he wanted to say, of course, but mostly, he just wanted to see her. He thought he'd give anything to see her.

By the time he turned and finished crossing the bridge, a light snow had started to fall. He had almost reached his truck when the heavy oak door cracked open behind him. He turned instantly at the sound.

It was Everett, and she seemed relieved to have caught him. "She's changed her mind, Ryan. I think she was just waiting for Mr. Harper to go. She'll see you now."

CHAPTER 58

LOUDOUN COUNTY, VIRGINIA

Kealey followed her up the narrow staircase. They continued past the second floor, up to the third. When the house was first built, the top floor had been used as a storage area for commercial goods, but since the extensive renovation in the mid-1970s, the open space had been divided into four large rooms separated by a single hall, each with its own private bathroom. As he followed her down the corridor, he was distinctly aware of a growing unease; Naomi had finally agreed to see him, but he had no idea what to expect.

He wondered if she hated him, if she blamed him for not taking the shot before Vanderveen could cut her. It was a distinct possibility, he knew, though the thought was almost too painful to bear. From her point of view, it must have seemed so simple. He had a gun; Vanderveen had a knife. She couldn't know that Vanderveen had given him no target, that he'd done everything possible to keep her body between them. Nor could he have explained it to her, at least not to any purpose. It would have sounded like an excuse, nothing more.

The hall ran the length of the building. They were halfway down when Everett stopped and turned to face him. It seemed as though her genial nature was relegated to the ground floors; up here, she was a much harder person. He watched as she adopted a serious, clinical expression, and knew at once that she was about to relay unwanted information.

"Ryan, before you go in, I want to make you aware of a few things. I know you've expressed no interest in her specific injuries, but—"

"It's not that I don't have an interest," he said. His voice was low but firm; he wanted to be clear on this. "It's just that I'm here for her no matter what. I don't see that knowing the specifics makes a difference."

"I understand, and I can appreciate your point. But I think you need to know."

Kealey took a deep breath. "Okay."

"Nearly all the damage is superficial. She was extremely fortunate in that respect. The knife missed the cervical branch of the facial nerve, but the wound to the cheek was very deep. There was no damage to the parotid gland, but there *was* some damage to the zygomatic muscles, both major and minor, as well as the buccal branch of the—"

"I don't know what any of that means," Kealey said, trying to push down his rising fear. "How bad is it? Just tell me that."

The head nurse blew out a short breath. "All of the muscle damage has been repaired. Her recovery should be in the ninetieth percentile, maybe higher. She's already made amazing progress. The buccal branch of the facial nerve—that controls movement of the mouth and nose—was partially severed, but the sutures held, and the prognosis is good . . . extremely good, in fact. The nerve damage is almost certainly temporary, but her speech is still a little off, so be prepared for that." Everett broke off, gathering her next words. "Most of all, it's just a very . . . traumatic injury. The way it happened, I mean. She's been having nightmares, insomnia, loss of appetite, things of that nature. And of course, the injury is to the face, so . . ."

"So what?"

"Well, she was a beautiful woman," Everett said uneasily, as if that explained everything.

"She still is."

Everett nodded slowly; Kealey's tone was tight and insistent, and she knew better than to argue. "I probably shouldn't be telling you this, but I have the feeling she's very nervous about seeing you. Or rather, nervous about you seeing her. I hope you can handle it."

He stared at her until she looked away.

"Sorry," she started. "I—"

"It's okay. Can I go in now?"

She nodded. "The door's open, but she needs to rest. You can have thirty minutes, but that's it. You can see her again tomorrow if she's up to it."

Everett turned and walked back down the hall. A second later he heard her feet on the stairs. Kealey put a hand on the door and took another deep breath. He thought about knocking, then realized that she might not want to raise her voice or even talk at all. In the end, he just tapped lightly and pushed inside.

The room was half in shadow, the curtains pulled back. Kealey could see snow drifting past the large windows overlooking the pond. The walls were the color of clotted cream, the furnishings simple enough: a large bed with a thick lavender comforter, an armchair and a couch against one wall, antique bookshelves against the other. There was also a small TV and a number of end tables scattered over the rough oak floor. Every spare surface was covered with floral arrangements in all manner of vases.

She was standing at one of the windows, facing away from him. Her clothing was basic and warm: a brown velour hoodie over a navy T-shirt, flannel pajama bottoms, and thick woolen socks. She didn't move when he closed the door behind him, but he saw her shoulders tense and knew at once that she was trying to summon the courage to turn around. This realization filled him with a bitterness he had never known; it felt as though nothing was right with the world, that she should be afraid to face him.

"Naomi?"

She finally turned, her eyes downcast. The entire right side of her face was covered in a clean white bandage. The wound itself wasn't visible, but even so, she looked incredibly different. Her face was gaunt, dark shadows under her pained eyes. It was immediately clear that she'd been suffering from much more than the physical injury, and Kealey knew why: the death of Samantha Crane—and to a lesser extent, Matt Foster—must have been weighing her down for weeks.

"Hi." She gestured at the vases that filled the room and tried to smile. "Thanks for the flowers. You might not have brought so many, though. It's starting to look like a funeral parlor in here, and that's an association I could do without."

He nodded slowly, aware she was joking, but unable to laugh. He took note of her speech. It wasn't as bad as Everett had led him to believe. In fact, he could hardly notice the difference at all. Suddenly, he was at a loss for words. What was he supposed to say in this situation? What kind of comfort could he possibly offer?

He started to walk over, but she seemed to retreat, putting her back to the window. He stopped, unsure of her reaction. "Naomi, I want to be here," he began slowly, "but if you need more time, I can—"

"What do you mean?" she asked. She was trying to keep her voice bright, but it wasn't working. "I'm fine. I would have seen you sooner, but I didn't want to scare you off with the swelling. For a while there, it kind of looked like I had two heads." She tried to laugh, but it didn't sound right at all. "How's your arm? Looks better, anyway."

He shook his head. "Forget the arm. Listen, you don't have to—"

"Ryan, I'm okay, I swear." But her smile was starting to slip. "I saw you walking outside," she said quickly, desperately. "Is it really cold? I heard on the news it's supposed to snow all night."

"Don't do this," he said softly, shaking his head. "Please don't do this. Talk to me."

"I *am* talking. I just . . ."

She tried to hold on, but it couldn't last, and she had pushed it down for too long already. Even from across the room, he could see her lower lip was starting to tremble, one hand tightly gripping the other. Then the façade gave way completely. She started to cry softly, and he closed the space between them quickly, putting his arms around her, pulling her close. Before long she was sobbing hard, hiccupping when she ran out of air, her hot tears dripping onto his sweater, soaking through to his skin. He felt a lump in his throat rising, but he pushed down his own emotions. He knew he had to be strong for her. He had already failed her twice: once with Crane and again with Vanderveen. He hated himself for it, but there was nothing he could do about that now. He only knew one thing for sure: that he would do whatever he could to make it up to her.

After about ten minutes, she pulled away and sat on the bed, her shoulders slumping. He joined her and took hold of her left hand, just waiting, letting her get control. When she finally spoke, her voice was exhausted and barely audible.

"I haven't slept in days," she mumbled. The emotional outburst had left her utterly drained. "He's there every time I close my eyes. And if it's not him, it's Crane. In some ways, she's worse. She doesn't say anything, but she doesn't have to. I know how much she hates me, Ryan. I took away everything she had, her whole life, and now I just—"

"Stop," he said quietly. "Don't do this to yourself." He pulled her close as the tears started up again, rubbing her back gently with his good arm. He knew she needed to get it out, but it was hard to listen to her talk as if these people were still alive in some kind of abstract reality, just waiting for her to fall asleep so they could continue tormenting her. He couldn't help but wonder if she would ever really recover from what had happened. The thought that she might have to live this way forever filled him with a sense of numbing despair, but at the same time, he knew he would never give up on her. He would do everything in his power to help her through it.

But only if she wanted him to. Once again, he wondered how much she blamed him for what had happened, and while it felt selfish to ask, he had to know. If being there caused her more pain than she was already feeling, he didn't want to stay.

She shook her head when he posed the question, but refused to meet his eyes. "I think I hated you for a little while," she admitted softly. "But not anymore, and I didn't really mean it to begin with. I know you would have stopped it if you could have."

"I should never have left you in the building," he said bitterly. "If I'd just—"

"Don't say that," she said. "It just worked out badly. You didn't make me leave the field office with Foster, and you couldn't have known that Vanderveen was waiting outside the warehouse. It wasn't your fault."

He nodded, not really believing her. He tried to shrug off his feelings, knowing it wasn't the time for self-pity. This wasn't about him, after all, and there was something important he needed to ask her. He hesitated, unsure if this was the right time, but it couldn't wait.

"Naomi, they're going to be releasing you in a week or so. I want you to come back to Maine with me. To Cape Elizabeth."

She didn't look up, but he felt her body tense. "Isn't that where . . . ?"

"Yes." Katie Donovan had died in the house on Cape Elizabeth nearly a year earlier. He hadn't been back since.

"Can you go there?"

She didn't expand on this, but he knew exactly what she was asking.

"I couldn't before," he said. "But I can now, I think. As long as you're by my side."

She looked up, and he went on. "Naomi, I want to take care of you. I want to help you through this, and I want to see you strong again." He hesitated, then said what he really meant. "But mostly, I just want you. For as long as you'll have me."

What happened next surprised him, though it probably shouldn't have. She pulled away, got to her feet, and walked back to the window. He stood up, confused.

"You don't mean that," she said, bitter regret creeping into her voice. "You can't possibly mean that. Not anymore, so don't pretend otherwise."

"What are you talking about?"

She spun around angrily, her eyes filling with tears. "You know exactly what I'm talking about."

He suddenly understood what she meant, but it left him in a difficult position, as he couldn't address it directly. There was almost nothing he could say that wouldn't hurt her feelings in one way or another. After thinking for a moment, he walked over and took her hand. She didn't try to pull away, but she wouldn't face him, either. "Naomi, look at me."

When she finally lifted her gaze, he didn't speak. Instead, he simply leaned down and kissed her. When he pulled away a minute later, a small smile appeared on her face. It was tiny and fleeting, but it was all he needed to see: a real smile, completely impulsive, not forced in the least. The reason for the kiss was simple and twofold: first, he had wanted it for weeks, and second, he felt the need to remind her of how beautiful she was. In truth, though, his feelings for her ran far deeper than she could have known, certainly much deeper than physical attraction. She was an incredible woman, and he'd take her any way he could get her. It was that simple.

"Are you sure about this?" she asked in a small voice. "I don't want you to feel that you have to do it out of guilt or because you feel sorry for me."

"Don't say that. You know it's not true." Very carefully, he touched the bandage on her face, selecting a spot that he knew wouldn't hurt her. "This will heal, Naomi. It's just skin-deep." He moved his hand down and lightly placed it over her heart. "I'm more worried about the wounds in here, but they will heal as well. You'll see. It just takes time."

The tears started again, and he pulled her close, stroking the back of her hair, murmuring all the right words, or at least trying to. He held her until she had cried herself out. Then he eased her over to the bed, sat next to her, and held her hand until her breathing assumed the soft rhythm of sleep. By the time Everett knocked on the door, Naomi was gone to the world. For now, at least, it seemed the dreams had released her from their terrible grasp. Kealey wished he could take comfort from her peaceful repose, but couldn't bring himself to do it. He knew all too well that the dreams would eventually creep back.

In the end, they always did.

CHAPTER 59
AL ANBAR PROVINCE, IRAQ

The Palestine Hotel, a squat, square building devoid of both character and charm, sits on the eastern edge of the town of al-Qaim, 200 miles northwest of Baghdad, less than 2 miles east of the border with Syria. In April of 2005, the town was the scene of intense fighting between Sunni insurgents and the 3rd Armored Cavalry Regiment, along with four other towns on the Syrian border. Al-Qaim, however, stood out in that particular group, as it was thought to be the temporary headquarters of Abu Musab al-Zarqawi. Ultimately, al-Zarqawi eluded capture, only to be killed little more than a year later in a safe house north of Baqubah, but the U.S. forces remained and established Camp al-Qaim on the city outskirts. The camp was now home to the 3rd Battalion of the 6th Marine Regiment, but while the gate was less than a mile from the Palestine Hotel, Ryan Kealey had no intention of visiting. He had everything he needed where he was, and in any event, he didn't plan on staying long.

He was sitting in a small courtyard to the rear of the hotel, his green plastic chair resting on two legs against the stucco exterior wall, a paper cup of weak lemonade in his right hand. He tilted his head back to the sky, searching in vain for a breeze. The temperature was 90 degrees Fahrenheit, cold for November, but not after the snow he'd left behind in the Blue Ridge Mountains. Propped up against the wall next to him was a well-worn AK-47 with a single 30-round magazine. The courtyard was enclosed with yellow walls of stone and mortar and topped with concertina wire, all of which had been strung by the building's occupants. On top of the flat roof was a guard shack surrounded by sandbags, manned by two men with scoped rifles.

Inside the building, however, lay the real security: an entire 12-man detachment of U.S. Special Forces operators, all of whom belonged to the 5th Group out of Fort Campbell, Kentucky. Six of the men were currently dressed as Iraqi soldiers, as was Kealey. The fatigues were almost identical to those worn by U.S. forces. In fact, the Iraqi Army's battle dress uniforms were supplied by the Department of Defense. Only the rank structure was different, but that had been factored in, and all the uniforms had been carefully checked for authenticity. Kealey knew it was all relative; despite his dark features and black hair, the only way he would pass as an Arab was at a distance. For today's work, that would suffice.

He had arrived in-country the day before, having spent most of the past week in Maine, preparing the house on Cape Elizabeth for Naomi's arrival. He had found a simple pleasure in shopping for her, doing the small things in advance that might make her life a little bit easier. He'd gone so far as to set up a room entirely for her and her alone, complete with a queen-size bed and comfortable furnishings. While he hoped their relationship would continue to move forward, he knew she needed time and space to herself: time to recuperate and time to move past what had happened to her, as well as what she had done. Harper had asked them both to come back to the Agency, offering Naomi a considerable promotion, but both had refused. Naomi just wasn't ready to even consider it, and Kealey wanted to devote himself entirely to her recovery. In fact, he wouldn't be in Iraq at all if it wasn't for the Agency's work in breaking Hakim Rudaki, the supposed Bureau informant.

Once the FBI leadership had washed its hands of Rudaki, the Agency had stepped in to take over. It had been made clear to the naturalized Iranian that failure to cooperate would result in severe consequences, none of which would end with deportation. The meaning of this statement could not have been plainer, and Rudaki hurried to appease his new group of handlers. In the end, his contribution was largely limited to putting the Agency in direct contact with his cousin, the Syrian defense minister.

Unfortunately, this was where the Agency lost the advantage. There was simply no proof that Reza Bagheri had anything to do with the attempted assassination of the Iraqi prime minister, Nuri al-Maliki. Nor did he appear to have any connections to the Iranian dissidents who'd claimed the life of Dr. Nasir Tabrizi in Paris. When Kealey mentioned the ongoing investigation to Naomi at Windrush, she absently suggested a possible link between Bagheri and the Iranian conglomerate that had purchased Rashid al-Umari's refinery near Samawah. It had seemed like a good possibility, but even that failed to turn up any evidence of wrongdoing. In short, the Agency couldn't prove that Bagheri was anything but who he claimed to be, so the man in charge of negotiations, the recently confirmed deputy DCI, had been forced to deal.

The first goal, of course, was to determine whether Bagheri had useful information to begin with. It soon became clear that he did, and his innocence was quickly cast aside when he requested personal immunity from U.S. reprisal in addition to a large deposit in an offshore account. Harper had agreed readily, eager to put the matter to rest. Once Bagheri had his money and his immunity, he proceeded to tell an amazing story. As it turned out, the bombing of the Babylon Hotel, Tabrizi's assassination, and the attempted terrorist bombing of New York City had all been masterminded by Izzat al-Douri, the former vice president of Iraq and a man believed dead since 2005. Since the invasion, al-Douri had been forking over large sums of money to select members of the Syrian government in exchange for asylum. His relationship with Will Vanderveen had resulted in the recruitment of Rashid al-Umari in Sadr City, and with al-Umari's large contribution of working capital to the Sunni insurgency, the plan, long devised, was set into motion.

The minister also confirmed that he had received five million dollars for his role in putting al-Douri in touch with the Damascus-based offices of Hezbollah, Hamas, and Islamic Jihad, all of which had received healthy infusions of cash in recent weeks. According to Bagheri, the cash was incentive for the various groups to cross the Iraqi-Syrian border in the last two weeks of September, armed with weapons brought into the region by Vanderveen and his European arms broker, whom Bagheri couldn't identify.

The one point that Reza Bagheri had stressed above all was his ignorance of the attack in New York. He had been paid to facilitate a meeting, nothing more, nothing less, and he'd had no desire to take part in a terrorist act on U.S. soil, especially an atrocity on the scale of 9/11. Harper wasn't sure whether this was the truth, but Bagheri had made it sound convincing. Either way, Harper had made his deal, and he intended to keep it. As far as he was concerned, Bagheri's story would ring true if—and only if—he could produce Izzat al-Douri, currently the most wanted man in Iraq.

Bagheri was quick to deliver. Within a week, he provided a current location as well as details of past movements. The former Iraqi vice president had moved several times since the start of the operation, from Tartus to Aleppo, Aleppo to Damascus, and from there to a town near al-Hasakar, where he'd inspected an arms cache delivered by Will Vanderveen several months earlier. That same cache—and many like it—had since been seized by U.S. forces sweeping over the border, but al-Douri had already traveled south to avoid capture.

Once Bagheri had turned over his wealth of knowledge, Harper pointed out that the Syrian government—culpable or not—would have to face some very difficult questions over the near disaster in New York if its relationship with Izzat al-Douri ever came to light. Bagheri had agreed. His first offer was to have al-Douri killed and the body produced for the purpose of identification, but that wasn't good enough for the Agency. For what al-Douri had tried to do, he would have to answer to the United States on a more personal level. And so a plan was set in motion. Once the arrangements were made and confirmed, Harper had sent for Kealey, which explained why he was now sitting outside the Palestine Hotel, on the Syrian border.

He looked up sharply as the door to his left swung open. Lieutenant Colonel Paul Owen poked his head out and nodded once. The two men had patched up their differences over the kidnapping of Arshad Kassem in Fallujah, and they'd resolved their dispute the way all soldiers did: by buying each other a few rounds. Just finding the drinks the previous night should have been quite a feat in itself. Alcohol consumption was strictly forbidden for U.S. soldiers stationed in Iraq, but while regular soldiers might have had trouble acquiring liquor, SF operators had no such difficulties, just as they had no problem getting Ethan Allen furniture for their safe houses and fully loaded Land Rovers for their daily excursions.

"Thought I'd find you out here," Owen said. "We just got a call from our friends in Damascus. Everything's on schedule, and there's a bonus."

"What's that?"

"Al-Douri has someone with him. A guy called al-Tikriti. You know the name?"

Kealey nodded. Tahir Jalil Habbush al-Tikriti, the former director of the Iraqi Intelligence Service, was currently number sixteen on the U.S. most-wanted list. It didn't surprise Kealey at all that the two men were traveling together; when the Baathists were still in power, al-Douri's considerable ties to the IIS had been confirmed on several occasions by high-ranking defectors, as well as in documents passed on by friendly services such as MI6 and the Israeli Mossad.

"Good. So we'll get them both."

"He's due to arrive in an hour. Our helicopter's waiting outside the base."

Kealey frowned. "They have a perimeter?"

"Yeah, of course. They're not going to land a chopper in an unsecured area. At least not this close to the city."

Kealey nodded and tossed back the last of his lemonade, crumpling the cup in his right fist. Then he dropped it on the ground, grabbed the AK-47 off the wall, and stood up. "Where's the truck?"

"Out front."

"Let's go."

Forty-five minutes later, a black Ford Escort whined steadily down a narrow, two-lane road running across the Iraqi-Syrian border two miles south of the Euphrates. The vehicle was occupied by three people, a driver from the Military Security Department in Damascus and two older passengers, both of whom sat in the cramped backseat. The mood within the car was tense; just sixteen hours earlier, the two senior occupants had been summoned to the presidential palace in Lattakia, where they had met with Syrian president Bashar al-Assad. What he had told them was partially true: their role in the recent escalation of violence in Iraq—as well as the attempted bombing of the Renaissance Hotel in New York City—had been uncovered by U.S. intelligence. On top of that, the CIA was aware of their current location.

The news would have been difficult to take on its own, but to make matters worse, it had been accompanied by an ultimatum. Both men were given twenty-four hours to get their affairs in order and leave the country. They were given the use of a private jet, provided their final destination was within Syrian air space and close to the border. Al-Assad had made it abundantly clear that he had never approved of the actions they'd undertaken, and for good reason; if the Americans had decided to strike before considering all the variables, his government would have paid the price. The meeting had ended on this sour note. As they were wordlessly guided out of the office, neither man thought to protest their swift expulsion from the safe haven of Syria. Both were silently surprised to be given the chance to leave at all.

Neither could have known that the car waiting for them at the al-Maze military airport was fitted with a GPS transmitter sending an intermittent signal to a satellite in geosynchronous orbit. From the moment the driver had started the engine, the young technician at al-Maze tasked with monitoring the Escort's position had begun relaying its coordinates by cell phone to a communications sergeant with the 5th Special Forces Group, the updates arriving in ten-minute intervals. It wasn't long before this unlikely partnership was able to pinpoint the Escort's likely first destination, a border crossing 2 miles south of the Euphrates.

Fortunately, the crossing was not on a major road, which would have complicated things. The border checkpoint consisted of nothing more than a sandstone arch over the road, a few date palms, and the rusted hulk of a T-72 tank dating back to the first Gulf War. There was also a small machine-gun emplacement, situated next to a prefabricated building supplied by the DOD. A few discreet calls from U.S. Central Command to select members of the National Assembly ensured that the Iraqi soldiers assigned to this particular sector were ready to move out on a moment's notice so that others might take their place. The outgoing unit received no information on the incoming unit, nor did they receive an explanation for the unexpected change in standing orders. The captain in charge of the displaced unit originally thought to inquire further, then decided against it. If the U.S. military didn't want him or his men in the area, then so be it.

The car approached the checkpoint slowly, the driver downshifting as the Escort rolled the last 20 feet, leaving the pavement for a temporary stretch of irregular, hard-packed dirt. The entire vehicle was coated in fine dust from the 40-mile run from al-Mayadin. Seven Iraqi soldiers with AK-47s stood in various positions around the checkpoint: two on the machine gun behind the sandbags, two more in the prefab building. Another talked loudly into his cell phone, and one provided cover for the seventh soldier, the *arif* tasked with identifying the vehicle's occupants. The driver slowed to a halt, applied the parking brake, and kept his hands on the wheel, obeying the soldier's familiar visual commands. At the same time, the man on the cell phone—an Iraqi army *naqib*, according to the rank on his Kevlar—snapped it shut and turned, screaming in Arabic down at the soldiers on the machine gun. Both men scrambled to correct something that the Escort's senior passenger couldn't quite see, but then the captain slapped both of their helmets and shouted again, obviously dissatisfied with their efforts to correct the unknown problem.

The older passenger handed over his passport absently, craning to see through the windshield as the staff sergeant examined the worn booklet through his open window. The sixty-three-year old Iraqi wasn't concerned in the least. The carefully forged document identified him as Khalid Abbas al-Bayad, a resident of Fallujah, and it had passed inspection before. But while he was distracted by the scene in front of the Escort, he didn't notice that the soldier next to his door had pulled a Beretta 9mm from his leg holster and was holding the weapon below the line of the window. Then the soldier murmured something in Arabic that caught Izzat al-Douri completely off-guard. To his credit, he assessed the situation with amazing speed, given his advanced age. His eyes opened wide, and he opened his mouth to shout a warning, but by then, he already knew he had made a fatal miscalculation.

When Ryan Kealey saw that the passengers in the backseat were distracted, he said the older man's name. Even if the former vice president of Iraq had not been instantly recognizable, his reaction would have made his identity clear. As he started to shout a warning, Kealey took a single step back, raised the Beretta, and fired twice into Izzat al-Douri's face. Tahir al-Tikriti cursed viciously as the back of the older man's head exploded 2 feet to his left, showering his own face and the front of his suit with blood and brain tissue. Al-Tikriti was younger than his traveling companion, and he was fast; he already had his weapon halfway drawn when Kealey swung the Beretta toward him and fired twice more, the bullets entering the former IIS director's chest less than an inch apart.

Tahir al-Tikriti inhaled deeply, his lungs filling with air and blood. He looked up at his killer, taking in the young American face, wondering what was behind those dark gray eyes as the gun came up for the last time.

The muzzle produced a searing, brilliant light.

And then there was only darkness.

CHAPTER 60

WASHINGTON, D.C.

It was just before 6:30 AM, still dark, a light snow drifting over the city as a white Ford Ranger rumbled to a halt on Q Street, just northeast of Dupont Circle. The driver, having just stolen the truck ten minutes earlier in Georgetown, blew on her hands to warm them up, scowling at the heater in the process. It seemed to be taking forever to warm up, but with any luck, she wouldn't need the vehicle much longer. Yasmin Raseen still had one good set of documents, including a well-worn Italian passport and a credit card issued by a bank in London. She'd already used the card to purchase a ticket to London, and she'd need the passport to board United Flight 920, departing for Heathrow later that afternoon. She was about to leave the United States for the first—and hopefully last—time in her life.

She shivered slightly behind the wheel, even though she was wearing a down jacket over a white woolen sweater. Her hands were pushed under both layers, resting against the bare skin of her stomach to keep them warm. Not for the first time, she wondered what would possess a man to wake each morning at this ungodly hour to run the frigid streets of Washington, D.C. Had she been a religious woman, she would have been used to rising even earlier in order to say the *Fajr* prayer at dawn. Although she didn't adhere to the faith, rising early for religious purposes seemed like a reasonable sacrifice. Prayer had meaning, after all, and could be conducted indoors, unlike running in this freezing air, which struck her as a strange choice of exercise. She could make no sense of the desire to invite a mugging or, barring that, a bronchial infection before the sun came up in the east.

It had taken her longer than she'd expected to track down the exact address on General's Row, largely because the street did not offer a great deal of cover. Wary of inviting unwanted attention, she'd been forced to limit herself to a few hours of surveillance each day, moving along the length of the street. She was also forced to work on foot, as she was without a vehicle and couldn't risk stealing one until it was time to act. After weeks of diligent study, she had finally narrowed it down to one probable address. Her suspicions were proved correct when the same black Suburban with government plates came to collect the deputy DCI four mornings in a row, depositing him at different times each evening.

From there, she began looking for weak points in Jonathan Harper's security. It soon became clear that the man was most vulnerable on his morning runs, which she had yet to see him miss. Not only would he be least aware at that time of day, having only been up for a short while, but the empty streets also provided a better chance for escape when her work was done. After finalizing her plan, she had booked the flight out of Dulles. Now all that remained was to carry out the act itself.

As she watched through the windshield, the door to the brownstone was pulled open, and a man came down the icy steps, dressed in tracksuit bottoms, running shoes, and a Boston College sweatshirt. He was also wearing thin gloves and a woolen watch cap. Harper seemed to look up for a moment, as though appraising the dark, empty sky. Then he began to conduct a series of slow stretching exercises, his breath steaming in the cold air, his body casting irregular shadows under the sidewalk lamps.

After a time he set off, walking north on 17th Street. From her position, she had a visual on her target for a long time. He broke into a run somewhere north of S Street, but then turned a moment later, fading from sight. Raseen wasn't concerned at all. She knew that he'd retrace his route exactly. She'd seen him do it on each of the past four mornings, albeit from a much greater distance. She no longer needed the binoculars, for when he returned in forty minutes or so, she'd be ready to greet him in person.

She found her right hand reaching out to touch the butt of her gun. Amir Nazeri had provided her with the Beretta .22 shortly before his death in New York. The plastic grip was cold to the touch, but she took comfort from it nonetheless. The weapon was resting on the passenger seat, covered by the previous day's copy of the *Washington Post*. The newspaper had been in the truck when she'd popped the lock. Her first act had been to flip the paper over, as the lurid headlines were hard for her to take. Izzat al-Douri had been shot to death at a border crossing in Al Anbar Province two days earlier, along with his chief advisor, Tahir Jalil Habbush al-Tikriti, the former director of the Iraqi Intelligence Service.

Yasmin Raseen had known both men for many years, al-Douri since she was just a girl. While she had yet to shed any tears over their deaths, she couldn't help but feel a distinct, but strangely indirect sense of loss. Since they'd been part of her father's life, they were part of hers, and with their passing, she felt a little more alone in the world. And there was something else to consider: al-Douri had been her primary benefactor since her father's capture near Tikrit, along with the last of the money he'd managed to personally carry out of the Central Bank before the fall of Baghdad. With al-Douri's passing, she was left with very limited means. There was no doubt in her mind that the Americans were responsible for the assassination of both men, even though al-Douri had yet to be publicly linked to the recent events in Baghdad, Paris, and New York.

As she waited for Jonathan Harper to return, her thoughts began to drift. Before long, they turned to Will Vanderveen, which didn't surprise her at all. Over the past several weeks, he had occupied most of her waking thoughts, as well as her dreams. One memory in particular stood out in her mind: the night at the Hotel Victoria in Calais. What a strange incident that had been. His violence had sparked something in her she'd long sought to keep down, but setting it free had done so much for her, both emotionally and physically. He was one of the most fascinating men she'd ever known, completely cold, without compunction, and yet she had also glimpsed an underlying compassion during the few intimate moments they'd shared. It was still hard to believe he was gone, and although he had died before achieving his goal, he had achieved something else that he never had the chance to know about. Something much greater than what he'd aspired to.

Her hands, warm beneath her layers of clothing, drifted over the smooth skin of her stomach. She smiled to herself, thinking about the life that would soon spring from her body. At thirty-eight years of age, she had long since come to the conclusion that motherhood wasn't meant for her, that she would have to find some other way to fill her barren inner landscape. And yet, now it seemed she had been given the chance she had always longed for.

She would not have to decide for many years, but she wondered what she would say to her child when he asked about his father. Would she tell him the truth? Or would she invent some acceptable version of events? Somehow, she didn't think she could stretch her imagination that far. After all, there was nothing acceptable about the things she had done. While her actions had never concerned her before, she couldn't help but wonder—in light of her recent discovery—whether it was time to put it all behind her.

It was something she'd have to consider, but for now, there was work to be done, revenge to be had. As she stared through the light dusting of snow on the windshield, a distant figure emerged from the predawn gloom, his feet pounding a steady rhythm on the pavement, his shoulders bouncing beneath ethereal light. He was obscured by a sudden gust of loose white powder, but then he reappeared, right on schedule, drawing ever closer.

Without shifting her gaze from the man jogging south on 17th Street, Nouri Hussein reached for her gun and pushed it under the folds of her coat. Then she opened the door and stepped onto the icy pavement.

The runner approached, unaware, and the snow came down in a great white cloud, obscuring the rising dawn.